Phil Stong

IVANHOE
KEELER

FARRAR & RINEHART
INCORPORATED
NEW YORK   TORONTO

CONTENTS

MELANCHOLY PILGRIM

I

"GOOD Lord!" said Ivanhoe Keeler, and then dully, "Good Lord!" He made the first invocation because he now saw from the river hill what he had seen only by darkness on his way up to the backwoods of southeastern Iowa—the city of Keokuk in a clear morning light. It was six o'clock; the sun had been up only fifteen minutes or so, so that the buildings of the little town doubled themselves with their own shadows, but still Keokuk was a metropolis compared with what it had been when he had last seen it by daylight two years before. It must have a thousand people, perhaps two thousand! The latter estimate was nearer the truth in the year 1839.

The docks were busy already. There were four boats in this morning, a small stern-wheeler pitifully crouched under a big side-wheeler and two small side-wheelers which would be headed for the Iowa towns on up the Mississippi, since they were to the north of the other boats. The little stern-wheeler, then, would be the Des Moines River boat which would presently paddle a few miles down the Mississippi and then turn northwest up the smaller Des Moines.

Ivanhoe Keeler said "Good Lord!" once more, faintly. His heart had been broken the evening before; the little boat would be passing within a few hundred yards of the pieces, up beyond Pittsville, sometime that afternoon.

Ivanhoe had been subjected to a series of shocks since his return, after more than a year of continual travel, to see his sweetheart in the wilderness. Where there had been a wilderness there were now farms as far as one could ride along the river; where there had been a trader there was a town of two hundred; most startling of all, where there had been his sweetheart there were also twin boys.

It was bad enough, he reflected, not bitterly but with a

3

small sense of self-pity, for Sue to marry almost as soon as his back was turned—after he had braved horseback blisters and other hardships to visit her settler family and her; it would have been still worse for her to show the effective warmth of the new attachment by having one baby, conservatively, in the brief space since he had left her, but two babies—both boys—at once crushed Ivanhoe.

He had learned the harsh details from "Fursten—Supplies and Dry Goods," around whose establishment a small village had sprung up, and he had not even troubled to visit his settler friends. He had, in a phrase which he suddenly thought of and which seemed rather good and tragic, turned and fled into the night.

Here he was in Keokuk at daybreak, weary and sore— and not footsore, either. One of the bitter things about it was that fairly good trails had been made and he could have used his buggy if he had only known it.

He reined up in front of the livery stable, whose doors were already open. At another moment his dapper clothes, his stock, his high gray hat would have made the tall young man seem dandyish, but now he looked like a picture of Uncle Sam, aged twenty-four, and all played out. Even his well-made clothes were loyal; they were wrinkled and baggy too, except for the trouser legs which were too tight to wrinkle.

With an effort he lifted off the two carpetbags that were balanced on a strap over the horse's shoulders and then with infinite care unfastened a violin case from a pillion of blankets.

The proprietor watched him seriously, without offering to help, till this was done. A livery stable took care of horses —men took care of themselves. The liveryman now took the bridle, led the horse inside and to a stall and took careful measures with a brush and currycomb. The horse ate the corn in the grain box and munched at the long prairie hay.

"Didn't stay long, son." The liveryman spat long and well against the angle of the stallboard and then put down the currycomb long enough to wipe his cud out of his mouth with his forefinger. He refilled at once from the pocket of his jacket and went on with his expert grooming.

Ivanhoe was about to ignore the remark when he noticed that the broad, red face of the big man was essentially kind, and under all circumstances Ivanhoe had to be gentle with good intentions, no matter how untimely or misapplied.

"No, there wasn't any reason to stay."

The man, down on one knee at a fetlock, clucked sympathetically. "Didn't catch her home, this Susan? Well, she'll have to be somewhere around, up there in Van Buren. There ain't no place to go visitin' for long. Why don't you go over and spend a day at the hotel—God save the name—a day or two and you'll be sure to catch her and the family."

"No, I can't stay." On his way through the day before Ivanhoe, in his exuberance, had told the liveryman a good deal about Susan while the mare was feeding, before riding on eagerly a few miles nearer her, in darkness and a threatening drizzle.

"That's a dirty shame! After you probably come a good long ways! I shined your buggy up. Pretty piece o' work but I could see by the mud you'd covered some ground and in a hurry. When you want the mare hitched? She could stand some rest." Ivanhoe knew that he meant that the rider could too.

Ivanhoe nodded. "Yes, she's done a hundred and twenty miles since I left here, on two feedings and no rest. I'll get a bite and find a barber and take a nap in the hotel." In spite of all determination his weariness now seemed more exigent than his sorrow.

"Oh, my God," said the big man, "you've picked the worst of everything. The bar here is stinking and the beds in the hotel are worse and the barber won't leave a bit of skin on you. If we could only have niggers—but they watch the gangplanks and the rails with pistols after the boat hits free soil or water. One gets killed trying to swim it every once in a while."

He thought deeply and arrived at a compromise. He

went to a near-by stall and drew out a demijohn, half-full of brownish-orange liquor.

"Take yourself a big shot of that—then you won't care— you'll get a good rest. Maybe, better than that buggy hotel, you could come back here and I'll smooth you out a place in a stall—" he measured Ivanhoe doubtfully—"maybe you're a little long, though, come to think of it."

"I'm six-two."

The proprietor shook his head. "You'd have to scrooge two inches and you'd still have your toes under the grain box. Let me think—and hit that jug."

"I'm too tired. This shape, I'd probably cry or something or start a fight."

"Oh—h! That's it!"

"That's it." Ivanhoe was tired; too tired for reticence or lies or concealment.

The red-faced man clucked again and exhaled enough of the fumes of the first course of his heavy Iowa breakfast— a half tumbler of Tennessee whisky neat—to convince Ivanhoe that he wanted none of the demijohn.

"Oh, well, son—they don't stay mad forever—or you don't." He winked his eyes and forehead together, confidentially. "You stay down here a week—it's a lot to stand but you look like you might have been through worse—and I'll bet when you get back she'll grab you like a drowning straw."

Ivanhoe laughed ironically. "She'll have to put her husband's twins down to do it."

"Unnh!" The big man ran the comb over the brush and absently pulled the combed hair off the dull forks with his fingers. "Got married. Well, now you can't help that." He beamed suddenly. "Why didn't I think of it! The cook's stove'll be going now on the *Excalibur!* The captain'll raise the barber up and you can change in the gents' saloon—and get a bath, if you need one, at the pump. You'll have the best meal I've ever tasted. Then come back up here before she puts off at eight, and I'll fix you a blanket in the hay—"

He paused at the look in Ivanhoe's eyes.

"She sails—pushes off—at eight?"

"Well, more or less at eight."

"Thanks." Ivanhoe stooped and threw the strap of the carpetbags across his shoulders. Then he gently recovered the violin case from the hay in the next stall. "That's what I want."

His legs were long and trained with all the years of riding and walking, but the livery-stable man caught up with him.

"You can leave your things here, son—they'll be safe. You don't need to lug them clear down there and back."

"I'd better take them with me. I probably won't be coming back."

"Not coming back—!"

"I think I'll go down to New Orleans and take a boat somewhere. They say ocean voyages are good for—for what ails you."

"Well—well, if you can afford them—maybe—"

"I can." Ivanhoe laughed briefly and bitterly; very well done. "I've got four thousand dollars in gold in these bags. Hah! I was going to buy a farm and settle down."

"For Lord's sake, sonny, don't tell anyone else that! There's men on the river would cut your throat for twenty dollars!"

Ivanhoe gave the stablekeeper a smile that was indescribably sad. "I know an honest man when I see him and I know when to keep my mouth shut. I've been tramping and fiddling since I was twelve. I know how to get around."

The stableman looked at Ivanhoe's lined brown cheeks and then at the naïve blue eyes which seemed unreasonably large because of blond lashes.

"Just the same, son—"

"What?"

"Why don't you have your breakfast and then come up and lie down and think things over? It ain't such a bad plan to buy land, at that. And there's more than one girl in Iowa."

"That's what I'm afraid of," Ivanhoe said. "I don't want to go through all this again, even if I can. I'm going on a ship and forget all about women. There's lots of ships haven't got a woman on them. Maybe I'll go to Texas."

The older man smiled and then resumed his expression of condolence. "Well, they say a hair of the dog that bit you— And what'll you do with your nag and the buggy?"

"You can use them till I come for them."

"Well—thanks." But even the man's honest sympathy could not restrain his feeling for this evident possibility of legitimate sport. "I'll tell you what I'll do—I'll deal with you for them."

"I don't feel like it," Ivanhoe said. "Most times I'd as soon deal as not—but not now. I'll take any offer you make if you want to buy them. Otherwise, you make them earn their keep."

The stablekeeper was depressed for a moment. "That way I'd just be dealing with myself. I'd ask too much and offer too little. By and by I'd pay what they were worth and not make a cent out of it. Don't you think a little dealing would take your mind off—things?"

"No, I don't."

"Then I'll keep them for you." He brightened. "That way I'll be making quite a lot off of you. There's getting to be a lot of smart boys in this town and your mare's the first English thoroughbred in this part of Iowa." He wrinkled his pink forehead. "No, I can't do that to you just because you got a mitten.—I'll tell you—I'll put up the horse and shine the buggy and do all the business dealings. And when you come back I'll give you twenty-five per cent. Now, that's fair."

"That's fair and more."

"Now, if something should happen to me, what do you want done with them?"

"I don't care—oh, yes, have them sent up to Mrs. Caesar Crawford at Pittsville. Maybe those damn twins can learn to ride a *good* horse."

"All right, son. You can count on me." They shook hands and Ivanhoe went on down to the river.

The captain of the *Excalibur* was a little gray man who bounced over his deck like a maniacal jumping bean. He and the mate seemed to be on almost even terms, except that the mate cursed him more quietly than he cursed the mate and the mate made guttural Teutonic-stem rejoinders in response to the captain's elaborate descriptive paragraphs. Sometimes they joined in tenor and counterbass to hurl blasphemies and obscenities at the calm file of men—three walking up the incline to the deck and three walking down—who were handling and stowing bales of furs and sacks of grain on the cargo deck of the *Excalibur*.

The men never raised their heads or quickened their pace. A captain had to be a captain, didn't he, so why should they resent his language? And a river roustabout had to be a river roustabout, so why pay any attention? The captains of the smaller boats leaned on the rails and listened attentively. They might learn something. At eight o'clock the captain would become a dignified gentleman—though not the lord of the boat and bridge that the pilot was—ordering everything about the boat except its navigation. The captain was responsible for the loading and unloading of the boat, for the cook, for the saloon stewards, for the engines and the fuel supply, which was rushed on board from corded stacks at every convenient landing. He could start or stop as he pleased but once the boat was started his problems were all social and economic—the pilot was the master of the vessel.

The captain was in the midst of a series of Biblical remarks when Ivanhoe Keeler arrived on the loading plank between an unsweet bundle of skunk hides and a package of twelve smoked hams. The passenger plank would be let down later but he was too tired to wait or to notice his company.

Ivanhoe saw dimly that he was on the wrong deck and pulled himself up to the saloons, step by step. In the men's saloon he changed worlds. Here, everything was jigsaw and gilt elegance. The stove had been kindled to take the chill off the morning, the berths were neatly made, the spittoons shone, the niggers had polished everything and one had only to call to be served.

He put his bags under a berth and lay down on it for the moment, having placed the violin between his body and the wall. He was awakened an hour or two later by the captain's hand and voice. The rhythmic roar and chug of the machinery, the hiss of steam and the rushing of water over the paddle wheels informed him that the ship was on its way to St. Louis.

"I say, mister," the captain said pleasantly, "are you for St. Looey? I hate to bother a man that snores with a genteel manner, but if you're for one of the landings I ought to know."

Ivanhoe shook his head and rubbed his eyes. He had barely had a good start on the sleep he should have taken the two nights before, but the saloon was full of the odors of buckwheat cakes, ham, catfish, the dark sugary smell of apple pie, the subtler traces of hot punch—he craved sleep and surrender to his eyelids but the idea of a crisped catfish, floured and buttered and browned, triumphed poetically over this fleshly weakness and his mind was made up immediately.

"Thanks, captain. St. Louis. I'll go up to the dining saloon. A little bit tired—rode all last night."

The captain nodded urbanely. He knew that Ivanhoe had been drunk in Keokuk all last night and Ivanhoe knew that he thought so, but drunkenness was considered an expression of virility and more a quality than a failing, in bounds, along the river. A two-bottle man who could speak intelligibly at suppertime was known to have hair on his chest, per se.

Ivanhoe automatically reached for his violin case. He completely forgot the carpetbags—they held nothing but his clothes and his four thousand dollars.

There were a dozen men in the room, talking, drinking, chewing and spitting. There were two games of euchre going on in the corners. A man was retching in the ordinary behind the panels. A farmer was drawing the boundary of some locality or possibly a route with his pipe, making a map on the air for another farmer with equally unruled whiskers.

Ivanhoe rose and started for the door, yawning splendidly. He turned on the captain, at his shoulder. "You got some nigger can take care of my whiskers and my clothes?

And I want a bath. I've got my own razors and brushes."

"Samaliel will fix you up. He's my man and a damned good one but I like to see him earn a few bits or so to buy himself back. I've give him a good low price, too."

"Buy himself back from where?" Ivanhoe asked sleepily.

The captain stared and then laughed. "From South, see? He's a slave. I bought him in Memphis for eight hundred dollars. He give me the best shave I ever had and I figured I'd make money on him, tendin' passengers—and I have and he has. He's the best valley anybody ever had and he can make a banjo talk; he's took in as much as five-six dollars in an evening playin' for singin' when the boys got a little happy. Why, he's kept up his interest regular and paid up four hundred dollars on himself—he's as much his as mine, now."

"Half his and half yours?"

The captain looked severe. "My folks are Yankee stock from Ohio—we don't hold with slavery. Samaliel's on my conscience, all right, but eight hundred dollars is a piece of money." The captain sighed. "Well, if luck keeps up he'll be all clear in a couple more years or so."

The captain led Ivanhoe into his own quarters. "I'll send Samaliel in with some breakfast and he can take care of your suit while you eat it and fix your whiskers afterward.—We got some sweet yellow cat down at Milam's Landing last night—and some bacon—and Samaliel's made the best open-face apple pie you ever tasted—and a big pot of coffee—and a mug of hot punch. You'll be a new man. Nothin' like vittles to take the place of sleep."

"Sounds great. Tell the man to bring my bags—I don't know which the toilet case is in—and tell him to hurry those catfish."

Almost immediately, before Ivanhoe had had time to do more than close his eyes, there was a gentle knock at the door.

"Come!"

"Good morning," a rich, deep voice said, with only the slightest intimation that "morning" was "mahnin'."

Ivanhoe turned his head slowly. Negroes were no novelty to him—round-headed, kinky-haired, shiny-eyed—the ordinary Negrito type from the Ivory Coast—but he had never seen a Bantu type before. Samaliel was almost as tall as Ivanhoe but obviously twice as powerful. His graying hair crinkled but it did not kink. His face was long and dignified —an arched nose, full, but not thick lips, gray eyes, a high forehead.

Samaliel flashed his teeth. "Your shavin' things, sir?"

"In one of the bags—you dig them out. What about that catfish?"

"The cook is fixin' the tray, sir—just in a minute. Hunnh!"

The Negro was fishing in one of the carpetbags. He straightened slowly. "You got anyhow a thousam dollars, sir, loose in your keester. Beggin' your pardon but you oughtn't to carry it like that. Some niggehs is honest and some ain't— and, beggin' your pardon, some white folks has got forgitful with theah fingers now and then."

"I'll bank it in St. Louis," Ivanhoe said sleepily.

A black waiter appeared almost instantly with a loaded tray and put it down on the captain's desk in front of Ivanhoe. There were two yellow cat still sizzling with butter, surrounded by slices of crisp bacon, two fried eggs, mashed potato patties, corn-meal muffins, raised biscuits, fresh country butter, marmalade, molasses, apple butter and a big pot of coffee.

Ivanhoe gave the waiter two bits. "Great heavens, man, you've brought ten times too much. All I wanted was just a fish to pick at and a cup of coffee."

The waiter smiled at Ivanhoe. "Wait, suh, till you try the feesh, suh. We'll have anotheh one ready, suh, when those is gone. Thank you kindly, suh." He disappeared.

Samaliel went out silently for his pressing irons.

Ivanhoe nibbled languidly at a catfish and a buttered muffin. Black coffee was best for a broken heart but he didn't like coffee that way. Why should a man drink black coffee because his heart was broken? he thought indignantly. There would never be any happiness in his life, why should he torture himself unduly? He took two spoons of sugar and a liberal pouring of cream. He realized that he was building himself up for further suffering but he simply didn't like coffee black. He stirred and chewed morosely and twisted at the knife in his heart. There had been a little while before Sue's family went to Iowa when he almost believed she would have him—no, he didn't really, his heart had been pretty badly cracked from the first time he'd ever seen Sue Ellison, now Sue Crawford. She might have married him just in her giddy way, though.

Iowa, damn the place! He'd seen the change coming over her the first time he'd visited the Ellisons in Iowa. She'd never be a wandering fiddler's wife, no matter how much money he made—back in Ohio she'd thought it would be fun. What was this settling business—some kind of bug that bit you?

It wasn't so hard to bear, though, as long as she wasn't irremediably lost, but if anybody could be loster than a married lady with twins he'd like to know who it would be, unless it was one with triplets. He laughed bitterly to himself—if she'd ever heard about triplets she'd probably have had them.

There was a soft cough at his elbow. "More feesh, suh? Here's a small one, very juicy." The Negro did not wait for instructions but slid two more fish on the plate.

"No, no!" The Negro looked disappointed. Never do to hurt his feelings. "Well, now that they're there I'll nibble on one of them."

"An' these muffins will be cold, suh—oh—" for when the napkin was lifted there were no muffins—"heah are some hot ones, suh."

"Well, just one or two—there, that's plenty."

Samaliel was stropping the razor with an expert stroke.

"That's good," said Ivanhoe. "My skin's as tough as leather—ought to be—but if it gets scraped it burns all day."

"Yes, sir. I'll be careful, sir."

Ivanhoe mopped up the last of the egg yellow with a

muffin, ate the muffin and leaned back in his chair. "All ready when you are."

Samaliel silently took the tray out and returned a moment later with a pitcher of hot water and a basin. He ran appraising fingers over Ivanhoe's chin and then went to work with the shaving brush. At the first touch of the brush Ivanhoe was reassured; Samaliel was no dauber, he worked the lather in suavely, gently and efficiently. At the first stroke of the razor Ivanhoe knew that he was in the hands of an expert barber—it was light as a feather. With a sigh of relief Ivanhoe sank back in the chair and returned to his reflections.

What should he do now? He had four thousand dollars in his carpetbags and three thousand more for security, in gold, in a bank vault in Cincinnati; and nothing to do with it. His world was all broken up around him—he hadn't a plan in the world. Maybe he could go to Texas and shoot Mexicans till he died a hero's death. Everybody knew there was going to be a war there just about any minute. He'd go down and join up with old Sam Houston. But would Sue ever hear about his death? He almost shook his head before he remembered the razor.

Somewhere he'd read that people with broken hearts took long sea trips. That was the ticket! He'd go to England and France and all those places and then go back to Pittsville and give a lecture. That was a lot better than being shot, anyway. He'd come back in a lot of English and French clothes with a mustache and a one-eyed spectacle on a ribbon and give a lecture. No good, either—everybody'd know from the Ellisons and Fursten about Ive Keeler the wandering fiddler and they'd laugh at him.

Then he had an idea whose simple brilliance startled him. Deep in his heart Ivanhoe knew that he was more than a fiddler. He liked his own improvisations and the folk music and dance tunes that made him better than a good living in bars and at small-town dances but he particularly liked the high-class music he occasionally heard in Cincinnati and he could play a lot of it. He was still young but he'd been playing ever since he ran away from home twelve years before, and playing for a living. His almost abnormally long fingers felt empty without a violin and they danced like elves when strings were under them. He had learned a good many of the tricks of bowing and sound production from the good violinists he had watched and he guessed that he could pass himself off as a pupil with some maestro over in Europe. He'd had only two years of formal instruction in his youth—before he could play better than the small-town music teacher—but he knew all the right words, and if he went to some foreigner, like in France or Italy, his mistakes would be put down to his being American.

A year with the Froggies and he'd come back Monsieur François Keeler, the celebrated French maestro, and give concerts in Cincinnati and St. Louis and Louisville and maybe sometime in Boston, and Burlington and Dubuque. Then, as a special condescension, he'd play in Pittsville which would have grown from a few hundred to several thousand by then at the present rate, and Sue would have to come with her farmer husband and her three sets of twins, or else—

"What! You didn't hear the great François Ivanhoe Keeler!" and then in the middle of the program he would have to stop patiently and wait while one—two—all the twins squalled.

"Never mind, madam, it's no inconvenience. They'll quiet in a minute."

"Excuse me, sir?"

"Hey? Oh, guess I must have been dozing. Rode all last night to catch the boat. Have to get to New Orleans for a concert."

Samaliel was snipping at the edges of Ivanhoe's hair. "You are an artist, sir, a violinist? I'm merely trimming, sir—of course you'll want it quite long."

"That's right."

But the daydream was irretrievably lost, for now he was fully awake. He shrugged his shoulders. Daydream? Hopeless dream, but he had nothing better to do. After all, Benjamin Franklin and Benjamin West and Old Hickory hadn't had any better education in their lines than he'd had in his.

And he had to do something. Wouldn't hurt anything. At least he'd be a better tavern player—

Tavern player. Wasn't there something he could do or be that would be great and noble—that Sue would hear of? Probably not.

The bitter moment was ameliorated by the fact that Samaliel was gently rubbing rosewater into his face and, however his heart was, his face felt definitely *good*. His pleasantly stuffed stomach and his cool, scented face were in rebellion against his melancholy and all his finer feelings. Why not surrender? The wound would never heal but the anguish might grow worn and dim as the years passed and he could lead a sybaritic life for ten years on the little fortune at his command.

Paris, definitely.

"Samaliel, that's the best shave I've ever had, and the clothes are perfect." Samaliel was holding up a fresh shirt. "How'd you like to come with me and be my body-servant?"

"That's very good of you, sir," Samaliel said, uneasily, "even when you're just jokin'."

"Joking, hell! I mean it. I'm going traveling and I need a man—watch out for my bags and clothes, and shave me. My chin feels like moonlight through the mists."

Quiet Samaliel smiled. "I thank you, sir, but I'm part free and I'm plannin' to take a place out in Iowa after I've made a little money. The captain, sir, is lettin' me buy myself off, fast as I ken. Thank you, sir, just the same."

Ivanhoe rubbed his cheeks and sniffed at the rosewater on his fingers. "I know about that. I'll give him the other four hundred and take a note from you. You come with me on salary and pay me as you can. Ten dollars a month I'll give you, and found, and my clothes when I'm through with them. I don't wear them very hard. You'll be all free and owe me four hundred dollars. We'll be all sorts of places and any money you can make with your banjo is yours, off service. Don't you want to go to England—and France—?"

The Negro seemed doubtful for a moment and then

shook his head. "All my plans is made, sir. I'd like to wait on you when you're travelin' the riveh though—"

Ivanhoe drooped his head. "All right, Samaliel—I know how you feel." He slid into his boots. "Good luck in Iowa. If I were you, though, I wouldn't try farming. I'd start up a barbershop, say in Burlington. Barbering is in its infancy in Iowa. You'll have 'em coming twenty miles."

Samaliel looked thoughtful. "It's a good idea, sir. Thank you."

"Here—don't forget this." He gave Samaliel a piece that looked like a diseased yellow dime but, happening to be gold, was worth $2.50.

"This is too much, sir. Four shillings is plenty, sir, fifty cents."

Ivanhoe smiled. "Why don't you come with me to England, Samaliel? Shillings are worth two bits there—twice as much."

Samaliel smiled back but shook his head. "Then, sir, I could only cha'ge half as much."

Ivanhoe nodded as the Negro closed the door. Not even a smooth chin was to be allowed him. Life wasn't going to do a damned thing for him—in the big, in the little, he was a dedicated son of misfortune and despair. First Sue and now Samaliel, and the magic fingers on the razor. No wonder the colored man was a good banjo player. He must have a separate brain in every finger tip. He'd heard they had good barbers in Paris—he'd get a book about French in St. Louis and look up "tavern" and "barbershop" and "violin teacher." That was all he needed to know. He wandered out to the deck, carrying his violin case—the instinct of the public performer was strong in him, but also, since his twelfth year his violin had been shelter and food and something a great deal more important to him. Everyone had gone to the bow of the boat to enjoy the warm spring sunshine and the sight of the wooded shores surging up before them and passing by.

No. He had no taste for it. Let them jabber, let them spit, let them warm their coarse bodies in a sun that could never reach their souls. Heifer-bound men and heifer-women, inconsequentially united by such terms as "good provider," "solid farmer," "fine cook," "figure of a woman," "figure of a man," "make some man a good wife," "there'll be plenty of little Smiths, or Joneses, or something." Groceries, progeny and prosperity—those were the terms of these cattle people in the most poetic and passionate relations they would ever know. He wouldn't play for them—he wouldn't play for any of them—he would play when he was an artist to prepare his reproach for Sue and the three sets of twins.

He went aft and sat down on one of the sacks of a load of grain. Fursten had said that the wheat crop had been extraordinary in Iowa last year. He had seemed to think that this was an item worthy of mention in the face of the catastrophe that had overtaken Ivanhoe. He had wandered on about many things—the dam that was building at Bonaparte, the rush for ferry licenses, the big school that was going up in Pittsville, the addition of more counties to the territory, the project for carrying navigation on up the river to accommodate arriving settlers, politics, prices, the continuing depression in the East—the hell with it all!

After the coffee, Ivanhoe couldn't sleep and it pleased him better, anyway, to look out at the wake of the boat and consider the miles that were separating him from Susan—and her husband and the two babies. The husband and the two babies he was unable to put out of his mind though they were utterly disconsonant. Babies seemed so materialistic—gross.

He tried to think of all the undesirable facts he could remember about babies and was slightly comforted. When he got back from Europe he would be tall, distinguished, saturnine, nestling his violin like a graceful lover; Sue—she would be putting rags on pink, moisty, squirming, shrieking things.

His sweetheart would sing for him chastely but amenably from her delicate brown grace—Caesar Crawford's brats would drool and holler at Sue.

He opened the case and lifted out the violin, put rosin on his bow automatically and began to improvise the great music he would write after he had been to Europe. He couldn't do anything in his usual three-quarter time—somehow it was nearly always gay in spite of the key and mood—so he turned to known music. He didn't know the title of Beethoven's "Pathétique" but he did very well with the major melodies of the "Andante Cantabile" from the work. He went on to some of the sugared tears of Schubert and to laments from the Tennessee mountains.

"Son," said the captain, from beside him, "do you know you're sittin' right over the boilers? And sometimes on these little boats they let loose. Not that I'm expecting it because we don't have to work the engines too hard in this current, but it's safer up by the forerail."

"I know," Ivanhoe said. "I'd rather be here."

He went on, continuously and softly. The wake of the boat spread out splendidly and fatally. Noon passed and the trumpet blew for luncheon. Ivanhoe went to the saloon.

"Gabbling" had been the right word. These people who had all been in the quiet, developing Midwest were enthusiastically eager to question and to tell. The river boat was a new experience to many of them, an annual experience to others, an unusual experience to everyone. The twenty people or so who made up the company were avid for new conversation, remote acquaintances or improbable relationships stemming from Ohio, New York State, New England or Virginia. There were generally pleasant arguments between the Whigs and the Democrats. There were discussions of farm prospects and general by-talk.

Ivanhoe ate silently and quietly because he was hungry. It didn't seem treason to his sentiments to eat lunch, since he had ridden all night and had nibbled only a few catfish and eggs and muffins and things for his breakfast. He trifled with a half-inch slice of roast, and some vegetables while he thought up a poem:

> "Now all the grace of life has fled;
> The rose has withered in the bud—
> Only the rueful, voiceless dead
> Know what men's hearts have harvested."

A bad rhyme that, but the only "bud" rhymes he could think of were cud, stud and mud—none of them suitable. He was too sad to try to think of an alternate second verse. He finished a pint of bitter ale and nibbled a quarter of a large mince pie—or rather, the last crumbs of what had been a quarter.

He waited till all the rest of the company had left the table so that his self-imposed exile would not be noted and then took his violin from under his chair and went back to his wheat sacks. He got the theme first and then the minor melodies which he made sadder and sadder until finally they would have brought tears to his eyes if he hadn't been making them up himself, and very busy at it too. On second thought it would be, "And roses are no longer red," which made a better show at rhyming with "harvested" and a complete rhyme with "fled" and "dead."

The thing was almost satisfactory now—a drooping of minor chords to the third verse which was lifting and oratorical, then somber minors on the G and D strings. Good! He sang.

The "Wanderer's Nightsong" made him feel still more agreeably desolated and "The Lorelei" finished out the luxurious mood. He merely jiggled on the strings after that, hunting mournful chords. A cough interrupted him.

The captain, the passengers and most of the crew of the boat were gathered behind him, listening. They had come up softly and he had been too preoccupied to hear anything short of a definite clatter over the hiss and churn of the engines and the water.

The captain extended a handful of change—five dollars at least. "The folks have liked your music—but ain't you going to play anything cheerful? It's still about six hours to St. Looey and staring at the woods along the banks kind of palls on you afterwhile."

It was Ivanhoe's first impulse to strike the money from the man's hands; his second was to give him a melancholy glance and shake his head at both the money and the proposal. Both notions took only a fraction of a minute to dispel.

The passengers were waiting not only with expectancy but with that quiet satisfaction that attends the conferring of a generous reward. He couldn't disappoint them—all his life would be devoted to appreciations of the acts of men of good will.

He took the change and dropped it into his breeches pocket. "I'll do the best I can. I rode all last night—I'm not up to myself—but here's a circle dance I learned in Louisville—"

"Let's go to the foredeck," the captain interrupted. "It's tallowed down if any of the ladies or gentlemen should want to skip it."

It was quite evident that most of them did want to skip it though there were only five women in the company of four times that many men and two of these were elderly.

"Every man under twenty-one has to be a girl," the captain announced. Three undeniable youths went to portside—three suspicious characters remained with the men. The captain eyed them narrowly but said nothing.

"I'll have to draft four of you," he then said, "to make it even."

"I volunteer!" said a grizzled old man in homespuns. "I can teach the young ladies somethin' about how they ought to do a dance."

Immediately there were too many "ladies," and it seemed possible that there might have to be a general election, but the great man, the pilot, came to the door of the glassed-in bridge and settled the matter.

"You, Jim Hargreaves, you'll be a lady," he said, selecting a long-bearded cattle shipper, "and Orion Gilbert and Carson Hughes." He went back into his sanctum and closed the door. The three veterans he had selected, tough old shippers and passengers on the Mississippi, took their places amid general applause.

"Take your places!" the captain ordered, though they had already done that. "Ready, music!"

Ivanhoe flourished his bow like a conductor and dashed off jauntily and somewhat hoarsely—because the music had to be loud—into the first of the many absurd and absurdly

titled tunes that he would have to play through the after-
noon, "Boston Streets I Once Did See," "Honey in the
Gourd," "They Stomp in Carolina," "Keep Away, Keep
Away, Sailing Man."

Ivanhoe was in no pain now. He was abstracted by the
rigors of his art, the cadenzas, the improvisations, the humorous prolonging of the two-file bowing of "ladies" to men,
the protracted whirling of the circle of dancers right to the
point of dizziness till his bow gave the signal to break for
the next figure and the gray old man, the volunteer who was
also self-appointed announcer, called, "One step forward and
one step back—hands on shoulders—watch your gait—" and
all the maneuvers of the circle dances and square dances were
achieved.

But after a while—after three hours—fatigue wore off the
edge of this excitement and Ivanhoe was tired. He rose and
bowed and made a final gesture by putting his violin in its
case. He accepted compliments gratefully, and the compliments were effusive enough to evoke gratitude, but he wanted
to get to a quiet place and think. To think, at last, not about
Susan but about himself.

II

"I'm sorry, sir, we'ah getting close to the city."

Ivanhoe shook his head and rubbed his eyes and instinctively reached for the violin case. It was safe at his head.

"Samaliel?"

"Yes, sir."

The strange, luminous blue-dark. When he turned his face
the yellow lights of the cabin windows were like a douse of
cold water, though they were far warmer than the dark skies
to which a man might send his thoughts without a challenge
of realism, life, fleshly necessities of light and warmth.

"All right, I've only the two bags and—I've got the
fiddle."

"Sir?" It was a humble request for permission to speak further.

"Yes."

"If you're still the same mind, I'll go with you."

Providence had been fooled, some way, or was fooling him. "You mean—you'd like to go with me?" Ivanhoe asked stupidly, still partly asleep. "What—uh—what changed your mind?"

"Deep South ain't good for colored folks, sir, 'less they know who theah with. I just as soon go along with you."

"What to hell do you mean?"

Samaliel cleared his throat. "Up close to the bordeh, you understand, I ain't worth but eight hundred dollars. A colored man gets so many chances to leave. Many's the time I could have left the captain if we hadn't had an understandin'. Five hundred miles south from St. Louis I think I'd fetch half again that. You have to have an understandin'."

"Why didn't your other folks sell you South?"

"Colonel Wormsley wouldn't do so. I'd been his man. Him an' the captain had an understandin', too. Now I've paid up half, sir, an' now if you'll take up the rest on a note you don't need to pay me no salary. I'll take good care of you an' I'll find a way to pay you back, little at a time. You can lend me around, sir; I can cook, play a banjo or a piany and be a gentleman's man. If you're going overseas, sir, they ain't seen so many niggers there and they'd come see—and when I'm not takin' care of you I can earn up on the debt."

"How do you know I won't sell you in New Orleans?"

The big Negro smiled briefly. "I was carryin' your bags with the gold in them this mornin'. Come around the corner, I heard you playin' your violin. I like music, sir."

"What in the name of the Creator were you doing with the bags?"

"You ought to be more careful, sir—excuse me—I couldn't see 'em layin' around. I kept bringin' 'em around and pilin' them close to you when I had to go and couldn't watch."

Ivanhoe kicked one of the bags. It was a handsome thing with a reticent worsted design on linen heavier than satin, protected by leather bindings and brass corners. The gold pieces inside clicked faintly.

"Said anything to the captain?"

"Yes, sir."

Ivanhoe was awake now and turning at the lock of a bag. "What does it come to altogether? I feel like a blasted thief, taking you off the captain—I'll throw in one of my razors, however the deal goes. They're Birmingham steel—you can chop wood with 'em and shave on 'em the next minute— settle my conscience, some, when you shave me."

Just as the boat whistled the captain came in. "You're takin' Sam?"

"If it's all right."

The captain sighed. "It's not all right, of course. I'll look up and down the river from now to then and I won't find another. But he'd be loosed from me come two or three years, anyway. And my wife won't nag me about owning a slave, every time I hit Keokuk." He presented a bill and a note. "The interest was paid in March. Counting the paper, four hundred and three-odd—we won't fool with the pence. And remember, sir, he owes you a debt but he's not your slave!"

Ivanhoe laughed softly and Samaliel understood. Samaliel opened the carpetbag and piled up gold pieces on the floor. He counted them three times and gave them to the captain.

Ivanhoe, watching this, added a gold piece and a dollar and the captain gave him the two documents he had brought. Ivanhoe tossed the note over the rail and handed the certificate of transfer to Samaliel.

"You're free, you understand. I'll have you taken back to Iowa. You can pay me when you can or if you want to."

"Sir?" The Bantu turned his head.

"Of course, I didn't mean you wouldn't want to—I meant when the money was convenient."

"Till the money is paid, sir, I'm still your slave."

Ivanhoe grinned. "Any way you want it—but only half of you is my slave at the most. I'd appreciate it if that half would get me my greatcoat and get ready to land us."

Samaliel hesitated. "One thing, sir—"

"What?"

"Would you mind, sir, if I brought my banjo? I won't bother you with it."

Ivanhoe gave him a stern look of reproof. "What kind of man do you think I am! How do you think I'd feel if somebody took away my fiddle?"

"Thank you, sir."

"I've got to get on deck and check cargo," the captain said. "There's just one thing I want to tell you—you don't know the nigger you've got there. Sam will be just as good to you as you are to him.—His father," he added quietly, "is a senator. He'd never admit it, of course, but if you ever go by Washington stop in the Capitol and you'll see which one. There's more to Sam than just nigger. If he'd happened to come light tan instead of brown he could fool anybody and he might be a bigger man than you or me."

"That's no business of mine," Ivanhoe said, drearily and pragmatically. "He can have his own head as long as he takes care of me."

The captain smiled enigmatically. "He'll take care of you —he's trained to that. But sometime you might need him for something bigger than a shave, and then you'll see about Sam—if you keep him liking you."

"I always try to be fair—and I don't—don't expect too much from anybody."

The captain nodded approvingly. "That's right. But Sam won't disappoint you. Well, sir, we'll be glad to have you when you're coming this way again."

"Thanks. The St. Louis & Keokuk line is my ticket from now on."

"It better be." The captain chuckled. The boat veered to port and thrashed at the water of the inside channel. "Unless you're a damn good swimmer. It's the only boat. Goodbye." He hurried to the front of the boat.

St. Louis was principally along the river front though its residences issued yellow oil light from the hills above the possible flood basin. The city had enough people to make a fair-sized army—some said as many as fifteen thousand—but since the budding of the river valley everyone understood that even this great figure was prospectively inconsequential. A transformation as swift as any magician could have achieved was going on in the Mississippi basin. Cabins were becoming villages; villages, towns; towns, cities.

"Sir?"

Ivanhoe lifted his head. "Yes, Samaliel."

"I can plan about the bags better—would you be stayin' long in town?"

"When can we get out?"

"You could catch the *Ed Shippen* in the morning, sir. A handsome boat and makes the downstream run in three days. Or we could wait off at Cairo for the *Sultana*, down from Louisville. Maybe you wouldn't want to be bothered, sir."

"No," said Ivanhoe, "we'll stay the night and take the other one. Do you know any place to stay the night?"

"There are several places, sir, but there's a little guest-house the captain favors—some German folks started it for their kin goin' up the river."

"All right. We'll get off last—I don't want to be in the jam."

"Yes, sir. I've got the bags. Your violin, sir?"

"I'll carry it."

Samaliel smiled slightly. "Yes, sir."

The boat warped in to the wharf. A rope flew out, then another and another so that the boat seemed to be pulled in to dock; the boat's plank was thrust down and a cargo plank was pushed up from the dock; shouting niggers swarmed up and down like army ants under the direction of an officer's corps of white stevedores. Grain sacks, cured carcasses of pigs and cattle, butter tubs, a few bales of furs, crude zinc and lead went out from the aft deck; the little company of passengers hurried down the mid-plank, either to noisy greetings or the shouts of carriage drivers.

Ivanhoe and Samaliel did not leave the boat till the dock was almost empty. The captain shook hands with Ivanhoe and slapped Samaliel on the back roughly.

"You do for him what you'd do for me, Sam. But you can always come back on the boat if you want a job."

"Yes, sir. I 'spect we'll see you again sometime."

Ivanhoe and the captain exchanged an amused glance. There was no question about the present proprietorship of Samaliel.

Samaliel loaded himself with Ivanhoe's bags and his own carrying sack and banjo and stood aside while Ivanhoe went down the gangplank to the wharf and the cobbled street. The crowd had largely dispersed and there was only one sulky-looking carriage driver near—his expression changed when he saw a man with a nigger and he drove up hopefully.

"Tell him where, Samaliel."

They rattled along a street that was bordered about equally with warehouses and gin mills and turned up the hill into quieter parts of the city, away from the continual commerce of the busy river. The driver stopped before a four-story frame building, painted fresh green and white, which displayed a swinging sign: ZUM GASTHAUS—Beds, Meals, Spirits.

"There are half a dozen German families in St. Louis, sir —very respectable people. They come here evenin's to see each other. The place is clean—and if you could bring yourself to touch a bite—"

Ivanhoe sighed and Samaliel was silent but theirs were the only silences in that part of the city:

> "*Im Zuricht auf de Heiden*
> *Ich nahm mich bis zur Leiden*
> *Und was war kuckelt is all' verrückelt*
> *Hei-oh-de-oh, hei-de-oh-ho!*"

> "*Holee-oh-lay-hee, lay-hee, lay-hee, oh-oh—*"

"What do those words mean, Samaliel?"

"Just singin', sir."

"Oh, sure."

The room was warm and damp with the big stoves in the mild spring evening and the effect of warmth was emphasized by the little company of twenty or thirty people who were surveying their beer mugs—two-pint affairs of crockery— laughing at each other and shouting quietly.

> *"Ich weiss nicht was soll es bedeuten*
> *Dass ich so traurig bin—"*

Glump!

> *"Ein Märchen aus alte' Zeiten*
> *Das kommt mir nicht aus dem Sinn—"*

A tall, bony-faced man with gray-brown hair and large iron spectacles hurried out from behind the bar at the sight of Samaliel and then stared myopically and blankly at Ivanhoe.

"Aber, the Herr Captain—?"

Samaliel bowed. "He'll be in by an' by, colonel, sir. I'm servin' this gentleman now."

"Ach, it makes goot. Now the hochgeehrte Frau Captain will not giff him any cuss any more for weil he should flesh and blood in bondage haben."

Ivanhoe laughed. "Nobody can cuss me for it, either. All I've got is a note for half of Samaliel. Can you find me space for myself and my half of him?"

"Oh, ja! We haff de two room zusammen. Very schön. Sie sind müde—all in—nein? Vielleicht gives a pig's ankle, mit Kartoffeln, mit sauerkraut, mit strudel, mit beer. Giffs here am besten beer in Missouri. I make him myself. Giffs then we should make a bath—nein? Denn man schlaft—nein?—wie in the Himmel mit the kleine angels zooping around and make Musik very sanft auf die Harfen. Ist ein very still Haus."

A stout boy hurried up and took the bags from Samaliel. He was obviously the product of some Turnverein or some hayfield, for he handled the heavy pieces almost as lightly as Samaliel as he started up the stair.

"Suite Zweihundert und vier, Werther."

"Two hundred and four!" said Ivanhoe. He knew this much German from his visits in Cincinnati.

The landlord laughed and Samaliel allowed himself a smile.

"We have not so great a building here but it makes big ven ve say hoondred after de' nomber de' floor.—Lieber Gott— ein Geige! Sie sind Spieler?"

He pointed at the violin so that his words needed no translation.

"I play," Ivanhoe conceded.

"Giff the coat—giff the hat. Friedrich—die sopper for de Herr! All of de best! Mach schnell!" His eyes, which had been respectful and humorous, were now entreating. "Verzeihen. I know well Sie sind müde—all worn—aber—the pig's ankle, he make you maybe so strong you play for us?"

"I'm not really hungry," Ivanhoe said, "but I'll be glad to play for you."

With appropriate weariness and heartbreak he opened his violin case.

"Sir," said Samaliel, "I'll go to the kitchen now and get my supper. You can have me fetched in a minute if you want anything." He took his banjo case, nodded to the landlord and went out.

The landlord drew a quart of beer into a covered stein and put it on the table before Ivanhoe.

"Drink first, Herr Geigenspieler. Comes easily laughing music."

Ivanhoe drank. The brew was pale, with a clean, grainy flavor, but Ivanhoe knew with the first long swig that tickled his solar plexus that this was stronger stuff than the heavy, sweetish, brown Bavarian stuff he had drunk in his earlier travels. He drank again quickly and found that the landlord was right—about the quality of his beer—his liver and his heart rebelled against his despondent brain and there was no doubt that there would komm mehr leichtlich Musik das lächelt.

The landlord tapped on the table.

"Verzeihen!" the landlord called. "Schweigen, bitte! Es gibt Musik."

The room quieted instantly. Ivanhoe had managed to do

for most of the rest of the quart in two great gulps. German —well, he couldn't speak German with his face but he could with his violin—

"I come from out the mountains here—"

——

"Where art thou—where art thou—my beloved land?"

——

"Where thou art not—*that* is thy home!"

The tension, the emotion of his audience grew as he played but with his chin and eyes down he could not see that. He himself was the Wanderer: the only possible home he had had for twenty years was usurped by—twins. He finished with tears in his eyes. He finished to find a row of steins and a pile of dollars and smaller change accumulating in front of him, silently deposited by big, square-faced men who were almost furtively anxious to hide their faces and what they showed.

Then applause started and grew into shouts of "Hoch!" and "Wieder!" and stamping, and shouted approval that Ivanhoe did not understand. A Negro came from the kitchen with his dinner—two very large pig knuckles, less than a bushel of mashed-and-baked potatoes, about the same amount of sauerkraut, a quantity of the first salads of the year, with some accompanying items of pickles and spiced preserves.

Ivanhoe had a drink of ale and looked at this pile of food. The smell from the pork ankles made him feel that he might be able to take a bite or two, untrue as such action was to all his higher instincts. Well, he thought, he ought to be kind to these people who were evidently well-intentioned and certainly appreciative. He would have to play at length after he had eaten and he must build up strength—a few bites.

He ate and drank hurriedly so that he finished in about three-quarters of an hour, with a piece of apple cake and a large piece of cheese. After that the landlord hurried up with coffee that was almost fit for a knife and fork, and a tiny glass of French brandy. Ivanhoe's wounded soul struggled with his replete body:

Soul: "We are wounded beyond all aid; life's fairest hopes are ashes."

Body: "The best beer I ever drank."

Soul: "How are the afflictions of spurned love to be endured?"

Body: "They certainly can raise a pig in Missouri."

Soul: "When love is gone, what remains?"

Body: "—apple strudel—"

These violently disparate opinions and attitudes shook Ivanhoe's being till the landlord brought a cigar from Habana.

"Sie—wird—you will give us some more the music?"

Ivanhoe nodded his long head sadly and picked up the violin. That moment all conversation and all laughter stopped. He tried his strings and found that the E was slacking too much for the time it had been tuned. He was pleased by this. He liked almost everything but cats. But—for the moment—this would serve.

Ivanhoe looked around at the expectant company. They were chiefly good broad German faces—family groups of solid burgher types, stout mammas, flaxen and towheaded youngsters, some pretty girls sitting at their mothers' sides, sipping at long thin glasses and pretending not to notice glances from a long table where ten dapperly dressed young men seemed to have a private club, devoted to collecting the largest steins in the world.

All the furnishings were green and fresh—cross-legged benches and tables, green walls garlanded with spring branches and appleblossoms. The bar might have been transplanted from Cincinnati—rows of steins and glasses, an inlaid ale pump and above it the inevitable engravings of Goethe and Schiller. Significantly, there were no political pictures, for politics in Germany had been in a highly feverish condition almost constantly since the Napoleonic Wars.

Ivanhoe addressed the room. "What do you want, please?"

"Tannenbaum—Stille Nacht—Lorelei—Heidenröslein—"

and a dozen others of which Ivanhoe had never heard—then everyone laughed and took a drink of beer.

"Um Gottes Willen," said the lanky host, "play was Sie wish—aber, nichts traurig—not sad, bitte."

A dollar bill floated down on the table. A voice said in perfectly good frontier American, "Kin you play, 'Oh, Wounded Heart, Wherefore Repine'?"

Ivanhoe turned and looked at the man in the dark corner. Even seated, slumped on his elbows over his beer, it was evident that he was enormous, with a long, raw, dolorous face framed by straight hair parted exactly in the middle; he was definitely lantern-jawed, hawk-nosed and even in his big, muscular neck a remarkable Adam's apple bobbed startlingly up and down at the moment, from emotion, not beer.

Ivanhoe bowed, retrieved the dollar, poised his bow and let the room have one of the elaborate and juicy laments that always took over American music when the Americans were not engaged in shooting up the militia of some other nation. The backwoodsman's nose drooped lower and lower toward his beer. When Ivanhoe had finished he lifted the sad eyes, without raising his face and said:

"Bully."

His voice was soft and husky. He waved a careless hand at the rest of the room and took a drink of beer. For one moment the two men looked each other full in the face—the big man's face had some foam on it—and knew that they were joined by irretrievable misfortune. Ivanhoe nodded that there would be a later meeting and turned to the room, noting with some satisfaction that it had become a dismal room; the wounded heart had filled it with repining and Sehnsucht—the search for an unknown fulfillment of emotion and desires—and that hardly a mouth was dry, or unmarked by the excellent ale. Even the young men at the long table stared at the board instead of at the ankles of the young maidens—they all had memories, ranging from curls to kisses.

Ivanhoe had a notion to play "The Wither'd Bower That Once Was Green" and make them all cry but he was sufficiently experienced to know that this spending of animal moisture would not be replaced by demands on the beer spigot—rather, by moodiness and reminiscence and early homefaring. This wouldn't please the landlord.

To change the mood, to stir the party, Ivanhoe played another song about bowers—the word had caught in his mind.

"Will you come to the bowers I have shaded for thee?"

He got no further. At the second phrase everyone knew the tune—the signal, played on a flute, that had sent Sam Houston's men to attack and rout twice their number of Mexicans two years before, when the Texans were "bottled up." Everyone in the States knew that tune. The Mexicans were driving nine hundred Texans against a river; the Texans were glad to go into an inescapable pocket because it brought in the enemy.

"Will you come to the bowers I have shaded for thee?"

The flute notes sounded the invitation and the pursuing army of Mexico fled on that daybreak; Santa Anna up from his breakfast table, guns forgotten, everything forgotten except flight, as a mob of Texans came down upon them in no formation known to gods or men, shouting of the Alamo and using the rifle, the pistol, the bayonet, the knife; far beyond the commands of the officers, till the stragglers of the opponent made the phrase of surrender, "No Alamo— no Alamo," to save their lives. They weren't there when Santa Anna killed every North American except one man and one horse.

The response of the Germans to the foolish song which had once had popularity was sufficiently stirring. Everyone knew what it meant—the light defiance of the States to everybody. They could raise two new Napoleons every ten minutes. If anyone wanted to fight Sam Houston or old General Scott he'd better bring his funeral wreaths with him, or they might stir up Andy Jackson.

They let Ivanhoe go on with his song after a few minutes, these people who had been exiled from their own countries because they felt that no man was incomparably better than any good man. They all sang, they all drank, and Ivanhoe fiddled. He played Mozart, he played the songs of Beethoven, he played "Honey in the Gourd" and "Missy"; he played "Cujus Animam" and Balfe and he played southern songs, "The Turmut Growin'" and "Scarlet Town."

Even the young folks paid him their respects and their shillings before they left but he went on till the room was almost empty and he was suddenly alone with the beaming host and the big man from up North. Both these people bore down on him as soon as the last party had left at the late hour of eleven-thirty.

"Prachtig! Herrlich! Vunnerful!" said the landlord. "This house, her is yours so long als Sie wish zu bleiben—to stay mit. I make you nun for nightcap de schönsten rum milk punch it giffs ever. Und also für dich, mein Freund Kolossus."

The frontiersman, big as he had seemed at table, now loomed gigantic in the candlelight. He was as close to seven feet as six but so proportioned that he seemed squat for his height—his chest and belly came down straight and full from his thick spreading shoulders; the mournful face seemed ludicrously improbable atop such evident efficiency and power. What was there the man wanted he couldn't take?

The landlord hurried to the kitchen to prepare the hot punch. As the door swung open and shut Ivanhoe thought he heard a twanging of music for an instant.

The stranger put out his tabletop hand. "My name's Charley—Charley Hoskin—from Michigan. You're the best damn fiddler I ever heard. I love fiddles—had one once but I couldn't do nothing with it. Anybody can learn to make music on one like you do's good enough for me. You don't know what you've did for me tonight."

Ivanhoe took the hard paw with some inward fears, but the giant's quick squeeze was deliberately gentle.

"My name's Ivanhoe Keeler. I'm from the Mississippi Valley—Iowa was the last stop."

The big man studied him for a moment with curiously perceptive eyes. "Girl?" he inquired.

"Yeah."

"Me too." Charley paused for a moment and then added

moodily, "She said she wasn't goin' to marry no covered wagon."

Ivanhoe laughed bitterly. "Hunh! Plenty of girls like a big fellow. I left my girl a year to fiddle enough money for a farm and when I came back she was spliced—and worse—"

"Baby, I bet you!"

"Twins."

Charley looked up from his stein with consternation. "Jesus! That's bad!" He ended the stein with a mighty gulp. "Two twins in a year—and married!" He had a consolatory thought. "Maybe they was early."

"Sue isn't the kind of girl—"

"No harm meant. Only if she hadn't been true to you till she was married it might kind of—you might feel—it wouldn't be—"

"Oh, sure. The twins make things some better."

"Esther Lou," the big man said somberly, "didn't even have another steady fellow. She turned me down for bein' a covered wagon—that was all."

"That's downright mean."

"Mein' Herren!" The landlord brought in a steaming bowl and glasses. "To your goot health. Sitzen Sie so long als Sie wünschen, aber tomorrow gibt a new day for me komm five clock." He yawned against his knuckles. "De black boy brings all other you tell him. Gute nacht."

"Good night," Ivanhoe and Charley said.

The landlord turned at the door with his candle. "The *Ed Shippen* fürht aus for New Orleans at neun Uhr—but if you could ein mehr Nacht stehen und de Musik machen de best it giffs me I giff you for de Musik."

Ivanhoe shook his head. "Thanks—I've got to get on. I'll come back sometime and stay longer."

"Ah—ist goot—come soon."

Charley ladled out the rich milk punch, aromatic with New Orleans rum.

He gulped a half pint of it and wiped his mouth with his hand. "Tastes to me like the landlord was tryin' to save milk," he commented.

Ivanhoe tried his. It was fire delivered in a velvet package but it was very soothing, eminently suited to take a man to dreamless and refreshing slumber. Charley filled up the mugs again.

"There's nothin' I admire better'n a good fiddler and you're the best of them. Here's your good health, Mr. Keeler, and if you ever see anybody you don't like don't risk your hands on them—just let Charley Hoskin know." They drank. "I'm conside'ed capable at changin' the faces and physiologies of ornery creatures of the human race."

He emptied his mug and ladled again from the gallon bowl. "What you goin' to do about—her? The twins girl."

Ivanhoe shrugged. "I read somewhere you're supposed to take a trip on the ocean if you don't take to drink. I can't play if I drink too much. I guess I'll go to Paris, France."

The big man looked thoughtful. "That's a good idea. I don't get no good out of drink—once I drank a couple bottles of apple brandy and they give me a headache. Dogged if I ain't a notion to come with you—that is, if you don't mind."

"I should say not. We're kind of two fellows in—out of a boat. I'll set you up to the trip if you want to come."

The big man ladled. "Now that's darn nice of you—but I'm heeled. I got a farm in Michigan that's goin' to be worth something. And I been loggin' in Wisconsin Territory. I rafted down a hundred cord or so of choice spruce and pine through Black River and the Miss' and what with my ready cash I dug up when Esther Lou turned me down I guess I'm set for about six hundred round dollars and always a farm to go back to."

Ivanhoe nodded. "That ought to be plenty—but if you run shy my coon's got three or four thousand of mine and I can make a little bit maybe, here and there, scratching on my fiddle—violin."

"Your *coon* has!"

"Yeah, in my bags—he takes care of them."

Charley gave Ivanhoe a look that was at once bewildered, suspicious and scornful. "You mean you're leaving a coon take care of three-four thousand of the needful for you? How long you had him in your family?"

"Yesterday and today."

"J. H. Christ!" The big man sprang to his feet and it was curious to see that stallion bulk move with the speed and lightness of a cat. "He'll be gone." He opened the kitchen door with such slow steadiness that there was no slightest rasp of the lifting latch.

"Go uway—go uway—bug don't bite the 'baccy,
  Go to chawin' on the leaf, I smash you up, by cracky.
  I tell him once—I tell him twice—old bug don't keep away—
  So I leave him in the master's field—but I leave him—to stay."

Charley tiptoed back. "Your nigger the big fellow with the banjo?"

Ivanhoe, preoccupied, nodded.

"He's got every nigger in forty acres in the kitchen listenin'."

Ivanhoe lifted his hand. "Wait a minute before you shut the door."

"Liz ain't true to me
  An' I'm so true to her—
  Someone'll work the other way
  Is what I'm lookin' fer."

The applause was whispered, as the strings and voice had been muted but it was an impressive volume of sibilance. Charley closed the door as carefully as he had opened it and tiptoed back.

"Ivanhoe, you ever beat that nigger?"

"I wouldn't beat a nigger. I'd kick his pants and tell him to get out."

"Maybe if you beat him he'd feel bad like us and play as good as you do."

Ivanhoe explained the arrangement of property values in Samaliel.

The punch jar was low. "You don't know which half." Charley sighed. "If it was top or bottom or either side you could slap it at him, but suppose it's checkered—he could say so—and you'd have to beat him with a pin. Oh, goodness! Music's all I got left—and he'd be another one if he was sad, like you. I guess I better get to bed if I'm going to catch old *Shippen*. See you at breakfast."

"See you."

Ivanhoe knew that his things would be perfectly disposed, as they were. He touched his fingers to the stair once in climbing unsteadily to his room. A warm brick wrapped in flannel, at the foot of the feather bed showed that Samaliel never let his art interfere with his solicitude.

Ivanhoe did not toss, yearn, or regret. He went sound asleep.

At his first stirring the next morning there was a soft rap on the door joining his room and Samaliel's.

"Come!"

Samaliel appeared with a steaming can of water, a pot of coffee and a large bottle full of white powder. "Morning, sir." He filled the coffee cup, put in the proper amount of sugar and cream, stirred it and handed it to Ivanhoe.

"Good!" said Ivanhoe and sipped the coffee gratefully. "What's that bottle?"

Samaliel was spreading out towels convenient to the wash-table and the easy chair. "Fizzin' salts, sir. I didn't hear when you came to bed."

Ivanhoe laughed and moved on the washbowl. "Darn good reason—you were playing your banjo to all the black folks in St. Louis in the kitchen."

For a bare second the white teeth flashed in a smile. "I hope we didn't disturb you, sir. We played soft."

"Me? A military band couldn't have disturbed me. But I thought you'd be dead on your feet this morning.—No, no fizzin' salts; my head's fizzin' a little but that'll clear up with breakfast." Ivanhoe settled down in the chair and enjoyed the caress of the lather and the soft brushing of a perfect razor stroke—all this for a petty four hundred dollars he didn't need any more anyway!

"Your hand's steady enough, all right."

"Sleep don't bother me, sir. I take it when I can get it.

If you'd got out of bed in the night I'd have heard you, sir. I learned in the war—I was with my colonel, sir."

"How in the world did your colonel happen to sell you?"

"Horses, sir."

"The gee-gees got him. I went through Kentucky once. Fine state."

"Yes, sir."

A hot towel and then the pleasant shock of a cold one and all the fizzin' went out of Ivanhoe's head. For one minute he felt on top of the heap—a sunny day pleasantly started, the assurance of indefinite perfect shaves, the bland odor of witch hazel, the prospect of new adventure, a new friend— and then God caught up with him and he remembered Sue.

His face changed so suddenly that Samaliel stepped back, alarmed. "Did I scrape you somewhere, sir? It burns?" He was referring to the lotion.

"Not the witch hazel, Samaliel. Go get your breakfast now. We have to be packed by eight-fifteen."

The guests in residence were all eating at the long table when Ivanhoe got downstairs, among them the captain of the Keokuk boat and Charley Hoskin. Charley had kept a place vacant next to his own chair by the simple expedient of spreading his shoulders till they took up two places.

"Old sock! What'd you do with your fiddle? We'd have time for a tune after breakfast."

Before Ivanhoe could reply the landlord was on him. "You haff well slept? De Bett is goot, ja?"

"The only decent bed I've slept on since a year ago in Cincinnati. Just any little thing for breakfast, mein Herr."

"Ach! Not even a poopy dog would we treat so!" He hurried to the kitchen.

The captain looked at Ivanhoe steadily and pointed to a razor nick on his own chin reproachfully.

The breakfast stretched out incredibly, with relays of cookery that would alone have justified the existence of the German people. The landlord was fascinated and delighted by the performance of Charley Hoskin—that powerful engine stoked himself as if he were a nigger fireman tossing on pitch-sticks for a race with the *Sultana*.

The big German youth began to carry down luggage and pile it at the door to the continuous urging of "Mach schnell, Werther!" from the host. Samaliel came at last with the carpetbags, the banjo and the violin.

At the door the host begged Ivanhoe to return quickly "zurück so schnell wie möglich."

In the carriage, Charley Hoskin leaned back and sighed, working a toothpick scientifically. "Not a bad Dutchman," he observed. "He sure puts out a square meal. I think he's got an ear for moozik, too—that says a lot for him."

Ivanhoe smiled. "Yes, I guess the twenty-one buckwheat cakes, four cups of coffee, two slices of ham, six fried eggs, two pitchers of milk and loaf of bread you ate to take the edge off your hunger would pass as a square meal—I don't know what you had before I came down—a toasted horse maybe. I hope the poor Dutchman doesn't have anything but consumptives now for a while, so he can catch up on his provision bill."

Charley looked at him with wide, concerned eyes. "Ive, I never thought of that. I bet you between supper, sheets and breakfast that poor fellow lost money on me—not to speak of his labor and his help. Have we got time to go back? I'll give him another dollar."

Ivanhoe pulled out his watch. "No, we haven't, I'm afraid. He didn't make any money on me, either, but don't worry—he enjoyed watching you eat."

Charley sank back again as the carriage rattled over the cobbles before the cathedral. "I always did get a lot of good out of my vittles. I guess I'm a borned hog but I don't like to leave table feelin' hollow—look at that! A meetin'house—fellow, is that a cracky! Oh, oh! Catholic for my money!"

Ivanhoe observed the cross on the steeple of the great pile and nodded. "Catholic—an old one."

"I don't see why us damn Congregationalists don't have churches like that."

Ivanhoe studied this. "I guess they're in a hurry and want to get 'em up faster and scattered around more."

Charley nodded. "That's it! You got it."

They digested quietly in a warm world of physical satisfaction that made their spiritual anguish dull and dim—a souvenir of unhappiness.

They came to the brow of the river hill and stared down at a busy inland port. Drays, horses, men and boats were swarming to make the most of the daylight hours, though there were usually flares burning and lanterns flashing about the water front throughout the night. Even in a city like St. Louis the docks and warehouses were still disheveled flimsy affairs with the exception of the big passenger companies' pavilions and elaborate loading arrangements.

St. Louis was a comparatively small city but it was growing with tremendous rapidity and growing first along the great, muddy river—the Mesesaba of the Indians. Its commerce was already large enough for a town three times its size; the quiet little administrative town of the old Spanish government and a scanty Indian-trading commercial center were being swept under by bales and rafts and sacks—wool, fur, hides, livestock, timber and all the rest from up the river. In the third year of the eastern depression distress had driven population into the upper reaches of the river with all the efficiency of Genghis Khan, and St. Louis was suddenly gorged and bewildered with marketable stuffs which paid their profits but demanded handling.

The tide had grown steadily without a recess. "Smart" men in St. Louis knew that it had to be a bigger city—rapidly; almost instantly. It had to house many more tradesmen, brokers, laborers, rivermen, lawyers, preachers, beggarmen and thieves. Boats were kept waiting till docks were free; warehouses ran up slowly and goods were piled along the river front awaiting storage space and men to handle the stuff. They needed more sawmills—they needed everything—and thousands of artisans and common workers who had set out grimly from the East to pioneer at unpracticed agricul-

ture on the frontier settled down to surprising prosperity at
the river crossroad.

While the East dabbled at currency adjustments and the
economics of despair, the great valley struggled under a
crushing overload of commodities—the hell with the green-
back; go shear a sheep, or saw a tree, or butcher a pig.

Some consciousness of this infant prodigality came to a
person as detached as Ivanhoe Keeler when the carriage
stopped at the entrance to the dock of the *Ed Shippen*.
Everything was frantic up and down the cobbled bank of
the river. Ivanhoe always compared everything urban with
Cincinnati—the most urbane city he had ever seen, perhaps
the most urbane city in North America. Sometimes its ordering was restless, along the Ohio, but it was never insane. You
might curse a man to get him to do more than a fair day's
work, but you never cursed him to do two days' work, at
fifty cents a day. These St. Louis fellows were getting special
pay—maybe six bits—because they tried harder and didn't
talk back.

Only, they didn't curse the niggers. These went in gangs
and they went by music. With a hundred pounds of wheat on
their backs they'd trot across the tricky flooring to a gangplank in an even file, the little man keeping his pace with
the big one.

There was a cough from a little distance and Samaliel
approached.

"Everything is locked in, sir, except the violin. The boat
is still taking wood, sir. It won't be off for an hour at least.
I've taken chairs in the saloon, sir, if you care to come in."

Ivanhoe turned his head to Charley. "Sixty minutes.
What we do?"

"Oh, let's run over to the tavern, there. We'll be on the
boat three days. Let's see a little of the town. Pick up your
fiddle."

Ivanhoe smiled. Charley knew that a tavern meant company and that company meant fiddling—the big man was
timid about asking for fiddling for his own sole benefit.

Seen nearer at hand there was nothing inviting about the

tavern except the large sign—WINE, BEER & SPIRITS—across the front of it. It had flush, vertical clapboarding; a windowed door had been let into the great double doors which proved that the place had once been a warehouse, probably grown untenable.

The inside bore out this promise. The only light came from the three front windows; the sawdust on the floor was soaked with tobacco juice; the plain oak bar, probably nailed together on the premises, was blotched with the soakings of many spilled drinks. Behind the bar, in obvious fear, a meek-faced little man with thinning gray hair hurried up bottles for a half dozen toughs, dockworkers, who alternated in cursing him and shouting at each other.

Ivanhoe had half turned to leave but Charley pushed on to the bar.

He threw down a quarter. "Double whisky."

"Yes, sir." The old man's voice was not quite steady.

Charley suddenly felt very sorry for him and when Charley felt sorry for anyone it was usually a good time for everyone to feel sorry.

"Nice little place you got here—" but at this moment one of the toughs noticed Ivanhoe and Samaliel.

"My God, men—a fiddler with a nigger! Come on, fiddler, don't be skeered. You play and we'll have the nigger dance!"

Ivanhoe was no coward—when he didn't have his violin. With that in his arms he was an utter craven. He shrank back.

One of the dock hands stepped forward and took him too politely, mincingly, by the arm. "Don't be afeard, sister, we wouldn't hurt a hair of your sweet little head—"

This was one of the moments that Ivanhoe most feared. It was when he forgot the violin, forgot politeness, forgot everything—sometime he might even hit somebody with the precious instrument and to destroy it would be like murdering an old sweetheart.

He struck with skill and power, with all the force of his free left hand, and the tough staggered, sagging, just far enough to make a perfect carom off the ham of bone and leather that Charley used for a hand. It was a perfect blow, with the snap and shock of a jab and the carrying power of a swinging hook; the big dock hand went a yard and a half without touching his feet and came to rest with the characteristic wet-ragginess of one who will not be troubled by the world's ills and worries for a half hour or so.

The room hesitated one instant after that terrible stroke and then they were on Charley altogether.

Ivanhoe was always hazy about what happened in the next two minutes. They were piling up on Charley—he put down his violin on the bar—saw Samaliel spring forward and bring down his man with a blow in the throat—and there was Charley with a firm clutch on two necks—the faces mashed together with a muddy sound.

Charley smiled gently at the proprietor. "Don't stir yourself—I'll drag them out."

Samaliel's victim and the parties Charley had introduced had staggered out on their own power but the other three were lying with their noses in the sawdust. Charley picked two of them up and dropped them on their backs in the mud, outside, so that they could breathe more freely.

Samaliel had the other one. He shook his head. "Kind of moved this gentleman's jaw out of place, sir."

"Hope it makes him talk quieter, after this."

But Samaliel shook his head again. He fingered the dislocation for a moment and then with a quick jerk put the jaw back in place. Then he placed the unconscious man neatly beside the others in the mud.

Charley looked on, wondering. "Where the hell did you get this coon, Ive? Sammy, you step up here and have a drink like a white man. It's good after exercise. What'd you do to that guy? I could hear him gruntin' like a jammed whistle."

"Adam's apple, sir, when he drew back to hit you. It hu'ts."

Charley bubbled with deep amusement. "Well, it didn't

seem exactly soothin'—what! Sherry? There's nothing in that."

"Excuse me, sir. This is an occasion, but beer and cider are enough for me, regular." Samaliel bowed and retired from the bar to one of the tables far back in the room. He was far more strict in watching the color line than the white men.

The proprietor was white and shaking so that the bottles rattled when he put them on the bar. "Gentlemen, these drinks are with my compliments."

"Your compliments," Ivanhoe said slowly. "Listen, sir, how did you get into this business in this hellhole, if you'll pardon the question? You hate it."

The aging man glanced up with surprise and appreciation. "Yes. It's too long to tell. I was a buyer's man in Syracuse till the great Van Buren and his depression came along. I lost what I had—my son too. He took to accountancy in New York. He was very well trained. I thought I'd find something in the new settlements. When I got here it wasn't hard to see what will finally happen—this town will certainly be a great town. I thought if I could find any little business that would keep me I could put the eight hundred dollars I had scraped out of the mess in some real property. In twenty years, gentlemen, which is as long as I will live, this privy will be worth a fortune. I'm informed on such things. But whether fifteen hours of daily terror are worth it—I doubt. There are assaults—well, leave that. I didn't realize when I bought it that a tavern in this place was something different from the old places back home."

Charley looked across his glass at Ivanhoe with full confidence. "All right, Ive, what can we do for this poor—this friend of ours?"

"If you gentlemen would share with me," the proprietor said eagerly, "I'd share with you. Come—I'll give you half-ownership; if order were kept and we had music, half the profits would more than keep all of us. We could clean the place and paint it—"

He stopped while Ivanhoe and Charley exchanged a long, sorrowful glance.

"I shouldn't have suggested it. Truly, in twenty years, gentlemen, the place would make your fortunes—but you're young; you can make them yourselves."

"Samaliel!"

"Yes, sir?"

"Go get me a thousand dollars."

"Uh—y-yes, sir."

Ivanhoe spoke to the proprietor. "What could you do with a thousand dollars?"

The old man's face was dull and then, abruptly, he began to cry. He stopped immediately. "If this is a joke, gentlemen, it's a joke in bad taste." His gray eyes burned. "You led me on—"

"Easy, partner," the great Charley said. "He has to think. Keep quiet."

Charley watched Ivanhoe reverently while Ivanhoe thought.

"We'll take half, but you spend the other six hundred on the place. Get it in apple-pie order. You can hire a dozen of the toughest bums in St. Louis to see that it's orderly. Fix it so you'll get the good trade of people stopping for a minute off boats. Put your prices up to keep away the toughs. Make it like the taverns you remember back home—they'll like that. Buy a good pine bar. Get a lot of liquor you could drink yourself. Hire a bartender—you mix with the folks. Put up a great big sign. Unnh—glass your roof and get some light; three or four windows would do it. Get somebody to shine the stove and clean the floor—every day. Will a thousand cover that?"

"And more, sir."

"All right. We'll be back in a year or two, maybe. Old man, you can keep the books."

"With a thousand dollars!"

He took a sheet of paper from the cupboard under the bar and made out a recognizance.

Samaliel returned with a paper parcel. "There, sir." He turned to Ivanhoe. "Ten minutes, sir—the last cords are going on."

The old man opened the parcel and the dim light glinted against the gold. For a moment the proprietor was frightened. He picked up a fingerful of the pieces and put them back again.

"A thousand dollars!"

"It's all right," Ivanhoe said. "Do the best you can."

III

The *Ed Shippen* was all engines and luxury. The breadth and height of the piston-rod housings told of the power below the elaborate and gilded passenger decks. Atop, everything that contemporary ornament could suggest; below, an eager, prideful hell. The wood was piled for its uses—slow-draft in one great stack to hold the fires if the boat had to stop for fixing or the boilers got too unreasonably high—a few points beyond the indicator's explosion point; pitch pine, hickory and elm for the controlled fury of the hot fires. The *Ed Shippen* was off its route on a trial trip: some smarty might be coming down from Louisville to meet them at Cairo—at the junction of the Ohio and the Mississippi. That was the *Ed Shippen's* usual route. Everybody was ready for trouble. Nobody ever beat the *Ed Shippen* on an even start.

The colored hands were humming, "Squat a niggah on de safety valve!"

They were the muscles and arteries of the boat. Its credit was theirs and was so recognized in every port from St. Louis to Donaldsonville and New Orleans by honey-wenches and black barkeeps in the river hot spots; the biggest levee loafer deferred to the smallest deck boy on the *Natchez, Ed Shippen, Empress* or *J. M. White* as if, somehow, the greatness of the boat must be subtly transmitted to the being of the man.

This part of life moved on the general aorta of the river, and every human affair, white or black, was interpreted in its terms. The boats could compete with any hotel in the world in elegance and frippery—this was one tone; but they could sprint like wild horses, they would scald, burn, or blast

life out casually for a trivial supremacy—that was the under-
tone. The same was true of the men who worked the boats.
The niggers were sporty niggers and the white men were
urbanites of the astonishing Mississippi Valley metropolis—
the well-populated flowing city between New Orleans and
St. Louis, the Paris that was 1,218 miles long and seldom
more than two miles wide. They were as gaudy, assured and
violent, with all the potentialities of explosion, as the *Ed
Shippen* herself.

Samaliel had secured two staterooms en suite, a large and
elaborate bedroom for Ivanhoe and Charley and a small, attached servant's room for himself. Charley gaped at everything with the astonished delight of a child, the gilding and
ornament, the draperies, the prodigally framed pictures, the
rococo furniture—he even admired the awful painting of a
clipper ship on the door.

"Gollies, boy! If the beds wasn't here I'd figure this was
the parlor!"

The "opera" houses Ivanhoe had visited in his travels
enabled him to be blasé in the face of this luxury. "Well
back in the boat. Sam thinks of everything. If the boilers let
loose we might have a chance to swim."

"Oh, hell," said Charley, "they wouldn't blow up a contraption like this. This carpet alone must've cost a hundred
dollars, maybe. 'J you look at your fiddle, Ive, to make sure
she was O.K.?"

Ivanhoe grinned and looked at his fiddle. He played
"Honey in the Gourd" while Charley beat time with his toe.
Charley sighed when Ivanhoe put the violin back in its case.

"That fiddle was sure sugar-cured." His long face grew
sorrowful. "She sounds just like Esther Lou singin'."

"It's an Italian fiddle," Ivanhoe said quickly. "Guarnerius,
or something like that. I bought it in Cincinnati from an
Irishman who stole it in Philadelphia. Hundred and fifty
dollars I gave him."

"Jesus Christ!" said Charley. "It's a good fiddle, all right,
but he stung you plenty! Ten dollars is a good price for a
fiddle."

"I liked this one," Ivanhoe said simply. "I threw in my old one on the deal."

Samaliel tapped at the communicating door and entered. "They're castin' off the lines, sirs, if you'd want to see. We'll be movin' in a minute."

The morning air was pleasantly cool on deck and the morning sun, starting its daily tour from Illinois to California, was dazzlingly crimson on the water. The paddles were turning slowly so that the boat's rudder could keep her nose up the river, to clear the dock, and the lap of water boiled up the sloping stone levee.

The last rope came in and the captain, saluting and receiving a salute from the impassive god of the pilothouse, shouted "Up anchor!" Four sweating niggers surged at the winch and immediately bells clanged, the water foamed and the boat described a shallow crescent and turned down into the Mississippi.

On the way to Paris, France! Ivanhoe experienced an objectionable lightness of heart. Down the river—New Orleans—Habana—Charleston—Philadelphia—New York—the Atlantic—Paris, France. That last rope had freed him of Sue and her twins—well, almost.

"I've been a fool all my life," he mentioned to Charley.

"Listen," said Charley. "I'd bet my bottom dollar that old guy will be good for the money. Anyhow, what d'you care? What d'I care? What good is money? You can fiddle and I can fight—why should we worry?"

Ivanhoe smiled a slow, sad smile. Charley's face grew dolorous and then he slapped Ivanhoe on the back and nearly knocked him into the thick, disagreeable water of the Mississippi.

"We'll forget 'em, hey, boy? They never done nothing for us but make us feel bad. Me—a prairie ship; you—twins. Just remember, in several weeks or so we'll be on the ocean and you say everything gets over when you get on the ocean —so why put it off? This ain't a bad ocean we're on right now."

"I courted her four years," Ivanhoe said. "She had molas-

ses-colored hair and her eyes were always waiting to laugh
when they weren't laughing. She could fix her little mouth so
funny when she played being mad and teased me. Charley,
she just raised hell with me. I guess I knew she wasn't ever
going to have me—but when she made it kind of definite,
this way—why, it was—upsetting, you might say."

"Sure," Charley said sympathetically. "That's about the
way it was with me, but her hair was light. She had big blue
eyes. She looked like a doll-baby that had to be tooken care
of, which I would. An' then she told me she was tired of not
seeing nobody because there was always a prairie schooner
in the house. I took the hint."

Ivanhoe was desolating in his sorrows. Even his tight trousers seemed lank and the longitudes of his face deepened and
drew together. "Her dad said—it came to me—that I was a
fiddler and nothing but a butterfly."

Charley forgot his grief and his face set ominously. "The
bastard!"

There were not more than forty or fifty passengers for the
downtrip. The boat would be jammed coming up from New
Orleans to the new lands of the West, but there were few
occasions for anyone to go down to New Orleans—trading
men chiefly, who would buy and ship from the gulf docks;
a scattering of defeated souls who had found pioneering too
difficult; some social callers and a dozen or so setting out for
the new cattle and cotton empires of Texas.

"I want to tell you one thing," Charley said, demolishing
the mood with his usual violence. "No one can lick five men
with his fists. When you hit that fellow you ought to've
known where you were puttin' your violin. Then when the
next two comes in you step back and give 'em a little yank
so they bang their heads together. Then you set yourself so
the next pair comes in opposite directions. Use stratecky."

Ivanhoe, glancing at the broad, thick shoulders and the
great hands, had some inner reflections but he said only,
"That's right."

It proved that there was no competition from the Ohio
River. For two days the sounds of the leadsmen were the

only noises of navigation on the boat, aside from the quiet, steamy rumbling of the machinery. In the main the party was not a happy one—hopeful people went *up* the river. Charley was taken in by two card sharks just above Donaldsonville and showed some signs of real impatience when Ivanhoe attempted to save him by mentioning berths. He was winning—a pigeon to the lure.

Ivanhoe stirred in his bed when Charley came down to the stateroom. The man was grinning.

"They wouldn't play honest so I didn't neither!" He dropped a heavy roll and fold of bills on the blanket. "Must come close to a thousand dollars, hey, Ive?"

"How did you—get away with this?"

Charley grinned again and threw a two-barreled pistol on the bed. When the trigger was pulled it fired a barrel and jerked a new barrel and cartridge into place. The bullets were bigger than peas—they'd make an inch hole in a man, going in, and a three-inch hole afterward if they happened to come out.

Charley wanted to tell about it. "Stud's a funny game. I get aces back to back. They raise and they raise and they raise. I don't get anything more but we keep on. Get about eight hundred in the pot and the slick fellow across from me puts down three queens. I put down three aces and take the pot—"

"Three! You had only two."

Charley put out his two hands over the berth, fingers spread. He moved his thumbs, almost indiscernibly, and the ace of spades and ace of hearts fluttered down on the blankets.

"Thought I might need them. Looked at my hand and swapped one of these fellows for something else—just ruffling the show cards. Then somebody noticed a seven was turned to ace." Charley picked up the two-barreled pistol and snapped the barrels so that they changed places.

"Had my feet fixed under the table—kicked it up under his chin. I picked up the plaything and took out the loads. His folks carted him off."

Ivanhoe was concerned. "We'd better sit up, Charley. They'll be back."

Charley shook his head. "No, no. I told 'em to get off the next landing or I'd throw 'em in the river. We wooded an hour ago and they went off."

On the fourth day the boat drew up to the moldy, stinking, discolored docks of New Orleans, where porters, whores, steerers and every kind of obscene assistant waited to lend a hand and a claw.

PART II

THE ANGEL WITH A COMB

ONCE the *Gulf Belle* was through the Delta Sammy relaxed and was his old efficient self. They all knew that it was almost as easy to steal a slave as a pocketbook in this muddy, dark, devious city, and Samaliel knew about the lives of black men in Louisiana and Mississippi. The whites were careful with their horses but they would light up a black man as carelessly as a Caesar illuminating his gardens with a Christian, or skin him with a woven whip till the bones of his back showed gristly white and bloody.

The dregs of black and white humanity settled out of the American nation here along the great gulf and they mistreated each other in ways that would have made an Iroquois torturer wonder and admire. The Negroes suffered most, of course, but they had their secret lodges and sometimes the body of a white man was found in a backwater or a lake— limbs crushed to ribbons, scorched eye sockets, tongueless, emasculated and half flayed. When one of the persecutors fell into their hands the black men tried to retort to the whole race, upon one body.

After such a discovery the whip fell mercilessly and sometimes fatally upon the innocent and the unknown guilty alike until some morning an overseer could not be found. He might turn up later, down the river, with the stigmata of crucifixion and other marks upon his body. It was an undeclared war of the most heinous cruelty. No good nigger was ever sold down the river any more than a faithful dog would be handed over to a vivisectionist. The black men who were condemned to the Gulf states were fitting companions of the men who bought them.

The *Gulf Belle* was a coasting boat, steam and sail, and sadly different from the *Ed Shippen*. Charley had a berth over Ivanhoe's and Samaliel had made himself a pallet on the floor to be ready for any call. A dozen passengers and the officers ate at one long table; the crew ate below on the next deck. The boat rode badly, with nothing but some cotton in the hold and the cargo line four feet above water, but the captain assured his guests that at Habana they would have heavier lading and the *Gulf Belle* would sail like a duck. Meanwhile, there were five hundred miles of the gulf, and the gulf was not placid.

Ivanhoe first noticed this when a small, disheartening tingle spiraled from his stomach to his ears. He shook his head and that threw his eyes out of place. They were very slow in returning to their proper situations. The boat lay over on a curious three-dimensional hypotenuse, jumped at the stern and then reversed. The tingle was up under Ivanhoe's breast-bone now. He felt like a top that had been spun off a cliff.

"That's the Delta, all right," Charley said. "Mud. I know mud!"

They were slowly drawing away from land, making south to the crow-flight route to Habana.

"How—how long does it take?" Ivanhoe asked.

" 'Pends on the wind. This is a head wind—might take four days. If she calms or changes it wouldn't be as much as three.—What's the matter?"

"I guess something I ate."

"That big fat pig's knuckle," Charley said deliberately. "Or maybe them buckwheat cakes all oozy with butter and splashed over with honey."

"You go to hell!"

The little landlocked ocean, full of its strange and beautiful plants and strange fish was curiously unperturbed by the extreme efforts of an artist and musician; its surface was beaten up, true, by a norther rushing down from the barricades of the Rocky Mountains, thrusting down on Mexico and curling up the waters between Yucatán and Florida with its long, gusty blows, but it was no more considerate of Ivanhoe Keeler than it would have been of Jean Viotti or Paganini.

The bitter and cruel part of the business was that after

Ivanhoe had rid himself of all but his spiritual content, the gulf seemed to want that too, without offering a means for surrender. Ivanhoe was indifferent about his life and so, it seemed, was the insanely frolicking ship and the hastening surges of blue-green water. Ivanhoe straightened out his bowed back and hurried to the railed ladder that led to his cabin deck. Better to die politely lying down than make a fuss on the bridge deck.

Samaliel was at his heels and puffed the pillow for his head.

"Sir?"

"Yes, Sam?"

"I been askin'. This is fizzin' wine, sir. Kind of settles down your stomach if you feel bad."

"Thanks, Sam."

He gulped the champagne. It stayed on his stomach but the walls continued to wave wildly and he belched and gagged with every wave and roller. The disorderliness and malicious persistency which voyagers since the time of Odysseus have noticed about large accumulations of water eventually aroused Ivanhoe's indignation but he was too weak to curse and he couldn't leave the slop jar long enough to jump overboard. He stuck his face in the pillow and moaned.

The door opened softly and Charley came in with Samaliel. Samaliel was carrying another bottle of sparkling wine and two lemons. Charley was carrying a very strong odor of corn whisky.

"Well, well, old socks," he said with more than his usual affability. "Now you've heaved you're feelin' better, I guess?"

"Go away, God damn you! You did this to me."

"I! What did I do?"

"You know what you did."

"All I did," Charley said innocently, "was to say you hadn't ought to have ate those pig's knuckles and pompanos and bushybase soup and shrimps covered with that nice creamy gravy and those pink cookies with the soft sugar stuff on them—"

Ivanhoe's boot caught him in the stomach.

"—and the oysters with ketchup on them and prow-leans—"

The other boot hit him behind the ear. Ivanhoe was briefly and fruitlessly occupied with the slop jar, which he intended to throw next, as soon as he was through with it.

"Now, now," said Charley. "Me and Sammy here come not as enemies but as friends and consolers. We have forged our swords into bar spoons. Sammy, the champagne! An' give him a suck o' the lemon!"

Samaliel timidly proffered the lemon, which was split half through from end to end. Ivanhoe caught Charley with it nicely above the eye.

"An' now the champagne," Charley said amiably, "an' keep out o' line of the bottle. You're too damn good a barber to die untimely. I think I'll have a little snort of corn."

He fetched a quart from his jacket and put back a pint and a half. Ivanhoe sipped at the champagne and gradually began to feel almost well enough to kill himself. The cursed room kept plunging and rocking. If he could nail his stomach to the floor, Ivanhoe thought vaguely, it would move with the boat and everything would be all right. He groaned and put his face back in the pillow. Maybe he would smother by and by.

"You see," said Charley, "you took the wrong tack, as us sailors say."

"Sailor!" It was faint and venomous as the hiss of a dying rattlesnake. "You Wisconsin woodlouse!"

"Oh, but Ive, I'm a rafter. I've took wood to Dubuque, Keokuk, St. Louis and landings between. Did you ever see a big blow on the Old Miss'? Waves rolling like cockroaches in a dishpan! The gale howling through the scrub willows! The logs scrunching and squeaking underfoot and liable to rear up and sock you in the seat of the pants any minute! Ive, if you'd asked me, I'd've told you what to do."

"Go away!" said Ivanhoe.

"All right," said Charley. "But I feel like talkin'. The system is to get just enough and not too much, so you don't know whether it's you or the boat that's rollin'. Now look at

you and look at me! I ate two stuffed ducks with onion
dressing for lunch just now."

Sheer anger strengthened Ivanhoe and he lifted his pallid
face. "Your head would look so nice in a coffin—same shape,
same material."

"You bet. And instead of this incense stuff you could
fry pork and onions in front and behind me."

Ivanhoe sighted for a shot with the bottle but Charley
went to the door. "G'bye. We'll come back an' see how you
are pretty soon."

Outside, he grinned at Samaliel. "Well, we done that
nice—he'll live. The worse he is the first day the better he'll
be the third."

"Yes, sir."

"Keep a kind of an eye on him. I got to go somewheres
and get some meddy down me." He patted the bottle in his
jacket. "Lord! I didn't know whether I was going to manage
or not when I talked about fried onions."

"Can I bring you some champagne, sir?"

"I guess you better. I'll try anything once. Soon as we
get to Habana I'm goin' to take this damn balky skiff to
pieces with my bare hands so we can't go on. The hell with
Paris, France."

"Yes, sir."

II

Three gentlemen adventurers glared from the rail of the
Gulf Belle at the verdure and white walls of Habana. They
hated the damn town on sight. The only thing that could be
said for it was that the blue waters of the harbor were completely motionless as the little ship warped in to the wharf.
Ivanhoe's rich tan and bloodless face gave him a disagreeable
yellowish look; Charley's eyes were bloodshot from continued doses of his seasickness remedy; even the impassive
Sammy looked none the better for wear.

"Hablo aguardiente," Charley said. "Hablo conac. Hablo
cerveza."

He had been taking lessons in Spanish from the bartender.

Cuba was doing a slow rigadoon for Ivanhoe. First it would tilt delicately to the south and then lurch sickeningly back to the north; then repeat.

Ivanhoe groaned. "This damned place is an island. How do we get back to shore?"

"Donde el fonda?" Charley inquired. "Tortillas con ron. Tomare una botella! Es demasiado caro. Donde una muy bien fonda?"

The great sea wall and the fortress waved in the breeze before Ivanhoe's eyes. He knew better now than to shake his head or shut his eyes—he stared fixedly at the diamond on his ring finger.

"Donde una cantina?" Charley inquired. "Hablo aguardiente?" he repeated pitifully. "Tiene oosteh un dormitorio?"

"What the hell are you talking about?" Ivanhoe inquired weakly and irritably.

"You'll find out, son. I've learnt to speak Spanish. 'Donde' means 'where' and 'hablo' means 'have you got' and 'aguardiente' means 'liquor.' "

"The United States oughtn't to be so far over that way," Ivanhoe said more hopefully, pointing toward Yucatán. "Maybe we could get soaked and reach it before we came to."

"Maybe," Charley said doubtfully. "One thing's sure— we got to figure out some way to get back. If I had a good tight skiff I bet we could almost row it. You don't get sick in rowboats."

Ivanhoe shook his head. "Too far. Sammy, fetch the captain."

The small, salty captain had turned the boat over to the pilot and the master. He came up promptly, smiling.

"Well, gentlemen, feeling better? Coming with me up to Charleston?"

Ivanhoe shuddered. "Not if I have to live here the rest of my life."

The captain clucked commiseratingly. "But you're over

it now. Takes every sailor a while to get his first legs. Besides, we're loading her right down to the rail—you won't feel a stir out of her—except, maybe, if we get a little blow above the Bahamas."

Ivanhoe shivered again. "What we wanted to know, captain, is which is the closest way to the United States?"

The captain laughed. "Well, that's not so serious. You can sail over to the Keys in a day. There's generally a few boats there—you can coast around to New Orleans or go the other way up to Charleston. If the Seminoles are behaving you could even go overland. Best thing, though, is to come with me up to Charleston. You can travel any way you want to from there. We're bound to have good winds this time of year. That is," he added thoughtfully, "if we don't get *too* good a wind. One trip I made in the spring I thought I was going to have to fish for a church steeple with the anchor."

"Thanks," said Ivanhoe hastily. "As long as we're here we thought we'd stop and see what Habana was like."

The captain nodded. "Nice town. Just one word to the wise—keep away from women and remember the men don't use their fists—nothing but knives."

Charley hardly seemed to move. "How do you like this one, captain?" The Bowie seemed to come from nowhere— the old sleeve draw.

"Very good, sir, very good. But if they catch you using it you go into the calaboose and God help you." He pointed vaguely toward Morro, standing bleak and impregnable upon its height. "I've heard there's a slide in there—goes right into the bay. It's slimy old stone and slippery. I don't know why sharks hang around the point there, just below the castle. Maybe they think some of the soldiers will toss them a banana. Trusting, those sharks."

Charley grinned. "We're peaceable Americans. We just want to see the town."

"Another thing," said the captain. "They hate Americans from the north. Why don't you stretch your legs, boys, and look very quiet into some of the cantinas and then come on with me?"

"I'll take my chances with the sharks," Ivanhoe said. "After the first two or three bites I don't suppose you'd feel hardly a thing. I like sharks but I don't like boats."

The captain grinned and frowned at once. "All right— but try to be careful. You—" he said to Charley, "you'll be marked out everywhere you go as a 'grande Yanqui.' You're just a walking temptation to any don with a girl. They know that if you bash them the military will take care of you before they can get up again. I'd hire a boat tomorrow—that would be the best thing."

"Oh, we might stay here quite a while," Charley said carelessly.

Charley relieved the Negro of the heavier bags. One of these jingled pleasantly in the melodious and persuasive tones of gold.

The captain stared. "My God, man, have you got money in that bag?"

"Oh, yes," said Ivanhoe. "Some!" He followed the others down the plank.

"Good-by," said the captain definitely. "Good-by."

The muy bien fonda to which the vehiculo took them at Charley's ostentatious request was set on a large square which in turn was built around a fountain that was not playing at this morning hour. A young Sancho Panza received them in the foyer, gave their bags to a porter and listened gravely while Charley explained that they wanted dos mucho bien habitaciones, una por el negro.

"We have a large room with two beds on the second floor and with a smaller room adjoining," the stout young Spaniard said pleasantly. "Only four suites to the convenience. Do you wish to eat in the house—or, no! Breakfast, perhaps, but you will please to see so much as possible of Habana. So we will make the rate by the room alone, right? Five pesetas, which is one dollar, for each—right? The mozo will bring the morning coffee, right? One peseta for each."

Ivanhoe laughed at Charley. "Understand English, Charley?"

"That's all right," Charley said sulkily. "I'll bet you'll

be glad I know all about Spanish before we leave. Una semana," he added to the manager. "Cual precio?"

The manager calculated rapidly. "For the week, with breakfast, I give you breakfast. Twenty dollars. Right?"

"We'll see what the breakfast is like," Charley growled. He took a bill from his pocket but the manager edged back as if it had been a snake.

"It is so difficult. One day it is this much—one day it is that much. If the gentlemen had gold? I have given you a very good price."

Ivanhoe twisted his head at Samaliel who instantly produced an eagle. The manager brightened and took it, ringing it on the table.

"The same in all languages," he commented on the sound. "The baths are no doubt ready. Afterward you will walk, right? There is the band at four in the park. At all times, what you please will be brought, but if you please, those dance well at the Hot Egg. The sign is Huevo Caliente, across the square."

"We'll try that," Charley said.

Some minutes later Ivanhoe stepped from the half-length iron coffin in which one squatted and bathed, and gave serious attention to Charley's ruthless conflict with his one ruffled shirt. Ivanhoe jerked himself into tight knitted panties and underwaist, slid on a shirt and wrapped a black stock around the collar, squirmed into his trousers and strapped his boots under the insoles.

They looked at each other, finally, with reciprocal admiration. Sammy had done some things for Charley's wardrobe—the hard, strong weaving showed out bright and crisp. There was a rough, easy, comfortable mode to Charley's clothes that was stylish and defiant at once.

Ivanhoe had always been a dandy. He had taken to black stocks since the Susan business—he was black, white and powder gray; his roach of dark hair carried out the scheme with premature silver at the temples. The sad gray eyes continued to question all the manners of heaven and earth.

"Let's go over to the saloon," Charley suggested. "We can't sit here. There might be some trouble or some girls or both."

Ivanhoe called Samaliel. "We'll be out, Sam. You fix things around and then do what you please. You got the money, haven't you? Take whatever of your salary you need. Have a good time. We'll be back late."

"Thank you, sir. I won't need anything."

They rode around the park two or three times in the vehiculo before they finally decided to go into the Hot Egg. In the first place, the Egg seemed to be dormant and they would have to wait for it to hatch. The hot lazy afternoon went on and the flowers and trees grew almost visibly while the vehiculo and its two horses furnished just enough movement to assure the passengers that they were not dead.

I could make the tour of this place by nose, Ivanhoe thought—foods, leathers, fresh water, paper, confectionery, hot iron—and he went to sleep. Charley snored to beat the devil. The thin little driver had had his information from the hotel. He walked and stopped his horses as he pleased, glancing at the sleepers behind him. A doubloon for the afternoon, surely. And the horses would be fresh for the concert in the evening. Three days' work in one and no trouble or labor.

Waking, Charley shook Ivanhoe. Ivanhoe was much better. He was accustomed to the motions of carriages and buggies; he was helpless against the plunges and spirals of boats. The natural and ineluctable gaiety that came to him happily when his limbs and his heart, his bowels and his determinations all seemed to say "Up and onward, Ivanhoe" were regaining their proper authority.

"The hell with you," Ivanhoe said at once, pausing to let his head catch up with him.

"That's right. We're at the Hot Egg, kid. Let's get down."

Ivanhoe dropped a gold piece to the driver—about twenty pesetas, the driver guessed, tossing it lightly on his palm. He asked for more, of course, and then inquired about when he should pick the gentlemen up and if they would like to see the amusements of the city. He knew the good companions, muy bellas señoras, dances as they should be, all that makes pleasure for the evening.

Charley waved him away while he was still orating and the two men climbed up the steep and narrow steps from the sidewalk to the door of the Hot Egg.

The place had barely opened for the day. There were a few men around in the big room, sitting in booths and sipping at coffee, and getting no pleasure out of the day which glowed so warmly and pleasantly outside.

The girl who came to the table wore a tight red jacket and a white skirt. There was a hint of contemplative sadness about her red mouth and her large, dark-brown eyes which always searched beyond her clients for the last slight and inadequate joke of all. Any man, looking at her figure, felt its warmth upon his palms; there was little doubt that she must open her lips when she kissed and was kissed. A tortoise-shell comb spread at the back of her crown.

"Señores?"

"Aguardiente. Tortillas con ron. Café. Everything."

"Bueno!" She moved away like a countess, head back, legs barely bending, the body drawn erect.

"Look at that," Ivanhoe said. "Isn't that pretty?"

Charley looked at him curiously.

Ivanhoe flushed and then turned on Charley. "It's pretty, damn it. Do you have to think about every woman like you were about to put your hand on her knee?"

Charley gave a resigned smile. "Yeah, I guess you do."

"Charley, I like you, but you're a damn swine."

"You bet," said Charley. "Everybody is."

"Mmmm," said Ivanhoe. He looked at Charley. Charley was a great mountain, subsiding with dignity and quiet upon its base, sloping down gently from summit to valley. His face was formed in the perfect mask that conceals every feeling. Ivanhoe realized what set him back about Charley; the man wasn't inhuman or "animal" but, except in moments of conflict, music or solicitude, he was virtually mechanical. On love, conversation and all such minor functionings he was a glib, sufficient, indifferent automaton. It didn't seem natural. It had taken him ten seconds to decide to go to Paris, France, instead of returning to Michigan. He had provoking assurance—the world would always make way for his big hands and his simple intentions. A straight course and steam power —that was Charley.

"Listen, Charley, I say that's pretty and I'm talking artistically. I could write a song about her—if she was my own great-aunt I could write a song about her."

"Sure," said Charley.

"What do you think," Ivanhoe demanded with muffled vehemence, "guys like Raphael and all of them were thinking when they painted pictures of lady angels and saints for the churches and so on?"

"They got them the right shapes just the same," Charley said.

"Oh, hell. How do you say 'thank you'?"

"Gracias."

Ivanhoe stammered and blushed. "How do you say 'beautiful lady'?"

"Now wait a minute, Ive—" Charley shrugged his huge shoulders. "Oh, well, it's none of my business. You say, 'Gracias, bella señorita.' "

"Thanks," Ivanhoe mumbled. He concentrated on scratching the top of his ear and did a very good deal of it before the bella señorita returned with a large tray on which there were a decanter of whisky, one of rum, a pot of coffee, a plate of small salty tortillas and tiny oily sardines, nuts, etc.

"Gracias, bella señora," Ivanhoe said faintly.

Charley grunted. "You dern fool, you should have said 'señorita.' You always say 'señorita' unless you know they're married."

The girl's laugh tinkled. "Ysobel ees not marry. You are Yanquis, sí? I haf known many Yanqui. I have some Eengleeth. Rum, beer, wheesky, ham 'n' eggs, you luf me lettle, Ysobel, what the hell, goddam, rough trip, hey, beefstik—oh, an' mooch, mooch more."

Charley poured himself a stiff hooker of rum and nibbled at an anchovy. To his delight it had a faint onion flavor. "Sure," said Charley.

"At night Ysobel dances for the company. You will come to see, no?".

"Oh, Jesus, Ive—she's a Spanish dancer. The captain told me about them. First they dance an' then they throw a rose at you an' then their hombre sticks a knife in your back. You don't want to get mixed up in this."

Ysobel pouted. "Ysobel has no galán to makes troble. Ees not good for dancer."

"He's joking," Ivanhoe said. "Sure, I'll—we'll come to see you dance—tonight."

She rewarded him with a smile. "Then I weel dance my best for the kind Yanqui gentleman." She left them to their bottles with a grace that promised well for the evening.

"Listen, Ive," Charley said desperately, "you're just fixin' up a peck o' 'troble' for yourself. The captain told me all about this. A wench that good-lookin' is bound to have a gallon somewhere around. Maybe she's a come-on—she gets you up some dark alley and he sticks a knife in you and they split whatever you got with you. These funny little yellow policemen wouldn't do a thing about it—just send a cart for the deceased."

"Not that girl," Ivanhoe said reprovingly. "You sound as if you'd been reading French novels. Not that girl." He gave her furtive glances as she moved around the room waiting on the growing number of Habaneros come for a restorative against the drowsiness of their siestas.

Ivanhoe drank his hitherto untouched jigger of whisky. "Charley, there's my remedy! I think that señorita might do a lot to make me forget all about Sue Ellison. Help a lot, anyway."

"She ain't goin' to make me forget Esther Lou or any part thereof," Charley said sourly. "An' she ain't goin' to make me forget that I'm a lot too young to die. I ain't ever goin' to forget Esther Lou or that I'm a covered wagon, but that ocean trip and this cantina have made me remember that there are still things in life to enjoy—dry land and ron and a good fight."

He tilted the whisky bottle toward Ivanhoe's glass but Ivanhoe hastily placed his hand over it. "I can't take much whisky, Charley, I'm not used to it."

Charley gave him a strange look. "Capacity's gettin' pretty short, ain't it? Seen you kill a pint of brandy an' never feel it, in New Orleans."

"Not on my land legs yet, Charley. Got to get organized."

Charley's face flushed with sudden anger. "What's the use of lyin' to me, Ive? Got to stay in good shape so you can spill a few drinks with the bella señorita this evening, ain't you? Of all the God-damnedest fools I ever saw you're the God-damnedest God-damned fool I ever saw! You think you know more about Habana than the captain? You're so God-damned stinking swell-headed rip-roaring bright in the brains you know more about town in half a day than he knows in twenty years!"

"I may not know Habana but I know a nice girl when I see one."

"Well, maybe you do—we'll find out about that when we see one."

"That's plenty, Charley, if you don't want a fight. This is my business."

"Fight. That's a good idea. I'll keep you in bed for a week and save you from gettin' killed."

"I won't fight till tomorrow," Ivanhoe said coldly. "And I'm no wilting violet, you big clumsy ox."

Charley cooled as quickly as he flared. "We won't have any more talk about fightin'—I'm sorry I brought it up—or took it up. I suppose I should have figgered anybody could fiddle as well as you do would be a damn fool." He poured gloomily and drank a half-tumbler of rum. "Señorita, the bill —the cost—how mucho?"

Ysobel came out smiling, glanced at the decanters, stared at Charley for a moment—he was evidently not feeling a whisper from more than a big pint of rum—and suggested three pesetas to the malo grande Yanqui—sixty cents, approximately. Charley threw her a silver dollar and rose with calculated rudeness to leave as quickly as possible.

Ivanhoe's eyes blazed but he smiled at Ysobel and dropped a small gold piece. "For your flower tonight, señorita."

The two men went to the inn in silence. They were both troubled by this breach of understanding—and both stubborn. Charley went to his room without a word; Ivanhoe went to his prepared to speak crossly to Sammy if there were the slightest fault to be found with his evening costume. There was none and almost as soon as he stepped in the room Sammy rapped at the communicating sill—the door was merely a curtain across a wide entrance in the plastered stone partition.

"Yes?"

"You'll be goin' out tonight, sir? The señor boss tells me there's the theaters—and places everybody walks—and the cantinas with dancers—and a concert right here in the plaza —I should touch you a bit with the razor and fix you?"

In spite of himself, Ivanhoe grinned: "You trying to make an elegante out of me, Sammy?"

Sammy smiled slightly. He helped Ivanhoe with his clothes. "Folks havin' fun have more fun if they know they look good—they best. I'll fix you, sir."

Ivanhoe lay back on the long chair. "All right, Sammy. We won't be here long. I want to see as much as I can. You brushed the big hat?"

"I think everything is all right, sir."

Sammy put on the lather and gave the razor a last caress or two.

"Sir, if you'll excuse me—Habana's a bad place. Would you want me to follow a little ways? I'd wait places an' you wouldn't ever see me unless some trouble happen to start up."

Ivanhoe started up so violently that Samaliel lifted his razor just in time. "The hell with that! I've been in worse places than Habana—and mostly I've got away alive. Very little of me, Samaliel, is buried between Cooperstown, New

York State, and Cincinnati, Ohio, and Pittsville, Iowa, and
Habana, Cuba. If I wanted a nigger mammy I wouldn't have
hired you. I don't want a nurse."

"No, sir. I didn't mean that—escusing me again, sir,
down from my heart I don't want to see nothin' happen to
you. If you felt undoubtful—"

"I don't feel undoubtful. You go on shaving."

The room smelled of dying stone, most ancient of all
smells. The place was two or three hundred years old and it
had accumulated a signature like a very old man. All its ex-
periences and reminiscences defied washing and refurbishing.
New paint seemed old the moment it was put on these walls.
The limestone had absorbed the centuries and breathed them
out.

A hopeless love, Ivanhoe reflected, is better than no love
at all. Better to have a broken heart and wistful reflections
than to go through life merely making a furrow like such a
plow as Charley. He pondered on the romance of himself
and Ysobel if it all came out properly. No farm—hell, no! A
farm was no place for her dark, brujo—witching—beauty.
She could dance and sing and he could play the fiddle about
as well as anyone he'd ever heard and why shouldn't they—?
No, he didn't want her dancing where he played. But her
strange loveliness would be noticed everywhere they went
along the Ohio and the Mississippi.

The countess who had given up everything for love!
Well, a queen had lost her throne and head because of a
weakness for violinists and Mary Stuart was certainly no
prettier than Ysobel. Ivanhoe shook his head again, and again
Samaliel's dexterity saved an artery.

Ysobel was the object. To possess that lightness, the
flickering that showed beauty in every aspect, to bring it to
his bow and strings, to warm the violin with her pretty
march, to lilt with the angle of her high comb—up in the
harmonics—to trip with the pitter-patter of the bow on the
short piano notes— He would degrade himself if he used her
for an advertisement, back in the river towns, but they would
both be proud when he made song after song out of her pres-

ence and his love. He renounced the silly idea of making her a countess. He could simply leave her—mysterious. That was honest.

"Your things, sir."

Ivanhoe rose reluctantly from his reflections and the sofa. He stripped off his daytime garments, sponged himself and slid into the gaudy evening costume that Samaliel had laid out, presciently. Sammy was a master hand with a stock and he was mildly regretful that the St. Louis niggers had not seen his master's best gold buckle with its small diamond. It would have raised Samaliel's considerable prestige.

"I won't need you this evening, Sammy. Take it for yourself and have a good time. You've been working pretty hard."

"Thank you, sir. I'll be back around eleven if that's all right, just in case you wanted me."

"Get back by morning, that's all. Need any money? You can take an advance on your wages if you want to."

Samaliel coughed and looked uncomfortable. "No, sir, I don't need any. In fact—sir—I hope you won't take it wrong—"

"Well, come out with it—take what wrong?"

Sammy pulled some bills from his hip pocket. "The folks in St. Louis and on the boat were very good to me, sir, and the landlord had me play in the patio this afternoon. I could pay you fifty dollars on myself, sir, if you wouldn't take it unfriendly. I expect to go right on workin' for you, sir, when I'm all bought back."

Ivanhoe laughed and took the money. "You're not paying on yourself—you're just paying what you owe me. 'D you get this with that banjo?"

"Yes, sir. Folks was good enough to say it made the ocean seem to be dancin' instead of rollin' an' heavin'."

"I'll have you play for me if I ever get on an ocean again," Ivanhoe said absently. "You keep track of what you owe me—figures make me tired."

"Yes, sir." There was a heavy step in the hall and

Samaliel took a fresh razor from the case. "If you're through with me, sir—"

"That's right—take care of Mr. Hoskin."

Samaliel gave him a startled look which grew into one of distress as the two men passed at the door without speaking.

Ivanhoe grinned at Charley's fears, in the Hot Egg at nine o'clock. The place was as safe, in a way, as a nursery. The crowd was cosmopolitan but it was obviously polite as befitted a better cantina in one of the great ports of the world. Though the Cuban-Spanish predominated, they were chiefly soft-voiced young men of means and good families. At least five languages—American, English, French, Spanish and Dutch—were being spoken by ships' officers and passengers at the tables. There were few bottles in sight—at this urbane hour most of the guests were drinking frappés and punches mixed with ice brought at great expense and waste from the icehouses of New England, or the Mexican mountains.

A small musical company was playing softly and quite badly in the corner and for a moment Ivanhoe forgot Ysobel and wished he had brought his violin. Still, the rhythms were interesting, and Ivanhoe nipped at his sherry and enjoyed the froggy sustained ploonkings of the guitars, the thin cantabile mandolins and the tambours and castanets—both strange to him. By and by he got the principle of the music—the suave opening, increasing volume and tempo, quick surrender to furious speed and skillful stridency. He forgot his sherry and lost himself in a scheme for the violin—entrance on a softly bowed D string, and G pizzicato and tentative in the introduction of the theme that would finally dominate passionately over the wild song of the E. He needed only two themes, which he invented at once, and his fingers were working at the problem of holding the bow strings and plucking the pizzicati—when the waitress of the afternoon moved between the tables and appeared in the center of the floor, bowing.

Her eyes passed him with no sign of recognition as she

smiled and bent to the whole room, impersonally. Ivanhoe noticed with momentary uneasiness that the first of Charley's legends was true enough—she had a rose in her hair. Then he looked at the sweet dark face again and shrugged; a man could be knifed for worse things.

Ysobel danced, not badly, a comparatively mild mala-gueñas and afterward a waltz. She played the castanets much better than the castanet player. The room applauded quietly and then outraged Ivanhoe by picking up its murmur of tattle with unconcerned unanimity as soon as the dancer had left the floor. Ivanhoe fumed inwardly and ordered Domecq. He drank a few gills moodily and estimated the number of people in the room he could whip if he made a general announcement that they were all pigs. The number increased and the bottle diminished with about equal speed.

Twenty minutes passed and Ysobel returned with the same impersonal smile and bow. The orchestra made indistinguishable small sounds and then a flageolet whined out a theme and after an instant the mandolina came in on thirds, while the guitars still beat a slow, broken, agreeable discordancy in the minor. Ysobel's head began to move to the music; she took slow steps, showing red slippers and an inch or so of red silk. The music went into full ensemble and she swept around the little space left for her near an empty table. The tempo went up with the volume, as it had done with all the music Ivanhoe had heard that evening, and it blew Ysobel lightly to the tabletop where she danced a very good bolero— not the bolero of such incredible beauty and temptation as Ivanhoe thought it, but creditable.

The room applauded more warmly and there were even a few shouts, but they were quiet, conventional shouts—amiable, appreciative, but governed. The talk picked up again. Ivanhoe reached for his glass.

A rose dropped on the table in front of him. The girl said, "I will be ready at the small door of the cantina in some few minutes. A carriage will not be needed. It is only a little way to the house. Remain for me."

She was gone before Ivanhoe could pick up the rose.

The young men were smiling discreetly but now he felt no inclination to whip them. He smiled back, took the rose from the table and kissed it with a flourish to the door behind which Ysobel had disappeared. He sipped his brandy—it would take her ten minutes, at least, to change her costume and he could afford to appear debonair, indifferent.

Later, he paid his bill and picked up his cloak. He went out as if he were on his way to buy a newspaper, the *Diario* or something from North America, but there was some low laughter from behind him which he didn't like but couldn't resent without making more of the incident than it deserved. He went out to the mist and moonlight, brought a carriage and its tired and disciplined driver almost to the sill of the small door of the Hot Egg. He ignored the remarks of people who turned out around the equipage and scuttled across the filthy cobbles of the street—the primary sewers of Habana—dribbling and washing unnamable filth to the great cesspool of the harbor.

Again he was troubled, however—it all came out too pat. He scrutinized the driver but the man was an utterly innocuous old fellow, certainly no galán with pistol and dagger. Still, it was remarkable that he had been so conveniently near the door. Ivanhoe did not notice that there was now another carriage conveniently near the door and others drawn up under the palms to take its place in their turns.

There was a twinkling of light as the side door opened and closed and Ysobel touched his arm lightly as she stepped up to the carriage seat. He sat down beside her and she leaned against him, all warmth and perfume.

"Did you wait long, my poor one?"

"It was not long, though it seemed long," he said automatically. He noticed that though no direction had been given the driver turned the carriage and started off with assurance.

Ysobel laughed. "Sweet words, Yanqui. I find myself fond of you—I am really verrry fond of you. You are so—how to say—with big eyes."

Ivanhoe puzzled over this one; his eyes weren't particularly big. "If eyes are to be spoken of, señorita, we must talk of yours."

She laughed softly. "In good time, amigo. Good, we arrive!"

Ivanhoe gaped at the great stone house while he paid the driver. Though the curtains were drawn, lights glinted all over the wide-flung building. Ivanhoe already knew enough of Habana to know that the walls of its single story must enclose a patio but the patio alone must be as large as a whole block of Cincinnati or St. Louis. He was bewildered—perhaps she was a countess after all.

Of course—a hotel. A fine one, at that. He tried to straighten these matters out in the instant before she took his arm. Waitress, dancer—there was the easy answer to that—the Hot Egg was owned in the family, but it now appeared that there was no family. Waitress—and she lived in a palace; the place was twice as big as the comfortable lodging to which the ship's captain had directed him and Charley.

The foyer did more than justice to the elegance of the exterior; or, perhaps it did some slight injustice to the handsome simplicity of the house. Ivanhoe had one fleeting impression of satin, velvet, brass, silver and then an oddly dressed and heavily painted old señora swept down on the two of them with an outburst of cordial but unintelligible Spanish.

Ysobel kissed the old lady and patted her bare back. "The señor does not have Spanish, mamá. It iss better we speak our poor Eengleeth, sí?"

Ivanhoe was embarrassed. There were music and laughing voices from behind the long draperies over the great door at the side of the hall—party going on without a question. With his dozen words of Spanish he'd be nothing but a nuisance.

"I just brought Miss—Señorita Ysobel home, ma'am!"

The old lady laughed. She must have been handsome at one time; her beautiful teeth had endured beyond her flesh as a clue to her earlier attractions.

"The señor moost remain for some while, I theenk. We

have wine and moosic and a good company. My yong lady has danced but she will attend at once."

Ysobel flicked Ivanhoe a kiss from her finger tips and skipped down the long hall.

Ivanhoe shook his head and dumbly followed "mamá" to the great door. There she turned with an apologetic but amiable smile.

"We have two Americans from your country weeth us, but if you do not weesh to come in it is as you weesh. Ysobel is a dancer—it is ten dollars, your money, or twenty if you remain to have coffee in the morning—"

Lightning finally penetrated Ivanhoe's insulation. He turned ungracefully and stupidly and walked out the door. There was a carriage waiting.

Charley was awake but apparently as drunk as two coots when Ivanhoe reached their room. He was perspiring eloquently—it had taken a bit of effort to beat Ivanhoe's carriage in time to jerk off his own outer clothes and pretend to be half dazed on the bed. Charley had had a lot of walking and running during the evening, not to speak of the worry.

"Habana's wunnerful town," he announced.

Ivanhoe looked him over. "Drunk, hey?"

"Good and drunk."

"Can't hold it, unnh?"

Charley managed to get his feet down to the floor so that he could squat on the edge of the bed, peering at Ivanhoe.

"Years creep up on us, Ive."

Ivanhoe watched the decreasing pulse in Charley's temple for at least three minutes. Exercise, not alcohol. It was an old test. The rhythm of aguardiente would not have varied perceptibly in that time.

"You followed me all evening—you know all about it?"

Charley straightened slowly. "Somebody had to take care of you, you blasted half-wit."

"O.K., Charley, O.K. Want any details?"

Charley smiled slightly but sympathetically. "Not many. I greased a carriage man. The bella Ysobel seems to put up at

the mooey grandest watchamaycallit for pooteys in Habana,
as well as I could make out. I figured you wouldn't stay long
so I came on back as soon as you came out." He smiled again.
"You damn near broke your neck coming down the steps."

Ivanhoe nodded briefly. "Do you know, Charley, I been
makin' my own living since I was twelve? Pa was a preacher
up in a dinky town in New York. He had me taught the
violin so I could play for services. Wesleyan bastard."

"That's Methodist, ain't it?"

"Yes, on both items. Anyhow, he had the powerfullest
right arm you ever felt—he used to lay it on with a piece of
inch rope till I couldn't hardly walk or sit; he'd lay it on for
anything and then give me a lot of pious stuff about saving
my immortal soul even if there wasn't much left of weak
clay. He'd have killed me if I'd ever told him the plain truth
—that he enjoyed it. He damn near did kill me once for going
fishing one Sunday. He beat me around the head that time."
Ivanhoe folded down his ear to show where it had been torn,
and Charley swore.

"I'm getting around to something, Charley. I don't think
the old man ever gave me so much as a shilling for myself in
his life. So when I got so I could fiddle pretty good I used
to sneak down to the tavern and play for the boys at the bar.
The old man was always wrapped up in his sermon Saturday
evening and some Saturday nights I'd make a couple of dollars. I used to make up songs about local people that tickled
them.

"Then I did a darn-fool thing—I bought a silk neckcloth
I just had to have. I hid it under my other clothes in my box
—he was always prying around—and, of course, that was the
first place he pried. I told him I'd saved up from doing odd
jobs and running errands but he took it for the heathen and
you couldn't have made another one out of what he left of
my hide."

Ivanhoe took a long, businesslike drink from Charley's
bottle. "He knew I was lying but I didn't know it. He
watched me like a hawk and one Saturday night when somebody opened the tavern door I saw him outside—listening. It

froze me. I figured he'd kill me when I got home and I was probably right. Ed, the bartender, figured so too. First he offered to let me stay with him but then we realized that though Dad wouldn't come in a grogshop he'd sooner or later send a watchman for me.

"Then Ed gave me good advice. He allowed I was a good enough fiddler to get along in about any tavern and asked me why I didn't cut through the brush. I mustn't go east because the old man might have me tracked, but to take country roads west till I got to Cincinnati or some place like that where there were lots of taverns. He told me to lay out for a few days' travel till I was out of likely catching distance. Then he gave me a basket of grub and two dollars and let me out the back way, to be on the safe side. Sure enough, there was the old fox, but he wasn't much at running and I slipped him in the dark. I had three days and nights of pretty tough going but soon I hit the Ohio and from there on everything was lovely. I could always get a barge ride for a tune and stop off evenings when we hit a town to fiddle for my supper. When I got to Cincinnati I sent Ed his two dollars and another for a bottle and had about thirty left. I've never had that little since."

"You will if you keep banking in a carpetbag," Charley growled.

Ivanhoe paid no attention. "I needed a new name—I never did like my old one, 'Shadrach,' so I picked 'Ivanhoe' for a book I liked." He took another drink and saw that the bottle wasn't going to hold out very long.

"There's two more under my bed," said Charley. "Go on."

"Well, you'd think that after all this batting around I'd be pretty well seasoned, wouldn't you? You'd think I'd begin to show some faint glimmerings of human intelligence."

Charley was uncomfortable. "Now, Ive, don't be hard on yourself. After all, this is a strange country—I was warned, but you wasn't." To save himself Charley couldn't suppress a grin. "Though I got to admit Spanish dancers didn't turn out to be exactly as described."

"All right, grin, you backwoods ape!" There was no rancor in Ivanhoe's voice. "You'd think that I'd be full of wisdom and experience and savoir-faire and whatchamaycallit after a life of struggle and privations. Well, I'm not— I'm full of sawdust and sachet and nonsense and vainglory. Everything's been made easy for me just because I can pull a horse's tail across a cat's guts and make noises. I'm glad," he said bitterly, "Sue didn't marry me. Instead of twins she'd have probably had a small china doll."

"Have another drink," Charley suggested. "You'll feel better tomorrow."

Ivanhoe poured the drink. "Tonight's the climax or something. This is about the worst damn-fool show I've ever put on. I start out for Paris to be a great violinist and then bust down because I got some bad fish in New Orleans and I don't like the way the boat rides. The first thing I do in Habana is decide a little coffeehouse—"

"Ramera—pootato, or something. The captain said I ought to know in Habana—I told him I didn't care about them, but he thought I'd want to know."

"—all right—potato is a sweet young thing fascinated by my terrific charm. Any jackass as much as a week old would have known it was a couple of gold pieces that made me so damn beautiful."

"That might be stretching it a bit," Charley said. He added dubiously, "I've seen some jackasses that age that were pretty smart, at that."

"O.K.," Ivanhoe said grimly. "You can do what you damn please, but I'm going to Paris and be a violinist. If I die in the middle of the ocean the whales can get some soft, juicy bites off me. If I don't die, I'm going to work like a dog and take pains to be a violinist—not a fiddler. I'm going to be some damn thing but a fiddling damn fool. I was all right before I left home and struck it soft." His eyes were hard and determined. "I'm going to be something yet—or buried, one or the other."

"What the hell, Ive? You take it too hard. She was a kind of a pretty little potato at that—I don't blame you—you wouldn't *want* to think what you might have seen she was."

"No more potatoes," said Ivanhoe, "whether they're women, work or foolery." He lifted his voice. "Sammy—Sammy!"

There was no answer and Ivanhoe suddenly remembered. "I told him I wouldn't need him. I'll pack my things—imagine hiring a nigger to shave you and pack your things! Fine shape I'm in."

"You honestly going, Ive?"

"I certainly am. My old man isn't here with his rope so I guess I better do the best I can by myself."

"Well, I can stand it if you can, kid."

They shook hands, had a drink, and began packing.

PART III

FORTUNATUS

I

THE trip from New York to Cincinnati was so absurdly simple that Charley taunted Ivanhoe about his early hardships. They had first a railroad coach almost as comfortable as the English cars, then a carriage over well-kept toll roads, then a stateroom on a river boat to the great Ohio River port, then a pleasant overnight stay in a Cincinnati hotel that was considerably better than anything they had found in London.

They put away their money in Ivanhoe's bank, except for the few hundred dollars Charley carried for emergencies and the few thousand Ivanhoe always kept in his carpetbag, to be ready for anything. Charley fumed and Samaliel worried about this but there was no moving Ivanhoe. Fists, pistols, and adroitness were good things, he admitted. Gold money was a good thing to have, too. His main line of defense was that it wasn't so heavy for Sammy to carry.

Both the friend and the body servant were concerned about Ivanhoe. He was in a depression that made him stand for hours at the front rail, as they paddled to Cincinnati and then to Cairo, and stare at the olive-dirty waters and finally turn away to his stateroom to lounge on his berth. He hadn't tuned his fiddle from Liverpool to the Ohio.

An hour or two before they hit Cairo, where they had to change for the boat up to St. Louis, Charley came down to the rooms with a big bottle of corn whisky. "Now, Ive—now we're back home. What the hell's the matter?"

Ivanhoe poured and smiled cynically. "Nothing's any good, Charley, if you must know. I think of Sue sometimes, but I don't care anything about her. Seven years is a long time. She's probably got the Indians jammed over to the ocean by now, with her twins. Charley, I'm going from nowhere to nowhere. You remember that Cuban potato—and

83

the stinky dames in the music halls that didn't want anything but the skin off your gizzard to be *nice*—and the pretty little half-cooked females around the dock in New York—potatoes and society all mixed up—and, Charley, I didn't give a damn about any of them."

"That's good," said Charley.

"It's not good. The thing is I suppose you get to a spot where you like folks but you don't like any women—and if you don't like them you haven't got any settled thing planned out, like a business or a farm. And when you're like that you're old."

Charley snorted. "For Lord's sake! So that's what's been the matter with you! How can you be old when you haven't ever even grown up?" He peered curiously at the brown liquor in his glass and then looked distastefully at Ivanhoe sprawled out on the bed again. "I thought you had some girl on the sly over in Lunnon—or were worried about having to shoot Mexes."

Charley scratched his head and then laughed disgustedly. "No girl is just about what the trouble is," he diagnosed. "You ain't been in love since you were going to see Vestris play-act every night and then coming home and mooning and writing songs about her. Not," Charley added reasonably, "that they weren't nice songs, though not enough snap in them for my taste."

"Hunnh!" said Ivanhoe. "I'd have had a hell of a lot of brains to fall in love with Eliza Vestris. Fine chance she'd ever have looked at me. I got more sense than that!"

Charley used his gesture of cynicism—he picked his teeth with his gold toothpick. "Maybe you have now, but you didn't have then. If you have, it must have come on to you all of a sudden. No, Ive, my boy, you're just like a cat— if you ain't interested in some woman you won't sing. Now, for Christ's sake, when we get to St. Louis try to find some female that you can't get along without. We're going to war, see, and that sets you up big. This is probably your last chance till we capture Mexico City and that might take months—it's so far to walk. There was a couple of nice-lookin' Fräuleins in that Gasthaus—they'll be married by now, but there ought to be more."

Ivanhoe lit a cigar, his first vigorous gesture of the interview. "Listen, my reverend friend, don't preach at me. You may be as innocent as an angel for all I know, but I never knew you to own a bottle of scent in your life and Sammy and I have smelled so many kinds on you and your clothes we could have started an apothecary shop."

"Now wait a minute, Ive. I had to please the customers an' I wasn't above makin' eyes at some of those wenches, but old John Jackson told me the first thing about the kind of stylish ladies that send notes to prize fighters. You get mixed up with them and, if milord the husband doesn't have you pistoled off, you wake up some morning with a nice case of pox. Not me. After this war I'm going to marry some good clean country female that can run a house and raise a family. Till then, I'll have my fun fightin'. But you're different—you won't be fit for shootin' till you're chasin' a petticoat again."

"Too much trouble," Ivanhoe said wearily. "Women see through me. Even Marie told me that as soon as she made enough money out of dancing and me she was going back to France and marry a bourgeois 'a man wheech ees soleed; arteest, non.'"

"That butterfly business upsettin' you again, hunh." Charley chuckled. "Don't you see, you bloody fool, what a great team we make—a pretty butterfly to make everything nicer and happier for everybody and a prairie wagon for heavy duty. If Sammy was only white he'd be the happy medium." Then he looked at Ivanhoe sternly. "Get that butterfly thing out of your noggin, Keeler. You're a stout figure of a man and if there's anybody fittener to live in this world than an 'arteest' I don't know who it'd be."

"Thanks, Charley, but it's not so. Just stinking parasites."

"Paris what? Still thinkin' about that French feeyuh d'jwah? W'y, the scum had to come to London to get a job dancin'—I bet in Paris her rump has shook hands with half the feather beds in town. I tried to tell you—but you ought to get over her now. We're on our way to war and a lot of fun. You're a fool for the dark ones and they tell me Mexico City's full of them." Charley always thought of the definitely impending war as simply an occupation of Mexico City. "I'll bet you won't be there a month before your heart's broke three or four times." Charley added, with satisfaction, "We'll be gettin' some good music out of you again—'Oh, señora—oh, señora—bella flora—I adora—' "

Ivanhoe fired the pillow and knocked Charley's drink all over his face. Charley wiped his face on the slip and cheerfully poured another drink.

"That's one trouble," Ivanhoe said listlessly. "I think you're right. I'm not only a parasite—I'm a damn fool. Every time I see a tasty girl I believe my own music. I start making angels out of cats because they've got good eyes or a nice walk or pretty ankles. If I do it again I'm going to smash my violin and go to California and raise cattle."

"They have señoritas there, I hear," Charley said maliciously.

"Then I'll join a slaver."

"The African girls are dark."

"You go to hell."

Charley bellowed and finished his drink. "Come on, butterfly, quit bein' a squirmy little caterpillar. We'll be docking pretty soon. Let's get a glimpse of the country." His face grew stern and thoughtful. "If you got to fall in love with something you better take a look at the United States. You'll have to kill men for it pretty soon."

II

Ivanhoe and Charley stared at each other. St. Louis—no! The pleasant little city of fifteen thousand, more or less, had swelled out to three or four times that number but the ferment of growth made it seem even larger than it was. The arrival of such a boat as the *J. M. White* would have drawn a great crowd of people in the days of Ivanhoe's earlier visit to the city; it still drew a crowd, but the crowd was lost in the bustle of the river front and the background of busy streets and many buildings.

"You go by a church," Charley said, half to himself.

"What?"

"To get to that Dutch place. We go by a big church, on about a little better than a hundred rods. There's a sycamore in front of a grocer's shop where we turn right and then left on a small street where there's a house that wasn't quite finished when we went by. What color would they have painted that, Ive? I remember the shape."

"White, I guess—it was pine clapboard." He counted on his fingers. "If they gave it the second painting it would be pretty fresh about now and if they didn't you'd notice it was shabby as the dickens."

"We can find the Gasthaus, if it's still there. Up the hill to in front of a big old Catholic church with a cross on it. Then we can steer it pretty close even if they've changed the landmarks. Anyway, the carriage driver may know."

"We ought to look in on that saloon," Ivanhoe said. "After all, a thousand dollars is a thousand dollars. That old man was all right—we both thought so. Maybe he made a go of it, if he ain't dead."

"Ive," said Charley, "we ought to have stayed here. They done a lot of things since we left and maybe we could've helped."

"Maybe. They seemed to do pretty well by themselves. Oh, well—just the same business of eating and sleeping and doing some fool thing, wherever you go."

"That's not so," Charley said definitely. The big steamboat, the little cities, the rich, wooded banks of the Ohio and the Mississippi had stirred him indefinably. He was about to become the first complete and devoted American. He hadn't seen a naturally assorted group of big trees since his rafting days in the great territory—Wisconsin. He wished that he had fought better with that little devil Bendigo to show him that everything grew big and strong in the United States of

America. Still, he reflected, he wasn't anything like the man George Washington was. George would have kept Bendigo on his knees.

Several brave and honorable Mexicans should have put their last affairs in order at this moment of Charley's regret and exaltation.

"What's not so?"

Charley waved an arm the size of a thigh. "Look what they've done. Where were we?"

"All right—there goes Sammy with his niggers."

Charley laughed at Ivanhoe. "Anyway, we went out of here with two carpetbags, two keesters, a banjo and a fiddle case. We get back with all of them and eight boxes and that thing for hats—it'll take three carriages."

Ivanhoe said vaguely, "What was the chap's name? Byerley—I've got the paper stuck around somewhere—I think it's with the rosin and strings in the case. That's the name, though."

"If he's still in business or alive, they'll know. The big thing is to get settled at the Gasthaus."

"Well, while we're down here—"

"Sure, we might as well see."

They were late in coming down the gangplank but Sammy was waiting attentively at the head of the first horse in the little procession of three. He stood by while they stepped up to their seats. Sammy was paid for and he had a few hundreds in drafts but he was Ivanhoe's slave and always would be.

"Byerley's first, Sammy."

Sammy made some quick inquiries down the line. The drivers shook their heads.

Ivanhoe rubbed his right eyebrow with his finger tips. "Charley, I think he'd have left something for us somewhere." He said to Samaliel, "We want to see the river. Maybe we can find the place where he used to be, anyway."

About four blocks up the street they came to a place which said: SERENADE BREWS—PILSNER, MÜNCHNER, ALES, PORTERS. In the next block they came to a door which said:

GENERAL OFFICES. IVANHOE KEELER, PRES.–RICHARD BY-
ERLEY, MANAGER. The red-brick fronts went for another
block along the river.

"Stop!" Ivanhoe told the driver.

Horses and great vans were pounding out and in a dozen
entrances; three great brick stacks were lifting smoke to the
sky; people came in and went out a dozen doors.

"I guess it must have been about here," Charley said.
"It's changed so. But there wouldn't be another Ivanhoe
Keeler."

Ivanhoe shrugged insincerely. "There would be, of
course. We might drop in and see him. That 'Byerley' catches
me. That was his name."

"I tell you," said Charley. "There's lots of people heard
you play and he probably figured you were dead, if he didn't
read any London paper—which he wouldn't—and he could
stick your name on the business to get it more popular. Look!
By golly, there's your picture with your fiddle and the face
has got a big beak and a long, sad look like yours. Holy
smoke—it's burnt on all the barrels, too!"

"It is, at that," Ivanhoe said feebly. "Let's look into this.
Sammy, keep the carriages."

They went through a rear door into the hullabaloo of
a great brewery and finally came out where they should have
started, at the little brick annex to the buildings where they
had first seen Ivanhoe's name. They questioned everyone
they met about where they could find Mr. Byerley but
nearly everyone was too busy to pay much attention and the
others thought it was a joke and laughed. At last they decided to dare the office itself. They could apologize if it was
the wrong party and buy a couple of schooners of beer and
leave.

Charley would cheerfully have taken on any three of
the van drivers but he shoved Ivanhoe ahead when they
entered a busy room with men at high desks everywhere
writing histories, or something, in big books and pausing on
their entrance merely to give them a disapproving look for
the interruption. If either had been alone he would certainly

have sneaked out again but neither dared to show a white feather in the presence of the other.

Finally a boy noticed them standing outside the rail. He appraised Charley's shoulders with some admiration and it was obvious that he was awed by the curled ear and the scars on Charley's mouth and eyebrows. He said respectfully, "There isn't anybody needed this time of year, but we'll be taking on some more men late in the winter if you want to come back."

Charley knew what was going on in the kid's mind when he stared at the curled ear—he'd been followed by youngsters in London and he recognized applause.

"Listen, squirt—is Mr. Byerley around?"

The boy gave an incredulous and then a frightened stare. "I—I think he's gone. Wait a minute—I'll ask inside, but I'm sure he's gone."

Charley shrugged his shoulders. The boy disappeared through a big oak door and minutes went by and by.

Suddenly they were both seized by the coatsleeves and Charley had barely doubled his fist when they heard a voice they knew.

"Ivanhoe! Charley! Come in—come in! This is the side door I use to get out of the office and home when drummers are persistent. Come in—come in!"

"Byerley, by God!"

"You remember the name, Charley! And you're back— you're both back! The papers said you were leaving—I've been getting a service from London since Charley started fighting the Revolution all over. I wrote, but you moved too fast. The letters came back. I knew that sooner or later you'd hear about Serenade Brews and Ivanhoe Keeler and drop in on me if you ever got west of Cincy."

The room was like a salon, full of crystal and plush and tapestry and wainscoted with shell mahogany.

"I'm sorry you caught me this way. It came to some expense, but it's worth it to show the big merchants that Keeler and Byerley aren't worried about pennies one way or another."

He pulled a cord and almost instantly a Negro came through the side door softly.

"Tea for the gentlemen, Orrel. Whatever they have for food in the kitchen—umm—I remember, Charley—a quart of Irish whisky and a bottle of the 1742 Jerez for Mr. Keeler and me."

"That's good," said Charley. "You got meals, too, now."

"It isn't quite that. Well, I won't make a long story of it. I went in partners with you, Ivanhoe, when you went partners with me. It wasn't hard to build up when I had a little money to use. If we sold out tomorrow we'd both be worth a hundred thousand dollars or so. But we'll both be worth twice that in five years. All of this is half yours. I've been as careful as I knew how to be and I've handled money a long time. We've got acres of ground down here that will sell by the foot before those white streaks get above your temples."

"He ain't old," Charley said suddenly, "I'm not old, and if you had any damn sense you wouldn't be old either. We're going to fight Mexicans—you are, aren't you, Ive? What the hell's a brewery? Just a nuisance. You're coming along, aren't you, Ive?"

"Sammy's got two or three thousand in the small leather case."

The little white-haired man suddenly beat the heel of his fist on the desk. "Oh, damn you! You're going to have all the fun. If you get back there'll probably be a quarter of a million waiting for Ivanhoe—and I'll be sitting here looking at figures."

"I wouldn't feel that way about it," Ivanhoe said quietly. "Every time I bust a bayonet I'll figure Serenade Beer has to pay on the new one."

Mr. Byerley laughed. He seemed to be at least two inches taller than when they had last seen him. They'd hardly have known he was the same man, in his fine clothes and with his assurance. But it was the nature of the two men not to be impressed by anything impressive and to be timid before the humbler orders of things.

"Get it through your head, man! You're one of the richest people in the Middle West. If you're worried about bayonets, we'll buy a thousand of them and men to go with them—you can be a colonel—"

"I don't know anything about fighting wars," Ivanhoe said. "Charley'd make a good colonel after he learned the system. I got to have somebody show me how to do in this war thing."

"Don't you realize," said Byerley, "that you're one of the big men in this part of the country? You're not going to march off just a common soldier—the first St. Louis man that heard your name would know you're Ivanhoe Keeler that owns the big brewery."

"I'll tell him I'm just a poor cousin. Charley and I decided we were going to get in this war and fight as much as we had to. We're not asking any favors. Anyway, after they see Charley fight once they'll make him a general. What's the difference? He can make me a colonel after he's a general."

Byerley looked at the two of them thoughtfully. "I've got a notion that you're about right. Some men are born lucky—they're the ones that think there isn't any such thing as luck, because they don't know what it's like to be without it. Well, your luck touched me and I'll never forget it. Maybe I think too much about money, but two or three times in my life I've been desperate for it. It's hard for me to realize that you don't understand it. You could buy twenty thousand acres here in Missouri and build a palace; you could have a hundred men working for you; every pretty girl for a hundred miles around would smile at you and hope you noticed her; you wouldn't ever have to do another tap of work in your life; you could go to Congress; you could be Governor of Iowa—"

"The hell!" said Ivanhoe. "They got a governor?"

"Just about—they think so." The servant came in with a tray of food and drink. "With your money and what you'll soon have you can get anything you want."

Ivanhoe and Charley looked at each other and then they both laughed.

"Hell," said Charley, "Ive wouldn't ever be a governor."

"Holy Mike, no!" His eyes narrowed as he concentrated. "You see, Mr. Byerley, you start making something out of yourself you're not supposed to be and you get yourself all mixed up and turned the wrong way. You know all about how to use money and build things like this and get us rich. But I guess you wouldn't be much on my violin and I don't think Bendigo would be so careful with his left hand now if you'd fought him instead of Charley. I'm glad you've made us a lot of money and got some yourself, but we're fixed and we just don't need it—anyway, at present."

Mr. Byerley rose from his desk. "You are two damn fools. I'm not idiot enough to try to stop you. The Lord or the Devil or somebody will be with you—but if you get in any trouble—sometimes money will help out."

"That's right," Charley nodded. "As soon as I get back from the war I'm going to buy the darnedest nicest farm in Michigan. I'm going to have the best oxen in seven counties and I'm goin' to buy the fastest saddle horse in Kentucky. I'm going to have Sammy dig me up two niggers and teach them to shave and take care of a man. Then if I got any money left I'm goin' to buy the biggest piano in St. Louis and hire an Eyetalian to teach me how to run it."

The other men looked at Charley's hands and laughed. "You'd better get the biggest and the stoutest. Why a piano?" Ivanhoe asked.

"Because Esther Lou always wanted one and she won't have any. I'll show her if I'm a prairie wagon. I'll make the Eyetalian teach me how to play those opera things, too. We'll see who's got the most sentiment—and the most piano, too. I might learn a little Eyetalian, so if Esther Lou happened to be going by I might happen to be playing and singing some of that devil thing you play—'O, Roberto—io adoro —in toto—ay so-so—' " The picture pleased him. "With a nigger pouring my whisky. I'll build a big bay window for the piano right close to the street." He sighed. "She's probably moved away."

Byerley laughed again but Ivanhoe shook his head glumly. "Twins are twins and all the pianos in the world can't change it."

Byerley looked at him shrewdly and made the right guess but he was far too much a man of the world to ask any questions. "Well, well. I'll have my carriage brought around and we'll go right out to the house. You'll probably not want to do anything much today but get your bearings, but tomorrow we'll see that you're entertained properly. I'll send word that you're here to the newspapers—they'll undoubtedly want to hear all about England—and Bendigo. We'll have a little turnout tomorrow night so that you can meet some of the St. Louis people. We're just getting into our season down here. The town's pretty gay—we'll have a lot of officers and volunteers here for the winter and I don't think you're likely to be bored."

"Soldiers?" said Charley. "Down here? I thought the war had started."

Byerley nodded. "You're too late for that war—it'll be over by spring and it'd take you a month to catch up with the army. Taylor can't get a fight worth mentioning and it's foolish to take all the trouble to get to Monterey just to spend the winter catching yellow fever—you can't catch Santa Anna. No, most of the folks here think old Scott will stop the excitement some time next year if the politicians will let up on him. If I were you boys he's the man I'd pick. My older brother—he's dead now—fought for him in 1812 and he called him the greatest general since Caesar. If you want to see the halls of Montezuma I'd go with him. In fact," he added, "there's not much else you can do. The first bunch of our boys pulled out months ago. They're halfway through Mexico now."

"My gosh, Ive!" Charley mourned. "We paid too much attention to the newspapers! But the way they talked America was sure to get licked and Ive and I couldn't let that happen. Damned Englishmen—why don't they print the truth?"

"A lot of people thought the same," said Byerley, "but no Americans. When our boys marched out of here they'd already started six wars—Illinois, Tennessee, Kentucky, and a lot of good farm youngsters from up north—to see whether the city folks or the farm hands got to lick the Mexicans first. But overseas I guess they didn't think much of our chances. Well, the war's not over yet—but I've got a sneaking suspicion that if they ever quit bothering old Winfield Scott it soon will be. He's never lost a battle. He's a fussy old codger, but when he fights he wins."

"That sounds like my man," said Ivanhoe. "Plenty of people can scrape a fiddle but the good ones never play anything till they know they've got it just right."

Charley laughed at that. "Haw! You better learn how to play some fandangos, Ive, if you're goin' to make the Mexes dance." Then his long face fell. "I guess we got here too late to do any good."

"No, I think not," Byerley said. "They'll need some more men by and by—and if you're set on this thing I can get you in. You'll meet several army officers tomorrow evening. They can place you. There's no reason for you to go in as common soldiers. There are flocks of colonels and majors and captains that don't know the first thing about an army. Half the little politicians in Ohio and Illinois are captains at least."

Charley shook his head violently. "No, sirree! I don't want to have to watch out for a lot of other fellows. Just give me my head and let me go. What say, Ive?"

"That's right. I wish we could be a company all of our own—I've got to take Sammy but I don't want him to do any fighting—I've got no right to risk his skin."

"If you were a major he could be an aide, or something," Byerley suggested. "You could leave him to watch your violin, somewhere safe."

"We'll have to think it out," said Ivanhoe. "Well, we'll

call in tomorrow for the party, Mr. Byerley—and thank you just as much as I can—"

"But you're going to stay with me! I've used part of my share of the profits to build a pretty comfortable little house —you can't go to a tavern—the carriage is downstairs this minute."

Ivanhoe looked at Charley but all he saw there was the same distress as his own. All that luggage—Samaliel—Mr. Byerley's house would never stand it. They were still quite unable to dissociate the confident, successful man of affairs in front of them from the defeated, timid bartender they had met for only minutes half a dozen years ago.

"Oh, nonsense," said Byerley. "Don't hesitate. If you hadn't come in that day I probably wouldn't be alive now. Everything I've got is yours, even if I hadn't been devoted to you for the way you handled those bullies. My son will be home—he wants to thank you. He sells our beers now and if I do say it myself he's spread Serenade Brews all over the West. We've kept a room for Ivanhoe and Charley ever since we built the new house. You may be here for months and I can't have you putting up at a hotel. I'll bring you both down to business with me—you've got to come—and you can see what Keeler and Byerley are doing. We didn't know whether you'd ever be back—you seemed to be so light about it—but I've kept my accounts and one of them was a place for all of you if you ever remembered me and came back."

"Wouldn't think of bein' such an imposition," Charley said firmly. "You see, we got our nigger with us and a whole flock of truck, not to speak of our rifles and swords—and Ive has to keep up his violin practice—"

Byerley threw back his head and laughed. "I'll give you a whole wing. Ive can play all night if he wants to. I won't take no for an answer. Where's your stuff?"

But Ivanhoe was preoccupied. "I just remember—we promised him we'd come back."

"Promised who?" Byerley asked.

"That German that runs the Gasthaus. I promised him I'd come back and play for him."

"Gasthaus? Good heavens, man, there are a dozen of them. Which Gasthaus?"

"The green and white one up beyond the church beyond where they were building a new house."

"But a Gasthaus that was here in 1839 might not be here any more. Who ran it?"

"That's right, Ive—it might not be. An' we forgot to ask the manager what his name was. The boy's name was Werther but he's growed up by now and probably got a Gasthaus of his own."

"Wait a minute!" said Ivanhoe. "That's what they called him. His name was Wirt—it'd be Wirt's Gasthaus."

"Every Gasthaus in town is run by a Wirt," Mr. Byerley explained. "That's German for 'host.' Wait a minute—I'll send for Herman. He used to run a Gasthaus and he might remember this one. Seven years is quite a while." He pulled a bellrope and a Negro appeared. "Run down and ask Herman to run up if he can spare a minute."

He turned back to Ivanhoe and Charley. "Herman's the best Braumeister west of Cincinnati—or east of it, as far as I know. He's one of the reasons we're rich."

There was a rap at the door. "Come on in, Herman—you're about to see our trade-mark and our president at last. This is Herman Staeger, our brewmaster, Ivanhoe—this is Ivanhoe Keeler, that started the business up, Herman."

Charley and Ivanhoe studied Herman and he studied them for a moment—then the fat, happy-faced old German's eyes fell on the violin which was occupying the softest chair in the room.

"De' Geiger—Herr Kolossus!" He rushed to throw his malty arms around Ivanhoe. "You haff komm zurück! You haff verinnert—remembert dot you muss spielen zum Gasthaus wieder. Hundert times I haff thought of you—effery time I see de' endt off a barrel mit the picture on I shake my head, I say to me, 'It look so much wie dot herrlich Geiger der hat such Weltschmerz' und I shake my head wieder und I dink, 'He is without kein doubt like Jung Werther—he hass jump off a britch or pop himself mit pistol.' Und now I know why he iss auf de' endt de' barrel."

"You don't mean Werther popped himself off!" Charley said with great concern. "Stout kid! Some girl, I bet you."

"Oh, nein! Not my Werther—iss only a Werther in a story—very sad—ach, nein—my Werther hass a girl but he will not pop himself off, I dink, because it gives quick his zweite baby und de' virst iss not so old to mach itself a living. Oh, no—not my Werther."

"I see you know each other," Byerley said. "I suppose I'll have to divide you with Herman. Werther runs the Gasthaus now—it's the best in town—and Herman makes the beer for it—and for everybody that ever tastes his Serenade brew. Well, I guess the best thing to do is for you boys to keep your things at my house and eat your suppers with Herman. He's talked about the prachtige or something violinist that was so sad and ate so much that I think I'll come over and take in both performances. Herman, will you ask me to supper?"

"Aber—ja!"

"All right. Let's get the baggage train started. If you've got carriages I'll ride with you and let my coachman show the way." He rang again and gave the instructions.

"How's that body servant of yours? 'Sammy' you called him. I don't suppose he knows that he nearly killed that man. Broke something in his throat."

"That was a jolly fight," said Charley with satisfaction. "You like a man big enough to bounce you a little when you hit him. Sammy's fine. He's bought himself now and got money in Ive's bank to boot. Ive's got to pay him a salary—we both give him a pound a month. He's a rich nigger. As soon as the war's over he's going up in free territory and buy a farm—might buy close to me, somewhere."

"The hell he is," said Ivanhoe. "I'm going to set him up in the barber trade somewhere close to me."

Charley laughed. It was an old quarrel. Both of them knew that Samaliel would never go far from Ivanhoe. The principal reason was that he wouldn't. The secondary reason was that as long as he belonged to Ivanhoe, legally, he was safe from slave catchers and all other persecutions that were inflicted on solitary black men.

They entered the procession of carriages and drove smartly up the hill. "There's the dern church," said Charley. "Hell, I could have found the Gasthaus on foot. It doesn't seem like no time—and here we are, Ive, and it's been seven years. Seven years we've lived—that's a tenth of all we're supposed to live—three score and ten, they tell me. And we're coming here just like we did before and planning to go again just like we did before—about all that's happened to remember is that I stood up to Bendigo and that Swedish guy said you were a good fiddler."

"That's all," said Ivanhoe, dismissing Ole Bull. "It doesn't seem like any time at all. Sometime I'm going to make a sad song about we are such stuff as dreams are made of and our little life is rounded with a sleep." He hummed a dolorous tune—accent on "dreams"—end of the crescendo on "little life"—double rest before "a sleep."

"Forget it," said Charley. "We want some cheerful music tonight, don't we, Herman?"

"Ja, wahrlich! Nodding traurig. Alles kommt out goot, nein? We make a Brauhaus—I mach beer—und you komm back zurück all safe."

"They came back a little bit better than safe, Herman," Byerley interjected. "Herr Kolossus has been schlaging Englanders wie skittles and Ivanhoe has spielt in the biggest theaters in London—and now the two Narren want to go to war."

"Eferybody does, aber we get dem in some way, nein?"

"Get us in?" said Ivanhoe. "Do you have to be elected to get into this war?"

"Yes, you do," Byerley said. "Tennessee had to vote for three thousand men out of thirty thousand that offered. The government wanted only fifty thousand from all the states just then. Illinois asked for three regiments and got fourteen. They've had to publish proclamations to keep men from mobbing the offices."

"Hell," said Charley. "Just what I said. Twenty-seven thousand guys looking for the job and we get back here a year late. We ought to've stayed. We're no better off than when we left and we're shoved out of everything."

Byerley hardly smiled. "We'll get you in if we have to make brevet colonels out of both of you. I know people who can do it. But some companies are forming just now—I think they'll let Scott out for Mexico City this winter. As long as you're going I'd just as soon you went with him instead of getting tied up with that immeasurable fool Taylor."

"Pour l'amour de Dieu," said Charley, who knew nothing about three languages except their profanity, "look at the place he's brought us!"

They had turned in to a beautiful Georgian mansion made of midwestern brick which seems aged the moment after it is baked. There was a cupola, naturally, over the central building and two gabled wings staring at them with white-painted streaks of lime between the salmon bricks. It sat softly and gently on twelve acres of wooded lawn which was barely yellowing.

"In my Father's house are many mansions," Ivanhoe said irrelevantly.

"And in my father's house there were many mansions," said Byerley. "You may think I talk too much about money, Ivanhoe, but this is the house I lived in back east—and this is the house I never hoped to have again till you and Herr Kolossus came into that awful kennel seven years ago. It's yours more than it is mine. You see why I want you to use it?"

"Yes, sir."

"Yes, sir," said Charley. He was just back from Europe and he knew manners from top to bottom. Never stomp a guy that doesn't stomp you.

III

Later, after they had left Byerley's mansion, they found that Zum Gasthaus was exactly as it had been, apparently, but as Herman showed the way the two young men discovered that it had gone through two buildings on each side and that it had a garden, now covered with straw, that made the Bellevue in London seem absurd by comparison. There were long stretches of roof on light wooden pillars and a place with flower beds and a fountain. The German had indulged his natural taste for landscaping as soon as he could.

All this was dark and cold now, but the original Zum Gasthaus had been made into a central hall with a dance floor in its middle and all the guests and diners from the four adjoining buildings came in and danced polkas, or even the waltz, as they waited for the hustling waiters to bring up another course of the interminable dinner that was being served. When the garden door was shut the interior closure still seemed like a garden of nodding heads and blue damask tables, surrounded by the comfort of walls that made the wind whine, and warmed by the four fireplaces of the central chimney.

"Got bigger, ain't it?" Charley said, asking for no answer.

Herman looked about without satisfaction. "Werther has done this. It makes a good deal money. I say—Pfulerei! Ganz Narrheit! We make good beer. We sell it. Aber de' Junge—Wand! All keerazy where de head is about."

"What's the matter with them?" said Charley. "They look like a pretty gay bunch of kids to me."

It was that indeterminate time of the evening when about equal numbers of clients were beginning and finishing their meals. Pretty blond girls were rushing around with trays of food and other trays of empty dishes. The columns and windows of the rooms were decorated with cedar sprigs and bayberry. Logs thicker than a man's body and almost as long were burning quietly in the great central fireplace and smaller fires were going on each side in the wings, mingling their glow with that of the big one through the wide double doors.

At one side of the central hall near the fireplace a white-costumed carver was working with a variety of joints laid out on hot slabs and a boy was dealing with potatoes, gravy, beans, applesauce and other such matters warming over charcoal braziers. The carver was waving a knife a foot and a half long and peeling off thick slices, now from venison, now ham, now beef, now roast pork, with swift but conscious grace.

"Vot's de madder vid dem?" said Herman. "Dere's nodding de madder vid dese—goot honest Volk come for de' sopper—but vait. Komms a hundert goot-for-nodding zoon now und trink beer und eat spiced ham und tanz bis ten, bis eleven clocks, bis midnight. Guest we do nod try to keep no more. Iss room for Herren und room for Damen to put powder on de nose. Iss rooms for help—fünfteen Herman needs nun—und rooms for banquet und Bund—zozieties. Besides, no guest would stand de' verwünschten commozhion! Und vot komms—macaroni dressed like barber pole—leedle girls all tee-hee—should be home in Bette. Tanz Saddurday night iss goot—is right—aber dies komm efery night. Im week ein man should vork—nicht?—und—"

Ivanhoe unconsciously interrupted Herman's tirade on the younger generation. He was fascinated by the carver.

"Andante cantabile—poco allegretto," he murmured.

"I'm hungry," said Charley automatically, in spite of his European manners.

"Um Gottes Willen!" said Herman. "I forget myself vile I breach sermon. Fräulein! De' Küchenzettel!" He turned to Ivanhoe. "Menu," he explained with a ridiculous simper. "You komm von Paris, nein?"

Ivanhoe grinned. "I still like German beer."

Herman slapped him on the back. "Goot—ganz goot! I knew de Französische vould nefer get you. Fräulein!"

The girl was just returning with the menu. "Ja, mein

Herr." She put down a long slip of paper, elegantly inscribed and illustrated, in front of each member of the party. Herman spoke to her rapidly in German and she turned and looked at Ivanhoe with wonder and awe—and she met his glance and blushed.

Alwine could blush better than almost anyone in the country and her blush came up to the boiling point almost instantly and wandered around her sideburns so that it was quite natural for Ivanhoe to look at the crown of braided, almost silvery blond hair, and wonder when the blush would show through. She would have been anywhere from sixteen to nineteen, with a pretty but pitiful small nose and a mere pink kiss for a mouth. One of her grandmothers must have been the model of the Dresden shepherdess—face, hair, taille, and all.

"Ja, mein Herr Onkel."

She turned and hurried away with porcelain grace. In a moment one of the beer waiters came in with mugs.

"Mein vife's sister's daughter," Herman explained. "A goot girl. Ven she can sprach English she becomes de Dame —wie sagt man?—she says 'Goot efening' to de Volk und seht aus dot alles iss goot by de' sopper—she iss lady of de house. Schön, nicht? Like ahnjel. Goot girl—goot girl. All de' family de same—mein Weib, de' sister—all goot, all schön like ahnjel. Nicht?" He appealed to Byerley.

"All good and beautiful as angels," Byerley said seriously. "What the devil was it you were ordering for us, Herm?"

Herman beamed. "Otto, de boy, keeps someding always for de old man. I order nodding—I say vas iss best he hass for old Herman, five times—twice for Herr Kolossus. Ah, we say many times about dot unglaubliche sopper he hass that night geeaten—und nodding in de Tash, de hat, de shoes— all in de stommick! Und braun beer—up from de Kellner comes vord dot his Fingern are vorn to be bone von de spigot. He said, Does de' man mach ein bahth in beer?"

Herman laughed heartily and Charley grinned. "Everybody says I eat a lot. You remember, Ive, the time the chef came out and kissed me—men kiss each other in Paris."

"He ate two dozen oysters, three bowls of mushroom soup, three omelets for four with wine and truffles—that's twenty-four eggs alone—he ate a meal for an intermit or whatever it is—he had some fish and some cold meat of some kind and when he said the roti was too thin the chef came out and kissed him," Ivanhoe explained. "Then he had a lot of ices and cakes and half a bottle of brandy on top of four pints of Burgundy. They cheered him on the way out."

"I was hungry," Charley said. "I licked a Frenchman that evening and the weather was kind of cold and sticky and no fire. I was afraid to go to bed unless I was pretty well filled for fear I'd catch cold."

"Has she been over long?" Ivanhoe inquired.

"She? Oh, Alwine. Oh, t'ree-four mont'. Already she can speech much English aber nicht sehr gut und she iss shy."

"Sure," said Ivanhoe.

The dinner-music of knives and forks was dying down before Alwine returned with a tray on which there were four plates and a great steaming bowl of river crawfish. She put a little bowl of hot butter at each man's elbow and retired with her tray.

"Prawns, by golly!" said Charley. "How did you get them clear over here? First time Ive got me to eat them I thought they were overgrowed crawjinnies." He took one by the tail, ducked it and smacked his lips over it.

"Don't be a jackass," said Ivanhoe. "They're river crawfish—better than any prawn you ever ate."

"Ump!" said Charley, dipping them as fast as he could move his arm and fingers. The bar waiter brought goblets of a white wine with the faintest suggestion of rosiness in it.

Charley drained half of his and went back after crawfish again.

"Don't spoil your appetite," Byerley warned. "If I know Otto there's plenty more to come that you'll want to focus on."

The three other men all laughed together. "Weren't you listening to us?" Ivanhoe asked.

"All right, but Otto's no French chef, and what he's likely to give you won't be a lot of whipped air with a little egg around it."

"Never mind," said Charley, rapidly reducing the gallon of appetizers toward its obviously approaching extinction. "I'll last a few more rounds."

Tobacco smoke was rising all over the room now and men had replaced the Fräuleins, since the business now was chiefly with the bar. The waiters were almost as nearly out of one mold as the girls had been, but these Germans were older, all slightly on the potty side as to figure, all pink-cheeked and mildly pink-nosed and all smiling.

Ivanhoe commented on the uniformities of the service.

"Ja. Vunce ve try to haff all raise de gross mustache." Herman sighed. "But dey vould not come oud de same." He lifted his glass. "Trink aus. Comes more Wein."

It was a jolly place, Ivanhoe thought. They were singing now in different parts of the room, various tunes, but rapidly one table joined in another's song and the scattered drops of vocal effort joined at the edges and ran together in a single pool of melody that shook the glasses. There was a good deal of shouting on heavily accented words and a good deal of banging of mugs but somehow the whole business did not seem noisy. It was orderly and good-humored, and extremely good counterpoint was going into the music.

"Jeez, Ive, why did we ever leave here? We wouldn't have spent two months bein' seasick and anybody couldn't forget his troubles here couldn't forget 'em anywhere. We could 'a' got jobs in the brewery."

"Yeah," said Ivanhoe, and then in spite of the crawfish and some sort of sourish, creamy, wholly magnificent cabbage soup he was eating, felt a strange sinking in the middle of his innards. There wasn't any such thing as true love or true romance. The minute before Charley spoke he had entertained the idea that a dim wistfulness he was able to evoke on occasion meant that he was and always had been devoted to Sue Ellison. Now he had to realize that he had not only been having a fine, warm, happy time—till Charley's remark curiously stirred him to a realization of his own superficiality —in this room, but that he had been having a very good time, generally, for five years at least.

It disgusted him with himself. He never worried himself about his peccadilloes with the Habana girl and with this one and that one in England and France—these were Byronesque; these were the natural refuges of a wounded spirit; these were desperate expedients to distract an irrevocably shattered heart. But now, he realized, he wasn't in love with Sue any more and he wouldn't have been if he had merely stayed in St. Louis and made a good living playing his fiddle.

Covent Garden and Ole Bull and so on were all very splendid and romantic but he might just as well have been stuffing out his lean belly with beer and picking up the Dutchmen's shillings so far as the final result was concerned. He was a shallow soul, fit only for fiddling and scraping in fips. He knew that any pretty girl, almost, could do as she pleased with him, just as most pretty flowers will attract a butterfly. A butterfly. That was what Sue's father had called him and Jesse had been absolutely right.

Ole Bull had said that he had a great natural gift—he had taught him the Bach "Air for the G String" in an hour, the afternoon Ivanhoe visited him to give him his Guarnerius, and said, "Now keep the violin and study for yourself from there." Mr. Bull already had a Guarnerius, and Ive's fiddle was the only compliment he felt was worthy as a gift to the man.

That was the only dignified thing in his life—"You have a great natural gift."

It must have been inspiration that had brought him back for the war. It is *dulce* and *decorum mori pro patria*. He hoped he would have time to realize that after they shot him so he could die happy—just ten seconds—that's all he wanted —to have one other thing to justify the brief fluttering of Ivanhoe Keeler, the butterfly.

He could have cut out a farm from the Ioway forests;

he could have been a lawyer and maybe a governor—they always liked his little speeches when he played his violin—like Sue's husband was going to be; he had never thought and did not think now of being a rich and important member of some worthy community, because he had never got beyond his first conception of money—if you needed some you went to a tavern and played the violin till you got what you needed. Every public place was one of his banks.

"You have a great natural gift." "*Dulce et decorum—*" Those were the two things to hang to.

"Ja, es kommt on ice von New Orleans."

"It's the best darn fish I ever ate," Charley was saying, "maybe it's part the sauce—"

"Vielleicht—somevat—but de pompano iss vunnerful fish. Must haff fish goot enough for de sauce."

Ivanhoe was aware of a heavenly flavor on his palate and a pile of bones on a plate. The singing had stopped and there was conversation—he knew the timbre and pitch of that conversation from many years back. Something was going to happen—the performer was about to happen. He nearly rose to his feet, instinctively, and then subsided and finished his wine.

A man came in from a side door carrying a violin case so old and weathered that Ivanhoe instantly reached down to his side and patted the disreputable little leather box at his side. Still there. A case grows to love its violin and fit it and give it assurances of safety. The violinist went over to the dais across from the fireplace and pulled out a music rack. A music rack? Ivanhoe lifted his eyebrows. He could stare at a blank wall and visualize every note and marking of any bit of music he chose to remember, from a two-bar tune to a twenty-page concerto.

"De Musikanten," said Herman. "Now it iss no longer a Gasthaus—it iss joost dance hall—moosik hall. Schnell kommt de jung Volk—hippety-hop. 'Kellner—Bier!' . . . 'Spielen de valse!' . . . U.S.W." He poked Ivanhoe gently with his elbow. "Tonight we giff dem sooprise—eh? Ei?"

"What?" said Ivanhoe stupidly.

The violinist, naturally the leader, was followed by a moldy little fellow with nothing but a portfolio, hence the pianist; behind him came a flautist who weighed two hundred and fifty pounds, as flautists do, and a cellist with a fine big head, silver-striped from the temples almost to the nape. The thin, melancholy violinist drooped his chin and shoulders with such a carriage that if his instrument had been pushed under his chin he would hardly have had to move a muscle except in the bow arm to hold it and play it. The lean face and big eyes, the hair waving back and down his neck, the gaunt body and long legs made him a success in one detail— he looked like Paganini.

There was an enthusiastic burst of applause, politely tempered but warm for all that, and the violonist hesitated in arranging his music and making suggestions to his colleagues long enough to give the three rooms a deliberate sad-eyed, one-sided smile. He brushed back his hair and went on with his work.

"After this night," said Herman, with satisfaction, "iss not so much broosh de hair back und bend de chin in dot fellow." He chuckled.

"Whatta that mean?" said Charley. He was uneasy and unhappy, in a way, because he had caught a glimpse of Ivanhoe's face and Ive was in another "mood." The best grub and the best company and the best luck since they had left America and Ive's face had set again like it was now—dead. Not sad enough to be good and sad so a couple of drinks would fix him up. Charley drank the rest of Ivanhoe's wine and having done so without arousing any protest he quietly drank the rest of his beer and put both glasses under his chair and behind it so that no one would notice that they were empty.

The room was in a quiet softly disturbed by the pianist's preparatory ripples and the C majors of the strings and the flute's B minor and whispers which were more than polite so that they should not disturb the preliminary twitters of the musicians. Charley held his mug over while the waiter poured another pint of beer in it. Then came the big tray on which

stuffed quail were piled like roasted oysters—dozens of them
—with a stamp of fat bacon across each breast and a high
bulwark of mashed and browned potatoes around the edge
of the yard-long platter to keep in the gravy.

The violinist nodded and the orchestra made sounds—a
mazurka—and the room slowly began to move. Almost everyone rose and bowed and began to swing about the floor.

"What's the matter, Ive?" Charley inquired solicitously.
The waiter had picked up the empty glasses and carried them
away, saving his words after a glance from Charley.

"It's just like it was coming down on the boat—the day
before I met you. Let them dance! Where'll they get with
it?"

"Listen, Ive—we're guests. You got to pretend you enjoy
yourself. Now come out of it—eiye?"

Two very beautiful young girls had appeared, as sleek
as lamb chops and as timid as quicksilver. One of them was
Alwine and the other was very nearly her blond, curly
double.

Herman laughed and seized Alwine and drew her down
to a seat between him and Byerley. "You haff an ice to eat
with us and some coffee, child. You, Ilse, you sit there
zwischen de big man und Ivanhoe. Es iss wunderbar how
you make from no minutes the toilet." He nodded and smiled
at Charley and Ivanhoe. "Sad, gives it, if you could not dance
tonight. I haff the yoong ladies, my niece and her Kameradin,
asked if they would not make Tanz tonight so that you
would not be sad since you komm back for soldier."

Byerley watched with detached, graying amusement.

Ivanhoe put his hand on the girl's arm and she rose with
her chin turned half away but with her firm young hand
clasped over his arm. Charley came up as he had come from
the turf within the ropes many times and Ilse had to laugh
at the way he took hold of her, as if he might break her firm
body if he put more than two fingers on her. It was a jolly
waltz and this wasn't the German girl's idea of how to dance
it at all. Shortly, she missed a step and Charley had to catch
her—after that everything went better.

Ivanhoe was one of the best dancers in the United States but the charming bit of porcelain in his arms was quite his equal and his heart could not stay very heavy when his feet were so light.

"You dance like an angel," he said but adding evident sincerity to the old flattery.

"Speak no English," the girl said but it was perfectly obvious that she had understood him. "Have you Deutsch?"

"Nein," said Ivanhoe, and sighed. "About zehn words."

She looked up at him from the corners of her eyes and smiled. "I have so much English, too."

"It's all right," Ivanhoe said. "We don't need to sprechen. We can dance."

Alwine was enjoying herself but she was concentrating seriously on the variety of exciting new tricks Ivanhoe had brought back from London and Paris; her face was lightly flushed with pleasure and triumph as she met the innovations and mastered them. Ivanhoe could not keep his eyes off her face; it changed all the time and each new arrangement seemed the prettiest—he was afraid he might miss an expression.

It was a good long waltz but it finally ended and Ivanhoe reluctantly took Alwine back to their table. The party had grown since the dance began. Werther had finally come up from the kitchen and the cellar and was standing exchanging good-natured raillery with his father in German; apparently Herman was criticizing the meal he was just finishing and Werther was criticizing his father's palate.

Again the passage of seven years was brought forcefully and concretely to Ivanhoe's attention. Werther had been a shockheaded lump of a youth when Ivanhoe last saw him; now he was a big, assured, barrel-chested man with a terrific blond mustache.

"Welcome, zum Gasthaus," he cried, and seized Ivanhoe's hand. "Thank God you got back safely to a civilized country!" He nodded to the waiter who stood smiling at hand and in a moment corks were popping like firecrackers. "This is the 'Ivanhoe Keeler' wine—laid down the year you first came here—a beautiful Hermitage. I've been saving it for you—I knew you'd have to come back to drink it."

"This is one of your hired help, Ivanhoe—or he was. My son, Captain Willis Byerley—pardon me, Elizabeth—with that uniform around it's hard to see much else—Miss Elizabeth Milman, my son's fiancée."

Ivanhoe bowed to the tall, serious-faced girl and shook hands with the thin-faced, black-haired young man. They were both handsome in a dark way and pleasant enough, but pretty serious people, he judged.

The thing that attracted Ivanhoe's attention and fascinated him was the young officer's uniform. Brevet officers were allowed limitless latitude in selecting their own uniforms, if they paid for them, in an army that was only about half uniformed anyway and Willis Byerley was a gorgeous sight—gilt facings on fine blue serge, enormous epaulets dripping gold braid, wide crossed bands of blue over his white waistcoat, cavalry boots that were dazzling black. The tailor had got his ideas from a picture of General Winfield "Fuss-and-Feathers" Scott but he had appropriated, as spoils of war, some of the more striking features of General Santa Anna's uniform. The Byerleys were important people in St. Louis and the epaulets were the biggest to be had. One of the Voltigeur companies had worn red sashes, so the tailor had added a red sash to the ensemble.

"By George!" said Ivanhoe. "The first thing I do tomorrow is to get measured for a uniform like that and the second is to enlist." A thought struck him. "I've got a sword. Do you carry a sword?"

Willis laughed. "Not to dances—they trip the ladies."

"Just so I get to wear one. I paid twelve pounds for one in London and it'd be a shame to waste it."

The music struck up again and Ivanhoe looked around. "I wonder what's become of Charley and Ilse—oh, there they are." The two appeared on the floor performing such a polka as had never been seen before outside Bohemia—they were giving their all and only Charley's expert ringwork kept them from bruising half the couples on the floor. At times the dance seemed to be a Graeco-Roman wrestling match and at other times merely a crime of passion by strangling; occasionally there was a fluttering Bacchanale and sometimes a charge of the Heavy Hussars, but there was one thing about the two—they both kept good time, so that Ilse knew when to get out of the way and Charley could feel that she had been warned. They were both laughing at the tops of their voices and the simply urbane company smiled, chuckled and warmed to them.

"Wahn!" Alwine said, releasing her arm for a moment to make the ancient gesture of the index finger circled about the ear.

"Sure. Charley's always Wahn. No harm in him though." She was so beautiful that he could hardly bear it. He'd thought so at first but now as the firm little back presented its corrugation to his palm and when she made birdlike pretenses of depending on his support he knew that she was the loveliest woman he had ever seen—and a hell of a long way the best dancer.

Yeah, it would be "Complaint of Pygmalion"—if he could get a rhyme—if he could get a rhyme the music would be easy:

"Chaste marble, gods have warmed for adoration—"

No. He hated "-ation" rhymes. And it had to be more personal. A "my" somewhere. "My marble, Heaven molded for my delight—"

That made her too secondary. Heaven would certainly be paying more attention to her than to him. And "his" marble gave him a shocking property right. Incidentally, the gods didn't do the molding—he did that—they merely did a little preliminary warming till he got around to a good job.

"Softness of marble lingers on thy throat
And all its whiteness lingers—
And something-something-something most remote
Beneath my fingers."

Get the third line later. "Remote" wasn't the only rhyme for "throat." There were—and then his damned brain which had been conditioned by sounds almost all his life—suggested: stoat, shoat, coat, dote, mote, rote, note—and such useless noises till he was sick of it. He could change throat to breast but that wasn't quite decent—or face—or arms—or cheek—well, he'd better work it out later—

Yeah, and change "softness." Too much "soft" in poetry.

"Pureness of marble lingers in thy question-mark,
And all its whiteness lingers question-mark, question-mark—"

Worse. Try a new meter:

"You were no more than marble but my fingers
Gave you a semblance that the gods themselves
Must animate and grant for my reward—"

Well, for Christ's sake! Blank verse. Never get anywhere that way. He must be getting a little out of his head about this girl. Blank verse! He'd be writing like Shakespeare the next thing he knew and you couldn't get anywhere writing Shakespeare's stuff. Shakespeare had taken care of that—nobody was going to squat on his property.

"Sie sind traurig?"

He was annoyed for an instant at this interruption and then realized that its source was the divinity for whom he had been composing the song.

"Traurig?"

She puckered up her face and made the signs of crying. "Traurig," she said in explanation.

"Nein. You're so beautiful I wanted to shut my eyes and forget about everything else."

She was puzzled and pleased because she suspected that the sad, serious face meant that he had fallen in love with her, as men did rather frequently, and that his moving lips meant that he was trying to formulate some sentence to cross the barrier of foreign speech. This was all profit for her normal vanity and they danced some more. He could dance—there was no question about that. But finally his silence provoked another question.

"De Augen—Sie sind müde?"

"Tired?" He came back to dancing with his mind suddenly shocked from his poem to its object. "I want," he said, "I wish to write about you the best Lied anybody ever heard. A Lied, see—about you. How ganz you are the schönste Mädchen im Welt. I want to write that. Schreiben, or something. Lieder—schönste Mädchen im Welt."

"Ach, nein—das ist nicht Wahr. You muss' not."

"I have to," Ivanhoe said dreamily. "When poetry gets the best of me I have to schreiben it. Then I make moosik to go mit. You wait. You'll see—as soon as I can get a rhyme. After you get one or two it goes easy."

"Wie?" she inquired doubtfully. The details of the divine afflatus were too much for her English.

"Ja. Wie."

To the great regret of both of them the music stopped at this point and they went back to the table. They had hardly reached their company when a shower—a hurricane of giggles—approached and Charley came up solemnly with Ilse who was pressing her hand over her mouth and giggling through it.

"Ich spreche Deutsch," Charley announced. "Listen—Du bist schön—dein Augens sind himmlische blau—Ich liebe dich—Wie geht's mit Ihnen—Leb' wohl—guten Morgen—haben Sie ein Schatz—ich bin dein Schatz—du bist ein Engel—ich wunsche Bier—Du liegst in mein' Herz. How do you like that?"

Ilse took her hand off her own mouth and put it over Charley's. "Schweig—you ask me, I haff told you. It needs not you should tell the world what such a fool you been."

"Hmm," said Herman. "Vielleicht, und maybe not. Charley learns schnell de right words for Cherman girls und Cherman beer. You are a goot professor, Ilse—ganz gut."

"He asked me," Ilse said in German.

"Ja—und you told him. Sitzen Sie—eat und drink but make no sound bis Ivanhoe hass de violin played upon."

"I—?"

"Natürlich. You cannot hope to komm here und not play. De Volk would not allow—I would not allow—"

Ivanhoe did not make any further show of protest. The bulky Werther led him to the platform and introduced him to Meister Arnold Schmidt, the pianist, and to the various other Meisters of the orchestra. The room had quieted while the curious audience studied the tall, lean young man in dandyish clothes, who clung to a patched old violin case and made European bows as he was introduced to the musicians. A joke, perhaps? A comedian? Perhaps a notable. Perhaps some finished pupil about to attempt his first performance before this friendly audience.

One of the great compliments, paid out of native courtesy, that Ivanhoe had ever received was Werther's simple introduction: "Ladies and Gentlemen: A violinist who visits us this evening." He lifted his eyebrows with a "Wait and see" expression and returned to his table.

Ivanhoe grinned as he tuned his A to the note the pianist gave him. At the first stroke of his bow the violinist's eyes had goggled; Ivanhoe smiled and nodded at him and said, "Guarnerius." The violinist rolled his eyes and folded his hands with a devout expression.

It was a cruel time for musicians. Any pianist who dared public performances had to know all the principal music of the time; had to be able to manufacture impromptus from any slender theme and the natural rhythm of his fingers; had to be able to arrange or transpose on the spot without losing any of the accents or intentions of the music. The pianist seemed nervous.

"What would you prefer?" Ivanhoe asked.

This challenge was met with a hollow, "As the maestro chooses."

"Something cheerful—the Bourrée?"

"Ah!" The man fingered a moment. "Your cadenza—?"

"Here." Ivanhoe played four notes very softly.

"Good."

With his chin over his violin Ivanhoe was as good as any

man in the world—defeated and ridiculous he might be in all other aspects but he knew that he was one of the great men of the world when he curled notes as soft and even as birch shavings out of the strings with his bow. When the piano halted for the cadenza he began to put in extras till the improvisation grew from a cheap display of dexterity to a cool little song, and another deeper one blended, and both songs danced with Alwine, the fairest girl in the world, skipping over harmonics so high that they were almost inaudible and pouring out worship in the deep G and D and concluding with a deep chord that turned into a brief minor, like a question—then he and the pianist went on and finished Bach's dance.

Someone started to applaud and someone said "Shhh!" He must be pretty good this evening; he had had the applause of silence just once before—in Paris the night he had found out about the little whore Malvina, and realized that he had always known that she was just that and had consorted with her anyway. He had played a violin arrangement—his own— of the furious final "Presto" of young Chopin's B-flat minor sonata and that evening he had been desperate because his fingers could not play it swiftly enough to make it one instant howl of disillusionment about a woman and despair about himself.

Now he realized again that even his despairs were thin and fragile. For this second time that no one would disturb any sound that might be left in the air he was telling a German girl that she was ethereal, and yet the depth of his soul, which required her, delighted in the delicate, light fragrance of her dancing and her beauty.

He had delayed for a moment but still there was no sound and he whispered quickly to the pianist and they took up an old gavotte which Ivanhoe could play almost perfectly and altogether passionlessly. At the end of this the clapping and the "Hochs" and stamping of feet thundered down. He played a slight encore of English country music he had acquired and fled from the platform with a pat for the pianist.

Alwine was dealing with some little tear streaks and he

distinctly heard Herman say, "He will komm back. Don'd cry."

Warmth and exultation filled him. It was all settled as quickly and easily as that. He saw Alwine and loved her; she heard his violin and loved him. They could be married right away—if anything should happen to him she would have a lot of money Byerley talked about and the memory of a hero. That's what he'd be, a hero. *Pro patria* and all that. He'd have his name on a monument and Alwine would go every Sunday and put flowers on it. He supposed she'd finally marry someone else but she could bring her children down on Sundays and tell them about how he had died bravely charging the trenches at Mexico City. Under these circumstances children would be permissible.

Herman was saying, "He'll be back in two months—he vas only a sigs mont' man und there are plenty der wünscht to fide."

Charley turned away from a discussion with Willis. "Ive, we got to be captains after all or we can't wear epaulets."

"Thunder!" said Ive. "I don't know how to be a captain. I'd probably get ambushed or something the first crack out of the box."

Charley nodded. "Me, too. Whadda you think about us hiring a real good captain to really run things and we'll be just assistant captains!"

Ivanhoe banged his fist into his palm. "I've got it! Sammy'll be coming anyhow. He can be our aide! His first owner was a colonel or a general or something; went through both wars. Sammy was with him in 'twelve—I bet he picked up all about campaigning; you know how quick Sammy is."

"I guess that's the answer," said Charley. "He'd have been around all the time when his master was planning. There's one thing, though—we can't have a working captain shaving us even if we only call him an aide. He'll be too busy."

"We won't have time to be shaved—this isn't a dance,

you know. We'll let our whiskers grow; Sammy can trim them when we're not fighting."

Charley snorted. "He won't have to trim yours for the first year anyway, and by that time the war'll be over. Come on, Ilse, they're getting ready to play again."

Byerley was laughing. "I think maybe we can settle you boys' troubles tomorrow. I'll get you brevets as captains and we won't bother about getting you any companies. That way you can wear your uniforms and not have to do any commanding. I'll get you under Major Curtin, as good an officer as ever tried a lawsuit. He'll understand."

"Bully!" said Charley. "That settles everything. Come on, Ilse, we'll have a dance in honor of Mr. Byerley." They stampeded across the floor, whirling and laughing.

"You're sure that'll be all right?" Ivanhoe asked. "I'd be in an awful fix if I ever had to give any orders. I don't know any."

"You don't need to," Willis said. "I've been training for three months now and they've got me training the new men. Half the brevets don't know any orders but 'March' and 'Fire' and 'Charge' anyway. The West Pointers will take care of the tactics and the formations and most of the companies are salted out with a few trained men that will tell the others what to do."

"That's right," said his father. "We've got a fine bunch of officers right from Scott and Worth and Pillow down to the captains and lieutenants—fine boys—Lee and Grant and Jackson and Beauregard—I guess Europe will think twice about starting trouble with America after those lads are seasoned up."

"Oh, var, var, var!" said Herman. "I vish dey qvit fiding so man could trink his beer in beace. Go on, Ivanhoe, tanz mit Alwine and forget de var."

"That's right," said Byerley. "In this country you can go to war about any time but you don't often get a chance to dance with anybody as schön as Alwine."

She was in his arms again and they were floating about the room. Ivanhoe was full content to be silent, pressing her hand and her waist and guiding her through the increasing crowd of dancers. Occasionally she looked up and gave him a little wondering, uneasy glance.

"You play anormously," she said at last.

"Wait till you hear the song—Lied—I'm going to machen for dich."

"Lied? Für mich? Nein, nein! Sie muss' nicht!"

"Ach, ja—"

"Verstehen Sie nicht—" She paused and then as the music stopped closed her lips. "Verzeihen. Bin ganz müde—"

"Müde" meant tired, he knew. "You better go to bed. I'm sorry—I didn't think about you working all day. You tanz so lightly I never knew—thought."

All she understood of this was "tanz" and his sympathy. "Danke."

When they came to the party Willis and his lady had left, deputizing their apologies to Mr. Byerley. Alwine spoke to her uncle in German and he explained that the girl was wholly tired and she wished to thank Herr Keeler for the very beautiful music and the very beautiful dances, and good night. She curtsied and disappeared and Ivanhoe pretended not to be looking after her but he could see the final grace of her head and shoulders and step from the corners of his eyes as she went up the stairs.

Thereafter for two hours, while Herman and Byerley, the older men, talked gravely about sober affairs and drank their own beer, while Ilse and Charley frolicked and romped about the floor, Ivanhoe sat quite silent and contented and preoccupied, sipping wine and finding rhymes for what was to be the greatest love song ever written if he could break out the feeling in his heart into phonetics. He had to give it up finally for the minute because after the second bottle of wine every idea seemed superb and he recognized the symptom.

The musicians put away their instruments at last and the crowd began taking its good-night punches and beers. Ilse and Charley returned to the party; Charley was shamelessly hugging Ilse under the pretense of supporting her with his arm and they were chattering in the gayest Deutsch-English that had ever been heard and understanding each other perfectly. When Charley's arm became too ostensibly affectionate Ilse would slap his face, so that there was a little pitter of slaps across the floor.

With each slap Charley registered more injury and distress so that at last Ilse was virtually dragging him. Ivanhoe gave Charley a mocking grin and Charley knew he was thinking about those classic sixty rounds against Bendigo, when even the world's master put his knee down some twenty times—and sometimes a wider part of him than his knee—before his cunning and resistless fist finally found exactly the right spot on Charley's jaw.

He glowered at Ivanhoe and then winked and with the next slap he sagged clear down so that one knee touched the floor for an instant. Ilse had won the first round.

They all had one last brandy to pick them up and get them home. Geniality was beginning to attack Ivanhoe. He said very little and tried to keep an even, agreeable smile on his face, so that he would not display with any unnatural enthusiasm his conviction that this was the best of all possible places and companies in the best of all possible worlds. Herman slapped him on the back regularly and roared at his own jokes, which were now wholly in German and Ivanhoe laughed back dutifully. Even Richard Byerley relaxed from urbane contentment to chide the schamlos Ilse for her assault on Charley—she might have hurt him badly. Charley puckered up his face as if he were about to cry and Ilse, whose hand might have been hurt on that granite face if her slaps had been more sincere, hastened to lift his brandy glass to his lips to hurry his recovery.

After that Ivanhoe remembered nothing but a stern inner effort to guard his behavior so that he could balance on the hairline between coolness and effusiveness and seem a man of the world—till they were out in the air and driving in Mr. Byerley's carriage over the cobbles and the slow swirling in his brain had become nothing more than sleepiness and a satisfied glow.

"What an evening!" Ivanhoe said. "Just right. Not like Paris—not like London—nothing too much excited—nothing tired. You'd hardly find it in any big town outside America."

"The Germans have sent us their best," Byerley said. "People who know life and love it have come here to make a good Germany. We get the cream—we can ignore the scum. How they strip themselves! If Prussia goes on there won't be a good German left outside America."

"Yeh," said Charley, who knew nothing about it, "that's right." He yawned. "They lost most of the Germans when Ilse came over." He yawned again. "Is she fun!" He straightened indignantly, as if someone had said something derogatory. "She can cook twenty things I never heard of. Pumpernickel, Wienersnitzel, Apfel things, noodles und strudels—" He laughed at some recollection. " 'Magine—she used to milk a goat—a lot of goats. All that trouble about a little thing like that. When she'd milked about a dozen I suppose she'd have about a pint. Then she made cheese out of it. Gee, she was smart to come to America. When I get rich and come back to America I'm goin' to buy her the biggest, darnedest Devon anybody ever saw over here. She won't have to milk it, see— the two hundred niggers will do that—but when she wants to she can get some satisfaction out of a real milch cow."

He leaned back and yawned again. " 'Scuse me—I'd just as soon milk a flea, if you give me my choice."

"I'll have them carry him up," Richard said softly to Ivanhoe.

"No, no," said Ivanhoe. "He's just happy and sleepy. But if anybody tried to carry him I won't be responsible. He'd resent it. I'll take care of him."

The humid air had continued to do its sanitary work on Ivanhoe. He'd had enough experience with Charley to know what to do on these annually separated occasions. His head was clear now—he wanted to be alone to think of Alwine. He could arrange that without bloodshed. Charley was the gentlest person in the world in both his cold and slightly aberrated senses, but if he thought he was being managed or handled, in any slight moment of sleepy drunkenness, no one could tell where the mauls on his arms might land.

Ivanhoe got a flickering impression of Byerley's sympathetically sardonic smile. "Perhaps you could have handled Bendigo better—but you know what you're talking about. Can I help you?"

"Yes. Have doors and lights straight to our bedroom and have Sammy there. I'll—we'll wait till you're ready. I'm sorry —I'm truly sorry, but he's just chock-full of being back in his part of America."

"No, Ivanhoe—don't make him any excuses. He's as quiet as a baby and even Ilse didn't know it was getting toward the rim of the pitcher. He's having a home-coming, like you say, and we don't need apologies. Ivanhoe—Ilse is a fine girl and she wouldn't play like that with a man that was very drunk or—dishonest. He's as straight as his big back. She came here five years ago when she was fourteen, and even then I told Herman—she's some sort of relative of his, that he needn't worry about her. Full-blown, men would come to her like ants to honey and my only duty is to see that she makes no bad mistake."

"In her choosing."

"That's right. Well, maybe this time, maybe another. If Herman's Kolossus wants her I think he might be very suitable. She's sense enough not to say yes in a minute but tonight, Ivanhoe, almost at once, they played like children. That is the most serious thing of all. They played and they laughed. Pardon me for being old but I think you're about to lose a part of a comrade. They're never quite the same. The last part of the old devotion goes to the girl. You're his comrade and she's his wife; she gets the last ten per cent."

Charley's breath was coming with deep inhalations and the quick exhalations that show it is best to take in outside air cautiously and throw it back swiftly. He couldn't snore if he tried. The English fighter, Wilson, had broken his nose just in front of the sinus and the surgeon had left both passages wide open in repairing the bone. The middle structure was still all right, so who cared?

Ivanhoe smiled in the darkness. He and Charley? What could happen? He motioned to Mr. Byerley. "The lights. I'll get him out all right."

Richard Byerley went up the steps and spoke to several men who had been summoned from the end of the house.

Ivanhoe spanked Charley with all the strength of his arm and then jumped out of the carriage and ran a few steps up the driveway. "Coward—coward—dirty little Yankee coward!"

Nothing intelligible came from Charley. He jumped from the carriage and fell down and plunged at Ivanhoe and fell down and chased him to the steps and fell down and hurt his shin—

"Coward, coward—dirty Yankee coward—"

Charley screamed like a woman and rushed between the two men holding candles to the first landing of the stair, where he fell down and slid back over the stairs like a hippopotamus on a mud-slide.

"Yah! Scared again! Come on, you dirty Yankee coward!"

Charley shook himself and now his face was fighting mad. The colored men remembered that he took the first four steps and the second four steps in two jumps.

"Where is he, Ive?"

"Come on in and keep quiet. You'll wake up the whole house. What's the matter with you? Come on, get your clothes off. There's your nightgown. You made everybody ashamed of you all evening."

"If I ever catch that—"

"Yeah, too much liquor again. Shut up and let me sleep."

"I'll get him if it takes me from now to Doomsday!"

"Go on and get him. Don't make any noise when you fall in bed."

"Someday I'll catch him. I'll know him by his voice. He was a fat guy with a little squeaky voice. Squinty eyes and short cut hair. I'll know him."

Ivanhoe made a slight snore, as if he were sleeping on his back and had had a bad dream in dozing.

"You bet you I will. Listen, Ive, I want to talk."

"Kerrrrrk!"

"Ah, you're a swell friend. This little girl, Ilse—"

"Kerrrrrk. Anhrwk."

"Here's his violin," Charley meditated, aloud. "I wonder how it would be if I bit right through it down here in the middle."

"Pssssooo."

"Well, here she goes." Charley grated his teeth on the pine knob at the end of the bed.

"You dirty Michigan bum! What right have you got to touch my violin! You put that right back where you got it—"

"I never touched it," said Charley, grinning. "Which way did the guy go?"

"I'm the guy, you big rummy. And quit making a noise in Mr. Byerley's house."

"I'm sorry," Charley said, and blew out the candles.

"Say, Ive, that little Deutsch girl—"

"Isn't she a stunner? Charley, I never thought I'd be in love again, but if this isn't it I don't know what could be."

There was a long silence. "All right, Ive. We'll always be friends. May the best man win."

"What the hell are you talking about? I thought you'd struck to that little hippety-hoppety Ilse—"

"Oh!" There was vast relief in Charley's voice. "You're talking about that little china saucer you were dancing with all evening. My gosh—Ilse was dancing like a house afire for two hours after she got müde and went to bed. She'd never do for me—she'd bust the first time I hugged her."

"All right—all right—I know how to handle pretty things—violins and women—without smashing them all to pieces."

"Unnnh!" Charley said sleepily. "Dainty little fellow. —Ilse—doesn't think I'm a Conestoga wagon. There's a woman for you!"

"Shut up and go on to sleep."

IV

They slept till noon when Samaliel came in, with a little procession of breakfast, basins, towels, coffee urns, fresh clothes and so on, following him by freight. The freight consisted of two colored men and a plump mulatto girl who obeyed Sammy's gestures and disposed of their burdens as he indicated. When they had finished Sammy motioned to the door and they all bowed meekly and hurried out. Sammy remained, arranging the trays and his barbering equipment silently and swiftly and hovering about to remove covers from the steaks and game as quickly as Ivanhoe finished a plate or Charley finished two. All the things were in hot dishes, frizzling over blistering slabs of stone or spirit lamps and Charley, wiping a bit of one of the half dozen eggs Sammy had just fried for him, off his nightgown, opined that this was his ticket and when he had chased the last Mexican under a cactus he wasn't ever going to get out of bed for his breakfast any more. Lying down, kind of, let your stummick spread out all over and the vittles had a chance to fill up the corners instead of dropping to the bottom and making you feel full when there was still plenty of room on top. He wandered on his theory of abdominal anatomy and put away the biggest half of the hot, brandied mince pie while Ivanhoe was jerking on his dressing gown and arranging himself in front of the mirror; then he was as quiet as a clam. There was something sacramental about Samaliel's performance with the razors—only the client had a right to talk.

"What'd you do last night, Sam?" Ivanhoe asked.

"Mr. Byerley—very fine man, Mr. Byerley—said his folks could have a dance in the main parlor, sir, in honor of the occasion, till midnight. I played some, sir."

"They liked it?"

"They complimented me, Mr. Ivanhoe. Sir, the houseman of a single man of this neighborhood—houseman's name is Bill—Mr. Ivanhoe, you might want to hear him play the piano—just a trick he has with syncopation, sir. Improvised on old tunes—any one you want."

"I don't like those symphonic tricks—I like my music simple. I'm no orchestra. It's all right for Schubert but there aren't many Schuberts. Leave syncopation to the highbrows. I like a steady rhythm—not gasps and hollers."

"Yes, sir. It was interesting, though."

"Hmm—well, I can't afford to just pass it up. When you finish that side get your banjo and show me."

"Yes, sir." Samaliel finished the shave, nodded apologetically to Charley for the delay and hurried downstairs. He returned almost immediately with his banjo, set it on his lap and began to play, crooning his song wordlessly. After a few moments Ivanhoe took out his violin and gave the beat nod to Samaliel, whereupon they took the old and silly air up together and made it magnificently hysterical and barbarous. It hopped and stuttered and hurdled the measures with the beats bleeding mortally all along the way; then Ivanhoe began to improvise with Samaliel bringing in mournful "Cluuuck-clucks" from the strings and the blackened head of the banjo and using his best tricks of knuckle-drumming till they whined out—here Ivanhoe missed because Sammy let the tune drop on a long, mournful accidental while Ivanhoe tried to wriggle back into the key.

"Whyn't you finish?" Charley asked aggrievedly. "It was good."

Ivanhoe studied. "There's something kind of polite about that, Sammy. No good music is ever finished. It's an idea. I'll have to hear this fellow. Go ahead, scrape that brush off Charley and we'll get along."

It was Ivanhoe's turn to be silent. Charley had a beard like a horse and Sammy worked it and softened it and then passed his razor about with hardly a sound.

Charley lay with his eyes closed and a look of deep content on what was rapidly turning out to be his face. "What d'you do today, Ive?"

"What do you do?"

"Well, I thought I'd leave you and Dick alone to talk

over the business and I'd just wander around and see the town. Might drop in to the Gasthaus for a bite in an hour or so. He'll probably take you somewhere down in the city."

"We might both go in and have something and go down together."

"Now, Ive, he wants to be hospitable and he won't want me bothering around while you're talking over your business. So you take Sammy and go on down and I'll be back in time for the party. I'm not in on your business—"

"Oh, yes, you are. He told me last night—you're in for a tenth of my share and a tenth of his. And he's been investing the thousand I loaned him for Sam—Sam's got nine thousand dollars in the bank."

Sammy lifted the razor. "Sir?"

"That's right. You're rich. With what you've brought back and everything, I guess you're worth eleven-twelve thousand dollars."

"You mean—that's mine, sir? With your permission, I could spend it?"

"Hell, you don't need my permission. You're free—it's your money. I wouldn't spend it all at once, though. You could buy a pretty nice farm with it and put in some good cattle and be a big farmer in the west parts."

"I should say so," Charley added.

"No, I can't do that. I can't ever do that. You please keep it a secret that a colored man has that much money? You see?"

"I see," said Charley, "but you buy a farm next to mine and if anybody bothers you I'll see he's buried on at least six different days, while they look for the other pieces."

"That won't do, Charley," Ivanhoe said quietly. "Outside of you, who'd he have for company? How's he going to manage his farm? He couldn't hire white help and if he got colored folks to work for him you'd have enough dirty Yankees and white trash from the South to hang him for planning a Slave Rebellion. He's got to stick with one of us, and he shaved me first. But I'm kind of thinking we'll settle together. I'll get Sam a good horse so he'll be at your place early."

Samaliel dabbed and brushed at Charley's face, with powder and lotion. "I could go back to England after we were all right. I could think of making a little shop in London and then Mr. Ivanhoe would be hoeing at his face somewhere, God knows where, and smarting like devils. And I'd be fat, somewhere in England. And you couldn't get through this war—you could, but who will polish the swords and clean the rifles? And you'll have uniforms, all out of shape. And your hair will grow, war or no war, and has to be trimmed. Perhaps you'd better let me stay?"

Charley was fixing his collar. "All right, Fiddler Keeler. I'll have to move next to your place. If you let one of your damn cows get through a fence I'll roast it."

Ivanhoe ignored him. He gave Samaliel a slip of paper. "Tell him I'll be there late in the afternoon. I want the bands closer to cerise than magenta. And you can pick the blue better than I can, Sam. And the heaviest braid."

"Yes, sir. And Mr. Charles?"

Ivanhoe frowned. "What do you say, Charley, we reverse the coloring—we don't want to look like twins. I'll use the blue and red and you use the red and blue—or whichever way you want it."

"Either way," said Charley. "Only we don't want them saying we went to fight for our country looking like a couple of bums. You tell him we've got plenty of money, Sammy, and to lay it on thick. Give him twenty pounds or so to start out with and say we'll be down this afternoon."

"Yes, sir. —Excuse me, Mr. Ivanhoe—I was talking last night—they say that red and white make a better sight for riflemen—"

"We've got to give the poor devils a chance," said Ivanhoe, who was thinking only that red and white made a better sight in St. Louis. "Now run along. We'll need you to dress us, about six. The evening's your own."

"Yes, sir. I was about to say—" He stopped in the obvious distress of some vital and dangerous revelation. "I was about to say—"

"Well, come on with it, Sammy! Who'd you kill?"

"Wait a minute, Charley. This isn't a man; it's a woman."

Samaliel stared at Ivanhoe. "Yes, sir. I don't know how you knew."

"What about her? Sammy, I didn't know you got into these troubles. By God, I'm surprised. What've you been doing?"

Samaliel looked at him seriously. "If I really have that money—she costs sixteen hundred dollars. She's with good people—but if anything happened to the family she's worth sixteen hundred dollars. I only saw her last night this time but we've got a liking for each other. Mr. Ivanhoe, you'll understand that if I don't have that money it would be fair for us to run north. I'd come back to you there, after this war, but it would be fair to run north."

"Well, for the love of St. Peter! Your money's tied up but there's enough in the grip to buy this girl and have her gold-plated. Open up the bag, Sammy, and take what you need, um Gottes Willen."

"Thank you, sir—but do you suppose—in case of any kind of trouble—Mr. Byerley would buy her for me now and give her her papers? He's an important man—they'd respect his papers."

"I'll tell him to do it right away, Sam. For Lord's sake, when did this start up? I thought you were going to be a bachelor forever."

"Well, sir, it was the other time I was here. She played the piano. She's mostly white—about the color of Mr. Charley here—and she plays very well. Well, it seemed I kept thinking about her all the time we were gone, sir, and it seems she'd kept thinking about me because when I got back she wasn't married. I asked her how it happened such a handsome girl didn't get married and it all came out that she had been thinking about me."

"Hell!" said Ivanhoe. "Some people have all the luck.

You fall in love with a girl in one evening and walk away for seven years and when you get back she's waiting for you. I fall in love with one for seven years and come back in two and she's got twins. If I could find a white girl like that I'd marry her if she was homelier than a mud fence."

"I tell you, Sammy," Charley said with enthusiasm. "Me and Ive has had our troubles in this world—we're goin' to buy this girl and give her to you for a wedding present."

Samaliel hesitated.

Ivanhoe spoke quickly and gently. "No, no, Charley. I guess Sammy would rather pay for her papers himself. We'll get him something else."

"O. K., Ive—set o' china dishes, hey?"

"Or maybe a silver teapot—what would she like, Sammy?"

For one instant, the only one in a long and honorable life, Sammy lost his composure or seemed about to do so. "I—" he smiled— "you see, I haven't known her as long as most engaged people know each other. I guess, like me, she'd like to work her fingers to the bone for you gentlemen all the rest of her life."

Charley, being enormously sentimental, simply couldn't bear sentiment. "Aw, hell, Sammy, we don't work you so hard as all that."

"Besides," said Ivanhoe. "Besides, they don't allow women in wars. You better figure to stay here with your wife, Sam, till we get back in a month or two. This war's likely to take weeks and weeks. Why, it's a long trip just to Mexico City, all by itself, and we'll probably lose a day or so every now and then fighting. No place for a married man. You go tell her to get ready to get married and we'll do the rest. Dick can give you a job in the brewery. We'll tell you about it afterward."

"If anything could make me surer I was goin' to see you gentlemen through the war, this is it," Samaliel said steadily. "I know all about wars from the colonel. I could be a help, gentlemen. The colonel always spoke well about my bayonet."

Charley shrugged his shoulders. "He's right, Ive, and darn nice of him. You remember those guys that used to fight with swords before the fist matches in Paris? There's a lot about that we didn't know and it's probably the same about bayonets and things. We'll better keep Sammy along to train us between fights. Get the war over quicker."

"There's just one thing," said Ivanhoe. "All the fun to one side, there's just a wild chance that one of those Mexicans might have an inspired moment and lay a bullet into one of us. This girl's waited seven years for Sammy and she's got something coming out of it. So you get a will made, Sammy —Dick'll find you a lawyer—and plan to get married tomorrow."

"That's how I planned, sir, since you said I had that money."

"Good! Take what money you need—Dick's got plenty more for you. I'll bring you the papers tonight."

"Thank you, sir. I'll be ordering the uniforms, sir." He paused at the door and bowed. "Thank you, gentlemen."

"Oh, go to hell, Sammy," said Charley.

Charley mused with his chin in his hand after Samaliel had closed the door. "That means about the time we get back we'll have a pickaninny, Ive."

"How do you know it does?"

"You never saw old Sammy flummox anything yet, did you?"

Ivanhoe conceded the point. "If you and me ever had any kids, Charley, it could shave them as well as he does us."

"Lots of people have kids when they're even forty. I knew an old goat in Michigan had two after he was seventy. We're not so damn old, Ive, not so old. Well, I'll be running down to the Gasthaus and see you later."

"I'll run along with you—maybe have a glass of beer."

"All right," Charley growled. "At it again, hey? Alwine, I suppose."

Ivanhoe whistled and looked at Charley from the sides of his eyes.

"All right—all right," said Charley. "But you sit at one side of the room and I'll sit at the other."

The two gallants straightened their neckcloths and went out together, with nothing concealed between them—again.

V

The night before the boats let loose for New Orleans they went to the Gasthaus for the last time. With one delay and another they had been in St. Louis for nearly a month so that it was Christmas so far as the Germans, who celebrated Christmas for a month, were concerned.

By the advice of the local residents and with the consent of their major they were traveling privately by passenger boat. Major Curtin was a Michigan lawyer with a big head, flowing locks, a chest like a beer barrel, and the fine, wiry hips and legs of a good pacer. He always seemed ridiculously overbalanced, particularly because he affected one of the big, narrow, plumed hats like that which General Scott wore, but his legs were cable stout. He had been a surveyor before he became a lawyer—his voice was terrific—and he had waded through enough head-high brush and grass to know that his big lungs and legs would get him almost anywhere.

Major Curtin and Charley had discovered that they were compatriots and they had soon thereafter agreed that the ultimate Michigan triumph over Mexico might be briefly delayed by the diddling and daddling tactics of a lot of feeble people from Virginia, New York, Pennsylvania and other effete territories. They agreed, also, that in an emergency it would be best not simply to tromple over these people but to respect their weaknesses and just slam them out of the way, on their faces, where they could lie and not get hurt. Major Curtin grudgingly admitted that Zach Taylor hadn't done so bad but he fooled around at it so long. With a division of men like Charley the war would have been all over by this time if Curtin had been managing things, he said.

The major's military knowledge was simplified to a few noisy orders: "Watch out for the bastards," which meant "Skirmish"; "Get ready, boys"; and "Charge" or "Fire." He had a bunch of tough woodsmen and farmers from the forest plantations and villages of Michigan mixed with a little supply from Illinois, Iowa and Tennessee to fill out his companies. Most of the men brought their own accustomed rifles with which to shoot Mexicans instead of squirrel or grouse. A few of them swapped for bayoneted guns but most of them figured that their own weapon and holster knife, which could be drawn more quickly than a bayonet could be thrust, were preferable to a strange piece of arms.

The major knew about Charley and was infinitely proud of him though he was sure that if Charley had stayed in the Northwest he wouldn't have got off so lightly as he had prize boxing the Britishers. The major had talked about the rugged sons of the wilderness so much in trials and in preparatory forensics for politics that he believed everything he said. In spite of the unconscious fictions, his command was one of those most noisily and sincerely eager to get to grips with the enemy, and they were chiefly frontier men who had learned to cope with hardship, pain and death and be eager still, up to the last circumstance—perhaps afterward.

From his first joining Charley had been a Moral Effect for the whole troop. He was what a Michigan man should be. If anybody didn't think so he could kindly walk up and be knocked flatter than a cedar-split. Some did a little bit of arguing with him out of sheer competitive spirit and the big man was gentle with them; he never used the real crushing power in his right fist—just gave them the slow, full-arm punch without the snap at the end of it. After all, he had studied under John Jackson and it wouldn't have been a nice thing to hit a man hard when he couldn't hit you back.

When they got up off the ground he would explain their faults and errors to them and they practiced with each other so that Major Curtin's force was soon known among the assembling Yankees as the Black-Eyed Daisies. They weren't quarrelsome but they had a great boxer among them and the same instinct which led the Midwesterners to build schools almost as soon as they had built cabins led them to take advantage of this opportunity.

"By the living Jehovah," Major Curtin said, "if we could get the bastards to do it we could settle the whole war with fists in two hours."

News came up from Mexico and Texas, and from Europe. No European country had any respect for the American power but all their journals represented the United States as a bullying, thieving great nation which was enforcing a rape on a smaller nation. In the same breath they noted the superior numbers of trained troops and the superior military equipment of Mexico and envisaged with satisfaction the humiliation of the Yankees.

All the foreign military staffs in countries of any consequence—Russia, Sweden, England, Prussia and France and perhaps others—had sent observers to watch the strength of the "United States" and see whether it might be easy to pick the young bones at some later time.

They had been disturbed when Zach Taylor's tough and unruly scoundrels had banished horse-lancers from warfare forever; a wild and deplorably criminal mob, looters, murderers and rapists, as it had proved, had several times overcome superior bodies of trained troops. There had been nothing commendable about the victories except the victories. "Me no Alamo"—the denial of a part in the old Mexican massacre of Americans—did not always stop the bayonet. There was the slight excuse that in one defeat—the only one—some of the Texans had seen wounded friends coolly lanced to death by the Mexican cavalry. They had paid their debt to the lancers. Zach Taylor brought in victory after victory and marched down through Mexico, and old Scott, who had never been whipped in battle and never would be, was stirring now, released finally from the foolish political webs of President Polk, to complete the campaign in the capital of Mexico.

Major Curtin, when he had had enough drinks of corn whisky, thought that this was all nonsense. He didn't know how many men he commanded because the lieutenants and things had to keep track of that. There was some colonel or something in charge of his outfit but he never paid any attention to him. He was a big political figure in Michigan. One of his captains or lieutenants or something had been to West Point and he knew how to fight on orders. The lieutenant told him what to do and he gave the orders. But he thought if he had been Zach Taylor they wouldn't have speared those fellows and he would be able to say, "Mr. President—here is the Throne of the Montezumas."

The major outlined these ideas to the party gathered at the Gasthaus. Ivanhoe, Charley and Samaliel were going down the river next day to wait for the slower transport boats. They were all in uniform. Samaliel was not present, of course; he had taken care of the men and then gone with Araminta, his new wife, to some rout of the comparatively new Negro society that was encouraged by the liberalism of northern Missouri slaveholders.

Ivanhoe and Charley were in their uniforms and so was the major. The Gasthaus was full of uniforms. The United States were preparing for the invasion that would surely be effected in the spring—Taylor and Worth to come down irresistibly from the north and Scott to take the first seasonable weather to cut off and invade Mexico from the gulf. The thing was as good as done for all these cheerful people in the Gasthaus; the dead, the wounded, and the "missing" were not considered for a moment, since there were to be none of these—only splendid charges and glorious triumphs.

Herman was at the table, late in the evening, and Richard Byerley and Ilse and Alwine and all of them who had celebrated the first evening. They had eaten well and drunk well and danced well and they already carried some of the nostalgia of imminent separation. In spite of this they could not help but feel the content of the place and the evening, and Ivanhoe, secretly and slyly touching his arm against Alwine's or turning so that his knee brushed her skirts, felt that was worth all the inconvenience that it cost—principally the cursed seasickness he would have when the boats went down the gulf.

He played for her that night the simple little song which had budded out of innumerable pretentious efforts, crystallized at last by the urgency of his time and place:

> "I put my life at little price
> So long as it is bravely given.
> Alwine, who should fear Paradise—
> Who knows Alwine and Heaven?"

And much more of the same regrettably inarticulate stuff intended to make her understand that he was engaging in a war, singlehanded, because his life had had its consummation when her eyes had opened at him or her tiny hand had touched his and such other affairs had occurred as might make a man breathe the word "Alwine" upon a desert battlefield and die without the slightest symptom of a groan.

This night, before he started for the war, she seemed more gentle, more kind than she had ever been before and her English improved remarkably; she did not speak much but she seemed suddenly to understand most of what Ivanhoe said, though it was true that Ivanhoe did not say as much as usual. The place was tremendously overcrowded, as it had been almost since Ivanhoe's arrival, and the noise was tremendous between dances. St. Louis was building up out of better-class Easterners, and European difficulties had furnished and were furnishing the city with the best of the German peoples. St. Louis was rapidly coming to Cincinnati's high appreciation of play and art. Ivanhoe was lionized almost as much as he had been after his first success with Yankee ballads in London and Paris, but as a musician now and not a freak. His original materials were considered funny interludes, but interludes with their own integrity.

Unfortunately, Ivanhoe's worst writing was done when he was in love. Ordinarily his writing was fresh and epigrammatic, but his bird wooings were filled with trills and semidemiquavers, as Pantagruel would have said. He was almost as helpless in speech. He was eloquent with Charley on Mexico and projected manslaughter but he was tongue-tied with Alwine on the subject which principally obsessed him.

It was not till their third dance that he sighed, "Mmmm —well, going away tomorrow."

"Ach, ja, it gives me so sorrow!"

He glanced down at the sweet face and was reassured about the world, its ways and himself. If there was "so sorrow" behind that loveliness on his account he must be more important to God than he had hitherto suspected.

"Alwine," he said, "Alwine—you will be here when I come back? I leave tomorrow—"

Some small perplexity and trouble wrinkled her eye corners and she seemed to draw in on herself away from his arms. Ivanhoe knew affected timidity and he also knew the real article, and this was it.

"I'm sorry, Alwine. I shall say nothing until I come back. Better not. I don't want you to be a widow just for one kiss. Anyway, my will's fixed so you'll get everything— if something should happen!"

All the bright color left her china cheeks. "No! That mus' you not do! Es muss—es gibt—it should be someone else! Bitte, Herr Keeler!"

"Ein andere? Wer wird es sein? Ich liebe dich, mein Alwine, and there is no one else in the whole world, no kinfolks, no one, du bist mein Alles."

The girl was genuinely distressed and with her distress there was mingled the shadow of perplexity, sitting curiously upon her white, marble-smooth forehead. Her face was so childlike, so innocent and delicate that Ivanhoe could not bear to see even this faint reflection of a secondary pain.

He patted the small hand which lay upon his arm. "We will not think more about it tonight, sollen wir? Tonight is für Freude, for dancing, for singing, for music and smiles— we will say nothing more."

Her relief was evident. She smiled up at him timidly and pressed the hand in her own. Ivanhoe stopped dancing and began flying.

It was a great evening, though some of the uniformed men present were amiably envious of the two officers who were taking a step toward the war ahead of their outfits. There was some complaint, too, about the fiddler taking his music away before it was absolutely necessary but Ivanhoe assured them that they would be sick and tired of his fiddle during the next month or two, before they got to the guitars of Mexico City. The Black-Eyed Daisies sent a committee with a gold stop watch for Charley and an elegant brooch for Ivanhoe and on breaking up the party added enough toasts to its cumulation of drinks to send everyone home pleasantly fuzzy at least.

"Where's Charley?" Ivanhoe asked sleepily.

Byerley smiled. "He's having a few last words. He'll be back home, by and by."

"Oh," said Ivanhoe. He didn't know whether or not he was jealous of Charley and his Ilse, whose heart had been openly and even ostentatiously on her sleeve ever since she had met the big man. In a way, it was nice; still, one of the dearest things about Alwine was her lovely diffidence.

Though it was eleven o'clock when they reached home, Byerley, that sober, orderly man, suggested that they sit up for the duration of a milk punch which, he said, would close their eyes tightly after the excitement of the evening. Ivanhoe did not feel that any additional means were necessary to this end so far as he was concerned, but he liked to talk to this man who was a perpetual curiosity to him.

Ivanhoe had never wanted money for his immediate purposes since his early youth and it had never meant anything to him especially. Byerley had more money than he could spend, and his son after him, in their two lifetimes, and yet he went ahead with determination and shrewdness—and what was more bewildering to Ivanhoe, with almost lyric inspiration—to double and redouble and pyramid the things he owned. He did not grasp money, but it was a circumstance of his affluence that he had a fine German piano and that the great room in which they sat down for the brewing of the punch was furnished with the work of Chippendale and his best pupils.

Richard Byerley caught his glance and smiled. "When you get back you must have a house like this, Ive. You can't be a wandering minstrel all your life. One of these days you'll want to marry and settle down—you'll have wandered enough and seen enough and it will be time for you to make a residence somewhere."

The colored man came in with the punch and served it. The two men lit cigars and sank into the pleasant, reflective warmth of the fireplace, tobacco smoke and a faint genial haze of liquor well treated.

"I've always been foot-free," Ivanhoe said. "If I had a house like this—well—I don't know whether I could get away from it or not."

Byerley laughed. "The last flutter of the captured lark, eh? Well, you're getting on in years, my boy, and my notion is that after you've seen this war you'll begin to recognize the advantages of a settled life. There isn't much more for you to adventure, anyway, unless you go southwest or to California and take up cattle raising. You've seen the settlement of this west country, you've seen the world, you'll see a war, and there isn't anything much likely to happen in this country that will be exciting after all that."

"Oh, I don't know. I knew an old frontiersman once, name of Eli Ledom. He was always kicking because there weren't any more Indians left to scalp or Britishers to knife. Said the country was all quietened down to a little sugar-pap country. Old Eli would turn over in his grave if he heard about this war, and him all dead and quiet."

Byerley smiled and shook his head. "This ought to be about the last one, though. The rest of this country's wars will be in trade and development. We're too far from Europe to get much mixed up with them. When we run our border down to the Rio Grande and out through California we'll have more country than we'll know what to do with for a hundred years or more."

Ivanhoe shook his head in turn. "There'll always be

some place where things will be going on and people will want songs played about them. I might go out and be a Mormon for a while."

"Mmm-mmm!" said Byerley. "After you got about seven hundred wives with some of that moony music of yours the Avenging Angels would make widows out of the whole kaboodle some night. Anyway, they'd want you to compose hymns. No, no, Ive—you'd better stick around and come into the business. We need a traveling salesman now and we'll need one worse and worse as time goes on. I've barely tapped the river markets. You with your fiddle—why, you could carry Serenade Brews from New Orleans to Dubuque and over to St. Jo and east to Cincinnati. Why, man," went on Byerley, his enthusiasm growing, "that's the very thing you're cut for! I'm not saying you couldn't be a great violinist just as a violinist, but you and that fiddle of yours could make Serenade Brews the great original beverage of the West. And it's going to be a big West, the way folks have been pouring through here the last eight years. We'll all be millionaires—millionaires two or three times over—"

"Now what in the world," Ivanhoe inquired, "could anybody do with a million dollars? That's just a figure. If you'd stand here pitchin' dollars into the fireplace from now till you were an old, old man, you'd get a cramp in your arm but you wouldn't hardly make a dent in the pile. A million dollars is a talk figure—what we poets call a figure of speech—a pardonable exaggeration to emphasize an idea."

Byerley laughed. "Nevertheless and notwithstanding, a good many men have had a million dollars—I wouldn't be surprised if we didn't have that many for you one of these days, to throw into fireplaces or whatever you want to do with them."

Ivanhoe shook his head. "Not as many as you'd think had that much. What you've spent is spent and what you can spend you can spend but what you're actually worth any minute is as much money as you need to buy something you want right then. If you want a quart of beer and you've got twopence, what good is the rest of a million to you right that minute? And that's the minute you're alive, you see. Not the minute before or the minute after."

"What if you wanted, say, to build a railroad?"

"Why, you couldn't build a railroad out of a million dollars. It's still not a million gold dollars. It's just an idea on pieces of paper that you're entitled to build a railroad. I haven't got any ideas like that, or any like building a railroad, so I still say a good fiddle is a very fine thing to have."

Richard Byerley let Ivanhoe's feeble economics pass and served the last of the punch. "Don't misjudge me, Ive. A million isn't a million to me, either. But I'm here in a kind of Golconda of possibilities, for me, and the dollars are hammers and shovels; I got here too late to raise cabins, even if I'd known how. A hundred years after I die there'll be fine houses and manufactories out where this town fades into the woods and the prairies, because I know how towns build and which way this one is going, and because I know what to do with dollars, even though I grant you that a million dollars is something that nobody can exactly apprehend."

"You to your business and I to mine," said Ivanhoe. "There's a lot in what you say—but in a lot of ways it's struck me that I have a funny kind of life, after all, and though I could think of ways to improve it, I'm not sure it would be what you'd call a lasting reform. Suppose I went out selling beer for you—one time or another, sure as shooting, I'd start for St. Jo and you'd hear from me next in Sacramento or San Antonio."

"Those are too far to cart," Byerley said practically. "The kegs would turn sour. Just the same, while you're down south making holes in your fellow man, I'd keep in mind what I was going to do when I got back. You've got the means to do just about whatever you please. You can't get away from the fact that the world has trusted you with a lot of its goods and you owe it some favors in return."

"I play my fiddle," Ivanhoe said simply.

Richard Byerley nodded slowly. "It's so impermanent."

For a moment there was deep wisdom on the young man's sad, droll face. "That's something that no one can ever tell. Maybe there's babies that will grow up to be presidents because I gave some young man an idea.''

Byerley smiled more broadly than usual—almost grinned. "Well, maybe. But those ideas usually work out whether there's music or not.''

"That's where you're wrong," Ivanhoe said earnestly. "Sometimes I darn near take myself seriously. This is a country chock-full of what not and vinegar, but it's a shouting country, and while hollering is all right most of the time, there's other times when it's not appropriate. You're not supposed to beller at a girl, 'Come here, wench, and fry me some sowbelly and raise me some babies!' That's why you need violins. That's why you find so many big guys like Charley that can lick everything they can get their hands on, but just stand around with their fingers in their mouths when there's a petticoat in the neighborhood.''

"Hmmmm. Yes," said Richard Byerley. "Yes, I suppose there's something in what you say. I suppose your violin might make them a little more—articulate.''

Ivanhoe sighed and smiled at once. "Getting back to my settling down, you see, for all you're clever, you hit me on the wrong tack. I'm going to when I get back. You could have made your whole argument with one word.''

"One word?''

"Yes. Alwine.''

"Oh," said Byerley tonelessly. "The little German Mädchen.''

"Yes. I got it all figured out. I'm going to be an artist impresario. The town's big enough for it, or will be. I'm going to buy close to the Gasthaus and build a concert hall. Then I'm going to get together an orchestra—you'll have to find jobs for the ones I bring in—and whenever there's any big singers or operas in Cincinnati, we'll bring 'em right down to the river and up to St. Louis. As long as it looks like we'd own the town pretty soon we want it to have music and culture and things.''

"Now, that's more like it! We'll call it the Serenade

Philharmonic Symphony Orchestra. We'll buy uniforms in our colors—scarlet and gold—"

"My God, Dick! Musicians wear tail coats!"

"Well—maybe it would be better that way—quiet and dignified. I'll hire a good commercial traveler from the East to go ahead of you and get out the advertising and another one to follow and pick up orders."

Ivanhoe shuddered but Byerley did not notice.

"It makes a perfect fit. All those German fellows used to drink beer—that's why they wrote such good music. The brewery will supply all the printed stuff and programs and down at the bottom, very quiet, we'll have a picture of a keg of Serenade Beer with our trade-mark—your picture—on it. Everybody will see how it fits in. Let me see—we'll have a trade motto—'The brew of the musicians'—that's good—or, 'Every glass a symphony.'"

Ivanhoe burst into laughter. "Dick—Dick—isn't anything in this world sacred but Serenade brews? I suppose you'll want to be buried in a hogshead and have me married in front of an ale pump."

Byerley chuckled. "Maybe I was carried away a little bit." His face grew sober. "Carried away by a tide of malt. Just the same, if it hadn't been for you and Serenade Brews I wouldn't be in this place tonight laughing with you. I'd be rotting in some ditch where they'd thrown my carcass years ago. You'll have to excuse me for being crass and mercenary. I'm a man of one idea."

"All of us are people of one idea—it's a good thing.—I wonder what's become of Charley. I'm sleepy."

"Oh, he'll be in by and by. We might as well go on up, eh? Sammy said he'd be back at six-thirty to get things ready. You better get some sleep. The boat pulls out at ten."

"That's all right. If it was anybody but Charley—I'd be worried. But if he was in any kind of trouble we could have heard it from anywhere in town."

"He wouldn't be in trouble. Probably he and Ilse have just forgotten how late it is. You go on and get some sleep."

They carried their own candles upstairs. In his room

Ivanhoe was surprised to catch himself with a little feeling of loneliness. Samaliel was not near him and Charley was out somewhere with Ilse. Alwine must long ago have turned her white cheek to the pillow and gone to rest with all the other angels, a very delectable but orderly lot. He had little time to reflect on this for his eyes were heavy with fatigue, emotion and the best liquors in the middle of the continent.

Samaliel woke him at six o'clock. It was ten minutes later that Charley came in, fully dressed but unshaven. His uniform was out of press but he was jaunty for all that.

"Hi, Sammy—get out your sadiron! Got to be got in shape before the boat goes." He looked at Ivanhoe. "Just jerked these on for a little morning walk while the house was snoring. How're you this morning?"

"Fine," said Ivanhoe absently. Charley hadn't had his collar and linen changed either, when he got up. Charley had not dressed freshly that morning. Charley had certainly not been home all night, till this moment.

Ilse! A little too excited with her voice and reckless with her laugh, perhaps, but a nice girl for all that.

That would be too bad—terribly too bad.

PART IV

A LITTLE WAR

I

THE sight was so good that it brought the usual tightness in Ivanhoe's throat. He wanted to cry or write a poem or play his violin. It was impossible to do any of those things well enough to comprehend all that was implied in the affair at hand. The surfboats sprinted over clear blue water to the sand of Mexico; the ocean surface rocked only slightly but somewhere—*somewhere*—in the hundred yards of blue between the squatty barges and the gray shore a prepared accident of explosion and death would occur; men would die at once or die drowning. The stout men pulling at the oars would give up the life of the fine shoulders and the eager bodies when the little floating wooden gourds, with fifty seeds or so in their bellies, smashed to splinters.

The day was calm. The beach was equally calm, running back from blue sea to yellow-gray flats to gray sand hills.

There was a flurry of cavalry on the hills, and the men, as helplessly enclosed in these cockles as they had ever been since they left the breathing and nourishing womb, made the pretense of gripping their rifles.

One shell flew.

The American ships could not yet reply to an unlocated enemy.

And Worth leaped from his boat to wade the swells to shore; followed in the instant, which is really many minutes, by the four or five thousand trained soldiers who had been prepared for this occasion.

The fire of the ships now broke at the ridges of the sand hills as the barges continued to pass to shore with the rest of a Ten Thousand.

Ivanhoe said, "Where is Xenophon?"

Charley said he didn't know. He was in a temper, and

since big men seldom have tempers they are not accustomed to them and control them loosely. "All I want is to get a bust at them and get it over with. The hell with Worth parading. Let me get over there for a minute!"

"You and I, Charley, are seeing the Anabasis all over again. The Ten Thousand against the older culture—the Persians and the Egyptians—the Greeks against the Persians."

"The hell with the Anabaptists or the anabastards or whatever you're talking about. Why don't they get our scow up here?" He went on fuming. "The best damned soldier in the whole army—stuck here with my knitting—what if the Mexicans charge on them now—serve them right if they massacred the whole bunch."

"All right, boys. Make it fast now!"

"About time," Charley grumbled. "Now you'll see some fightin'."

Major Curtin, who was going off with his own first fifty, chuckled and poked Charley in the ribs. "Never mind, Michigan. You'll get your chance to lambast a Mex or two. Over side! Hey, Ive—not you. They'll get you and Sammy a little later—"

"What the hell—Charley and I stick together—"

"Not this time, Ive. We don't want to chance gettin' that fiddle wet. We'll take you off as soon as we're set in and see what's up."

"For Christ's sake! I came to this war to fight—not to fiddle."

"He's right, Ive," Charley said. "There'll be plenty of Mexes for one and all but if your fiddle gets busted we've ruined the whole regiment. Watch out for him, Sammy, till I get through takin' Vera Cruz just now. See you this evening, Ive."

"I won't stand for it!"

The major barked. "Sergeant! You and Jimmy Thompson keep this man under arrest till further orders."

"Aw, maje, ain't we goin' on this boat?"

"You heard your orders—shut up, Dave. Ain't you ever going to learn any discipline?"

"Aw, hell—when we get there it'll all be over."

"Shut UP! And guard your prisoner."

Dave subsided and stood scowling at Ivanhoe. The boat loaded rapidly and they heard a parting yell from Charley. Ivanhoe, standing disconsolate with his violin in one hand and his musket in the other, said a rude word.

"Give way!"

"If you'd of learned to obey orders when you're told this never would have happened," Dave said bitterly.

"I'm your superior officer," said Ivanhoe, "and not only that but I can punch your nose in with one hand if you don't close your lip."

Since there was considerable truth in both these statements, Dave shut his lip and looked after the departing surf boat.

Samaliel, who had been standing with one leg pressed against a certain one of Ivanhoe's bags, in the mess of duffel, took a small glass from his eye and turned to the other soldiers with consoling news.

"Beg pardon, gentlemen, but it don't look like there would be any fightin'. The scouting party has just come back from over the sand hills."

The whole mood of the abandoned men changed in a moment.

"Skedaddled, by Jimminy!" Dave said jubilantly and embraced his prisoner and superior. He and Ivanhoe did a short dance.

"What a sell on good old Charley! Like to see his face when he gets off the boat and there's nobody there but our boys!"

Now there was cheering from all the ships and suddenly they heard the band from the flagship, *Massachusetts*, strike into "The Star-Spangled Banner."

They all came to attention, but Ivanhoe dropped the posture in a moment—it was beyond endurance—his heart was about to break. With two snaps and a jerk he had his fiddle out and in another instant the song was pouring out of it, above the music of the band across the water. The few scores of men and sailors left aboard the boat began to sing.

The song had barely ended when Samaliel reported the landing of Charley's boat. The big man and his mates had jumped into the surf like the others, under instructions, and run up to join the formation. They emerged from thigh-deep water like unusual Tritons, with their rifles and powder boxes held above their heads. It had been assumed in the issuance of the original orders that there would be an immediate engagement on the beach with no opportunity for rifle fire so that the arms were unloaded but tipped with their long, triangular bayonets.

Ivanhoe remembered this detail and began to yell with laughter. "Can you see Charley, Sam? He must look so damn silly standing there with that bayonet—"

Sammy permitted himself a chuckle. "Can't make him out, sir—they're dressing the squads—now it appears they've been given 'Rest'—the others are digging into the sand, sir—oh, they're handing out sappers' tools."

There was a howl of delight from the abandoned men.

"I'd give a thousand dollars for a semaphore," Ivanhoe said. "That big ape telling me I got to stay here and keep my fiddle dry!"

A grinning ensign paused and touched Ivanhoe's shoulder. "Something you'd like to say, sir? We've appreciated your music, sir, and the flags aren't busy. I'm sure the captain—"

Ten minutes later Captain Charley Hoskin, sweating dutifully at a shovel with the rank and file, got an unexpected message delivered by a grinning orderly:

"DIG ONE FOR MY FIDDLE IT MIGHT GET WET IVANHOE."

II

The first mails came a few days after the landing, on ships by which Polk and Scott's other political enemies were tardily and inadequately yielding up the supplies agreed on for the campaign. Ivanhoe had a note from Richard Byerley, rushed into the army mails by some wonder of money and method which only Byerley and God could manage.

"MY DEAR BOY:

"Tell Charley that Ilse is fine but wonders why he hasn't finished the war and come back—as I write this he has been gone almost ten days and she wonders about the delay. I have explained that the voyage takes time and it will be some days before he can catch Santa Anna even with the fellow's wooden leg. She inclines to doubt this; she feels that if they will only put Charley—'Sharley'—down somewhere on the edge of Mexico he will find the scoundrel out in a day or two and settle the war at once with his 'dukes.' Seriously, she is very well, and as good a soldier here as he is there.

"Tell Samaliel to be easy about Araminta. She is managing this household now—her earlier people are kind and good in every way but I thought it best to have the wife of a partner in genteel service. I have written to my son. Araminta and Elizabeth have a sympathy between them. Tell Samaliel only that; he will understand. They are both waiting for their husbands to come back—and waiting—

"It seems ridiculous to speak of Serenade when you are probably camped between a cactus and a rattlesnake, but there is some little movement of population to the West, even since you left. Taylor and the crazy California affair have made migrators feel that all of the West will finally belong to the United States. I am strongly inclined to agree and I have set up branches at the principal crossings of the Missouri River. With your approval, we might go even farther toward the West. If U. S. finally occupies the upper part of Mexico permanently there will be ports and an important population there. If time and chance favor I may send a cargo and a few managers to Tuleberg in California, to be ready.

"At any rate, my boy, try to care for yourself as best you can in your circumstances. There is hardly a young man in this country more fortunately situated than you are at this moment—a soul that moves all others with music, devoted friends, great wealth, great experience of life at the best part of your youth. And now you are adding the satisfaction—not for display, because you are Ivanhoe Keeler, but for yourself—of mortal courage. But don't waste all of these things including courage in some demonstration of recklessness.

                    "Yrqwlxy,
                              "RICHARD BYERLEY."

The norther which had been tearing at the American camp all day had finally defeated its own purposes by building up sand weather strips against the exposed sides of the tents. The candles hardly flickered at the howls which made the top poles swing against the guys.

Samaliel was busy with the uniforms and rifles. He listened in silence to the paragraph that Ivanhoe read him about his Araminta and looked up only at its conclusion.

"You will write him, sir, that I understand?"

"Good!" said Charley. "Took the words right out of my mouth—at least, I was tryin' to think what to say back to him. You're a handy fellow around, Sammy. Anything else in the letter, Ive?"

"Business," Ivanhoe said briefly. It was time for lights out.

III

They took Vera Cruz with an ease and a simplicity that seemed quite natural to them but not to the amazed European observers, quartered on the ships of their own nations or those of England, well under land-cover but out of range of the fire that was frequently exchanged between the little mosquito fleet of the Americans and the guns of the fortress of Ulua, guarding the gate of Mexico, Vera Cruz, on the seaward side. Old Scott, taking his time, had thrown up batteries day after day till the threat of serious bombardment made such a massacre of civilians unnecessary.

"A hell of a war," Charley said. Worth and Quitman and the rest of the generals had been saying it for days, but Fuss-and-Feathers was an economist; he used days instead of assaults. There were a great many days and it was foolish to have people killed, Mexicans or Americans, to make a show and save a little time. Besides, he never fought except to win and never fought at all unless it was necessary.

"What are you crabbing about?" Ivanhoe inquired. "We've got Vera Cruz, haven't we?"

"We could have had it a week ago. Jesus Christ, Ive, do you know we've been here close to three weeks? And it's still a good big week's march to Mexico City? With foolin' around it's going to take us more than a month to catch old Pegleg and put a halter on him."

Ivanhoe smiled. "Yes, it's going to take us more than a month. What do you think we're going to march on for a month? We can't go any faster than the guns and the supplies. And it's just barely possible, my fine oversized ox, that the Mexes may interfere with us here and there and hold us up."

The Americans were well accommodated. The major and his staff, with Ivanhoe, Charley and Samaliel, had a big house near a square where they all messed together. It was a palace on the outside and a sty on the inside; an elegant sty with fine furniture and decorations and a century's accumulation of casual dirt. The owners had taken their movable valuables up to the capital with them when the town was first invested so that the men ate out of camp dishes on great mahogany tables with finely cut bronze sconces to hold their lights.

They had cleaned out the place as the army had cleaned the stinking streets, not with their own hands but with those of the inevitable criminals in any army who think that a victory is necessarily a sack. Scott had appealed to the "ninety-seven decent men out of every hundred" to restrain the other three; there had been only one murder, a few rapes and a good deal of pillage in the first few days of occupation. The murderer was hanged; the rapists did not ordinarily survive for court-martial; the pillagers and bullies were set at garbage work.

Now the streets and buildings of Vera Cruz showed unusual cleanliness and food was plentiful, as it had generally been, but increasingly expensive as the conquered population learned that the Yankees must pay money for what they took. A fantastic idea—to take a city and then buy its wares! Fuss-and-Feathers, aside from his innate decency, was thinking of a long march which could be sped if supplies were eagerly fetched from the countryside, rather than concealed or destroyed before the invader.

Charley had joined this program with vast enthusiasm; partly out of indignation at the army's first evening's excesses, which he had ameliorated but could hardly stop, and partly, in all honesty, because it sped up the work of cleaning Major Curtin's quarters—and those of all the rest—at no more expense than the collection of a few culprits.

The result was thoroughly satisfactory. The big house was shining and the dinner was elegant. The army had picked up a fair percentage—higher than Scott's estimate—of the worst Americans to be found, chiefly from the cities, but they did not desert from Charley. They had his simple assurance that if anything went deliberately wrong or if any of them was missing from duty, he or Ivanhoe or Curtin might see them in St. Louis or Philadelphia or New York—or Mexico City. He would glance toward where Orizaba Mountain had been arranged by God, white and hard, and then he would take a loop of string out of his pocket and do "cat's cradles."

It was fascinating to see the big knuckles as he managed the string. He could make the "cradle" and the "seesaw" and the resolving twist that brought it all straight again in a loop over the four fingers of both hands. And they looked at the hands and remembered that an American soldier had been found dead, that first wild evening, with only a little bruise on his neck, at the back. Not strangled or hurt. Backbone busted.

All the debris of the few shells was piled away. It didn't amount to a lot. A mud city and the mud people were as much used to this bombardment as ants still making their towers of excreta between the bricks of a sidewalk. It hurt Ivanhoe. Don't they have any lives, or don't they have any places? My God, we've blown down their own places to live, as politely as possible, and we probably have killed a dozen or so, and they simply charge us higher prices.

He thought, What would I do?

He thought, They're absolutely right. I'd go somewhere else if I could but if I couldn't I'd charge the other guys every cent I thought I could get.

Samaliel was waiting at his side with the wine bottle. Charley said, unhappily, "Ive, this ain't a good idea. Let's get back home. This is no good. I've had more fun in the States."

Ivanhoe drew the picture for himself—the streets, the squares, the cathedrals, the fortess. They must all be motionless and dull for this man who had been born up toward Wisconsin Territory or Michigan. The very sight of a cathedral, no matter what had been blown off it, must give him a dismal sense of a culture, a religion, a way of thought which he disliked by habit and hated by tradition.

"What are you talking about, Charley? You're going to fight out the war. What'd you come down here for? Sammy and I counted on you—"

Charley said dully, "They won't let us fight. I like a fight when I have to have one. This time it was for the United States. This Scott can do his own war. He's all right, but the low-down buzzard wants to do it all himself. I'm just here, if they want anybody—"

"Well? What do you want? If you weren't here the Mexicans might fight. D'you ever hear about John Milton? He said, 'They also serve who only stand and wait.' "

"I don't want to stand and wait."

"And a lot of boys would get killed because you'd want to mix up in something you don't know anything about. Look, they've promoted Lee and Grant and Jackson and a lot of West Point regulars because they know how to fight— and when. Will you please, Charley, just try to use your brain for thinking?"

"I can lick anybody outside England and maybe inside."

"Not all at once. We've got a scrap we can't settle that way."

Charley grinned slowly. "This is all cut and dried, but

you can't get around the plain and simple fact that I'm just an extra mouth to feed in this army. And this war bores me to death. We'll be scratchin' through cactus for the next month and then what'll we have? Another dump like this up in Mexico City and nobody to lick but a lot of our own damn thieves."

Major Curtin roared from the end of the table. "Just hold your horses, Charley. Old Pegleg will show you some action up at Cerro Gordo in a week or two. We're not in the City yet by any manner of means."

"Never will be at this rate. Why doesn't our bunch go on ahead if old Scott's got to wait for go-carts for his New York babies? Here I bring a sword all the way from England and the only time it's been out of its skibbard was when Sammy was cleanin' it up."

"If you'd throw the damn thing away it'd be less trouble to you," Curtin suggested. "When you do fight it'll have to be with a bayonet and that thing will just be around your legs. You farmers got the damnedest ideas about war."

Ivanhoe and the young lieutenant from West Point who had been attached to Major Curtin's command grinned at each other quite openly.

"All right, all right," Curtin growled. "Maybe I don't know all the fancy tricks like Captain Lee and Lieutenant Grant and the rest of your pretty boys from the Academy but when the time comes, mark my words, all I'll have to do is tell the Daisies to go and they'll chop up as many Mexes as your voltigeurs and dragoons and high-sounding regulars."

The young West Point man said, "But, major, sir, perhaps it's in the general's mind to keep as many of your Daisies as possible from being chopped at the same time."

Major Curtin grumbled. "Like to see them try it—oh, I'm not objecting to the Old Man, Heaven knows—greatest general in the world—but he's too confounded deliberate for my style."

"He's deliberate," the lieutenant agreed. "He was too deliberate for the British back in 'twelve and he's too deliberate for Santa Anna now. Do you realize, sir, that out in the harbor there, there is a clutch of Europeans—English, French, Prussian—waiting for this enterprise to crash so that their governments can revise their policies to the States? And what have they had to report? 'Scott has taken the great sea-port of Mexico and the Fort of Ulua with a loss of nineteen killed.' They're waiting like buzzards, sir, for an American debacle and my opinion is that General Scott will not fur-nish it—and that, by God, in spite of all the politicians on his rear."

"Now you've said something!" Charley approved. "Maybe it would move things along if they'd send some of us up to Washington to fight Democrats."

Major Curtin lifted his earthen cup. "Here's to General Scott—our next President!"

They all drank and smashed their cups—an inexpensive gesture since they cost six cents for ten in the market—and Charley disavowed any doubts about General Scott's military policy, though he still felt a bit swindled on his war.

Ivanhoe rose from the table, buckled on his sword and picked up his fiddle. The American bands had merged their resources and gave the people of the town a concert in the evenings—"El Violin" was known all over the port as well as the "negro norteamericano" who played the banjo, a strange instrument like a flat, round guitar. Some said it was a kind of guitar and some that it was a kind of drum but it was most noble for the dance.

"Off to our chores, Sammy."

The dozen-odd members of the party rose and Ivanhoe led them out the door to the great cool loggia, still compara-tively unaffected by the dangerous heat of April that would shortly bring the fever. Sammy, out of his serving coat and magically recoated as a soldier, appeared almost instantly with his banjo. He bowed to the company, Ivanhoe flipped his hand at them and the two went out to the street and the square. The others finished their cups of stiff native brandy and prepared to follow.

The young lieutenant saluted the volunteer major. "There's somebody assigned to see that they're safe, sir?"

"Yeah—Obie Tremaine and Clarke Davis—two tough boys. And Charley's right behind. Though I don't think any of these folks would bother El Violin."

"Neither do I," said the professional soldier, who had been assigned to manage the lawyer, "but Scott told Wynkoop he would rather have them than two brigades and a battery of twenty-four-pounders. Nothing must happen to El Violin or the Negro—nothing. And we will move tomorrow, sir—a matter of strict confidence, of course."

They looked at each other thoughtfully but with slight smiles.

"I can't put him in supplies, lieutenant. He'd blow straight up through the roof. Sammy, the nigger, is easy—he's to go to hospital duty—you wouldn't want a better doctor—say, maybe—"

"No, Keeler can't doctor and he'd go through the roof twice if he were nursing with Sammy doctoring. You'll have to assign him every time. Watch out for the wagons—stay back to guard the wounded—any damn thing—I beg your pardon, sir—"

"I cuss, too, sonny, without even going to the Academy. I wish to Christ you'd quit 'sirring' me, too. Of course you're running this outfit—I'm just a backwoods politician with a pull—and a lot of interest in the United States of America. You're a soldier—you might be a Quitman or maybe a Scott sometime, at least a Lee or a Jackson, so don't let's have any 'sir' foolishness."

"In front of the men, though—"

"They don't give a damn about it, either. They call me by my first name as often as not, but they do what Quitman tells you to tell me to tell them to do. The Daisies haven't had a disciplinary order in Vera Cruz. Good boys. All farmers—too bad some of them came from Ohio back east."

The lieutenant nodded sympathetically—pleasant young fellow named Pickett with some Pennsylvania outfit. "Still—I think we'd better stick to 'sir,' major. Those of us that stick in the army have to get used to it, you understand. Slip up and we get disciplined. But about this Keeler—we probably won't have more than three or four battles to the City. You can use him for dispatch duty once or twice—back to headquarters or somewhere—put him to guard the wounded—and of course you can always arrest him for something or other."

"I thought of that," said the major, with a good deal of satisfaction. "But I used it once."

"Oh, well, it will stand using another time or two, sir."

"Sir be damned," Curtin growled. "Still, all right. I get the point. I'll take care of it—but if he ever finds out—next to Charley he's as bad as any man in the brigade."

The lieutenant smiled slightly. "We could give his violin a separate arrest if desperate measures seem necessary. He'd never leave it."

Curtin slapped Pickett on the back. "Boy! I'm going to take some tactics myself! I've got him under the heel of my thumb! If Keeler gets a scratch during this campaign it will be following a general rout of the American army—but for God's sake, sir, don't let it get to him. He came down to fight and that's what he plans on."

*   *   *

Jalapa was a pleasant place. Ivanhoe and Samaliel had ridden hell-for-leather at Cerro Gordo, away from the enemy, according to their instructions to tell an artillery supply to go somewhere else from where it had been sent. There was no one at the destination and they rode back, after some hours, on their undersized ponies and found a confusion which left them no direction or any direction in which to turn. However, that did not last long. A flag had been raised over the hills and the troops were all charging up the dunes from the direction of the Gulf of Campeche toward the mountains.

"What do we do now, Sam?"

"Wait and see what to do, sir."

The view ordered itself in a little while and Samaliel and Ivanhoe took to their tent for the night.

The next day they were in Jalapa: a peaceable entry with flowers blooming and girls smiling; Charley still making a fuss about getting a tussle, in spite of a uniform that was definitely dirty and a smelly bandage just under his elbow where he had been scratched by a bullet when he went out to save Pillow and the Second Pennsylvania. He was full of the most vicious kind of language.

But mail reached them at Jalapa and this time Charley had his own letter. So did Samaliel. So did Ivanhoe.

"I hope," Alwine said, "that everything will go well for you. All must go well. You are so noble to me. If you were wrecked in fight you would still be remembered, do not forget that. Sincerely, Alwine."

"Jalapa," said Charley. "How much farther, Ive, to Mexico City?"

"About a hundred and fifty miles."

"We could make it in five days if we tried."

"And get killed somewhere along the way. You figure out a war for yourself—I'll stick to this one."

"Never mind, Ive. What's the home news?"

"The Mississippi is still running. The Ohio goes into it. New Orleans still trembles on the edge of the Gulf of Mexico."

Charley took his letter and gave Ivanhoe a careful glance. "Ive, why don't you go out and get yourself a girl somewhere around? They're crazy about the Yankees. Or stir up something for yourself. You've been a graveyard since St. Louis. You don't pay any attention."

"Oh, the hell," said Ivanhoe, and went to bed, under the scented trees.

Everything dragged. Supplies were slow. Scott's reinforcements from the States were slower and payday was an old joke. The Daisies had long ago learned of the stack of golden eagles in Ivanhoe's luggage and it would have been worth a man's life to be found trifling around that portmanteau; anyway, it was easier to ask Ivanhoe for ten dollars "till pay day." Samaliel finally hinted to Charley that Ivanhoe was financing an undue share of the Mexican expedition and Charley spoke to Ivanhoe.

"Aw, I got plenty more back in St. Louis."

"Yeah, but why get taken for a fool? These boys ain't using the money for anything they need—they're spending it around the tabernas and giving it to the señoritas."

"Well, you got to have a little fun in your war. Anyway that isn't true about the tabernas. I loaned Jim Trebilcock ten dollars to buy a pair of shoes—his toes were sticking out—and he bought them."

"Ten dollars. Hell, he must own the finest pair of shoes in Mexico!"

"I didn't ask him for the change," Ivanhoe said loftily.

"You know how much you've got out to this crowd of pickpockets?"

"Sammy makes a note."

"Well, you've got better than two thousand dollars. You'll never see a cent of it back."

"On payday—"

Charley snorted and laughed. "On payday you won't get paid if there ever is any payday. Why should anybody pay you? You got money and they know it. You're a nabob—why should they give you any of their hard-earned pay? Don't be a half-wit all your life."

"I don't suppose anybody's touched you for as much as a shilling."

"Well," said Charley, "that's different—when they really needed it."

"You didn't get forty guys roaring drunk the last night at Vera Cruz?"

"That's not fair—that was social."

"You didn't lease the biggest taberna in town the night we got here and invite all the Daisies to come and take what they wanted."

"We don't want them looting and rioting like these other fellows did at Vera Cruz. I kept them out of trouble."

"It sure didn't look like it at formation yesterday. If the major hadn't had a horse he'd have had to come on his hands and knees."

Charley gave a grin between embarrassment and pleasure. "But he was very quiet and peaceable when I put him to bed. He's going to make me Secretary of War when he gets to be President. The best thing we can do, Ive, is to cultivate these influential fellows and not squander our means on a lot of rowdies and nincompoops."

"Well, let's not hear any more lectures, anyhow."

"All right—all right. I'll see you get a nice room in the Michigan almshouse when we get one."

*   *   *

Santa Anna would not fight at Puebla, either. Ivanhoe and the Daisies reached the city in the middle of May with Worth's regulars and some of the better volunteers. There was no battle at all; the Pueblans had had considerable property confiscated by old Pegleg, and the priests welcomed the Americans and prepared the people to do likewise. The church bells rang and Charley cussed as they entered the rich cathedral town. They sat there doing nothing for weeks on end. The volunteer terms expired and Charley was threatening to go back to Vera Cruz till he noticed that too many other soldiers were planning to go back with him; men sick and tired of the treatment of Polk and the Democrats who had authorized the war and then cut off supplies so that the Whig, Scott, should not win it.

When the others prepared to drop out, Charley prepared to stay in. Aside from his natural dislike of Polk he had no political feelings of any kind. He would have voted for Scott at the moment, or for Clay or Harrison, poor old fellows, if they had all been running, or for George Washington if he had been alive. Charley wished he were alive and running; that would settle all his doubts.

Puebla was sufficiently comfortable but it didn't get the war anywhere. They sat around waiting for Scott and hailed him when he arrived but then he put his whole army back to drill and the long days passed. They were not disturbed by the fact that seven thousand of them were invading a nation of seven millions but they had a cumulation of minor irritations: Worth with his "scarecrows," which were minor alarms that kept up excessive sentry duty; the absence of mail, since it took an army to bring it from Vera Cruz; and most of all, the complete failure of any pay system.

Then they got almost three hundred thousand dollars in gold granted by the Democrats, their enemies in the bipartite political system of a country that boasted about its union.

*   *   *

"I'll raise five dollars," Ivanhoe said. There were twelve or fifteen playing behind the six players and making the bets with the players.

"And up five."

"And up."

Ivanhoe raised another five and another. When the bet had gone around someone rapped. Twenty-five dollars more came down to see the man who had bet.

"Little straight flush," said Ivanhoe.

The cards were folded and shuffled but before they could be dealt Ivanhoe yawned and rose from the bench.

Someone said, "Quitting winner, huh?"

Ivanhoe said simply, "I've won three thousand dollars tonight. If I stay I'll double what I'm owed—anybody knows when a fellow's luck's running—you ought to be glad to get rid of me. I just wanted to get back what the brigade owed me—I've done that and half more. I'm quitting winner—but I'm letting you boys off light."

"So—try it again," Alvin Krestchler said.

Ivanhoe won forty or fifty dollars on the hand, and went to bed.

*   *   *

Puebla had been a conquest but it became a habitation. Weeks passed and Ivanhoe became increasingly conscious of the dull, monotonous nature of war. Occasionally on the little walk they had had up from Vera Cruz someone took a shot at you from the chaparral but he always missed. They caught a deserter one morning and Worth had him hanged but no one cared. The deserter was too hot and tired to care himself. On the scaffold he looked as if he were ready to go to bed and wondered why they didn't turn down the covers. It wasn't even a good scaffold.

Interminable delay—waiting—waiting—till the United States government decided whether it was more important to win the war or the next election.

The mails came with the delayed reinforcements but no one bothered too much about them. The States were a million miles away where people were still living, where some curiosity probably still existed about the little band of men, detached from real life, who had traveled far for a triumph and found themselves sleeping through endless afternoons in an air that was half perfume and half stench. The military routine was so small that it was hardly noticed. The first pleasures of life were only occasionally observed even in the cold evenings when the tabernas were ready with roasted pig, cold wine and warm girls.

Scott came and waited, too. "The want of salt meat" brought dysentery. Finally, in July, the trains arrived and Scott moved.

"Scott is lost," said Wellington, who had beaten Napoleon.

*   *   *

It was all just dreary so far as Ivanhoe was concerned. "Does Ilse ever say anything about Alwine?"

"Why—she says she's all right. You got a letter from her, didn't you?"

"It sounded peaked. She wouldn't have a decline before I got back, would she? This damn business—Charley, she didn't look like she'd have a decline?"

"She wouldn't get any decline. She's just blond. Ive, when we get back let's start a farm in Michigan—you and me and Sammy and Ilse—I mean, unless—you got some other idea."

"Why don't we all stay in St. Louis, Charley? Ilse and Alwine and you and all of us could have a good time."

"You bet we could. Get that fiddle ready, Ive. The boys'll be waiting."

*   *   *

They had hard grins after the King's Mill. Too many of their friends had been killed. "Molino del Rey" prepared a vicious answer for Chapultepec. Even Charley conceded that Contreras, Churubusco and Molino del Rey were something to talk about, but he always spoke of the war in the past tense now that Mexico City was at hand.

"A week from now we'll be startin' home," he assured Ivanhoe on the same September evening when the American staff was consulting anxiously on which was the best of the bad ways to approach the capital and, after the plan of battle was made, even Scott was confessing that he had his misgivings. He had decided to storm the guarding hill fort of Chapultepec at the west of the city rather than attempt the flooded and fortified swamps to the south.

Charley was in comfortable ignorance of the doubts and fears of the officers and he would have pooh-poohed them if he had known of them. Charley was a success as a soldier— he had smashed half a dozen rifles in hand-to-hand fighting and he made a superb leader for the shock platoons of the Daisies. When he started out to go any place it was unfortunate for anyone who happened to be in the way. He had two or three scratches for his exploits—his luck would have been incredible except that it was most likely that when the Mexicans saw this wild bull with his howling crew of attendant fiends rushing down upon them they did not pause to take careful aim or to contest long with steel.

"Quite a little war," Charley said with prevaledictory satisfaction. "It was worth comin' to."

"It was for you," Ivanhoe said sourly. He took a mouthful of chicken and a pull at the wine that Sammy had miraculously been able to beg, buy or plunder. "I might just as well have played my fiddle at home."

"Don't say that, Ive. Captain Lee said your fiddle concert at Puebla when the short-timers began to quit saved the army at least two regiments and maybe more."

"The hell with the concerts. If they'd let me fight they could have spared one of the regiments. There's something damn funny about all this, Charley. You don't suppose that

Byerley paid the major to keep me out of trouble? No, if he'd done that he'd have paid for you, too."

"Of course, he didn't. You're imagining things."

"It's darn funny just the same. Where was I at Contreras? Back tending the fires we built to fool the Mexicans while the fighting men—the fighting men—sneaked up on them. Where was I at Churubusco? Forty miles away guarding the hospital train. Where was I at Molino? Under arrest because some fool aide got some names mixed. Do you realize I haven't been in one single battle?"

Charley finished his supper and picked his teeth. He was quite as little aware as Ivanhoe of the musician's status. "Well, cheer up, old boy. We'll probably have another battle tomorrow when we go into Mexico City and whichever way we go—through the mud or over the hill—they say we're going to have a good tussle."

"If they try to keep me out of this one," Ivanhoe said gloomily, "there's going to be trouble. Hell, what will I tell Alwine when we get back? You with four scars for Ilse. When they ask me what I did I can say, 'Why, once I got so close to a battle they could almost reach me with cannon-shot.' "

"You've done more good doing what you did," said Charley. "What if the bandits had got you while you were keeping up those fires? Those things have got to be done and the generals just don't think it's strategy to have the army's fiddler shot. It would have a hell of a depressing effect on all the boys if they can't even take care of their own fiddler."

Samaliel came in from his own supper to take care of the men's clothes. He had his own tent for cooking and his chores and for living, but its most important function and the reason that he had it to himself was that in his spare moments he shaved a select clientele of officers.

"Samaliel hasn't been in a battle yet, either, Ive," Charley mentioned.

"That's a lot different. He's the best nurse and about the best doctor in the army. The Medical Corps would raise the devil if they risked Sammy's neck and so would the officers. That's got something to do with fighting—patching up the cripples, but all I do is fiddle."

"If I may say so, sir," said Sammy, "that's got something to do with our fighting, too—don't you think, Mr. Charley?" Whenever Sammy uttered anything remotely like an argument he gave it as an adopted child to one of the white men.

"There was never a truer word spoken! Now you calm down, Ive, and do what the officers think is best. I think when I was smoking back in Puebla you was sayin' something about Jackson and Grant and Lee and Scott and the rest of the regular soldiers knowing how to fight—and when. When they want you to do some fightin' for them they'll let you know—and in the meanwhile lay back and quit criticizin' the way I been handling the fightin'."

"Conceited big ape! Just because you clubbed a few poor little Mexes over their pates with a musket—"

"Just what I was saying—nothing to it. No reason why you shouldn't do what they tell you and make yourself really useful."

Ivanhoe was caught on both flanks and subsided into grumbles. By and by he spouted out, "But this is the last chance and I'm going to get into it, one way or another."

"Maybe so and maybe not," said Charley. "We'll ask the major what kind of chores he's got for us tomorrow."

But at the major's tent they found that that officer had not the slightest idea of what the morrow would bring. He had lost Lieutenant Pickett, who had been assigned to more important work, and he now depended on occasional messengers from Colonel Reilly, who was a brevet officer like himself.

The whole situation was utterly confusing to the major, but then it was bewildering to much better military heads than his.

"Hello, boys, sit down."

"We won't take a minute of your time, major—"

"Might just as well—take all you want. I'm just waiting to find out what they want me to do. I'm just the head hired hand as far as we're concerned. Nobody knows what they plan. Couple of the boys from the Point were in a while ago and they don't know—each one says he does and then they start arguin'—I don't know what about; they were in too deep for me in about a minute. Seems we're pretty likely to split up and try to fool the Mexicans about which way we're going to put on the main attack, no matter what happens, but just how nobody knows. One of the boys says we'll wade through the mud over to the highway and the other boy says we'll climb the hill and cut up the Mexicans there if they can fool old Pegleg into moving his men down to the highway. It's all Dutch to me."

"Well," said Charley, "we'll know in the morning. Wherever Worth's got us, that's the way we're going."

This simple analysis, founded on the fact that the Black-Eyed Daisies and Charley himself were with Worth's command in general, finally proved correct though not so soon as Charley predicted. Scott kept Santa Anna churning his men around all day till the American army was nearly as dizzy as the Mexican general himself. There were several severe but small and indecisive engagements on the south and southeast and bombardment on the west but it was morning of the following day when Charley found himself with Worth's troops behind a little grove halfway between Molino del Rey and Chapultepec to the east.

At four o'clock in the morning an orderly came to Ivanhoe's tent with Sammy and two privates.

"Formation at five, Charley. Ive, you and Sammy will be assigned at the surgeon's headquarters tent."

"I knew it!" said Ivanhoe. "By God, I'm not going! I get the dirty work every time and Charley gets all the charging. Where's the major? I'm going with Charley!"

"No, you're not. Major expected this. You're under arrest. Boys, take him to the hospital tents and turn him over to Greenbaugh and Vickers—they're not bad hurt. He'll be their prisoner till further orders."

Ivanhoe noticed at this moment with some pleasure that the major had chosen two of the larger and tougher Black-

Eyed Daisies to be his guard in each instance, but this did not prevent him from swinging on the nearest one and putting him down on his back. The other fellow, however, was on guard. He sparred till his partner got up and then they moved in on Ivanhoe and pinioned him.

Ivanhoe surged and grunted but he could not get his arms free.

"Charley," he said. "Help. Aidez moi," he added to remind him of the past face of battle.

Charley shook his head. "They could shoot me. Better go peaceful, Ive—they need you over there and me over here."

"Oh, hell," said Ivanhoe, crushed by this treachery, and he dragged along peaceably.

Samaliel followed. It did not occur to Ivanhoe to ask the black man for help or to Samaliel to offer it—Ivanhoe because he knew what was only a scrape for him would be a serious affair for the Negro and Samaliel because he preferred to see Ivanhoe safe at the tents for the wounded.

The tents formed a considerable city, more because of the rich profusion of Mexican fevers and the dysentery than because of the accuracy of Mexican shooting, though Molino had swelled the place. It was not the pleasantest spot in the world. Whisky was the common anesthetic for major surgery, such as probings and amputations; hot oil was the disinfectant to bring on a "laudable pus" which smelled to the heavens. There was a good deal of noise from some of the fever patients and from men dying of gangrene or of peritonitis-induced delirium. It did not require the least heroism in the world to work frantically in this place and to work indefinitely without rest. After a time one ceased to notice the smells and the noises because fatigue became more exigent than anything else and furnished its own anesthesia for other disagreeable things.

Ivanhoe's two grinning captors turned him over to two glowering successors. He looked at them surprised; they were usually good friends of his and he had visited them with the other boys regularly since Molino.

"We know, we know," they said to the first guards. "Git out!"

Big Jake Greenbaugh had caught a bayonet at Molino—through his cheek and partly through his jaw muscle from the front; in sliding out the point had made two jagged flaps of his outer ear. While the jaw was healing he talked with difficulty from one side of his mouth without parting his teeth. It was healing well but not handsomely. Hal Vickers had caught some canister in his neck and shoulders which had promptly "pizened" and his life was given up. Had the wound been in his leg it would have been amputated but amputation of the neck is not practicable. However, he had pulled through and it had been some time since Churubusco; he was in uniform again and feeling chipper but the doctor was taking no chances on a renewal of the fever.

"If you make one move to git away," said Jake, "I'll be pleased to death to stick this bayonet in you, you God-damn fiddler!"

They were leading him toward headquarters where he would be watched till the wounded began to arrive; then there was work for him and he would not want to escape if he could.

Ivanhoe stopped. "For the love of God, Jake, what's got into you? I didn't murder anybody—I didn't do a thing. I certainly never did a thing to you."

Jake mouthed. He had used the bad jaw too violently. "Tell him."

"If we didn't have to mammy you, you bastard, we were going to sneak a few loads for these rifles and get in the shooting. There's nothin' the matter with either of us but the damn doctors and their 'pizening.' Now we got to stay to watch you."

"Now wait a minute, boys. I'll escape—then you have to go down report. Maybe you might run on a little shooting before you could get to anybody."

"Have to report here," said Big Jake. It sounded like "affareporeah."

"Well, you were going to skip anyhow—I got another

idea. I'll give you my parole. I'll report at headquarters and tell them I gave you my parole—they all know it's good and you'd be justified in taking it—and I don't know what became of you."

The two men looked at each other and then they both grinned together, or at least Hal did and Jake tried to, and stuck out their hands as one.

Ivanhoe shook but as he was doing so his face changed. "Wait a minute, boys. I was thinking when I said that there was no use for you two to miss out because I have to—but I got a new idea; I'll go too!"

"Ey! Ca' do 'at!" said Jake.

"Naw, you can't do that! You're a prisoner."

Ivanhoe smiled blandly. "Sure, you got to guard me. But did anybody say where?"

*   *   *

They did not dare to join any of the formations but lingered behind Worth's on Charley's say-so as to the outfit which would see the most action. From five-thirty in the morning till eight the heavier part of the American artillery thundered out shells against the fort, first, and then canister and grape into the grove ahead. Only the heavier part because similar attacks were going on from the south and quartering to the north, and they had to make almost equal noise to keep Santa Anna's forces divided; from the noise the Yanquis might almost as easily have designs on the swampy road to Mexico City as on the west gate of the fort—or they might storm from some other direction.

At eight o'clock the American guns all stopped for a minute, as a signal, nearly at once and the men of Pillow and Worth took the grove and the outworks of Chapultepec in their direction on the west.

Behind them to the edge of the trees, stealthily, sheltering themselves unnecessarily from observation, since the rest of the army was all intent upon observation of the battle, came the three strange companions, the prisoner and his guards.

The motion of the battle quieted curiously while the firing continued.

Before the Americans came out from cover their ladders had to be ready to throw against the wall and the ladders were not ready. There was no perceptible pause in the battle because the forces to south and east attempted to improve their positions and the fire was as heavy as ever on the west, but the men on the west were content to keep cover and lie firing and cursing about the ladders without which they could not hope to scale the steep walls of the forts at the top of the hill.

"Wa uh heah you sink, Ive?"

"Maybe Santa Anna's coming this way—no, that couldn't be—he's got heavy fire down below there—oh, ladders! They were waiting for the ladders to get over the walls. My God, boys, you realize we ain't got a shot between us? I'll pick up a gun from some of these fellows—we haven't got time for ammunition. Come on, and run like hell—we got to catch up with the ladders if we're goin' over the walls with the first."

"Come on!" said Hal.

The rest of that assault was inarticulate to Ivanhoe then and forever. He remembered that it was strange that a man who could not talk except in grunts and hisses could run like a deer. He distanced the other chap who was limping slightly as they came to the ladders. They passed some of the formation and chose viable ladders as if they had been choosing unpreoccupied waiters in a London pub. The rifle was in his way and it was not loaded and would never need to be loaded, anyway, so he dropped it at the foot of the climb, dodged a bayonet and hit the glaring young brown face behind it with his fist and swiftly drew the fine English sword that Sammy had been polishing so vainly all these months.

It was a good sword—faster than a pistol in this jam of stinking bodies. He could whip it into the disabling thrust-cut in carte, hamstringing the muscle under the right shoulder, far more rapidly than a man could aim and fire a revolver or recover from a bayonet lunge or even hit with his fist. He remembered vaguely that he had not wished to kill anyone and it comforted him because he also remembered, afterward, that some of them were very young—the cadets in the Military School on Chapultepec. A good many may have bled to death afterward if his edge had caught the great vein under the arm—but there was no time for "Ecole" accuracy, no guards and certainly not dull blades. He had not lunged for the heart when there was an alternative.

He thought afterward that he must have been on that terrace or tower or whatever it was for two hours but it turned out that it was only ten or fifteen minutes. He was looking down now over a great lovely valley, with mountains to the west and a high-spired cathedral city almost a stone's throw below, something like a town he had seen in France or Scotland, perhaps. It was very quiet except for a patrol of yells below and toward his left—but looking over this broken stone parapet those were inconsiderable and so was the dry heat.

His arm was very tired and there was a dull and not unpleasant pain in his thighs. He must have been on his legs for a while. There was a noise of steel against stone and he whipped about and gripped his sword. The sword was not there—it had dropped out of his fingers on the flagging while he was busy thinking about things. The blood on it was already dry brown. He wiped off as much as he could on the uniform of a Mexican who was through with a uniform and put it back in the scabbard.

There was a terrific din going on all around which he had not noticed while looking at the valley. Quitman had gone on down after the Mexicans to follow them through the gates of the City. He came near succeeding, but he did not. It was an old habit of Scott's rival subordinates to take long and independent chances—if they succeeded it showed what a fool Scott was and if they lost Old Fuss-and-Feathers could get them out of the pickle—and no credit to the damned Whig.

Ivanhoe paid little attention to all this bother. He had not seen Charley but Big Jake and Hal must be somewhere around. He suspected that Charley was somewhere down below there, chasing along the viaduct to Mexico but he and Jake and Hal had been late and his latest companions had been recently wounded so they must be around the place.

He finally found Big Jake, tying up his ear in his dirty handkerchief. The bottom part of it was about to fall off entirely—it must have been hit in the fracas. Ivanhoe had a cleaner handkerchief and he adjusted the fragment and the cloth carefully.

"Come on, big fellow, we got to find Hal and get out of here. Hal's all right, isn't he?"

Big Jake pointed. Hal was propped up against the wall, gasping for breath. "He wasn't as good off as he thought he was—he'll be all right in a minute. Boy, what a fight, while it lasted! We'll hold him between us. Let's get back over and get dressed—your nigger's the best hand around at it and afterward we can say we fell down or something. Maybe they won't even miss us if we can get back."

Ivanhoe looked at himself and laughed. A few pistols had gone off too close to his second-best uniform; he was scorched and dirty and torn all over and, by the great grace of God, a bayonet had creased his chin and cheek—by the stinging he could tell that it would make a scar. What luck! It might have been inside his clothes or even on his hindseat!

*   *   *

The fighting was not over on the next day, by any means, but the troops who were not immediately engaged felt, as Santa Anna himself did, apparently, that he was merely disputing a *quod erat demonstrandum*. The capital surrendered and then, after some rioting, succumbed in a day or two. The Americans took over the rule and all that followed was anticlimactic, but, as Charley had not suspected, vital.

The results of Ivanhoe's escapade were all agreeable. Vague as his intentions had been he had come to the aid of a Daisy, without noticing it, and had been observed just at the end of the fight when observation is possible. Young Hal had collapsed almost immediately upon reaching the roof but had taken no evident harm by it and Big Jake's ear would never have been handsome, anyway, and the man had done some good and useful fighting.

There was nothing the matter with Hal except that he had overtaxed a heart which had already strained hard to pull him through a moderately fatal infection. He walked the last few hundred yards to the hospital tents quite naturally, though breathing hard. The hospital behind Worth's position was a shambles. It didn't seem to Ivanhoe that there could have been so many hurt in the battle and then he remembered that most of the injured were concentrated here. The healthy Americans were still fighting around the City.

"Wait a minute," said Ivanhoe. "They won't know anything about it, I guess, but Jake's got the best wound. You and I'll take him in, Hal, just in case they're looking for any of us. Take off the bandage."

They encountered a harried surgeon. "A God-damned ear! This cheek is old! We can't fool with ears—oh, Keeler. Listen—you got a camp kit. Stitch it so it won't fall off—just like sewing a patch—and pour some whisky around it—the water's got fever in it. I can't bother—we've got heads and bellies and legs and Christ knows what! We can get around to the scratches tomorrow. I'll sew up your cheek then, fiddler—"

He rushed away to the next row of tents.

Ivanhoe tied up Jake's ear again. "Let's get out of here. Come on over to the tent. Hal needs a drink and I want to swab out this cheek. Samaliel's got some good clean thread in his kit and I can sew you better than any of these buzzards. We've been recognized on duty, so we're all clear."

The battle still thundered, but they were content with their warfare for the day as being something over what had been required of them and satisfactory in its conclusion. They were convinced that the firing around the City meant nothing—pursuit, and replies to guerrilla firing. The generals would take care of that. They were over Chapultepec and on the broad road to the City and now Ivanhoe shared Charley's feeling that the war was over.

They got magnificently drunk on some brandy Ivanhoe had bought from the French observer. Young Hal was all for going out and joining the pursuit, since he had had no part in the day's battle except climbing up a ladder and falling off a wall. Ivanhoe vetoed this.

"We have our duty to our friend here." He sewed up Jake's ear with a heavy needle that would pierce the edges of the cartilage, and Jake did not murmur though he refreshed himself once or twice from a cup of brandy.

"It's going to leave a big scar, Jake."

"What'd we come here for?"

Ivanhoe laughed and fingered the plasters over his own cheek.

*   *   *

Ivanhoe was mistaken about Charley's pursuit of the Mexicans to their city. Late in the evening, while Ivanhoe, Jake and Hal were singing in Ivanhoe's tent, Major Curtin led in a glowering man with a web of bandages about his head.

"What the hell's all the noise about? I got a headache."

Ivanhoe leaped up eagerly. "Charley! I thought you'd be settled down in Mexico City! Didn't expect to see you till tomorrow."

Charley put himself down on his blankets. "Mexico, hell. I was goin' to be first up the first ladder and then they shoved it over on me. I banged my head. I'll get 'em tomorrow. Chapultepec—I suspicioned that's what it would be. They better be out of there by tomorrow."

Charley was so aggressive that it was apparent that he was not hurt seriously.

Ivanhoe laughed. "Don't worry. I just took it myself."

"You! You was supposed to be back here. Whadda you mean?"

Ivanhoe realized that Major Curtin was present. "Why, just kidding, Charley, but we got Chapultepec and probably

Mexico too, by now. You mean you weren't on Chapulte-pec?"

"Hell, no, I was off of it. Wait till my head's all right. I'll chase Santa Anna clear to Philadelphia."

Major Curtin's big face opened. "Could you see the battle, Ivanhoe?"

"Yeah—sure, we could see it. It wasn't far away and uphill."

There was a moment's silence and Curtin said evenly, "You scratch yourself, Ive? You're plastered up."

Ivanhoe laughed. "That's right. More than one way. But, my dear major, when you put me under guard you didn't name the place of confinement. The boys and I decided that the Castle of Chapultepec would be a good place to chain me up, so we went there."

Major Curtin, the lawyer, studied this over. "I'm a son of a wild jackass," the lawyer murmured. "Give me a shot of that brandy, Ive. Is Big Jake's ear all right? He looks like a mummy."

Big Jake answered for himself. "Thousands of lives and ears would be saved every year, sir, if Captain Keeler was in command. My ear never felt on so tight in its life. I defy any son of a bitch to bite it off—at that, I kind of wish they would. It's in the way and it hurts."

"Shut up," said Charley. "Got another bottle, Ive? Where's Sammy? Have him fetch me a bucket of water. My head hurts. So you really got up the hill? Damn funny—I don't suppose I'll ever see the top of it. And you supposed to be sitting back here quiet. Good boy, Ive."

"Go to hell," said Ivanhoe. "If I'd waited for you to aidez moi I'd still have my lovely girlish face. I used my head the right way instead of trying to bust rocks with it. Sammy's up taking care of the wounded but he left a tub of water and some towels in his tent."

Major Curtin put down an empty bottle and opened a full one. He filled the cups and then lit a large cigar. "Get a good rest, boys—we start again tomorrow. The storming party is supposed to build up its strength and come in as reserves first thing in the morning—Santa Anna's still meandering around with a hunk of army—may have some more fighting tomorrow."

"Bully!" said Charley. "I won't rest easy till I've given him a good bust over the head for this one he gave me." Charley always regarded his injuries as coming from the Mexican general personally.

"What a wonderful, wonderful day," said the major, who was warming rapidly on repeated gills of brandy. "What a wonderful, wonderful, wonderful day."

"Wonderful day," they all agreed together.

"Wonderful," added the major. They all sat for a moment in warm, silent retrospection.

A man appeared in the lanternlight at the front of the tent and saluted. All of them, including the major, jumped to their feet to return the salute—it was the hero of the day, young Lieutenant Pickett, who had seized the colors when Longstreet fell and carried them to the top of Chapultepec.

The major rushed to embrace him and bang his back. "By God, sir, you're a credit to your training in the Black-Eyed Daisies."

"Thank you, sir." Pickett smiled but the major did not know that it was because Pickett reflected that, if he had done anything commendable, some years in the United States Military Academy might have had something to do with it. "I came over for a special reason—two special reasons, major. In the first place I wanted to hear Captain Keeler—Ivanhoe—play a couple of tunes before I went to bed."

Ivanhoe winced involuntarily. "Good God—" he said and stopped. His right arm, the bowing arm, felt as if it had been torn out by the roots.

Pickett laughed. "Not feeling like playing tonight? I saw you doing some fiddling this morning and you seemed to be healthy then. You were supposed to be on hospital duty—that came straight down from Worth."

"The hell it did! So that's why I've always been somewhere else when the shooting started! I thought so! They can't do this to me!"

"Apparently not."

"But I wasn't on hospital duty, lieutenant; I was under arrest for insubordination and was under surveillance all day —I still am," he added, motioning at Big Jake, who was grinning, and Hal, who had, unfortunately for Ivanhoe's demonstration, fallen sound asleep.

"I see," said Picket, staring at Hal fixedly.

"Well," said Ivanhoe, "if I made a false move he'd wake up and halt me."

"Let's try," said Pickett.

"He might shoot me before he thought."

Pickett hooted and then went forward with his hand extended. "With that brandy bottle, I suppose. Well, Ive, Hi Grant—that is, Captain Ulysses Grant—and the fellows sent me over to compliment my old comrades and say that they thought your bowing was better than ever this morning."

"I—I—thanks!"

"A trifle staccato, perhaps—a Tartini cadenza, no doubt. Where in God's name, man, did you learn that thrust-cut? I got a glimpse of you and you reminded me of home—the first slice when you carve a turkey."

"Hey," said Charley. "Ive wasn't fiddlin' this morning— he was in the battle." Charley was frequently confused by double-entendre and that day he had taken a terrific bump on the head.

"So we noticed," said Pickett.

"You see, lieutenant, Charley was a pugilist in Europe and in France they always had some fencing with the boxing. So nobody in France could stand up to Charley fighting and the only way to keep up interest was to issue a double challenge—saber and fists. He went to the salle or ecole or whatever they call it and I didn't have anything to do in the mornings so I went with him."

"And it didn't do any good—we had to go back to London," Charley said glumly.

"No—when they jabbed at him he'd get excited and double-beat and knock their swords away. Nobody was going to pay cinq francs to see ten seconds of fencing and ten seconds of boxing. Charley tried to hit soft but he couldn't do that, either, when the other guy was serious."

"Hunnhunnh," Charley agreed. "I can only hit soft when it's fun or I'm sorry for somebody."

"You didn't hit soft this morning," the major observed. "From the size of that lump."

"It wasn't in fun and he wasn't sorry for anyone," Pickett explained.

Charley chuckled. "Thanks, lieutenant. That's right."

"Well, I just came over to extend greetings—I'll go back and write some letters. Oh, there'll be a mail out and probably one in tomorrow if you want to send anything to the States, major. You can send the whole packet for your boys under your own cover—they can distribute it in New Orleans and St. Louis—in St. Louis—you haven't got any Southerners in your outfit."

"No; all volunteered in the North—started with a regiment from Michigan. Some of your Carolina and Alabama boys I'd like to have for the Daisies."

"You'd like to have every good-sized tough in the army. Well, I guess all Americans fight about the same," said Lieutenant George Edward Pickett. "Oh, speaking of that, major, one of the English officers was laughing at our rough mess this evening about the Prussian observer's report on the battle. Will you tell me what order you gave for the charge?"

"Why, I don't remember. Something about giving them hell, I suppose."

Pickett chuckled. "You're the one. The Prussian said, 'What can any army hope to do with a force containing a brigade with a *major* who is a lawyer by profession, who, at the crucial moment of combat gives such an order as "Come on, boys, give them hell"; upon which they charge up an unassailable height, scale an unscalable wall, and rout superior numbers of prepared and highly trained troops?' That's the Britisher's translation. No reflection on your military experience, sir; it's a compliment and a high compliment."

The major came as near simpering as he could with his big rugged face. "Thank you, sir. I don't know much about the phraseology of military orders but if orations are required I can, sir, soar to the highest eminences of elocution." The major took a big drink. "However, it doesn't take an abracadabra or an oration to get the Daisies to fight."

*   *   *

The Americans marched into Mexico City the next day and quickly quelled the little uprising which old Pegleg had planned against them—a resistance of beggars, convicts released for the purpose, and classes in the city who might profit and could not lose by any civil disturbance. The looters, who were shot on sight, were not Americans, certainly, while revolt threatened within the city and Herrera and Santa Anna threatened outside and discipline was the price of life.

Ivanhoe and Charley did not see Scott's entry into the city. They were technically hospitalized and none but active fighting units moved to the town for several days after it had actually fallen. Then they were all moved in but quartered in the larger buildings in numbers. No one knew what might happen—even the "noble" people were capable of cutting a few Yankee throats if they found a few Yankees isolated.

Scott put a stop to this in a calm and economical way. When a shot was fired from a building the American cannon blew down the house on the theory that the sniper was not also a housebreaker. Citizens found at large with arms were hanged or shot, since only one kind of game—Yankees—was at large within the walls of the city and there was a strong presumption of murderous intent rather than love of sport.

Things quieted down. The Mexicans reverted to guerrilla fighting, which had been successful against France and Spain—but now they were fighting backwoodsmen and pioneers from a country smaller than their own, but more exacting on its settlers. Step by step, cruelty by cruelty, shot for shot, the Americans crushed this campaign.

Charley said one night, "I would like a sock at this son of a bitch." He was reading an old paper.

"Which one of the battalion, Charley?"

"That little New England louse, Daniel Webster. Listen, 'California and Texas between them are not worth a dollar.' "

"He's nothing but a thief and a drunkard and a dirty politician. Don't worry about it."

"We got to fight this war in the United States, too?"

"Yes. Every war. Every kind of war. People being what people are they'll always be unreasonable and ruthless if it gives them more chance to bellow. That will always be true, I think."

Charley frowned. "It might be why I fight and you fiddle—"

"No. We're honest. We want to bellow like Webster, but not with lies and foolishness to help us. Because we can bellow better if we live long enough to learn. Webster can squall these things because he wants to be the biggest bellow in the United States. All the dead boys strung from here to Vera Cruz don't mean as much to him as the fluff of his coat over his little ass the day he's inaugurated President."

"He won't be," Charley said grimly. "Not if I have to grow wings and canvass the country."

"In a way, he's an artist," Ivanhoe said regretfully. "If only he weren't such a liar— What did you hear from Ilse?"

"Oh, nothing much. Nothing new after the last mail. Sammy's wife is still with the Byerleys. They all expect us home."

"Nothing about Alwine? She hasn't written me—"

"Yes. She said she was too tired to write but, as far as I can make out, the Blessed Savior should take care of you and everybody."

The doubts were stirred again in Ivanhoe's mind. He turned on Charley abruptly. "Charley, let's pack and get out."

"Like that!"

"Hell, we haven't been in the army since Puebla. This war's over for all practical purposes. We were enlisted for three months and we've been serving ever since. We haven't even got a right to wear these uniforms. Let's go back with the mail convoy tomorrow."

Charley nodded slowly. "There's an idea. There's no scrapping to amount to anything—we haven't tried to draw pay—our term's out—and I'd like to see Ilse."

"So would I, because Alwine would be along."

Charley's face changed. "Ive—you can go anywhere, you know, and do anything you want with your fiddle. And you're smart. Look at the way you got up Chapultepec. We might get separated sometime—but it would be me that was lost from you. You've always got the fiddle, like that guy in the fairy story that could rub the lamp—you rub a fiddle, instead. Ive, you're all right, you know, but you don't know—"

"What the hell are you talking about?"

"I'm tucking in."

PART V

HOME-COMING

I

THE *Missouri* raced up the river from New Orleans to St. Louis at ten miles an hour or better but Charley had mortally insulted the captain by offering to get out and push and Ivanhoe had exceeded this by thumbing his nose at Almighty God—the pilot. In spite of these outrages and sacrileges, however, at the end of five days, late in the morning, the *Missouri* headed in to the quay of the little city.

"For the love of Mike, Ive—you can't leave this country be a minute. Is this St. Louis or Philadelphia?"

The town was toward the end of a decade, in which it multiplied its sixteen thousand inhabitants by nearly five and it was putting on long trousers. Since the progression was more or less geometrical, the evidences of growth were more marked in the later years. The year that Charley and Ivanhoe had spent away from the place this time had changed it again, almost as radically as it had been changed in their seven-year peregrination before.

"For God's sake," said Ivanhoe.

The whole sky line of the river floor was dominated by one tremendous posting—SERENADE BREWS—and the boat passed building after building and dock after dock ornamented with the same legend in dull crimson and green-gilt.

"What the deuce has Dick done now? Bought the town?"

They were interrupted by an urchin—a well-dressed and healthy urchin but still an urchin.

"General, I wonder if you would write your name in my autograph album?"

The thing had a pencil and a little blue book which he offered hopefully. Ivanhoe took them as he took everything that was pushed at him, whether it bit or not.

187

The child was encouraged. "If you would, sir, any little sentiment—?"

"Sentiment," said Ivanhoe. "Listen, I'm not a general and I haven't got any sentiment. Ummh! Or have I, Charley? What are you laughing at?"

"I'm not laughing."

"You were."

"What the"— Charley noticed the urchin—"dickens! You can't tax a man for laughing because he saw something funny long, long ago. You can't bring a man's past up against him."

"Oh, let's forget it. All right, sonny."

"We thought you were a general, Mr. General, on account of your uniform but Mamma says you're a great French violinist unkoneeto."

"They're both right," said Ivanhoe wearily.

He wrote quickly:

"Never eat mud. General Winfield S. Tartarini."

"*Thank* you, mister—general—"

"A compliment—thank *you*."

The brat departed. "Jesus Christ," said Ivanhoe. "Nobody can figure out what I am—not even the babes. I'll be the last to learn, of course."

Under the apparent blankness of Charley's face there was a granite base of understanding.

"I think that's right, Ive. But as long as you *will* learn, everything's all right."

The boat bounced. "Well, here we are. She's hitching up."

One of Charley's deficiencies was that he could not get through crowds unless they were inimical. He always had to get out of the way of some woman or a little man in a hurry. Ivanhoe had learned a simple method of dealing with the contingency. He was a tombstone that moved. He never ran into anyone and no one could object if they ran into him. Whenever there was a trifle of space he became an adjoining tombstone in the proper direction, and by this method he could move more rapidly through crowds than people who shoved.

The technique was useful on the St. Louis dock for at least two thousand people were jammed there for the arrival of the *Missouri* with another cargo of returning heroes among its passengers. The city was able to supply a few regular ambulances and others extemporized from wagons and carriages to take off the wounded men and those with whom fever had lingered. Only one man had died in the five days up the river, so three of the four waiting hearses went away hungry.

Charley fell in behind Ivanhoe, meekly, and Samaliel behind Charley. Samaliel carried the violin, the bag and the banjo. The three men had accumulated a small mountain of luggage in Mexico but that would have to wait till they could send a wagon for it. The *Missouri* would be tied up for two or three days.

The crowd had been speculating on Ivanhoe and Charley and their uniforms and scars and their odd luggage. Some thought they were entertainers up from New Orleans but their browned faces gave the correct clue and there was a murmur of applause and a way was made for them as they approached the flagged riverside.

Someone from that other year recognized Ivanhoe as the "Geiger" at the Gasthaus and the crowd began to murmur like a tree suddenly touched by a breeze, leaf by leaf and then branch by branch.

The three men barely escaped a reception. Six husky "Dutchmen" suddenly rushed down on them and barred them off from the crowd. Before Charley could knock any of them down, their leader, beside Ivanhoe, said, "To Mr. Byerley's parlor, sir."

Two or three minutes later the steam lift was taking them up to the tower which housed the water tanks and malt mill. Here they found that Richard had built a whole suite of reception rooms on the adjoining roof of the main brewery building. The whole construction was so new that it still smelled faintly of mortar and plaster. The whole brewery that they had wondered at the year before was now only a wing of the main plant.

"He sure keeps hopping," said Charley. "That's a joke, Ive."

"I know," Ivanhoe said kindly. "When you have one of those brewing I don't know whether I can beer it. For Lord's sake, have we come into the nursery?" There were, indisputably, two women carrying children bearing down on them over the heavy carpets that carpeted the long hall between the tankhouse and the offices.

Charley said, "Ilse!" and Sammy said, "Araminta!" and the next instant Ivanhoe was alone, ten yards from the nearest person in the world by space and an infinity by all other gauges. Only for an instant, for Richard Byerley came from behind, smiling, with both hands out to Ivanhoe.

"My boy!" Then he looked at the scar down Ivanhoe's cheek. "You were hurt! I told Curtin—"

"I thought so," said Ivanhoe. "It didn't make any difference. General Worth wanted to keep me to play the fiddle anyway. But I got in the scrap at Chapultepec. They were trying to kill me at Chapultepec and I didn't lose my head— I maybe killed a few fellows accidentally but mostly I just put them out of the game."

"Ivanhoe—my dear fellow! I couldn't explain to you— there are a million people in this country that can shoot a gun, but you can play a violin or make a song. You should never have been in the war—"

"Among the million people in this country who can shoot a gun," Ivanhoe said steadily, "I'm not the worst shot. I didn't go to war to play études and toccatas."

"No, Ivanhoe. Whether you wanted to or not, you went to lift the hearts of a thousand Americans who could shoot a gun as well as you and needed your fiddle as much as they did their rifles. Won't you ever understand?"

"I understand that if I hadn't got into Chapultepec I'd have thrown this uniform in the gulf before we climbed on the boat back, and the sword along with it."

"Well, well," said Byerley. "If they ever have another

war I won't interfere. But I guess that will be a long time. You boys gave Europe a good scare down there."

"Well," said Ivanhoe, "I did get in a pretty good battle, so there wasn't as much harm done as there ought to have been. Now, what in God's name is this business about Ilse and the baby?"

"They were married two afternoons before you left. There was a special reason why we couldn't tell you—but I'll tell you about that out at the house over a drink of rum."

"Alwine isn't here! Is there—was there anything the matter with her?" The first thing Ivanhoe thought of was that porcelain complexion and the dreaded "decline."

"No—she's in good health but she couldn't come. I'll tell you about it when we get settled."

Charley came over and shook Ivanhoe's hand and this unusual gesture—for they didn't need handshakes between them—was even more ominous than Alwine's absence or Byerley's secret.

"I'm going up with Ilse and Charley Junior," Charley said in the suppressed roar that served him for a sober voice. "We'll all have supper and the evening together though, hey, like the last time."

"Sure," said Ivanhoe. "Congratulations, Charley. One thing and another sort of took my breath away."

Charley grinned. "If you'd known I was a married man and the father of a family you'd have been worrying and worrying me about my taking chances. I kept mum. Good-bye till supper."

Byerley made three or four attempts to start casual conversation in the carriage until he saw that Ivanhoe did not want conversation but the information Byerley had for him. Even in the study Byerley was slow with his story. First they had to drink a big toast to Ivanhoe and Charley's return; then another to Serenade Brews which was now a million-dollar business in both its aspects, brewing and real estate, together; finally, a third big noggin of rum to the United States and General Scott, its next President.

Ivanhoe's head began to spin but the world brightened.

If Alwine was all right and he had plenty to keep her with he couldn't think of anything much that could be wrong.

What was the man saying? "And now, Ive, there's some bad news for you. I don't know whether we did right or not but we knew you were going off to war and you might not come back. And Alwine thought, and I couldn't disagree with her, that if her letters would make you any happier— then if you didn't come back they would be that much to the good, and if you did come back it could all be explained to you."

"You mean she didn't care—all along?"

"She was fond of you, Ivanhoe, that was why she wanted to write."

Ivanhoe nodded his head. "I should have known by this time. That's the way it always happens. But where's Alwine —it wouldn't be in my cards to change her—I've held the same hand too often—but I could try—"

Byerley shook his head. "It wouldn't do a bit of good, Ivanhoe," he said gently. "You see, one reason she felt she ought to write you is because she was writing to her sweetheart down with Taylor while you were here and you didn't have a Schatz! He's back now, short an arm, and they're married."

Ivanhoe poured himself four fingers of rum and gulped them down. Then he stared out the window for a long moment. "All fooling. Jesse Ellison was right—the fiddler is just a butterfly. Well, Dick, I'll go wash up. Is there a Keokuk boat tonight?"

"Keokuk? Why do you want to go to Keokuk?"

"There's an old settler up there called me a butterfly once. I'm going up and settle a farm somewhere near by and play at the tavern if they've got one yet. I want to be where I won't forget again."

*   *   *

A large, very sober-faced young man in incongruously dandyish clothes stood at the bow of the little Keokuk boat as it pulled in to the pier. Behind him was a big light-colored

Negro guarding a great pile of luggage—the captain, a new one since Ivanhoe's last trip this far north, had warned the violinist about the danger of bringing a slave into the free state and had subsequently reported to the curious passengers that the nigger's name was Samaliel and he was a freedman working for pay.

Upon which there would probably have been a little horseplay with the nigger from some of the inevitable rowdies on the boat—if he wasn't property he was just a nigger—but neither the black fellow nor his employer looked as if he would stand for much, even if the white man did carry a fiddle. Someone also noticed that the fiddler carried a sword strapped to one bag and that the scar on his cheek was not excessively old.

They guessed Mexico—they guessed all kinds of things—maybe he was a Frenchman though he looked more Yankee; the cruelest thing Ivanhoe ever did was to signify by his utter withdrawal from everyone that he wanted no questions and no conversation.

The captain got up courage as they were pulling in to suggest that he might be taking the gentleman down the next day—the boat went at nine—but he reckoned with that store of dunnage the gentleman would be planning to stay in Keokuk awhile.

"No," said Ivanhoe. "I'm storing most of this in Keokuk and going on west. We won't be back till we're settled and come back for my man's wife."

"Then you'll be taking the Des Moines River boat in the morning, sir? There'll be a lot of roustabouts on the pier. I'll shout some of them up for you, but keep an eye on them or you'll miss things. But they can put it on the boat now and it will be safe."

"But I don't know where I'm going—oh, do you ever carry anything for a trader named Fursten—Philip Fursten?"

"Oh, yes, he's well-known. At Pittsville, about fifty miles up."

Ivanhoe smiled slightly. So they'd gotten boats to the place since he left, nine years before. Probably taken up most of the land near by, too. He'd stop there, anyway, and see how many twins Sue had by now and how they all were. It wouldn't hurt this time.

"I wonder if I could have this stuff freighted up to Fursten?"

"I can take care of that myself, sir, that's our business. My own boys will handle it and there'll be nothing missing."

"All right, thanks." Ivanhoe handed the captain a ten-dollar gold piece. "Give them that for their trouble. I've got to buy some horses but I'll beat the boat to the other end if it doesn't start till morning, to pay the freight and receive it."

"Thank you, sir, they'll handle everything carefully— mighty carefully after this." The captain hurried away re-gretfully. He was getting somewhere on Ivanhoe but he still couldn't make him out. But the pilot had touched the pier and now the captain truly became the captain, with a multi-tude of duties.

A few moments later Samaliel and Ivanhoe with two bags and two instrument cases strode down the streets of Keokuk. It had grown but not impressively after St. Louis, though it was a busy little city near the docks and on the commercial streets.

"Think I can find this place," Ivanhoe said to himself more than to Sammy. "It's only been nine years. It's part stone so it wouldn't likely be torn down so soon. If that dock's the same place it's straight up the hill and beyond about two blocks or so."

Ivanhoe would have missed it, however, if he had not been looking closely, for now the stone barn was only a wing of a considerably larger frame barn. Odds on it had changed hands but Ivanhoe had decided that the former proprietor, the custodian of his horse and rig, was a trust-worthy man who would furnish them two good horses at a fair price.

The place was being tended rather languidly by a boy of fifteen or so who was reading a newspaper and occasion-ally spitting into the cuspidor near the stove of the bright, warm little office. His spring chair squeaked as he let his feet slide off the stove guard and climbed to his feet.

"Well, you're lucky," he opined. "Not much call yet tonight and you can have your pick of the stable. How far you takin' 'em? Appears to me you never been here before." Then he noticed the grips. "Strangers? Pa'll want to know who you are before he lets you take a team."

"Where is your father? He might remember me. I left a horse and rig with him here several years ago, if he was here then."

"You left— Hell's fire!" He pointed at the violin case. "Are you that fiddler?"

"I suppose I am."

"If Pa's wondered and speculated about you once he's done it a million times! The fellow that trusted him with his mare and rig—you the one that got a mitten—girl had twins?"

Ivanhoe smiled. "That was about it."

"Well, I'll be cussed. Pa had about give you up—Ma said long ago you'd never be back—probably went and drowned yourself or hung yourself, because that's the way musicians acted. She was for spendin' the money but Pa always said, 'No, sir! Ain't nobody goin' to be sorry he ever trusted Joe Baker, an' your money's in the bank drawin' interest and you still got your horse and four others left an' your rig's ready to go—many the times I've shined it—"

"Here, here, what's going on? You talkin' the gentleman's arm off about the fiddler? Good evening, gentlemen— I've been having supper—I hope the boy— Well, for the love of God!"

The big man's eyes goggled. "The fiddler!"

"Haven't I changed at all in nine years? You've filled out."

The horseman's eyes went over him keenly. "Yes," he said slowly, "you've changed. I'll bet you wouldn't go to Texas if any girl gave you the mitten now. You rounded out fine in the barrel, but the main thing is the cut of your muzzle's changed and you ain't got that colt look in your eyes."

Ivanhoe winced, though he knew that this final "trip to Texas" was at last legitimate not only because of Alwine but on grounds of his own disappointing personality. "Thanks," he said abruptly, and then more kindly, "I hear you've taken good care of Nelly. I knew you would."

Baker chuckled. "I was going to give you one more year and then she'd have gone to that lady up in Pittsville along with your twenty-five per cent, and the rest of the money."

Ivanhoe puzzled. "The rest of what money?"

"I've got it all kept in books. I waited a few months to hear from you and then I had her bred—too good a horse to be wasting her time. Not to speak of seven children, she's got grandchildren and great-grandchildren. She's only missed one throw and her young ones do about as well. I've picked good sires—all of 'em straight from Messenger if you could believe the fellows that brought them through, but good sires, anyhow. And I've got a little bunch from some of the grandchildren by a Morgan that seemed to be a real Morgan—beauties. I kept a stallion out of the first batch—"

Ivanhoe laughed. "Man, you're getting me all mixed up."

"Well, I didn't have any authority, but I could see from the first that they would get too many for me. I sold my own geldings and worked yours for the board and keep of the lot of them—but altogether—" he fished in the countinghouse desk for a book—"deducting all charges, stud fees, veterinary care and so on, I owe you $4,048.67, five horses, a rig, and God knows how many colts anywhere from seven to nine months old—I got them out on the farm—I sold a bunch of mares this summer and fall—the business was getting too much for me. I paid you for your geldings for the stable at the highest I could get anybody to offer—"

"Wait, wait. Suppose I take your two best saddle horses and we call it quits."

"My two best saddle horses belong to you—shame of it is they'll both be foaling around May so you may not get more than three months' use out of them."

"Have to get some draught horses anyway," Ivanhoe

said. "And we've got to be moving. Got two good saddles to sell? And bridles?"

"Not so fast. I've been handling this whole thing for you and I won't take what's not mine. I've made plenty out of the whole business. That's flat. When you send for the horses I'll send you a draft. You might want me to take care of the colts—bring them up and sell them for you? Anybody'll tell you I'm a good hand—and I do like to see good stock—good as this—treated right and sold for what it's worth.—If you don't send for your stock I'll bring it up myself after the Sunday rush—and I guess I better bring the money in gold.—Yes, I show some stuff for the saddlery here. I'll fix you up with the best we got. And I'll charge you a fair price for it and take the money like I expect you to take yours."

"Oh, hell," said Ivanhoe. "Anybody can see it was a partnership deal—share and share alike. We'll split it right down the middle—horses, colts, money and everything. It was your brains and work and all I put into it was one mare. Half and half or I'll walk out of here and you'll never find me again."

"That ain't fair."

"You heard what I said—how about those saddles?"

"Ain't you going to use the rig?"

"I'm going on where there aren't any roads. Give the boy here the rig—and give him one of my half of the horses. He's old enough to start sparking and he needs a rig."

"Jesus Christ!" said the boy.

"Everything I touch but girls," Ivanhoe said, a few minutes afterward, outside.

An hour or so later, after a deliberate and reasonably appetizing supper, they rode in the dark toward Pittsville. The road was so rough that Ivanhoe congratulated himself on leaving the rig behind and a fair share of the ride had to be made without moonlight, so they did not reach the frozen ford till the sky was graying before daybreak. Across the river as they rode down toward the ice they saw the sparkling of many lights.

PART VI

PITTSVILLE

I

"THAT is Pittsville, Sammy," Ivanhoe said as the last stars grayed out. "God knows what it is. You can see the lights. When I first saw it there would have been only the trader's light and when I last saw it there would have been five or six lights and now—what would you say?—two hundred lights, or more. Come on, let's cross; there are fresh, hard wagon tracks on the ice."

"Were you going any special place, sir? It's early."

"They're burning lamps," Ivanhoe said. "Yellower than a good candle. Oh, where we're first going—to the first lamp, of course. The law of this country is that wherever you knock you're haled in."

"You say it has changed, sir?"

"No, that wouldn't change."

While they walked their horses slowly and carefully across the wide river the gray foredawn began to sift away like a slow fog; first Ivanhoe saw gables along the crest of the hill and then square blocks of buildings in the valley, great cubes in the path of the approaching sunrise but without the advantage of a silhouette against the sky in any direction.

"We'll have to ride a long way from here, Sammy. I didn't realize—"

The nimbuses thrown out of the lighted windows were contracting rapidly and the first sunlight appeared in the east well before the sun.

The horses stopped and even the men smelled open water. "Now what the devil is here—it's a little bridge to land!"

"Looks solid, sir. It's well out on our side and over to the pier. Little bridge they can move over the path of the boat, sir."

"That's right, Sir Isaac. They pull the outside end up-stream to bank till the boat gets by and then let it slide back again till it hits this pile. Well, a wagon's gone across it— I'll try it first."

Without waiting for the objection Samaliel was sure to make he touched his horse with his heels and went at a walk-trot across solid timbers that made a noble noise. Samaliel did not follow till his weight was off the pontoon, for both their sakes. The horses leaped up the steep cut in the nearly verti-cal bank and came out on a level road that was obviously a street, by the regular lights which glowed in parallel lines for a few hundred yards and continued, rising, till they disap-peared a few hundred yards still farther away, up the hill.

A great block of a building with lights glowing here and there all over it was immediately ahead of them.

"A factory warehouse, by George, or a tavern—and right at the ferry it would be a tavern. Sammy, our ride's over!"

They found the double doors a dozen steps on and swung off their horses. Ivanhoe loosed his violin from the pillion he had made for it and Sammy took the straps off his banjo and the bags and put them down so he could hold the horses.

Ivanhoe rapped at the door and then opened it. It was the ordinary big central room of a hotel with inelegant chairs scattered here and there over the wide painted boards of the floor. A tufty old man of amiable but sleepy appearance was behind the desk. He was hairy here and there—nose, ears and the ridges of his pate, and nowhere else on his face or scalp. He pushed a yawn into a smile with the help of one hand and hopped off his stool with a great assumption of wakeful-ness and vigor.

"Well, sir, beautiful winter morning—"

"It will be by and by when the sun comes up," said Ivanhoe, who was tired and cross. "Will you have a boy stable our horses and help my man with the bags? A room for me and one adjoining mine for him and have baths made in each of them. And good beds in both of them—we've ridden all night. Wake me at three o'clock in the afternoon for breakfast. He'll wake himself."

"Yes, sir— Jake!" The porter looked across the table which he was swiping casually with a gray-brown rag. "Take the gentleman's horses over to the livery and then come back and take the bags upstairs—I'll bring them in."

But as he came around the desk Ivanhoe noticed that he was slightly rheumatic and he motioned him back. "No, you won't, Sammy and I'll bring them in. You got to stay on duty. Is it too early to get a good strong milk punch?"

"Oh, sir, Mr. Dunshee—he's strict—"

"Mr. Dunshee the owner?"

"Yes, sir. He's a very big man in this county and state. He doesn't allow liquor in this hotel."

"No?"

"The kitchen fires are lighted. I could have the porter bring you up some hot milk or coffee—the cook and the waitress would be glad to fix it for you."

Sammy spoke gently. "Sir?"

"Yes, Sammy."

"I did some talking, sir, just as we left St. Louis. Iowa is a very curious state, sir—fine people and a fine state, but curious. I don't know whether they'd fix your milk just the way you like it, sir."

"All right for my man to fix my hot milk?"

"Oh, certainly, sir. Your man will find the kitchen out this door."

Sammy took a grip and disappeared. "I knew all the time—I can smell kitchens." It was the first time Ivanhoe had ever heard him boast but the boast was not about kitchens; it was about a different foresight.

"Carries a special kind of cinnamon I like," Ivanhoe said when Sammy picked up the bag and took it with him.

The milk punch had about as stiff a lacing of brandy as Sammy had ever put in one. The clerk vowed and swore it was the best cinnamon he'd ever tasted. By the time they had finished it the porter had returned with word that the fires were lit and the baths ready. Ivanhoe left instructions about his luggage in case he did not wake by three o'clock and the porter led him to his room—a pleasant enough little room with south and east windows looking out over the river.

The rude awakening occurred when Ivanhoe climbed into bed. It was a spring mattress and not in good repair. Nothing larger than a rabbit could have slept on it without distortion. Ivanhoe got up and looked for the bell cord but there was no bell cord. There was not much sense in protesting anyway—Sammy had unpacked him and it would cause a lot of useless work if he changed rooms. He could camp for tonight, or rather, for today, and arrange for a new mattress when he woke.

Ivanhoe made himself a pallet on the carpet and with a short curse and a short groan settled down for his rest.

*   *   *

Sammy kept on shaving steadily.

"—of all the God-forsaken, misbegotten, pock-pitted arrangements since Procrustes—Sammy, just lie down on that bed, will you?"

Sammy applied the lotion. "It wouldn't do any good, sir; mine was just the same."

"Well, all right, but there couldn't be another one like it." Ivanhoe arose from the chair and put on his coat. "I'm going down and give that clerk a piece of my mind. And after he helped me drink up the hot milk!"

It was a sunny winter day, crisp and stirring. Ivanhoe felt that he would be moved to do a really good job on the clerk—at the same time he thought he might do a better job if he had a bite to eat first. He told Sammy to get his breakfast in the kitchen while he got his own in the dining room and to meet him in the lobby to confirm the deplorable condition of the mattresses. He picked up his violin to be sure that it would not be stumbled over by some chambermaid and went downstairs.

There was a printed card on the dining room door: SUPPER AT SIX.

The door was locked.

The clerk hurried over from the desk, beaming but apologetic. "We don't serve except at the regular hours, Mr. Keeler, but I can have something sent to your room from the kitchen." He lowered his voice. "But confidentially, if I were you I'd go up to Butchin's Coffee House—they serve at all hours—quite passable food, I've been told." He paused. "You can buy hot milk there, too."

He turned back to the desk but Ivanhoe put a firm hand on his shoulder. "Wait a minute, my friend. I appreciate your suggestion—but what was your idea in putting me up on that infernal contraption that looks like a bed? You must have known about it. Everybody in town must have known about it. Everybody in the world but me must have known about it—it's the worst mattress in the whole world."

"I'm sorry, Mr. Keeler. Perhaps it isn't quite up to snuff but all the mattresses in the hotel are the same. Mr. Dunshee is quite proud of them, sir. They're the first spring mattresses west of the Des Moines River in Iowa."

Ivanhoe was appalled for a moment and then he recovered. "They must be the first spring mattresses east of the Styx River in Hades, too, but what has that got to do with a man's getting a night's rest?"

The clerk shrugged apologetically. "It makes Mr. Dunshee furious if any suggestion is made—I'll tell you what, Mr. Keeler—we have plenty of good thick blankets. I could have the maids store a good thick bale of them in your room."

The old man's evident and pathetic anxiety to please touched Ivanhoe. "All right, old chap—that will do for a night or two till I can make this fellow Dunshee see sense."

"Oh, Mr. Keeler! I wouldn't mention it to him—if you're planning to stay in Pittsville—settle down anywhere in the county."

"Eh?"

"Mr. Dunshee's very influential, sir. He's a very wealthy man. He owns over four thousand acres of farms as well as the steamboat and this hotel. He has the biggest store in the county and does the shipping for everyone. They say he came here with a hundred thousand dollars and that he has twice that now. He's a friend of the governor of the state."

It was evident that while sympathizing with Ivanhoe the clerk was proud of the status of his employer.

"All right," said Ivanhoe. "I suppose a lot of important people owe him money, too."

"Yes, sir."

"All right," said Ivanhoe. "I see I'm going to stay in Pittsville longer than I planned to. Where can I find this Dutchman?"

"If you must, sir—in his store. It's the biggest brick building in town—on Water Street, a block up."

"Good! Where's this coffee house?"

The clerk gestured. "Foot of the next block."

"Foot, eh? So everything heads from Dunshee's."

"Yes, sir."

"When my man comes into the lobby tell him to watch out for the boat and our things and that's all for this afternoon."

Ivanhoe sauntered out and down to the corner. A few passers-by stared at him but he was used to this—it was because of the violin case. At the corner he began to appreciate the changes that had come to Pittsville in nine years. He had left a trading post, a church, a school and four or five little houses. There were now several business blocks, two-story brick and one-story frame, and the residences stretched up over the river hill. But the traveler Ivanhoe was immune to such transformations.

The fact was, the abominable bed had changed his plans. Such things simply should not be. He was the Hercules to bring this Procrustes to grief. He probably would have thought little of the matter and passed on if the ogre had not seemed so particularly disagreeable in all aspects. The man seemed to need tearing apart.

Perhaps a life of good works would dull the memory of Alwine. Perhaps that was better than going into the wilderness and brooding about her, however bitter-sweet that brooding might be. At any rate, there was an immediate business to attend to and he could plan more profoundly after this was given his attention.

He went into Butchin's Coffee House and moodily ordered a venison steak with all the fixings—he didn't know what they ate out here and he didn't want to embarrass the man—and a mug of ale—as an afterthought he said, "Serenade Ale." That would help good old Dick along.

"Sorry, mister," the waiter said. "I haven't heard of that. We've only got our own brew in the pump and Illinois ale in bottles."

"I'll try yours," Ivanhoe said, "but you ought to have Serenade. Finest ale made. You can get it from St. Louis."

The waiter nodded amiably, meaning he would give the matter deep thought without intending to do anything about it, and went back to the kitchen.

The pea soup was fair, the steak, which came with succotash, mashed potatoes and gravy, cole slaw and dumplings, was very good and the mince pie was superb. The ale was awful.

I'll correct that, Ivanhoe thought. Have old Dick send me up a keg for a sample and he'll sell these people right along. He can't say I'm not keeping him in mind. Then he remembered those kegs with a fairly recognizable picture of himself burned on their ends. No, they would think he was a bigbug and showing off.

Dunshee's "Drygoods, Hardware, Etc." store would have been much too large for the town—1,500 people or so— if it had not also been the financial, real estate and importing capitol of the county. It was stone and brick—two stories with a flat sloping roof that ran down to warehouses in the back. A series of large-paned windows centered bow windows on each side of the double doors at the entrance. Behind the windows on low platforms were displayed special selections of goods from the merchant's stock—shoes, fabrics, a stove in each of the bows, chinaware and some smaller pieces of furniture.

The place was dusky inside and in the corners the lamps were lit despite the sunshine outside. There was a pleasant smell of leather, fresh cloth and all the "newness" that filled the place. Two or three clerks were busy with customers and two or three were busy at the ordinary occupations of unoccupied clerks, with feather dusters and cloths.

Ivanhoe got directions from one of the dusters-up who pointed with a brush of turkey feathers to a stairway and a long balcony at the far end of the store.

"I'm not certain that he's there, sir, but Evelyn will be. She's Mr. Dunshee's daughter and his secretary and she can take any message."

Not this one, Ivanhoe thought, as he went back toward the stair. The balcony was quite dark except for its central part where a girl sat on a high stool working over a counting desk. There was a skylight here. Beside her was a great flat desk and heavy chair which Ivanhoe judged must be Dunshee's.

At the sound of Ivanhoe's footsteps the girl put down her pen and turned halfway and then the whole way toward him.

And she was young Susan and Alwine and Eliza Vestris and all the women Ivanhoe had ever loved or thought of loving—even a little bit of Marie, though it seemed profane to think of Marie and this girl at the same time. He stopped dead and stared at her without any sense of impropriety, as he might have looked at any other familiar person.

Instead of blushing or frowning or turning away, she looked back at him. Ivanhoe did not know it but his face was interesting, with its artist's mouth and eyes framed by a long scar, the fighter's chin and the strong grace in every inch of him. And he was carrying a violin case though he did not remember it, any more than he remembered his little toe, which went with him wherever he went.

How pleasant of God to put them all in one person, Ivanhoe thought. And this was the reason I did not marry any of the others.

His heart sank. And I won't marry this one, either—this is the last one I won't marry, because there can't be another. This is the climax, largo con forza. But not lamentoso, by

God; he would always know that she had existed, after all.

"Miss Dunshee?"

"Yes. My father is at the coffee house. He always has coffee at four."

"Well, it doesn't matter. It wasn't anything special. Just came to make myself known—I thought of buying a little farm, but there's no hurry. Tell him I called and I'll come back tomorrow a little earlier."

Now *she* was staring at *him*. He wished she would do that permanently. He wished he were a sculptor and a painter both—the beautiful small body perched on that high stool, the dark, lively cameo of face and hair, her eager eyes which were laughing and questioning at once.

"Pardon me—but you *are* Ivanhoe Keeler?"

"Yes," he said stupidly. "How did you know?"

"There couldn't be two of you and Sue Crawford has lau— talked about you a hundred times."

"You started to say 'laughed.' "

The incredibly swift changes of her face were almost as beautiful as the face itself. "I'm sorry. But these old love affairs really are funny when they're all over, aren't they?"

"All right," said Ivanhoe. "That wasn't why Sue laughed, but that's neither here nor there. What I really came for was to tell your father that the hotel clerk says he couldn't do anything about the mattresses—they're atrocious."

Her face was suddenly alarmed. "Please don't say anything to Father. It makes him furious. He doesn't abide criticism of anything, I'm afraid, and the mattresses are a sore spot."

"They're a hundred sore spots if a man is idiot enough to sleep on them."

"I stayed at the tavern one night when the governor was here and the house was full. If you'll put four or five blankets over the springs the beds are comfortable."

Ivanhoe frowned thoughtfully and nodded. "I didn't think of that. You're a genius. Thank you, Miss Dunshee—it was silly of me to make such a fuss when I'll be here only a day or two, anyway."

I must get out of Pittsville, Ivanhoe thought, or I'll act like a fool and say something silly to this girl and remember it always after.

"Only a day or two! But then you must come out and play for us—could you tonight? Sue says that you are a real minstrel—you make your songs as you go along. I think that's wonderful—I can't improvise worth a cent. If you can possibly come tonight I'll send a boy out and ask the Crawfords and the Ellisons over and anyone else you'd like to see again."

Ivanhoe shrugged. "I haven't anything to do. You see, Miss Dunshee, I came up here under the impression that there were still claims and cabins. It seems your father owns all the claims and cabins are passé. So I think I'll go back to St. Louis and ship for Independence—there's still a lot of room in Kansas, down toward Pike's Peak—they say it's good country."

"Oh, don't do that! Father will sell you one of his farms, on time, and you could do well around here, playing for dances and funerals and weddings and so on. You wouldn't want to do your own farming, anyway, and there are lots of good tenants coming through all the time.—And you will come tonight, won't you? Emmy wouldn't have time to arrange dinner now, but just after dinner—around seven?"

Ivanhoe shook his head. "No, I'm not used to settled country—but, yes, about playing tonight. I judge you play, too."

"A piano—not very well. Father brought it on from Wheeling. I guess it's the only piano in the county—the county ought to get a pianist."

Ivanhoe smiled. "I imagine it has one. We'll see tonight."

"I'm anxious to hear you play."

He could feel her smiling as he went out. What a damn fool he was to get into a thing like this! This time he would have to go to China, at the very least.

*　　　*　　　*

He had studied the dress problem carefully. His usual tails, white waistcoat and monumental collar were out of the question. In the first place, he always had to break the collar to hold his violin and this time there would be no dressing room to make a quick change in. The tails were out of the question and so were pumps. He decided on an ordinary short-tailed jacket of dark serge, a soft ivory waistcoat and a black stock, a small lapis brooch and similarly elegant and unostentatious fixtures in the way of trousers, shoes, etc.

He was glad that he had done so when Dunshee met him at the door of the great white house, for Dunshee was wearing very nearly the same costume except that his brooch was a simple gold bar.

Dunshee smiled without parting his lips and then clipped out, "Mr. Keeler, sir." His face was as long and gray and lean as the limestone slabs in the retaining wall of the house's terrace. He had allowed the whiskers to grow down to the points of his jaw and they were gray and lean, too.

"Mr. Dunshee." They shook hands.

"The Ellisons weren't able to come" (Try to get Jesse out to hear a fiddler, Ivanhoe thought)—"but the Crawfords are here and we've asked in a few friends—not old settlers like you"—the thin smile again—"but what Evelyn calls music lovers."

The great parlor was elegant in a way; not like Dick's down in St. Louis but good in some points and not especially wrong in any. The piano was a big square Babcock arranged diagonally across a corner of the room at the end farthest from the fireplace. It looked like an ebony coffin for a flat elephant, welded on trestles.

Well, thought Ivanhoe, taking in the wallpaper, the rug, pictures, piano and furniture at a glance, even elegance must go pioneering. He was glad, when he noticed that Dunshee was studying his face, that the look on it must have been mildly approving.

"Ivanhoe! Why, you're getting positively fat!"

Good God! And this was the girl who had sent him all over half the world! He shook both her hands and noticed that they at least were about as he had remembered them—smooth and firm. Her face was a hint rounder but the hint was sufficient. She was a beautiful woman, still piquant, still laughing, but she was not a companion for Ivanhoe Keeler's adventures—she was a chatelaine.

This other—this nut-brown girl with the wide eyes that were not brown and not quite black, with her small mouth that could be either firm or whimsical—why, she would dare the devil for any man she cared to companion.

He laughed with Sue. He was nothing like fat but he had filled out in the eleven years since she had seen him. Things happen to a man between twenty-four and thirty-three and Ivanhoe was not unconscious of the fact that lines of his face that had been concave were now straight from eyes to chin.

"Well, Sue! What was it I was playing for you yester-day evening?"

Sue laughed. "The same Ivanhoe. Ivanhoe, this is my husband, Caesar Crawford."

He was a solid young man with a face that was pleasant but slightly too sober for Ivanhoe's taste. Yes, if a girl married a man like that she could expect twins. They shook hands warmly and the introductions went on. The Methodist and Congregational preachers and their wives; the organ player at the latter church, a sweet-faced old woman to whom Ivanhoe took an instant fancy; a lawyer who spoke of Caesar as "Senator"—it turned out that Caesar was in the young State Senate—and some oddments of Pittsville culture who were simply free bodies floating in space to Ivanhoe, then and forever after.

"Miss Dunshee." At the very last she brought forward a young man over twenty and well under thirty with the forehead and wide upper face of a German and a well-shaped head and chin that might have belonged to any good human species. One of the right kind, Ivanhoe observed.

"Mr. Keeler—this is Ernest Bogel. We had to ask him because if he'd heard music, even a mile away at the farm, he'd have been here!"

Not quite that, Ivanhoe decided. The music of Evelyn herself would have drawn him without any sound. That settled that point. Leave town tomorrow on the horses and catch the boat in Keokuk in the morning.

Bogel said, "Sometimes when there isn't too much to do on the farm in the winter I practice on a violin myself. I've never heard anybody that really knew how to play one."

"I wish I were going to be here longer," Ivanhoe said. "I had twelve lessons from David and six from Spohr—I might be able to help you out with what they told me. And Ole Bull had some good ideas—"

"Oh, yes, I have a magazine at home with his suggestions."

The other names had made no impression on the young farmer but Evelyn looked at Ivanhoe curiously. "You had lessons from Spohr?"

"Only six. Charley, a friend of mine, had to make a business trip and I couldn't stay any longer."

Ivanhoe saw that he was in for a cross-examination the next time he saw this girl and it was a joke on her and a bitter joke on Ivanhoe that he would never see her after tonight and all her questions would remain unanswered.

The assembly chattered dutifully; it would have been impolite to ask the fiddler to fiddle for the supper that would come along about ten o'clock without establishing the pretense that the meeting was purely social and that Ivanhoe was merely meeting old friends for whom he would doubtless play a few songs when the fancy struck him.

"Bogel's all right," said Dunshee. "His dad is a German—got twelve hundred acres over toward Brunswick—one of the biggest farmers in the county. The old man got caught in some kind of political trouble in the real Brunswick, in the old country, and had to skedaddle but he had a good head and he brought along fifty or sixty thousand dollars in gold and English drafts. Wouldn't be surprised if he wasn't worth a hundred thousand!"

"Really."

"Yes; it's a pile, but he's probably got it. Germans are

funny people. He's about as good a farmer as you could find but he's full of all kinds of nonsense and moonshine. Whole family's crazy about music and that fellow there knows Latin and Greek. I hope you can fiddle well enough to get the violin bug out of his head—discourage him. No offense intended—fiddlers are fiddlers and farmers are farmers—you can't be both—and he's as good a farmer as his father. Caesar's got plans for him and"—the slit smile which Ivanhoe now understood was intended to be amiable—"so have I."

Ivanhoe nodded. "Seems to be a fine chap—but don't you think, Mr. Dunshee, a man is entitled to his hobby?"

Dunshee seemed uncomfortable for a moment. "Well, you see, Mr. Keeler, in this rough country we leave music more or less to the women. I know all the big fiddlers are men, but out here it would be better if Ernie liked hunting and fishing, or stock breeding, or something like that. We might want him in the Legislature sometime, or he might build up to governor, or go to the United States Senate after we got Caesar there. And among our farm folks—well, he might just as well play the piano, almost."

"I see. You want a solid man."

"That's it—no reflection on fiddlers, you understand—but this is farm country and when the time comes for Ernie's advancement we wouldn't want him to have anything—incompatible—in his background."

Ivanhoe smiled. "I'll do the best I can to discourage him—but I'm not a concert violinist or Paganini or any of those things."

"Oh, the Ellisons say you can fiddle well enough—and what about a tune? I've been watching Evelyn and she's been waiting all evening for you to get started. She's a fine pianist, that girl. Studied since she was almost a baby till we came here—ten years or more. She plays mostly classical music, Mozart and those others, but she can make up an accompaniment for any old jig you want to play."

Ivanhoe went to the piano and fingered at the music there. Nothing much. Heller, Liszt, piano arrangement of "The Damnation of Faust," some ballads, book of hymns—

he looked at the heavily loaded stand of shelves and found what he wanted on the second rack. He put it out on the piano and waved at Evelyn.

"Come, give me some practice."

All the chairs were turned at once. Evelyn's eyes were speculative, but at the same time that they told him she was curious about him they notified him that she knew a great deal more than he had mentioned.

Her shoulders, the rounded nape of her neck, the dark hair, her position at the piano were all utterly lovely, Ivanhoe observed. She gave him the A for his violin at once and Ivanhoe reflected that this must have been learned from Ernest but he went ahead and tuned through GDAE—"God Damned Apple Eater" he had used to help memorize it a hundred years before.

The ballads, he assumed, must be the latest ones popular in Iowa and ones with which Evelyn must be familiar. "Green Grow the Rushes, O!" he had heard in the army till he was sick of it, but he played it.

She was about to ask him something when Sue came over and patted him on the cheek, his hands being engaged with the violin and bow. "Oh, Ivanhoe, you play just as well as you ever did—better, I think. It reminded me of the old days. Please play one of your own—I always loved the ones you made up yourself."

Ivanhoe grinned at her. "You didn't love me."

He fingered out a theme. "Improvise on that four-four with a new phrasing on each sixth—you know, simple ballad style—ta-da-dee-ah-da-da—ta-da-dee-ah-da-deeee—and put in decorations at the end of the two fourth phrases. Understand?"

She played softly.

"A little sadder—minors at the ends of both quatrains!"

She was capable of a brief, delicious giggle. She played again.

"That's fine! That's sadded about right."

Evelyn played and Ivanhoe played and sang:

"Now that my years are spent,
Now when the ceaseless wrack
Ceases, my course is bent—
I shall go—back."

Evelyn created a passable interlude, not too lengthy.

"Back to my homing land,
Vineyard and catacomb,
Boundless, without a strand—
Silence! My only home."

Ivanhoe was particularly proud of "wrack" and "catacomb" and "strand." Good poets like Edgar Allan Poe used words like that. "Boundless" was pretty good, too. You were always reading about the boundless sea, and the boundless this and boundless that.

The applause was led by the preachers and the organ player, all of whom knew what "catacomb," "strand" and "wrack" meant. Young Ernest seemed unhappy. It sounded like a good translation of a bad Goethe poem—he did not suspect that it was other than original, but he worshiped Goethe and he tried to believe that all his bad poems were good.

The dignified old Congregational minister, who affected a small mustache and goatee in the French style, went so far as to pat Ivanhoe and Evelyn on their shoulders.

"You have a real talent for song, my boy. The violin is pleasant but the important thing is that you have a singing mind. Sing some more."

"I'm tired," Ivanhoe said to Evelyn when they were again alone in the corner of the room. "Let's really play them something and then I want to get to—my floor."

She made a beautiful scowl. "You said silence was your only home. You'd better go to it if you plan to talk about mattresses. There are lots of better rhymes for 'home' than 'catacomb,' too."

"All right. About two years with Czerny over in Paris wouldn't hurt your touch a bit, either. The expression is fair but the legato sounds like a pretty poor corduroy road."

He caught the barest glimpse of unmatched pink between her lips before he picked the piano arrangement of the Chopin E minor Concerto from the top of the piano and spread it on the support in front of her.

"I can't play it—and the violin part is written into the keyboard!"

"Then fake it and don't worry about the violin. Play the introduction and then try to come in on time. This is for the violin—the orchestra doesn't amount to a straw."

She gave him a thoughtful look. "You can do it?"

"Yes."

With no more words she brought down the resounding chords of the introduction and played a page and a half before she gave the lead to Ivanhoe—he had a feeling that she had thrown the rest of the music at him. He had played this for David but not so well as he played it now—plaintive, pleading, gay, despairing, furious in the succession of themes.

Evelyn had been quite correct when she said she could not play the transcription, but Ivanhoe helped her with the rapid passages, stealing them from the piano. She was adequate enough on the passages that were not definitely virtuoso.

There was a patter from the listening group when her last chord had died out.

"Evvy! You play beautifully!" said Susan. "And Ivanhoe, too."

They were all bored.

"Who are you?" Evelyn asked in what was almost a whisper. "Sue thinks you're her Ivanhoe—but you must be almost the greatest artist in the world."

"You haven't heard them all. I'm a poor second fiddle to the first fiddles. I almost busted up this box when I first heard Ole Bull—and Bull was nothing to David in actual interpretation—wait, let me show you—" He whipped out a few phrases of one of the Bach Solo Sonatas. "Bull was a gymnast but Ferd was an artist."

"Ferd?"

"Ferdinand David. We got to know each other in Leipzig."

"Leipzig in Europe?"

Before Ivanhoe could answer Caesar Crawford appeared, laughing. "If you folks don't get in there you're going to miss out on supper and if anybody here needs it, it must be Ivanhoe. Thought he was going to rip every string off his fiddle with that last fandango or whatever it was."

"Concerto," said Ivanhoe automatically, offering his arm to Evelyn.

"All right," said Caesar, "have it your own way—it certainly was some fast fiddling. Evelyn, you ought to get around and give concerts; maybe you and Mr. Keeler could team up and give dances and concerts."

"How would you like to give a concert with me, Mr. Keeler, with Czerny and Spohr and Chopin in the audience?"

Ivanhoe grinned at her and shuddered.

"Oh, don't be so modest, Ivanhoe," said Caesar. "I'll bet you play just as well as a lot of those Italian fellows."

Evelyn laughed. "You're barking up the wrong tree, Caesar, as Father would say. Mr. Keeler is a very fine musician but I think he was expressing doubts over his accompanist."

"Well, what's the matter with Evvy's playing?" Caesar asked, puzzled. "It's certainly the best around here!"

"Around here isn't around far enough," Evelyn said. "Mr. Keeler is a finished musician and I'm only a third-rate amateur."

"I like that!" Dunshee had come from the dining room to retrieve his messenger, Caesar. "After you've studied under the best teachers in Albany and Wheeling and Cincinnati!"

"Father, Mr. Keeler has studied under the best teachers in the world."

"What—in Boston and Philadelphia? Didn't know you'd been in the East, Mr. Keeler."

Ivanhoe nodded. "Coming back from England. But the best teachers in the world are in Leipzig and Paris. I didn't really study much with them though, and Miss Dunshee overrates me. I'm a passable amateur as good violinists go."

"You're a virtuoso as good violinists go," Evelyn said warmly. "I've heard good violinists and my legato may be terrible but I know enough about music to know that."

"Not questioned—still, you're too kind. I didn't mean to criticize your playing—the expression is very good indeed."

She looked up at him with a smile. "I'll get to work on my Bach and Czerny tomorrow and you can come and criticize—I want you to—and bring your violin."

Ivanhoe bowed. Dunshee gave his daughter a quick, uneasy expression.

Then he shook his head wonderingly. "Traveling all over the world to learn to play a fiddle! I could think of better things to do with my money. Evvy, I think Ernest has loaded a plate for you. Come on, boys, I guess there's plenty of it but there's no use taking chances." He gave his daughter a little shove and took Ivanhoe's arm himself.

The crude and unnecessary stratagem sent a shock of anger and determination along that Keeler spine which had been so foully wronged by Dunshee's unspeakable mattress. By God, he might not be good enough to take Evelyn in to supper but his violin gave him a standing invitation to her presence and he would use it. It was too bad for Ernest—his evident courtship was going to suffer frequent interruptions from now on, but until she decided to marry the man, Ivanhoe decided to stay around and be as annoying as possible to Dunshee. He would give him a scare until he was either thrown out of Dunshee's house or Ernest was installed in it.

*   *   *

The next morning Ivanhoe told Samaliel to unpack the baggage and toward noon he sent him up the hill with a note:

"Mr. Ivanhoe Keeler sends Miss Dunshee his compliments and his thanks for last evening's entertainment. If she intends practicing her Bach today and has no engagement for the evening it would give Mr. Keeler great pleasure to call and comment on her improvement."

Samaliel came back looking faintly troubled. He had seen Miss Evelyn Dunshee and he had also seen another period of a melancholy Ivanhoe not too remotely in the offing.

"Miss Evelyn Dunshee, though she does not expect to have made any remarkable improvements by seven o'clock this evening, will be at home to Mr. Keeler at that time."

After that the day crawled. Ivanhoe and Sammy took a short ride in the country but the day was overcast and the fields of dead cornstalks and pastures of leafless trees were depressing. They rode a mile across the great oxbow of the river, listened for a few moments to the chopping that was going on down in the timbered valley and returned to Pittsville for a late lunch. Ivanhoe ate his in the coffee house but Sammy was influential in the Ferry Tavern's kitchen and lunch was kept warm for him there, since he had explained that his hours were his master's. Sammy had let it drop that he knew something about French and Spanish cooking and though the cook sniffed at "foreigners," she was tremendously intrigued. A banjo concert given in the kitchen during Ivanhoe's absence the evening before had fixed Sam firmly in the regard of the cook, her stone-mason husband, the two maids and their "fellows," the porter and the porter's wife, and the village handy man, who had dropped in to make some small repair or improvement on a cupboard.

Not the least of Samaliel's qualities was that, although he could maintain a pleasant reticence, so that no more of Ivanhoe's affairs got out than Ivanhoe chose, his manner and his various talents always won special treatment for him and his master in strange places.

Ivanhoe did not suspect, but Sammy knew that the whole village must be speculating about the two of them; very well, they could go ahead and speculate till Ivanhoe chose to furnish them details. Knowing how easily Ivanhoe was "pumped," Samaliel guessed that this would not be long.

The afternoon passed somehow and at three minutes of seven Ivanhoe rang the bell at the Dunshee home. Evelyn herself answered the door and gave him his "good evening." She was wearing a somewhat simpler dress than on the previous evening, but all the styles of the day were flattering to women—round bosom, high collar to accent the throat, slender waists, belling skirts.

Ivanhoe shook his head. "No, I'm afraid I won't find any improvement. No one could practice Bach seriously in the afternoon and be so fresh and lovely in the evening."

"I'm interested in only the musical part of your Parisian studies, Mr. Keeler. What a beautiful greatcoat!"

"Yes, the fellow was a good tailor. I was a kind of walking advertisement for him—played in the music halls and people noticed what I wore."

"Music hall—that sounds like England."

"That's right. I was a Yankee novelty—so was Sammy, my colored man. He played the banjo and sang southern songs—great novelty, especially since a lot of his songs were American variants of old English songs. They wrote some pieces about him now and then for the weeklies and things!"

They sat down by the fire.

"How in the world did you ever happen to go over there?"

Ivanhoe laughed. "I was young—Sue!"

The girl did not laugh at once. "Silly," she said finally, "but romantic."

"I didn't go over to play—I went over to study and be a great violinist and make her sorry. Then they got me to playing in a little bar one night—I used to be a tavern player through the Reserve in the old days—that's how I lived after I was twelve. Struck me I might as well make a little money in England before I started spending it on teachers on the Continent, so I started playing around the alehouses. A manager heard about me and I played for three years—all the houses. We made three farewell tours after the first one and came out mighty well.

"The manager—decent chap for a manager—suggested I disappear for a year or two and make a triumphal return so I went to Paris to study like I'd planned—there was a manager met me in Calais. I finally got away and made a special trip to Leipzig to see Spohr—Ole Bull gave me a note."

"Ole Bull! Where did you meet him?"

"In Paris. He was interested in American music."

"So he sent you to see Spohr—to tell him about American music."

"No—to learn to play a violin. Spohr gave me six lessons and sent me to David—David's very strict. What with loafing around playing concerts and so on I'd been gone from England quite a while and my London manager sent for me. David said there wasn't much he could do for me—it was natural for me to play rubato and my technique was good enough for that. But," said Ivanhoe with a sidelong smile, "I went on practicing my Bach anyway."

"In just a minute—then what?"

"Well, we went back to England for a couple of years and then Charley and I decided to come home. Now about Bach—" The questionnaire was beginning to trouble Ivanhoe. He knew the old female trick—get you to talk about yourself till they knew more about you than you did—too much more.

"Charley—was he a violinist, too?"

Ivanhoe laughed at this incongruous idea. "Lord, no! He was a big farmer from Michigan. His heart was broken, too, and he was bound for Texas where he could have seven fights every day to forget his troubles. He decided to pitch in with me and come to England instead."

"But how could he get along in England?"

"Charley got along as well as I did. He had a notion he could lick any Englishman that ever lived—mighty near turned out right, too; he could, all but one—and he took up boxing. With prizes and betting and the presents the sports used to give him, Charley came home well fixed. He won nearly two thousand pounds on one match alone—better than any fiddler could ever do. He lost a thousand on himself in the championship match but that was the only match he ever lost!"

"A boxer and a musician! What a combination!"

"Not at all," Ivanhoe said quietly. "They're both arts.

Charley is as quiet a gentleman as you'd want to meet and as good a friend as anyone could have."

"Where is he now?"

Ivanhoe chuckled. "He fell in love with a little blond Fräulein in St. Louis. Now he's married and got a baby. He'll never get back to Michigan to show his old girl his London clothes and his French. The worst French," Ivanhoe added thoughtfully, "anyone ever heard. Even seems funny to me. What about your lesson, young lady?"

"I'm frightened—your teachers' accompanists must have been artists themselves."

"There weren't any Liszts or Chopins in the bunch. Don't worry. All I know about piano is what I've heard. 'Mein Gott! Dummkopf! Wie spielt man de Violin zu solche Musik? Wirst du nimmer lehren?' That was Spohr's style, but I won't bite your head off."

She smiled to herself. She suspected that he was not so diffident and timid with all women as he was with her—about anything but music.

As she seated herself at the piano she asked, "Did you come to Pittsville to show your London clothes and your French off to Sue?"

"Indeed not! I didn't realize this country would all be settled. When I left there was still prairie grass a dozen miles from here. I came because—ah—I came to take up a claim."

"In Heaven's name, what for?"

"Well, growing country—and all that—I didn't think it would have grown so fast, though. Charley's all settled—I didn't have anywhere to go!"

Ivanhoe pulled up a chair beside the piano seat and took a gold pencil from his pocket. "Some simple Czerny to warm up."

She had hardly hit the first solid chord in the exercise, however, when a roar arose from two rooms away.

"Evvy! Will you please quit that damn-fool twiddling and play something Ernie can play?" The roar diminished but the voice drew nearer. "Ever since that fool of a wandering fiddler got impertinent last night you've been doing nothing but 'da-da-da-de-da-de-da-de-da'—it's enough to drive a man out of his head. What do you care what a vagrant thinks— Hey! I say! I thought it was Ernie!"

Ivanhoe had risen and now Evelyn stood up, her face white with anger.

"I thought it was Ernie, of course."

"It wasn't Ernie," said Evelyn.

They stood in silence for a moment. "Well, dash it, can't you recognize a man's apology, sir?"

"I can't recognize that as an apology," said Ivanhoe, "but I can't use the customary method of getting a better one from you. If you'll stand out of the door, sir, I'll get my coat and my—fiddle."

"Please do, sir!"

Ivanhoe took two steps before Evelyn seized his arm. "Promise me you'll come back tomorrow evening when Father is himself and will do what a gentleman should."

"I'll send my man up in the afternoon to see if I should come back. I'm very sorry I caused you this scene, Miss Evelyn. Good night."

Dunshee had not made a fortune by letting his temper get too far beyond his discretion. The prospect of twenty-four hours alone with his daughter in her present disposition appalled him. He would be given the silence—nothing reproachful or undutiful—and, confound it, if Evvy had been fool enough to ask this fiddler to the house, both of them had some right to feel angry.

"Just a moment, Keeler—I'm sorry. Evvy was playing those twee-twees for an hour before supper and they got on my nerves. And the evenings Ernie gets off he likes to play tunes—not that stuff. It seemed inconsiderate to me and I flew off the handle. I don't know anything about you, sir, and I had no right to say what I did."

"Thank you, sir. In some respects you were justified—I *am* a traveler and I *am* a fiddler but I try not to be impertinent and I'm not a vagrant—I tell you this because, as you say, you don't know anything about me, and I try not to seem surly. Good night, sir."

"You *will* come back," said Evelyn. "Tomorrow—and finish the lesson?"

He bowed and went on out.

*   *   *

The note asked him to come at six-thirty rather than seven because Miss Dunshee was expecting additional company at seven which would preclude a piano lesson after that time. For this reason there were no more questions when Evelyn led Ivanhoe into the parlor—some light talk to relieve them of the flavor of the last leave-taking and then they went seriously to work.

Ivanhoe was a good piano teacher for a violinist. In thirty minutes they had marked up a Bach Prelude and Fugue and a flowing Chopin Nocturne for further study; Ivanhoe bowing out the phrases on his violin and valuing the notes with swift pizzicati, and Evelyn marking at his direction the passages in the music where her execution was at fault. They had finished this and were playing a foolish little Gigue together when the bell rang and Evelyn hurried to the door to admit Ernest Bogel. Of course, that would be the visitor, Ivanhoe thought.

They shook hands with both hands, Ivanhoe observed. Well, why shouldn't they? He cased his violin and brushed down his coat.

"Mother sent you over these," Ernest was saying, beyond the arched entrance. "She's got so many pots of them now it takes all her time watering them."

What was the damn weed? Probably a geranium or a verbena, or a delphinium or a banyan tree, or something. Ivanhoe had racked his brain to think of something procurable as a tender for his two visits to Evelyn but there were no flowers for sale and the small boxes of bonbons were probably ordered in cases and kept for months. He thought of a handkerchief but Dunshee had the only stock in Pittsville—it would be like taking a bottle of scent to a chemist's daughter and frail as a handkerchief was it seemed too substantial for the circumstances; what he needed was something perishable—some fruit, candy or flowers.

He felt that Ernest was being unfair because his mother had potted plants and then smiled at himself. Ernest was only an innocent victim of circumstances.

There was one thing certain at the moment—nobody but a boor would remain here when a gentleman with an intended of long standing had called on her by appointment.

Well, thought Ivanhoe, she could make a worse choice. The younger man stood in the light of the double arch, smiling down toward Evelyn who was turned toward him and talking; Ivanhoe paid no attention beyond hearing that it was some light social pother of the town that did not concern him. Then she led him over toward Ivanhoe, who was standing at the end of the piano, smiling. The blond young man had quality—a face that was at once strong and gentle and certainly intelligent. His big body, perhaps as heavy as Ivanhoe's, though he was two inches shorter, moved easily and well.

He smiled a genial greeting. "Well, this is luck! I've been telling the folks about you and they don't want you to fail to come over and have supper or a Sunday dinner with us before you go. Dad will kill the fatted calf and the fatted cow and bull to hear a real musician again. All we've got's a Steinway organ but you don't need much accompaniment."

They shook hands warmly. "I'll be delighted," said Ivanhoe. "I'd like to meet some Pittsville people in case I ever come through again or happened to want to settle here."

"Again?" said Evelyn. "What about my lessons?"

"And what about mine?" said Ernie. "We thought you might be with us a few weeks, at least. I counted on at least getting a study program from you. You'll certainly have time to hear me before you go—won't you?—and put me on the right track?"

"The fact is," said Ivanhoe, "I don't know whether this is a headquarters or just a posting stop for me. There are more things I can attend to conveniently from here—but I've got to catch the morning boat to St. Louis and wind up some things I left at loose ends down there."

"Why don't you stop around here somewhere?" Ernest asked. "This country's growing hand over fist. You could make a good living here now, giving lessons and concerts and dances. In the winter you could tour the river towns from Dubuque to St. Louis and come back to the inland towns out of season."

That, Ivanhoe thought, is what he thinks of me as a possible rival. For a moment the butterfly was near rebellion but it was too well-conditioned to rebel seriously. Here was a fine young fellow from one of the county's best families; a solid fellow; a good farmer who could nevertheless speak Latin. He was an important part of a locale, whereas Ivanhoe was not and never could be a part of any locale. Sometime he might be a senator in Washington and Ivanhoe might be playing his fiddle in far Cathay by that time. Fine husband and father—playing a fiddle in far Cathay.

"I don't know what I'll do," Ivanhoe said. "I wouldn't like teaching steadily"—he glanced at Evelyn—"except under special circumstances. And I wouldn't have the patience to start youngsters out. I came up here with the notion of making a settlement for my old age—of course, I didn't realize that it would all be civilized after nearly ten years. Still, I might do worse than this county. I liked it the other time I saw it. Buy a good farm ready settled and fix up the house for a kind of refuge when I want to rest and when I get too old to finger my fiddle."

"You could do a mighty lot worse than this county," said Ernest.

"Well, I've got to go down and talk to Charley—and a real estate man I know in St. Louis. The few times I ever expect to want to get fixed in a place for a while, I want it to be a home I want to be in."

"Right," said Ernest. "I've already got the plans worked out for the place I want to have—sometime."

Ivanhoe moved toward the door. "Well, good night,

folks. I've got to go down and see that Sammy is putting the right things in the bags."

"But I thought I'd hear you play at least one piece!" said Ernest.

"It isn't near eight o'clock yet, even," Evelyn said.

Ivanhoe hesitated. They both seemed sincere. The question was whether it would seem parsimonious to go or an intrusion to stay. "All right, one. What will it be?"

Both men looked at Evelyn. Ivanhoe opened his case and resined his bow abstractedly and carefully as if he were playing a tune on the cake. Evelyn went over to the piano and struck a few chords; then looked at Ivanhoe inquiringly.

"Good! Second stanza solo violin."

She gave him his A and a moment later they began to play Schubert's "Ave Maria." Ivanhoe kept a pure tone through the first stanza and then took the song into his own hands, carrying the harmony himself and ornamenting the theme; Evelyn came in for the third and last stanza which he played in harmonics, with the tone dying as it sank in the last phrase and note.

There was the proper moment of silence till Ivanhoe said casually, "The left hand was quite good—better than I expected. If you can learn to run your phrases in abstract music the same way!"

He tucked away his violin and loosened his bow. "Now I'll have to leave you folks."

"Not yet," said Evelyn, and Ernest echoed her.

Ivanhoe smiled. "I'll be back in a few days—perhaps for quite a little while—perhaps for a few days, but I'll see you both then. Good-by for a few days." They all shook hands and he left Evelyn with Ernest.

He was very thoughtful going down the hill toward the hotel. When a man is finally in love his first instinct is to fence off all intruders, however innocent or dangerless they may seem. There was something about Ernest that was not quite compatible with this notion—it was as if he had attained some late status of marriage with Evelyn in which he still

loved her but was quite used to the sensation. As far as Ivanhoe could see she accepted the idea—emotionally their wedding would be supererogatory; they were fond of each other
and took it for granted.

If Ivanhoe had not been finally in love with Evelyn he
would have begun with the aphrodisiac of music and gone
on to others merely to see what a little excitement would do,
tossed into that admirably serene situation between her and
Ernest. It might drive her to Ernest or it might more probably bring her to him but it would be unfair and artificial
whether it succeeded or failed. He couldn't play the violin
for her every moment of their lives, and that would be his
promise if he won her that way.

He was not the man to make up fifth-act speeches about
giving her up to the better man, but when he gave a concert
he liked the last number to be as moving as the first, with the
audience still pleased and eager—not weary of eccentric and
long-drawn melodies. Let her have Haydn—he would continue to be Tartini.

Damn that man Dunshee! If it weren't for him, Ivanhoe
thought, he would know exactly what to do, but for Ivanhoe
no crusade was small, and Dunshee needed correction. Ivanhoe could not bear dissonances and little ones were dissonances just as much as if someone had ripped up all the strings
of a violin by the roots. If it weren't for Dunshee he could
do what Dick had suggested—make himself a small, very
good orchestra and go about this culture-hungry country,
winning, no doubt, the acclamation of multitudes. There
were plenty of towns for annual tours between Pittsburgh
and St. Louis, with summer concerts in the latter city to hold
his company together.

Dunshee was the reason he couldn't do this—absolutely.
He would do it afterward, if he didn't go back to Europe for
some more lessons, but right now there was the matter of this
big toad in a small puddle; this very offensive toad in a puddle that deserved something better. The crusading spirit grew
in Ivanhoe. He might still build his own hotel even though

it would keep him in Pittsville three or four months and he would probably have to give Evelyn piano lessons and Ernest violin lessons the whole time.

He grinned at himself. Dunshee did need a spanking, but he knew that if Dunshee's daughter had not needed piano lessons he would have thought only vaguely of reprisals. Oh, hell, he might as well go through with it. He had with all the others and they had cured themselves as this one would not, but he would rather have a permanent clean wound this time than the troublesome scars of an old hurt. He would go back and take all the delight he could from loving her as long as it lasted—till she married the fine big blond—and when it was no longer decent to love her and he had had a modicum of fun in torturing the man who had thus directed her affairs, her father, he would go away again and stay away.

He went to the desk in the hotel and cleared his throat at old Jake who was already beginning to nod. Jake worked from four in the afternoon till eight in the morning, but he had a spring office chair in which he got most of his sleep during the quiet hours after eleven o'clock. He also had his meals and ten dollars a month, which was a good wage for a man close to one side of sixty or the other. He slept and wakened easily so that his hours were really not a hardship; as a matter of fact he was the least bit jealous of his hours off the desk when the vivid, brilliant life of the tavern went on without him.

Jake jumped out of the chair at the low billing desk and met Ivanhoe at the clerk's desk which joined it at right angles.

"Mr. Keeler. There're two gentlemen waiting for you— since seven."

Ivanhoe glanced about and saw two men, about middle-middle age bearing down on him from the table at the right center of the room. His eyes narrowed. What would anyone want with him? Farmers, undoubtedly, in rough homespun which was nevertheless their "best"—faces burned gray-brown—heavy bodies—old felt hats for Sunday, for years of

Sundays. He thought they might somehow have heard that he was interested in buying a farm.

They paused with the diffidence of men who are assured with large animals but timid with human beings and each looked to the other for speech.

"You Mr. Ivanhoe Keeler, the great fiddler?"

"I'm Ivanhoe Keeler. What can I do for you?"

There was a long pause; finally one of them spoke. "You see, Mr. Keeler, my girl's marryin' his boy a week from to-morrow, on a Saturday morning. We got the arrangements all arranged and a good lot of food for the wedding break-fast—why they call it breakfast at noon, I don't know—and we want to do our best for them. We wondered if we could hire you to come play some music, wedding music like, be-fore the wedding and have breakfast with us and maybe play a little before they drove off to the boat."

"My boy's taking them to Keokuk for their honey-moon," the other farmer said with no little humble pride.

"Andy's a good boy," the bride's father confirmed, with the same pride in what his daughter had captured.

Ivanhoe smiled and frowned at the same time. "I'd like to play for your wedding but I'm starting for St. Louis to-morrow morning. I don't know whether I can make it back in a week."

"We'd make it worth your while," the bride's father said eagerly. "We could pay as much as five dollars."

"Apiece," said the groom's father as he saw that this offer left Ivanhoe unmoved.

"That isn't the question," said Ivanhoe. "It'd give me only a day in St. Louis—well, I'll try to make it if I can—I won't promise. But since I can't promise I won't charge you anything if I do get back."

"Mr. Keeler, we'll count on you, whether you promise or not. It's the nicest thing you could do for the young couple—and the nicest thing we could think to have done."

Ivanhoe laughed. "All right. I'll be there, if we have to blow up the steamboat. I've got a horse or two in Keokuk—I'll pick one up and ride the last stage to get here in plenty of time. One of you will have to see about shipping my saddle and bridle down to—here's the address—I haven't time to take care of it."

"We'll see you get 'em if we have to carry 'em down."

"Who'll I ask for when I get back?"

"Oh! Excuse us. This is Colin Beggs and I'm Jim Agnew. The wedding's at my house, about two miles out of town to the north—you can't miss it if you just ride about two miles. Anyway there'll be a lot of rigs there—we'll have a lot of relatives staying with us."

Ivanhoe shook hands. "Saturday morning, then, about eleven, I suppose."

"If you could make it ten-thirty, before everybody gets there, Colin and I will find a little something to oil up your elbow and we could kind of look the premises over."

"You see," said Colin, the groom's father, "the women planned to do it like back east. First everyone gets seated— they come in out of the front room to the parlor. Would you want to play something then?"

"Yes," said Ivanhoe, "but we'll let that wait till the day that we do this oiling you spoke of. I've got to find my man and start packing if you'll excuse me. I'll see you next week."

"Thank you, Mr. Keeler. And say, Mr. Keeler, if you happen to settle down with us, Colin and I will see you don't lack in any way for eatables and cider and things like that. We sure appreciate it, Mr. Keeler."

They shook hands all around and the two farmers left. Ivanhoe went over to the desk. "Who were they, Jake?"

"Good solid people, Mr. Keeler—both old families. They're related to half the people in the county. Colin's on the Board of Supervisors. That will be a big wedding—you ought to see one of our big country weddings, Mr. Keeler. And if you do stay among us it won't hurt anything to have Colin and Jim your friends for life, which they'll be."

"They looked solid— Sammy in the kitchen?"

"Yes, sir—I'll fetch him." Jake chuckled. "Young Andy courted Evelyn for a while but the Bogel boys sort of crowded him out—it was kind of cut and dried between the fathers that Evelyn would marry one of the Bogels—I wouldn't want that to go any further."

"Boys?"

"Oh, yes. Old Ludwig's got three. First the oldest one courted Evelyn but she wouldn't have him, and then the next one, but she wouldn't have him, and now it's Ernie, but I guess she'll have him."

"I guess so. Don't close my room account, Jake. I'll be back for that wedding and I'd just as soon leave my stuff where it is."

"But I could have it stacked away for you, Mr. Keeler, and I'd see personally that your room was ready when you got back."

Ivanhoe gave him a gold piece. "That will take care of the room and buy yourself a cigar with the rest."

"That's too much, sir—thank you, sir." Jake nearly made speed to the kitchen.

Samaliel appeared immediately, carrying his banjo and its case.

"Sammy, we're catching the boat down to St. Louis in the morning."

"Yes, sir." A look of relief and satisfaction spread over Sammy's face.

"Just pack your own things and a bag for me. We'll be back next week."

"Yes, sir," said Sammy in a very different tone.

*   *   *

The precipitancy of Ivanhoe's departure made it impossible for any post to precede him to St. Louis, but when he announced himself at Dick's outer office it was almost as if he had just returned from Mexico, for his brief pause in St. Louis ten days before, or a little less, had not seemed a return at all.

"Well, well, Ivanhoe! You didn't stay long! Good boy! Good boy!"

Ivanhoe suddenly realized that he hadn't stayed long; it seemed to him that he had stayed for centuries. Three days in Pittsville—it was incredible that three days should change a man's character and dignity as his had been altered.

"How were the frontiers?"

Ivanhoe blushed and grinned at once. "There weren't any. Just the same, I think I may dig myself a hideaway up in Iowa. I'm no damn good, Dick—I'll never settle down—not in any respect. But I'll have a place to keep a good bed and this ton of music poor Sammy has to lug around whenever I want to sit down for a little while."

"Not a bad idea—though why in Iowa?—oh, I forgot." He pulled a cord and a colored servant appeared. "Get Mr. Hoskin."

"How is Charley—and family?"

"They're fine. It would be a pretty cranky Frau that couldn't get along with Charley, and Ilse isn't. Charley's taking care of Carriage for the plant and you never saw a better behaved bunch of van drivers in your life. Also we don't lose any more kegs from the wagons in the tough spots around the river front. Charley rode out with the drivers the first few days and he nearly killed four or five ruffians who tried to cut the ropes before he was six blocks from the plant. The next day a fellow in one of the gangs drew a knife on him—we sent our doctor to the fellow and he will probably live to go to jail. Serenade vans are sacred now."

"What a bully job for Charley! He must love it!"

"He does. I hope the supply of toughs lasts. He's got them scared to death here on the riverside but we have some other bad spots in the city."

They were interrupted by the gentleman in question and Samaliel bringing the luggage. Charley rushed to grab Ivanhoe by the shoulders and shake him this way and that till Ivanhoe let loose a straight right on that iron chest with every ounce of strength he had. Charley fell back and squared off.

"Whoof! What they been feeding you up in Ioway?"

"Tigers' blood and tenpenny nails. If you can't stand a little tap like that you better keep away from Iowa—you big tough, you still wear that piece of iron plate under your shirt." Ivanhoe wiggled his fingers.

"Say, Ive, come on up to my house and see how the boy's grown since you left."

"Grown? In a week? Well, I can just dash up—I came down to do some shopping, dearies!"

"Shopping! You mean you're not going to stay?"

"I planned to for a few days but I've got to play at the wedding of the Beggs boy and the Agnew girl next Saturday. It's an engagement."

"Who the hell are they and what the hell do you care? Come on, Ive, you can't let us down like this! You can't let the Gasthaus and everybody down. Boy, you look ten years younger since you left!"

"I'm a hundred years older," Ivanhoe said soberly and then laughed again. "That little cabin town I left is full of brick buildings now; still, it isn't a bad little town. I think I'll play around there a while till I decide where to go next."

A quick look of intelligence passed between Byerley and Charley.

"Why don't you come here right away and save a lot of trouble?" Charley suggested. "I saved room for you and Dick's saved room for you and Serenade has been building some nice new houses—we could build you one just to suit you."

"Might get to like it. You, Sammy, put those grips down and go find your family. I won't need you till tomorrow morning at—"

"At my house," said Charley.

"At my house," said Dick.

"At Dick's," said Ivanhoe. "Sammy knows where that is. Get out, Sammy."

Charley grumbled. "The last time you saw little Charley you didn't hardly see him. You didn't say a damn word how good-looking he was."

Sammy disappeared and the three men leaned back in their chairs.

"Now tell us how you come to get back so soon," Charley suggested.

"Had to buy some music and things. But listen, there's a damned old hellion named Dunshee up in this town, Pittsville, and the beds in his hotel are awful and he won't change them. Seems they're pioneer beds."

Ivanhoe went on and on without ever mentioning Evelyn. "—now the Ellisons may have been the pioneer farmers, and old Dunshee may be the pioneer Shylock, but I intend to be the pioneer Tonkünstler of that county." He grinned. "It takes a kind of courage and hardihood those others will never know."

"Come through—come through!" said Charley. "Any girls up there?"

"I don't know why you ask that. Of course, lots of them."

"Any special ones?"

"I don't know what a special girl is. One with stripes like a zebra, I suppose, or with gold-plated ears."

"You know what I mean."

Ivanhoe patted a yawn. "I got to be up and doing—lots of buying to do before I start back."

"I want to show you our plant," Byerley complained. "You haven't been through it since before the war. I work and slave down here building us up a nice brewery and you won't even look at it. I'm in this business for money but I'd like to get some fun out of it, too. We got the finest plant between here and Philadelphia and all you've ever seen is practically the woodshed now."

"I've seen how big it is—but all right. If I can wind up my shopping fast enough I'll come back early and see the brewery before I take you up to the Gasthaus for supper. That includes you and the missus, Charley. And the baby, too, if he drinks beer and appreciates Beethoven."

"He loves beer but he probably couldn't stand your fiddling, since you turned farmer almost a week. Come on, we'll get my carriage and run up to the house and then I'll take you around."

Byerley rang the bell and gave instructions about Charley's carriage.

"We'll have a nip while we wait for them to get the outfit ready," Dick Byerley suggested, and shortly afterward there were glasses and decanters and biscuit on the table. "Any chance to sell some Serenade up in Iowa, Ive?"

"There's a darn good chance, if my picture wasn't on the end of the kegs. If they'd see that they'd think I was a famous something and it wouldn't be the same."

"What wouldn't be the same?"

"Oh, they'd think I was somebody. I'm a violinist. That's the way I've always got by and that's the way I always will get by. Everybody in the world can think it isn't important, the damn fools, but to me it's the most important thing there is, almost."

"Did you say 'almost'?" Charley inquired casually.

"Well—if it was a choice of whether I'd rather have my violin shot or me, I guess I'd have to give up the violin."

Charley peered at him.

"If there's any market up there we can arrange to have a special brand made—maybe a violin instead of your picture. And I'll have some special tags printed without your name on them. We've been waiting on the river markets above here till the towns got worth a special salesman, but they've got a little brewery at Quincy now and maybe we ought to get into that territory before it's too late."

"It's not too late yet," Ivanhoe said. "The brew's just passable."

"By George!" said Byerley. "You wouldn't have to sell this stuff, you know. We've got a smart little new icing keg —the beer keg itself sits inside a jacket—there's a long stout spigot that goes through the jacket and the keg both—then you put ice between the keg and the jacket. I'll have our head cooper put silver bands on one of our display models— red and yellow mahogany—and a name plate on top of it— and all you have to do is just have it and have it set up in the taverns you go to to furnish your own tipple, because you like this special kind of brew. The barmen will steal out of it, of course, and when you've been around up there a little I'll send a traveler through. Nothing commercial on your part."

Ivanhoe and Charley roared together. "Not much," said Ivanhoe. "But—all right. After all, I've got a share in this business."

Byerley was so excited that he sent for the cooper at once and gave his directions. By this time the chaise was hitched and Charley and Ivanhoe mentioned a revoir and took the lift.

"My God," said Ivanhoe. "Dick will have barrels of Serenade Brews at the Second Coming of Christ."

"You bet he will," said Charley, "and you and I will pocket a bit of the change—you to buy some more music and steamer tickets and me to buy little Charley some kind of a course in Harvard College or Academy or whatever it is. He's a smart codger—Dick. He doesn't need any more money —none of us need any more money, but he keeps on making it."

"I suppose it's an art," Ivanhoe said thoughtfully. "I suppose I don't have to play the violin any more—I don't have to and I'll never be any better. I've reached my limit, a little bit too soon. But when you get used to playing games you have to keep going on with it. You don't ever have to hit another guy in all your life."

"I see what you mean—let's don't talk about it."

It was a curious kind of chaise in which they rode to Charley's pleasant white house well back from the crest of the river hill. It had the ordinary double seat but behind, elevated so that he could see over the roof of the vehicle, even if the roof had been lifted, a Negro rode in solitary splendor on a small single seat.

Ivanhoe shook his head. Even in ten days Charley was beginning to show signs of decadence.

Charley noticed it. "The lines are long enough so he can drive from back there when we bring the baby. Don't want to be elbowing and flapping around with Ilse holding little Charley right next to me."

"You've got too lazy to get out and tie up the horse," Ivanhoe said.

They stopped at Charley's house only for an inspection of the premises and the baby, which looked very much like a baby, though Ilse pointed out special features and advantages about it, contributed by "Karly" and by her Mutter's Vater who had taken the classical course at Göttingen.

She sparkled at the mention of dinner in the Gasthaus. "Oh, so gay. All as it was once since, one time. We dance, not, Karly?"

Karly grinned. "We dance."

"Oh!" She had thought of something but she covered the thought with her bright smile. "Well, we dance. Will you dance with me, Herr Geiger?"

"I certainly will, if I have to choke your husband." He knew what that swift and passing cloud meant. "We'll all have a good time."

Ilse looked at him with pitying admiration for his courage. Two weeks had not passed since Ivanhoe's heart had been broken and here he was brave and apparently gay—what Gemütlichkeit, what Herzhaftigkeit!

Karly kissed his wife good-by and he and Ivanhoe set forth—first to the music store where Ivanhoe bought an armload of music including the new Paganini Etudes of Liszt; then to a candy store where he bought a dozen of the very largest and best boxes of bonbons, and then to a hothouse where he bought an orange tree, a lemon tree, rose trees of several varieties, a cyclamen, a camellia tree, in bloom, and several love-apple plants with their fruits just turning red. These were to be delivered at the boat in the morning.

"Where to now, Ive?"

"Furniture dealer."

Charley looked puzzled but gave the necessary directions.

To the salesman who hurried over to the two elegantly dressed gentlemen, Ivanhoe said succinctly, "I want the two best spring mattresses you've got in stock."

Charley whistled. "Mattresses! Jesus Christ, boy, those are nice flowers, but ain't you a little overconfident?"

Ivanhoe grinned and patted his violin case.

Charley shook his head.

*   *   *

Ivanhoe rode into Pittsville alone on the following Saturday morning. Sammy was on the boat taking care of the precious flowers to see that they did not get too cold and the bonbons to see that they kept cold enough. Ivanhoe was whistling, "Dir töne Lob"—

> "Thine be all praise,
> Thy wonder ever treasured—"

from the bewildering but lovely opera *Tannhäuser*. There was a piano and voice score in the packages which Samaliel was attending.

Evelyn was a nice girl and so was Elisabeth in the opera but the knight sang all his best songs to Venus.

Ivanhoe had the deepest respect for Evelyn but if Tannhäuser sang his most lyric passages to the profane goddess that was all there was to it so far as Ivanhoe was concerned. Implications might be implications but music was music.

He was in a cheerful mood. Once an utter hopelessness is definitely and finally established it leaves room for some slightly compensatory amusements. Byerley had been delighted by Ivanhoe's exclamations over the magnitude and perfection of their brewery. Alwine had delicately but unnecessarily stayed away from the carnival at the Gasthaus; she had missed a magnificent evening. The war hero-violinist had been toasted from all over the place and his music acclaimed to the roof.

Well—when the brief project at hand was concluded, perhaps he might come back to St. Louis. What were the plans he and Dick had had for an orchestra? One would certainly thrive in St. Louis. Ivanhoe had treatises by Habeneck and Pasdeloup in his purchases and he had ordered one of those "baton" affairs that Beethoven and the late Mendelssohn had used. They would have to have an elegant one made in the East—Ivanhoe had seen a few in Europe but even with the great authority of the two masters they were still regarded as an affectation.

Ivanhoe saw the advantage of the weapon, the implement, at once. It was crisp and singular and it was a scepter—no blurry paw that pointed vaguely and bred doubt by its very emptiness. The baton was an instrument which pointed out the fact that the conductor was playing on an orchestra.

He had also bought a flageolet as a guide to the qualities of the winds; he understood the strings and brasses and he could learn the delicacies of the reed, from the half-human clarinet to the flute, out of this facile, vulgar little instrument. He was prepared to study a month on his scores to see how a few of them should be presented in their true meanings.

He felt good about Charley and about Sammy, too. Good old Charley was having the time of his life; he was finding adventure in the city that he had not imagined could be found inside any of the country's many frontiers, and with it he had the adventure of Ilse and the baby. As much as it was in his reticent nature, Samaliel adored Ivanhoe. Because of the fiddler's twiddles on catgut and wire, the slave was a comfortable, even wealthy, freedman, married to a free wife and father of a free son. Actually, he was more enslaved than he had ever been, but enslaved by devotion.

It all came out well. Despondency was forever out of Ivanhoe's life. He patted his fiddle case on the pillion behind him.

"If you got busted right now, signorina, I wouldn't cry for you. You've done all that could reasonably be expected even from a Guarnerius. You've had a good, exciting life and it hasn't been wasted—look at Charley and Dick and Sammy—not to speak of some other folks. I'm the only one you've ever harmed, old darling, and I guess I shouldn't mind it—you've been a beautiful and faithful sweetheart."

He interrupted these highly sentimental reflections as his horse's shoes clattered on the river ice. He was on a mare again, this time because his partner in the horse business had suggested that he start a branch office in Pittsville the first time a good stallion came by that way. The idea struck Ivanhoe; it sounded substantial and solid and earthy and it wouldn't be much trouble. There were enough prosperous farmers around Pittsville to buy up all the fine geldings he could produce—if he had luck and got mares from the other two mounts he might go into the horse-raising business, which was about the highest class farming there was, as even Dunshee would have to admit.

He played with this idea, as he came to the boat channel and crossed the little extemporized bridge from the ice to the bank. To do the thing properly he ought to buy a fair-sized farm, put up a house that would serve for the refuge he had imagined, a good horse barn and a good hay barn and granary, have a few pigs and a few chickens and some peacocks for ornament like the handsome creatures he had seen on some of the English estates where he had played. He would have the livery-stable man hire him a good farmer and hand with horses to run the place and go into the business of settling Iowa with fine horseflesh. This way his sitting-down place would not be an empty and useless spot when he was not using it.

The fine mare under him had made excellent time so that there were still several hours for a fair night's rest when, after leaving his horse at the livery stable, he crossed the vacant block to the hotel. Old Jake was burning a low night light and sleeping with his head down on his arms, folded over the desk. He awakened at once when the door opened and jumped up to take Ivanhoe's light bag. He already knew that he could not take the violin.

"Morning, Mr. Keeler. You must have had a good ride up."

"Fine—roads are in good shape for winter and I had bright moonlight the biggest part of the way. Do you suppose there's any coffee left in the kitchen?"

The old man's eyes sparkled. "Yes, my pot's still hot over the coals. I'll be right back." He hurried to the kitchen.

Ivanhoe grinned and got the brandy bottle out of his saddlebags. When Jake got back with two steaming cups he laced them generously and they both sat down at the long table.

"Any news since I went away?"

"Any news? You're the only news around here, Mr. Keeler. You got everybody guessing. Seems you been all over Europe and there was a drummer through here since you left said you was a fraud unless there was two Ivanhoe Keelers. He said the real Ivanhoe Keeler owned a whacking big brewery down in St. Louis and wouldn't ever drift off into a little town like this."

"Yeah," said Ivanhoe, without turning a hair, "that's a funny thing. I've seen the signs, too, and I will say the man's Serenade Brews are the best beers I ever tasted. Keeler isn't such an uncommon name and if you were born about the time the novel hit this country your ma might call you Ivanhoe. Think of all the Andrew Jackson Smiths there must be in this country."

"That would be about the how of it. Well, young fellow, if you're going to fiddle for the wedding tomorrow you better get some sleep."

"You're right. See that I get up in time."

Ivanhoe was glad for once that he was a fiddler and obviously not a brewer. They would probably catch up with him some time but not immediately. It would take shattering proofs to make anyone in Pittsville believe that the inconsequential musician owned a substantial percentage of the St. Louis river front. Somehow he felt that the little association he was to have with Evelyn and the feud which he planned with her father would be more pleasantly conducted if he fought only with his usual weapon, and more honest, for he was really not a brewer—he was a violinist at best, and at worst a fiddler.

Ivanhoe slept soundly from three o'clock till nine-thirty when he woke as automatically as if the hotel had given him an alarm. He bathed, put on his gaudiest fiddling clothes and went downstairs with an intention on breakfast, but Colin and Jim were already waiting for him.

"Just as soon as I get a bite—I rode half the night."

"Never mind about your bite—you come on out to the house and we'll give you a real country breakfast—we got a rig outside."

Ivanhoe smiled. "My horse is ready over at the stable. You start with your rig now and I'll tell them to have the coffee hot for you when you get there."

"We planned to haul you," Colin said, "but I guess no white man could take a remark like that standin' up. Come on, Jim."

As Ivanhoe walked over to the stable he heard the rig roaring out of town. He hurried very little, untied his mare and then set her at a two-forty run. He passed the rig about a mile out of town; Jim was crouched above his seat, whistling the whip over a good-looking pair of bays and yelling at the top of his voice. The sound became fainter as Ivanhoe went on to a big red-brick house which was surrounded by buggies, carriages, chaises and wagons. A tow-haired youngster came out to the yard gate and Ivanhoe tossed him the bridle.

"Get her out of sight—they thought they were racing me."

The kid chuckled and led the mare into the barn quickly. "Mr. Keeler?"

He did not pause at the door. "How d'ye do, Mrs. Agnew?" He could hear two voices shouting wildly down the road. "I'll explain—but get me half a cup of coffee this very instant—they're almost here."

He pushed past her and settled himself in a rocking chair in the midst of a startled but slightly amused company. The gracious big woman hurried in within the minute with the coffee.

"Sugar and cream?"

"Not a word—this is the third cup you've given me—please."

There was a noise in the carriage yard.

Ivanhoe turned to the company. "And as I was saying about the federal debt: I think that in order to assure a community of nations—oh, hello there!"

Jim and Colin stood in the doorway and looked at him grimly.

"I believe I *will* have another cup of this delicious coffee, Mrs. Agnew—I don't suppose it's good for me—"

Mrs. Agnew played up. "Five cups of coffee before you have a thing to sit on your stomach!"

"Don't you five cups of coffee me, mamma," said Jim. "We been humiliated enough without a lot of fictional cups of coffee. I don't suppose you had time to meet any of these folks, did you, Mr. Keeler?"

"Oh, yes—plenty of time. Don't know I got all of the names just correctly—there's Mrs. Beggs—and her sister—and the bride's uncle—and the groom's uncle and aunt and cousin —and—but I'm starving—"

"Well, dog my cats," said Agnew. "He really—he must have flew the rest of the way. How many cups of coffee did he really have, Mertie?"

"It's not proper to count a company's food," said Mertie Agnew. "You'll have to ask him."

Behind them as they went into the big kitchen for breakfast, not a "saved-over" breakfast but a brand splinter new one, a murmur of surmise arose. "—But nobody told him— how did he know I was Mertie's brother?—how did he know I was Andy's mother—?"

Perhaps they never learned in all their lives that there are blond Scotch and dark Scotch and that Scotch family faces are likely to be as definitive as family plaids.

Andy's mother was quickly signaled into the kitchen where the two fathers and Mrs. Agnew were watching Ivanhoe restore his forces, with delight and awe. Ivanhoe wished that Charley were here. While the performance was not up to Charley at his best or even at his average, Charley would have respected him a little more if he could have seen him putting down one waffle with sorghum, the next with honey, the next with maple syrup; swallowing an egg or two, obliterating a piece of ham, swallowing magnificent biscuits in two swallows, with fine sweet butter and mulberry preserves to ease them along the esophagus, rinsing from a jug of wild grape juice, bitter-sweet and treacherously potent, and generally replacing sleep with provender, which was the best way to do it, as Ivanhoe had discovered long before.

When Ivanhoe had finished and devoted himself to his coffee, thick with cream and well-sugared this time, Mrs. Agnew suggested that she get the "children" who had been properly sequestered, after the first greetings to the house company, in the funeral parlor—the big cold room at the end of the house which was never used for anything but ceremonies—to comfort each other in the face of the imminent ordeal. They had done this splendidly; i.e., they were both about to faint.

Dorothy was a sweet young girl, holding up her head rather better than Andy. She was nervous as the deuce, of course, with considerations of the fact that a bare dozen hours would include the greatest change that would ever occur in her life—birth and death are not changes, since there is no consciousness before one or after the other—but there was no question that she regarded the change as an achievement. She had lived the life and been the person that fine young Andy wanted to guard and keep.

Stout Andy, with his long head and wide blue eyes, was in far worse case. When he forgot to close his teeth together there was an almost imperceptible quivering of his jaw—it was like the trembling in the knees of a buck brought to bay.

Ivanhoe coughed, touched his lips with his handkerchief and snitched a piece of reasonably warm bacon off the egg platter. "D'ja hear about the race?" he asked Andy cheerfully.

"Race?"

"You kids' folks tried out their buggy against my mare Mazeppa. I gave them about a mile start. Tiresome waiting for them while I had my coffee."

The girl laughed softly. "Dad will steal your horse. That's supposed to be the best buggy team in Iowa."

"Sit down. Let's have some coffee and plan on this. Now, you two have got to be the star performers—don't look so glum. Don't pay any attention to the people—just think about each other. You think about her and you think about him."

"Yes, sir."

"Now when I want you to come downstairs, I'll step in the parlor and raise my hand to get them quiet. Then I'll step back in the hall, where they can't see me and I'll play like this—DEE-dee-de-dee-di-dee-dee, Dee-diddle-omp-dee-dee-eye-do! Mendelssohn's Wedding March. Don't pay any attention to anything before that—those will just be incidental. I'll give Mrs. Agnew a signal so you'll know when to come down and go up front to the preacher. Then he'll marry you. Then I'll step in the doorway and play and then the preacher will bless everybody and then you can be congratulated and we'll have some lunch. Will you tell the preacher, Mrs. Agnew? Andy, come here and let me fix that stock—and keep your chin up off of it after this. Head back."

They met in the hall and went up the stairs as brave and straight as if they were merely going to be shot.

He thought they had all gone as he stood looking, almost wistfully, at the confident bend in the knees of the tight trousers and the almost flippant swirl of the long skirt as the reassured couple mounted the stairs.

There was a touch on his elbow and a glass was thrust into his hand. "Come on, Paul Revere. They'll be half an hour upstairs getting the last touches. Colin and me don't approve of drinking, but we thought the fiddler might like a little warming and we can't be unsociable."

"The fiddler is always a good excuse," said Ivanhoe, but he went back to the kitchen with them.

There was a pint of whisky from the Pittsville grocery and a gallon of sweetish, heady cider that had been corked until it was like a rich and nutty champagne. It appealed to Ivanhoe.

"Listen, Ive," said Jim. "When I die, will you come arrange things and play for my funeral?"

"He's a born manager, Jim. My God, we were all at sixes and sevens—"

"Don't tell me. The only kids we got, Colin. If we had ten apiece we'd probably know how to get the last ones married—but I bet we wouldn't. Mr. Keeler, we've heard a lot about you in this country and we don't know anything about you; but Colin and me are behind you whatever you plan to do, if you happen to stay here."

"I don't know what I'm going to do, but I appreciate what you've said—maybe you'd better wait, though, till you hear me play."

"Hah! Listen! We know about that! You played in Europe. Colin, we better get to our seats. I got to get up and say 'I do' when they give Dotty away."

"I'll be right alongside you—don't get nervous."

"Poor old Andy. He looked kind of pale-brown one minute and kind of pink-brown most of the time!"

"Hell," said Andy's father, "I was married in a log cabin by a travelin' preacher. Nobody else there but Addie's mother."

"You scared? Don't lie."

"Well, hell, she was comin' with me to live. How would I know whether I'd suit her or not?"

"Get out," said Ivanhoe. He looked at his repeater. "It's almost time."

He went almost as far as the door with them; then lingered in the hall. The big parlor was sweet and colored with cuttings from all the potted plants in the neighborhood. He observed with regret that someone had brought lilies—he should have thought of those in St. Louis. But the bride was wearing the poor little bouquet of camellias he had carried almost as carefully as his violin from Keokuk last night, and today. Sammy was bringing the tree from which he had culled this gift.

A head nodded over the bannister. Ivanhoe stepped into the buzzing room and played one sharp note on the D string.

He nodded gravely and disappeared into the hall. That was very surely Evelyn, whose face had been more startled than those of the others—she must have known the violin.

He began very gravely with the apostrophe to the plane tree from *Xerxes*, and drifted through Mozart to the Liechtenstein Sonata of Beethoven and from there to some Berlioz —the *Faust* opera, he could not identify the aria precisely, except that it was warm and sweet.

He lifted his bow and everything was silent. The bride took the first step down the irrevocable stair. Then the Mendelssohn March from *A Midsummer Night's Dream* came from the violin and anyone there would have sworn that a splendid parlor organ was blowing out deep and true behind the theme.

Ivanhoe noticed with satisfaction that, though Andy was more pale-brown than pink-brown at the moment, his hand was steady as he held Dorothy's. They went up and stopped in front of the preacher and the Satisfaction of the Rites went through smoothly and even with a kind of touching dignity.

At the end of the prayer and blessing, just as the young couple rose, the minister held up his hand. He was willing to help even a Samaritan, since the Samaritan had made this one of his better services.

Ivanhoe played from Schubert:

> "Thou art the Rest
> And gentle peace;
> Now you will still
> Wistful desire.
> I dedicate
> To what thou art
> Here in its dwelling
> My heart and seeing—
> Here in its being—
> My feeling heart."

Ivanhoe played three stanzas with the normal variations in treatment—the simple song, the variations, and harmonics, the final treatment, gravely on the G and D strings.

For the third time in his life he had the applause of a moment's silence. He let it last long enough and then he stepped quietly into the room with the violin and bow at rest.

He had done it too well. Everyone in the room seemed about to cry. Ivanhoe came forward with his bow in one hand and his violin under his arm—how well he knew those sweet, deep curves at the sides of the bridge,—and gripped Andy with his free hand while he kissed the bride.

Thereupon everyone rose and shouted and overwhelmed the newly married couple. Ivanhoe could never remember afterward how long the wedding breakfast lasted, except that it must have lasted for some time since he was ransacking for jolly Scotch tunes before it was over, and in spite of great sops of grouse, quail and roast beef, with five or six kinds of pie, the ostensibly innocent ciders and punches which Jim and Colin thrust at him from moment to moment got him into a condition where everything he said had to be weighed, censored, reweighed, rephrased, recensored—and then they were all talking about something else, so he did not need to say anything.

They finally drew him away like conspirators. "Listen, Mr. Keeler—Colin's thinking some of running for the Legislature. You'll be playing around here all winter, maybe, and if you'd say no more than that you played for Andy's wedding—why, you'd be know up in Iowa City when Colin gets there. You could be a big figure, Mr. Keeler. If Colin gets it, he'd see you'd be a major in charge of all the state military music and so on."

Ivanhoe put up his hand and felt the scar that ran along his chin and up his cheek.

"That wouldn't be fair to you," he said. "I'll be glad to say what I can for either of you—you've certainly been good to me—but I'm a tramp; I don't know where I'll be this time next month—maybe two hundred miles from here. I'm a little too much of a flutterer to count on. Thanks."

"No, you won't," Jim said confidently. "You won't ever leave us and this place here. We'll talk to you afterwards when we're in town, hey, Colin?"

"That's right," said Colin, and they both withdrew with magnificent tact.

The party began to thin after a while and Ivanhoe was ready to leave when the bride and groom, prepared for flight, approached him. The groom was conscious of his tall gray hat but no more conscious than the lovely bride was of her gray watered silk traveling dress and a tiny black pancake that was pressed to her fine dark hair by a ribbon under her chin.

"We can't—" said the groom, "we can't—tell you—"

"Yes, we can," the bride said, and she jumped up and kissed Ivanhoe with a loud smack.

"When I get to be a millionaire I'll give you the change," Ivanhoe said.

They both giggled, free at last from the tension of their day, and Andy grasped Ivanhoe's hand firmly. "I want you to play at our anniversary next year."

"I'll play," Ivanhoe assured them. "For all three of you."

The bride ducked her head and dashed for the carriage and the groom, after a feint at Ivanhoe's chest, dodged after her. And then there were cries and harmless missiles, and the team tapped away.

Ivanhoe put his violin under the other arm—his left arm was tired from grasping and protecting it from the party—and started toward the kitchen door and the stable where his mare was haltered.

" 'Thou art the rest,' " someone said. "They don't un-derstand that."

"They understand the music—or they will, in a little while."

"Romantic."

"The word itself is its own best rebuttal. It means, prac-tically, fantastic. Did you ever hear of a romance written about anyone my age—an antique who has seen all the sor-rows of this doleful world? We get realistic as we go along. I was just playing something calm and soothing. It's too bad that when two kids are crazy about each other they have to start them out by scaring them to death. If I had the doing of it all marriage ceremonies would be banned by law."

"What would the bride have to talk about the rest of her life?"

"Serve her right. All I ever heard any of them say about their weddings was how scared—ha, ha—the groom was."

"You are extraordinarily cynical for a man who has just played 'Du Bist die Ruh' like one of the better angels."

"Sublimation, my good Evelyn. All of the best hypocrites are artists, and vice versa."

"Well, come up and practice some hypocrisy for me this evening. Ernie is going to bring along his violin. Both of us worked like mad while you were gone. Perhaps my legato won't be so distressing."

"Distressing. Mmmmm. That's good and feminine. A man says excavating implement and you throw it back at him as a spade—or a muck shovel. All right, about seven."

"Perhaps six-thirty, for my music lesson?"

Ivanhoe bowed and bowed again to Dunshee who was just emerging from the press of people about the door.

"Hello," said Dunshee with the smile that he used for Ivanhoe—the resigned, disdainful smile that one would give to a child dirtying itself up at making mud pies. "Mighty nice fiddling."

"Thanks. My fingers were a little stiff. Rode up from the Keokuk boat last night and didn't have time to warm up. Nice wedding."

"Yes. A good wedding. Ties up two of the best families in the county—there'll be no Yankees or speculators on Beggs or Agnew farms for a long time to come." The thin austere face broke into a smile. "We'll have some more Democrat votes in the county, too, when us oldsters have to go. You a Democrat, Mr. Keeler?"

Ivanhoe's eyes narrowed. "General Scott was my commander."

Dunshee smiled. "Well, well—he was commander of all of us for a while. Thanks to Worth and Quitman and Taylor we came through that affair without much damage—except a lot of desert unloaded on us."

"You don't know what you're talking about," Ivanhoe said with reprehensible abruptness. The boy had brought up his horse. He took the reins, jumped into the saddle and rode off, before his temper led him to further indiscretions.

* * * .

He had not been long in the tavern before he heard from Dunshee. Sammy had arranged the new mattresses on their beds and Sammy's room looked like a greenhouse. The old mattresses were standing on their ends against the walls, awaiting removal. A fragrance of oranges, lemons, camellias and assorted flowers lingered in the room. The new music was neatly stacked on Ivanhoe's cabinet and the bonbons were set outside the window in their original package, to keep cool.

He had barely changed his clothes when there was a knock on the door and Sammy hurried to open it.

It was old Jake, shakily perturbed. "Mr. Keeler, sir, I'm terribly sorry but Mr. Dunshee told me to tell you—that is, I find that this room has been engaged. We didn't know whether you'd be back."

Ivanhoe sighed. "Well, we'll have to take other rooms."

"That's just it, sir—we haven't any room. All the rooms have been engaged."

"Well, well. Busy little town, Pittsville. Right at the end of winter, too. But since this room's paid for the rest of the month, I don't think I'll move."

"I told Mr. Dunshee. He says he'll refund the balance or the whole month's rent—"

"But he can't refund it if I won't take it. I have a freehold, lease, mortmain, assignment, tenure and habeas corpus on these rooms. Is Mr. Dunshee greater than the Constitution of the United States? Is he greater than Blackstone and the Magna Carta, the Lex Romana and the Salic Laws; the Pandects of Justinian and the Zend-Avesta? I think not!"

"But Mr. Dunshee says—"

"I have behaved myself in a becoming manner—there is no damage to the property and so my contract is neither null nor void nor outlawed."

"I don't know, Mr. Keeler. It's not my doing or wish, you know. But I have to work here—"

"Tell Dunshee to come up and explain himself. He's waiting downstairs right now to see me packing out. He'll wait till the icicles of hell are longer than the stalactites of the Great Caverns. Tell him to come up—but if he doesn't come up and annoys me any more I'll sue him for upsetting me and damaging my art." Ivanhoe leaned back in his chair. "It's pretty certain that one of the people at the wedding today would be on the jury."

Jake barely smiled. "No doubt, sir. I'll tell him you want to see him."

He had barely hopped down the stairs, it seemed, before he returned. "Mr. Dunshee says, sir, that if you have anything to say to him he'll speak to you in the lobby."

Ivanhoe picked up a Chopin cadenza again softly. "Tell him I haven't a thing to say to him and I wish he'd go away and quit bothering me."

"Leave the door open," he added. "That will get him," he told Sammy. "He'll count on pounding it. Nothing more disconcerting than to figure on pounding on a door and then find it's wide open. Leaves you wondering what to do—you can't just stamp in, but you're in plain sight outside."

Mr. Dunshee solved this situation by banging loudly at the side of the door.

"See who it is, Sammy," Ivanhoe said languidly. "I'm busy unless it's something important." His voice was high and clear over a twittering con brio.

"Mr. Dunshee, sir."

Ivanhoe put his violin on the bed and rose. "Show him in."

This hardly seemed necessary since Dunshee was plainly visible in the frame of the door, his face glacial except for the eyes which were hotly furious.

"Mr. Keeler says to come in, sir."

Dunshee strode into the room. Ivanhoe put down his violin and bow and looked up with blandly questioning eyes.

"What is this nonsense, Keeler? I want you to pack your fiddle and the rest of your trash and get out of my tavern at once."

"So Jake told me. These rooms are let and paid for till the end of the month—twenty-seven days. If you don't want to renew your contract with me at that time, I'll find other quarters then, but I don't believe there's much you can do about them till then, unless you want to bring a civil complaint about my behavior."

"I don't know anything about your behavior or care. I have other use for these rooms and I'm telling you to get out. Your whole month's rent will be refunded."

Ivanhoe picked up his violin and softly picked, "When Marlb'rough Went to War," high up on the fingerboard. "I won't get out," he said gently, and picked up his bow.

"You won't, eh? We have a sheriff in this county—a friend of mine, Mr. Keeler. Will you get out quietly?"

"Yes, sir. At the end of the month. And now if you don't get out of my room I'll throw you out first and sue you afterward. These premises belong to me as long as there's no complaint about my behavior. I've been quite aware, sir, that you thought very lightly of me, but I didn't think that your petty contempt would lead you to an indiscretion of this kind. If you annoy me, sir, I have the means to take you from court to court for the next five years and I think that you will pause before satisfying your puny malice at such a cost. After all, your business is here but I can play my violin anywhere to which you may be subpoenaed. We fiddlers have some advantages."

"I'll have you taken up for vagrancy."

Ivanhoe rose so suddenly that Dunshee started back toward the door. "Sammy—my personal portmanteau."

"Yes, sir."

Ivanhoe snapped open an inside compartment and showed Dunshee about twenty pounds of gold eagles. He picked up a handful and dropped them back. "Vagrancy?"

He smiled. "I'm an investor. Do you know anyone around here who would like to sell a farm? I have three mares, two in foal, over in the livery stable and I'm thinking of going into the business—I've got a dozen or so more, all pure-bred from the dam, down in Keokuk."

Eager speech formed on Dunshee's lips before he remembered himself. "You can stay here then, till the end of the month. I'm not accustomed to being told that I don't know what I'm talking about, young man."

"That comes with years and experience, sir. Good day."

Dunshee went away, fuming and bewildered. Ivanhoe turned toward Sammy languidly.

"We'll get him down yet, Sammy. Can't afford to have our free frontier dominated by a lot of little Caesars.—Yes, sir!"

Dunshee had reappeared at the door. He pointed to the wall. "Is that the mattress that belongs on the bed?"

"That is the outrage that belongs in the river. I got my own mattresses in St. Louis—"

"Not for the beds in the Ferry Tavern. I'll have that replaced at once."

"That's all right," Ivanhoe said wearily. "The mattress I got sleeps just as well on the floor."

But Dunshee smiled thinly and went back down the hall. He had won this trick, at least.

*   *   *

That evening as Ivanhoe and Evelyn were discussing the phrasing of the Adagio in Beethoven's von Browne Sonata, Op. 22, the doorbell rang, not at all to Ivanhoe's surprise.

"Oh, my!" said Evelyn after she had opened the door.

In came the orange tree, with oranges; the lemon tree, with lemons; the camellia tree, with camellias; the rose trees, with roses; the cyclamen, with cyclamens, and all the young greenhouse that Ivanhoe had bought in St. Louis.

"Oh, my!" Evelyn said again. "Over in the bow window with the other plants. I'll sort them out tomorrow."

"What in the world possessed you?" she asked Ivanhoe, after the two draymen had gone.

"An accumulation for past, present and future—I can't get cut flowers whenever I call up here so I thought I'd have some you could cut for yourself whenever I'm asked up. I don't think those oranges will ever be big enough to do any good but the blossoms are nice."

"Do I have to have you here before I can take any of the flowers?"

"That is an excessively rude question. When the flowers are ready to pick I'll be kind enough to come up and give my sanction. Now let's see if you can get that left hand so it won't sound like a military parade."

"Yes, sir." She beat the chord easily and Ivanhoe came in with his violin on the air so evenly that only the very worst pianist could have marred its smooth and level statement.

"That's better. Keep up your practice. You'd better begin to work on Chopin's Number Three—the Prelude—that'll smooth out your left hand. In a few weeks I'll break your heart. After you learn the Third you can get after the Revolutionary Etude. You'll never learn that."

"How do you know I won't?"

"No one ever has. If you do, I'll let you tour with me this summer."

"Thank you. Oh, dimme!"

The edited oath, which might have been "dear me" or "damme" was evoked by the ringing of the doorbell. Before Evelyn could rise the door was opened and they both heard the heartiest voice Dunshee could make, "Hello, Ernie!"

"Of course she is. She's got company, but I guess that won't hurt. Come on in, boy. Evvy! Ernie's here!"

Evelyn smiled at the door as Ernie and her father entered and went on fingering the inhuman bass that Chopin had written for his G major Prelude.

"Well, Evvy, aren't you going to get up and speak to Ernest?"

"In a minute." She began to catch the thirds in the right

hand—abandoned the left hand and began to work out the simple melody. Then she played three measures complete.

Ivanhoe laughed. "That'll keep you out of mischief for a while. Good evening, Mr. Dunshee—hello, Ernie."

Dunshee and Ivanhoe bowed to each other. Ivanhoe shook hands with Ernie cordially. "Didn't see you at the wedding."

Ernest shook his head. "Mother was there for the family. We had to stick to our chores—we'll be plowing soon and the place has to be plotted out for the year's crops."

"That," Dunshee said impressively, "is the reason the Bogels are the best farmers in this part of Iowa. Everything planned, production, prices, and the whole business. When pigs are dear and corn is cheap they've got pigs and little corn. When corn is dear their pigs have been sold and they've got grain to sell. Your father and you are wizards, Ernie."

Ta-de-da-de-da-de-da, deda-de-da-de-da-de-deee-oh. She was getting it.

"There are five of us," Ernie said. "In times like this it isn't hard to guess what will be needed one year and another. Of course, no one could have guessed the drought, but we came through all right. Dad always keeps what he calls a Disaster Minimum. If a volcano started we could feed."

"Evelyn! What in the world is all this stuff?" Mr. Dunshee was over in the bow window.

"Mr. Keeler brought me some plants from St. Louis."

"Eh? Oranges. Not much juice in them, I'll bet. Shiny, but no sap. Sit down, Ernie. I guess this music will be done in a minute."

"It's done," said Ivanhoe. "Get the left hand, Miss Dunshee—the right is easy going. Be careful with the thumb—don't overaccent. Now I've got to run along."

"Going? You've only just got here!"

"I brought my violin," Ernest said mournfully.

"Oh, well," said Ivanhoe. "If you'll play for a minute I might be able to suggest something in the way of exercises."

Dunshee laughed. "Ernie doesn't need anything in the

way of exercises. Look at the boy! There's a picture of a
man for you."

Ivanhoe smiled at Ernie and lifted his eyebrows very
slightly. "Let me hear you play for a few minutes."

Ernie fussed with his violin. Dunshee sat back with his
rocky face; the fiddler might ignore him for the moment but
there were innings to come.

Ernie was not a good violinist—he wore his heart on his
fingerboard. He could hit the right notes and lament or re-
joice but it was beyond him to take the music as it stood
and play it as an abstraction; he could not add two and two
if they were represented by X's but if they were represented
by apples, which had flavor and odor and texture, he could
get to the sum of four apples.

"That's good," Ivanhoe said. "You should work on
Lieder. You will never be able to make the violin do more
than sing. That is enough. Hold the wrist higher so that the
stops are more nearly vertical and there is no slide in catching the tone. The double stops in a song should be struck
together—not with the tone first and then picking up the
harmony. I can hear you again in about a week."

"Thank you, Mr. Keeler."

"So that's how you do with a violin," said Dunshee.

Ivanhoe paid no attention to this. "Work on Mozart.
I'll send some out to you by Sammy. Keep the chords tight
and exact."

"Yes, sir—you'll tell me some more next week?"

Ivanhoe smiled. "I think so. I may settle down here."

"You're going to start that horse farm?" Dunshee inquired.

"Oh, I may dig for gold or raise pineapples. I think I'll
stay around Pittsville for a while till I find some better place
to go."

"There may be better places for an artist, Mr. Keeler,"
Ernie said eagerly, "but you won't find a much better place
to live. If I were you I'd buy up along the river somewhere.
There's going to be a big steamboat traffic as the state fills up.

You can sell timber and ship your crops or horses or whatever you raise right out of your front yard."

Ivanhoe shook his head. "I don't know but what this is a railroad country, especially when it begins to settle back of the rivers. It would be easy to lay tracks on the valley."

"Nonsense," said Dunshee. "We'll have railroads, of course, to feed the river ports, but those tooting things can never compete with boats on freight rates. It's natural for us to go to the rivers. Look you, we send down heavy cargoes of raw supplies, with the current, and we haul back light cargoes of manufactures, against it. It's in nature."

Ivanhoe laughed. "There was an old preacher who said that the graciousness of God was shown by the fact that He always had fine harbors near great cities. But you may be right—men turn to rivers naturally. However, the railroads will certainly build in, in time, for express services and rapid passenger service. Now, if I were a clever man I'd buy a long stretch of land along the river somewhere along here between Keokuk and Ottumwa. Even Des Moines may come to something like a town in the next twenty years. That way you're safe both ways. The railroads will have to use some of it for their tracks, on account of the river hills beyond the lowland, and you'd have an outlet to the river."

"Nonsense!" Dunshee said again. "You overestimate the steam cars. Give me a good horse and I can short-cut over the hills from here to Keokuk faster than any railroad that can ever be built—short of an enormous investment for cuts and tunnels and gradings; why, man, think of what it would cost to build a track even seven miles from here to the corners at Brunswick. And there's your river, practically level except for the fall above the bend where there will certainly be a dam and locks for water power, anyway."

Ivanhoe was thinking. He would have to look at a map of Iowa again. "You're probably right—but if I decide to buy I don't see how I can go wrong by getting a slice of river front."

"More expensive, that's all. If you're going to buy you'd

better do it soon. We've had a few of the boys from the war drift in and take up their bounties west of us."

"Bounties?" said Ivanhoe.

"Yes, some of them get as much as a hundred and sixty acres. It will send prices up around here."

"Well, I'll be darned. I looked at the papers but I didn't see anything about it."

"There would have been your chance," Dunshee said, smiling. "Officers, musicians and the men mentioned in orders get the maximum. If you had twiddled your fiddle down at Vera Cruz you could have your horse farm for nothing."

"Hunh! Yes. Well, well, I'll write to Burlington tomorrow—a hundred and sixty acres will make a nice little beginning of a farm."

Dunshee brought down his thick Scotch brows incredulously. "You mean *you* were in the war—"

"Charley and I both got the Order of the Purple Heart —started by Washington, you know. It was a bully war—I learned a lot of good Mexican music—gitanas and boleros and malagueñas and so on. They don't dance like us—they get a lot more out of it."

"Please play some!" Evelyn demanded.

Ivanhoe glanced about. "Well, one or two—then I've got to go." He played a gypsy song that began with melancholy, worked up to frenzy and faded again in melancholy; then a suave aragonnaise and a wild bolero.

"You really need castanets and a tambourine to get the whole effect," he explained. "You can't quite make up for them with plucked strings."

"Did you see them dance?" Evelyn inquired.

"See them dance? Every gallon and neenyah in Mexico can dance like a tarantula. They've got some sense for it we norteamericanos missed out on."

"Do you mean," Dunshee asked with casual incredulity, "that they gave you a decoration for fiddling crazy jigs like that?"

Ivanhoe's face set hard and grim. "Not for that alone,

sir." He ran his finger along his scar, from cheek to chin. "It's late," he added, "and I have business. Good night, all."

Caesar Crawford's home was on the hill among the houses and offices of the county's other lawyers; the farm to which he had first taken Sue Ellison Crawford had been rented years before when Caesar's legal practice leaped into immediate prosperity. The house was lit so that Ivanhoe went up to the front door and knocked without an appointment.

Sue answered the door, matronly but charming in a loose house dress. "Oh, Ivanhoe, how nice of you to come calling —and with your violin! It's like the old days when you used to come around with new songs. I hope you've got one this time. The youngsters are all in bed but you couldn't wake them with a cannon. I hear you've been to St. Louis—tell me about it."

Ivanhoe laughed. "By and by. I want Caesar to do some business for me."

She pouted. "It took business to bring you here. All right, but we'll have a visit and some music afterward."

"We certainly will. Hardly got a word with you the other evening."

"Caesar's in his office—do you want to talk to him in there?"

"Yes—we won't bother you with a lot of business."

Caesar's first reaction was flippantly cheerful. "Well, well, Ivanhoe. What have you been doing? Not five-card monte or illegal sale of liquor, I hope. Those are pretty terrible crimes in Van Buren—at least that's been our crime problem for the last ten years. Sit down, man—want a cigar?"

Ivanhoe waved away the package and held out his own case filled with thin golden cigars. "I like a light smoke. Try one of these—they're wrapped in Habana for Dick—for a friend of mine."

They both lit up and Caesar glanced at his smoke appreciatively. "Don't blame you for refusing these stink-sticks we have up here. Well, let's get the business over with. Sue will want to hear you play."

"All right. I want to get a farm around here—need a

tenant, of course—I don't know a pig till it's roasted with an apple in its mouth. I'll need a good man with horses—I've got a nice bunch of thoroughbreds and thoroughbred Morgans down at Keokuk. Apparently I've got a hundred and sixty acre claim against the government for service in the Mexican War."

"In the war!"

"Captain of Michigan Volunteers—three citations—I'll bring you the papers tomorrow. You can take care of that for me. But that won't be enough. I figure about two sections but not in sections—six hundred and forty acres along the right bank of the river—say a half mile deep, roughly, and two miles long. Then we'll figure another section of wooded pasture—rough land but back so there won't be too many gullies. I understand that goes for a song."

"Do you know what this is going to cost? I can assemble it for you but the old dollar and a quarter days are over. The wood pasture—yes—we can get that for a song—fifteen hundred will be plenty, but you'll have to pay as high as twenty an acre for some of the good bottom land—it will average better than ten."

Ivanhoe took out a notebook and wrote:

"DEAR DICK:

"Am buying a farm. Please send me $8,000 in negotiable form. All well. Will be back as soon as I get the farm to going.
                                                                    "IVE."

He showed this to Caesar. "You better send a messenger, I guess, so the money won't get lost in the post. I'll give you a thousand dollars in the morning to guarantee his expenses and your fee."

"A messenger! Good God, I'll go myself!"

"Well, then catch the morning boat. I want to get this through. I'll send Sammy up with the thousand first thing tomorrow morning—six-thirty too early?"

"No—but I've got to clear things at the other office and pack—"

"Sammy'll pack for you in ten minutes—shave you, too —best shaver in the world—and see you on the boat. When you get to St. Louis go straight across the street from the dock to the brewery—the biggest one there, called Serenade Brews. Ask for Dick—Richard Byerley—the manager, and give him this note and he'll give you the money any way you want it—gold, draft, anything. Then you hustle back here and if I were you I'd try to get all the options and claim receipts the same day before they see what you're doing and raise the prices."

In spite of his professional aplomb, Caesar Crawford's eyes had widened. "By the Lord Harry! Then you *are* that Ivanhoe Keeler!"

"I suppose I must be the only Ivanhoe Keeler there is. Right name's Shadrach—I changed it to Ivanhoe when I left home—great book. Now, Caesar—you don't mind, do you—" Ivanhoe smiled friendlily—"after all, we're courters-in-law— not a word of this to anyone, see? Confidential between attorney and client when it comes out you've bought the land. I want you to get me the data on the stables and equipment I want to keep, say, about a hundred horses, self-sustaining operation. You might talk to Mr. Bogel and Agnew and Beggs—they're good farmers. You can do it casually, maybe laughing about my horse-farm project. I'll draw some plans for the house when you get the land. You'll handle that for me, too. I think we'll use the hard limestone from up Chequest, rough-cut—something that won't burn down or blow away."

"Sue knows you came here and that you're talking about a horse farm. She'll put two and two together when I begin to buy up the land."

Ivanhoe frowned. "Don't tell her much of anything. Whoever you're buying it for it's mostly a credit deal till the farm gets running. That impression won't hurt anything. Now I won't see much of you for a while—so there'll be no talk. Everything straight? I'll play a few tunes for Sue and you."

*　　　*　　　*

It was nearly ten o'clock before he got home but when he did there were three people waiting for him in the lobby. They were all talking together amiably and rapidly but with the courtesy that marked them as strangers with common interests.

They advanced on Ivanhoe together. The spokesman was a middle-aged to elderly man in eastern clothes. He wore a signet ring that was too large for his stubby fingers.

"Mr. Keeler, sir. These gentlemen and I have each ridden a considerable distance from different points to talk to you. I hope it isn't your bedtime."

"Not at all," Ivanhoe said, puzzled, considering that the news of Serenade must have got out and he probably had some promoters on his hands. "Anything I can do."

"We happened to get here almost together tonight—my name is Bakeless—from Ottumwa. I have the mill there. This is Mr. Lightscombe from Agency, and Mr. Pfeiffer from Farmington. We've got it all figured out that if you came to Ottumwa for a concert on Friday night—it's under a four-hour ride—you could make Agency the next day for a concert and dance there Saturday evening and Farmington Sunday evening for a concert there on Sunday evening at the church."

Ivanhoe laughed. "Well, that's pleasant but it sounds like a lot of riding. I'm up here unprofessionally. May I ask how you happened to hear of me?"

Mr. Bakeless smiled. "You're pretty well known in this corner of Iowa, Mr. Keeler. There are a lot of us that like music and remember it from the old days farther east. At fifty cents you could easily take fifty dollars in Ottumwa; with the dance in Agency you'd do as well or better there. They'll pay a flat fee of twenty-five dollars at Farmington, and that will leave you only two hours or so from Pittsville. Entertainment in each case of course."

"I'm here on other matters."

The big clerical-looking person from Farmington said, "No, no—but we can't have a European artist out here in our new country and not hear his music. Aside from wanting to hear the music—there hasn't been any of consequence around here yet—we can't let you go back to wherever you came from and report that we're a lot of unappreciative barbarians out here in Ioway. Wouldn't do."

Ivanhoe laughed. "Well, we'll figure out some programs. Jake! Will you get our coffee and the brown bag—you know which one."

*　　*　　*

It grew to be one of the busiest winters and springs of Ivanhoe's life and also of Sammy's. The colored man's expertness with banjo and guitar was celebrated from Dubuque to Keokuk, Peoria and Quincy, and his interludes for Ivanhoe's concerts grew to be almost as famous as the concerts themselves.

The gold pieces piled up in the bag but they were not allowed to rest there long. Two miles from Pittsville on a high hill overlooking the rippling "rapids" of the river half a dozen of the county's masons were chipping and fitting blocks of the almost granitic limestone of the creek ledges into the finest house the county had ever seen. There was some suspicion abroad that Keeler was building the house and going in over his head to do it. The county was settling rapidly; there was already an organ teacher in Bentonsport and the novelty of good music would not again pay four or five thousand dollars in a season as it had this year.

Late in March when a fine slate roof had made some of the rooms of the house fit for occupancy a farmer came in from Illinois with his family and began, with the help of his three sons, to break three hundred acres of flat bottom land and sloping hills for their crops. The farmer was no help; all he knew was that he had a fair contract with Caesar Crawford. Caesar was absolutely silent—no, it was not his farm; it was the farm of a client. The next rumor was that Ivanhoe had formed a company in his travels, or that Caesar was acting for some rich man in Dubuque or Burlington.

All they could get out of Ivanhoe was, "I'm a fiddler— what would I be doing with a farm?"

The only clue, and it was not highly regarded, was that the Crawfords suddenly developed an interest in music and Caesar bought Sue a piano on which she hammered faithfully and finally with some success for two hours every day, including Sunday.

Gossip started when Evelyn, Ivanhoe, and Samaliel gave a concert at the community church five miles from town. It was a great event—all the people from two towns and half a dozen villages crowded the little building and the yard outside the windows and doors. It was, fortunately, one of the balmy March evenings which are quite frequently followed by April snowstorms in Iowa. The newly formed Ladies' Aid took in nearly a hundred dollars, by the sale of sandwiches, coffee and lemonade, toward the building of a fine new brick church.

Miss Dunshee and Mr. Keeler played things from Chopin and Mozart; then the colored man played some Mexican tunes on his guitar; then Miss Dunshee and Mr. Keeler played a potpourri of songs everybody knew and the Kreutzer Sonata by Beethoven that had some lovely religious music in it.

When they finished it Keeler lifted Miss Dunshee's hand, as they bowed for the applause, and everybody thought for a minute that he was going to kiss it, as he might have learned to do in Paris, France.

He was overheard by the preacher and the deacons on the platform to say, "You'll be good enough to tour with me next winter," and she said, "Maybe I'll be so good I won't need a fiddler along."

Agnew, who was one of everything, from supervisor to deacon, whispered quite contentedly to the preacher, "If Ernie doesn't watch out he's going to have his girl fiddled away from him."

Samaliel played some curious toe-tipping music to his banjo and crooned funny little verses with it, with the names and foibles of the county's prominent residents represented and the audience rocked the poor little wooden church. Then

Evelyn and Ivanhoe played Schubert's "Good Night" and spent half an hour taking handshakes and congratulations as if they'd just been married.

Ernie drove Evelyn home while Mr. Bogel and Mr. Dunshee and Samaliel and Ivanhoe fussed at getting the piano back on a stone-boat headed for the Dunshee home. The tuner from Keokuk alone had cost fifteen dollars for the two tunings—they said that Mr. Keeler had arranged for him and paid him to help out the church. A fool and his money, a lot of them said, but the opinion at the Four Corner Church was that Mr. Keeler was certainly going to heaven, even if he wasn't churchgoing, though without the embarrassment of having to ride in on a camel through the eye of a needle.

Sammy managed some punch in the tavern kitchen, after his exertions with music and the piano. He brought it to Ivanhoe steaming.

"Sammy, sit down."

"I've been sitting, sir. I'd as soon stand, sir."

"Don't be so God-damn punctilious. You're a free man—if they knew what you had here you'd pass for a rich man. Sit down."

"Yes, sir." Sammy put a flange of his hips lightly on the edge of a chair.

"The house is about finished, Sammy; we'll send up a piano and some furniture from St. Louis. I've got fifteen fillies that'll be ready to breed pretty soon coming up from Keokuk. We'll buy a good stallion in St. Louis. That'll give us eighteen mares, two foals and a stallion to start out with. If they build the bridge they're talking about it will be down toward the mill and the ford—fine place for a tavern. I've—Caesar got me four lots there. I think I'll have you and your family"—Ivanhoe grinned fiendishly; Charley had written him of his discovery through Ilse and her devious female sources that there would be still another Sammy along toward autumn—"fix me up a hotel there."

"Yes, sir," Sammy said faintly.

"Don't try to fill the whole damn thing all by yourself.

That finishes us up here. If I stick around here Dunshee's going to go crazy and do something silly. I didn't plan that. It would upset Evelyn. I've had my fun—he'll never be the same little Dunshee he was when I came here—and I'm going to let it out who owns that limestone house, so that he won't forget me. You're a married man with a family—it's time for you to settle down and run this bedless tavern out of business —oh, give Jake a job when you open—and take care of your friends out in the kitchen—I'll turn it all over to you. You've got a better head than me, anyway, except for music. You're always running after novelties in music."

"Yes, sir."

"Spend ten thousand if you want to. I'll be back up in the fall."

"Back up, sir?"

"I'm taking the boat day after tomorrow. I'll send your —family—mmm, your family—back right away. You deal with Caesar Crawford and get things moving on the tavern. Oh—Sammy—you might have a little subbasement in case any of your friends, of color, happen to pass by this way, leaving the South."

"I'll pay for that myself, sir. But, Mr. Ivanhoe—"

"Good boy. That settles everything. I'm leaving most of my razors—I'll be in and out of here toward the end of the year. I may even stay here a while next winter. But I haven't played fair, Sammy. It's time for me to get out."

"I beg your pardon, sir. It's not fitting for me to say— I'm sorry, sir. Do you think Miss Evelyn will be surprised?"

"That's all right. Yes, she will be. Sammy, we've been through enough—well, an artist has a false advantage. She likes music, God bless her, and I'm a better musician than Ernie. But old Ellison was right. Why, for Christ sake, if I had to stay here and actually run that horse farm or do anything solid or important, even in this half-tamed jungle, I'd be the most miserable failure that ever came into Iowa. If I just disappear for three or four months she'll get her senses again and when she and Ernie get settled I can come back.

This is a good place, Sammy; and it's very safe for you—handy to Charley and Dick, too."

Sammy moved his lips and Ivanhoe smiled and waited for his protest.

It was a very faint and dubious, "Yes. sir."

PART VII

DEATH OF A MISTRESS

I

A MAN who is about to destroy himself may sometimes have an instant's pride when his finger pulls on the trigger or his foot kicks away the bucket and leaves him on the noose. These are the finalities which are far above the braveries of chance—a man who knows he has no chances in a hundred is incomparably braver than a man who has one chance in a million, in any circumstances.

Ivanhoe looked with a kind of relief at the bags and boxes that Samaliel had packed so carefully. If it were done, then 'twere well it were done quickly, and after all the futile little fevers of his life it was good to know that he had finally found his true love and that she was as much lost to him as if they were both where they would, after all, finally be—neatly dressed and handsomely cased and shedding their graces and the fine needlings on their brains into digestive earth.

It was good to have found her and known her for his beloved; to have defined his futility and incapacity for himself; to know that his life had been destined for nothing and had come to nothing while small, pleasing achievements and gaieties were still in his reach. Now he had no responsibility to himself—God would probably give him twenty years or more as a favored and delighted observer of people who were cursed with duties and immortality and permanent affections. There was some story about an Undine who went to unreasonable extremes to gain a soul. Whether the soul was actually delivered was highly speculative.

He was old enough to know that the little pain in his heart, which would be with him all his life, would come to be a treasure; the memory of beauty that always defeats desire and the childish craving for possession.

This was concluded and he had serenity once more, and his violin.

He said, "Come in" quite calmly to the knock at the door. He was dressed for the day's good-byes.

Old Jake held out an impressive envelope. "It's a telegraph from Burlington, Mr. Keeler. Governor Briggs is going over the state. Bet anything they want you to play."

"That's right," said Ivanhoe, glancing at the message. "I'm going to St. Louis tomorrow morning for a few months. I can't do it. Tell the messenger to put that on the wire wherever the wire is."

"But the governor—?"

"Too bad. I'm leaving tomorrow morning."

It was not ten minutes before the jerry line up the river brought a message from Iowa College in Davenport. A little later Ivanhoe heard from Dubuque and Keokuk, also on the governor's route—fifty dollars and entertainment. A rider came in from Farmington, down the river, with news that Ivanhoe might appear in Keokuk with Mr. Lincoln, the Illinois politician, if Mr. Lincoln could arrange his speeches. Ivanhoe answered this bluntly, "I fought in Mexico, so Mr. Lincoln would consider me unconstitutional."

It was near noon when the handy man came from Dunshee's store to tell Ivanhoe that Mr. Dunshee wanted a few minutes with him.

"Anyone can speak to me that wants to," Ivanhoe said, while he arranged some music for packing.

"But he wondered if you could come over to the office for a moment."

"You can see that I can't. I've got to catch the morning boat."

The man was appalled. "But—it's Governor Briggs! He'll be here in four days!"

"He'll miss me by three," Ivanhoe said. "If he and Dunshee want to see me I'll give you my address in St. Louis."

It was bitter, after all. His temper was not good.

"It's very important, Mr. Keeler. Mr. Dunshee and Mr. Briggs are old friends. Mr. Briggs asked particularly if he could hear you at the reception. I think that Mr. Dunshee assured him that he could—"

"Mr. Dunshee must have been a bloody fool if he did."

"Mr. Keeler. Everyone has heard about you. The governor particularly wishes—"

"If wishes were horses beggars could ride. I'm leaving for several months tomorrow morning."

"But, Mr. Keeler. It's the governor of Iowa!"

"Hell's fire! I never heard of him. I couldn't fool with him if he was the King of England. I've got pressing affairs."

"Mr. Keeler," the man said piteously, "I can't take that answer back to Mr. Dunshee. Don't you see—?"

"Oh—I see. Sammy!"

Sammy would never get used to Ivanhoe but he kept his face perfectly expressionless except for his eyes, which widened and moved while he waited for the newest wonder or monstrosity.

"Sammy, you go with our friend here and tell Mr. Dunshee that I can see visitors in about half an hour. I'm very busy, preparing to leave."

There were two hard vertical lines down the sides of Sammy's face. He broke them with crisp little dashes in the middle. "That's all, sir? I have no authority to say anything more?"

Ivanhoe compressed his lips and bulged his cheeks with a laugh. "Don't stand there and ask me questions. Were you a soldier or weren't you?"

"Very good, sir."

"Don't say that, either. It sounds like the damn-fool butlers and things. You tell him what I said and then you say 'Very good, sir' to him—don't say it to me."

It was twenty minutes before Dunshee's chief clerk found Ivanhoe in the lobby, where he was quietly drinking hot Bourbon and lemon. The chief clerk of the Dunshee company was a moderately important man; he had a small share in the business and other resources.

"Mr. Keeler, sir!"

"Go up and see my man and find out whether I'm busy. Hey! Sammy!"

From upstairs there came a faint "Yes, sir?"

"I'm busy. I can't be seen unless Old Dunshee comes over."

"Yes, sir."

Ivanhoe raised his brows and turned to the clerk. "You can go see Sammy if you want to, but I'm sure I'm busy."

"Mr. Keeler—Mr. Dunshee will pay anything in reason."

"Tell him I'll give him fifty dollars to play the fiddle himself."

"But he can't play a fiddle!"

"Tell him I'll give him a hundred. He can learn. That's all—good-by."

Ivanhoe glanced at the Dubuque newspaper. Primitive Cistercians that didn't speak settling up by Dubuque—well! —example of piety no doubt, but if you wanted to keep these Iowans from spouting, paralysis would be better than piety. Vows of silence—Ivanhoe laughed. Hell, one-fifth of a man's life is sound and out here where little news was all the news, talk and noise ran well over the physiological ratio.

He was still smiling when the faint rottenish smell of camellias intruded upon the nutty flavor of his latest cigar.

Evelyn was across the table. "What is this foolishness about going away and not playing for the governor?"

He gave her a friendly smile—perhaps it might be possible to like Evelyn after a while, without loving her. "I have to go away."

"Dad was wild but he had to settle down. The beauty of my smile and the soft words from my coral lips are supposed to fix everything. You won't let me down and shatter my father's trust, will you?"

"Why not?"

"You're going—you won't play?"

"I think these things ought to be talked over by the men concerned." He touched his fingers to his lips. "I'll come up and say good-by before I go, if you'll let me."

She looked at him directly with the funny little twisted

grin that she could command when she pleased. Her face was so bright and lovely!

"If I go out of here now, with that for the last word, you'll please not try to talk to me again."

Ivanhoe shrugged. "I'd like to keep a better memory but it's all right. A clean break. A clean break of nothing. You still need to work on your left hand—it would be a shame to give it up now when it's coming—"

"You're a little butterfly like they said—a kind of dusty little butterfly!"

"What's the matter? I've never done anything to you!"

"You're just spoiling my father's whole party. The governor mentioned you especially. Father knew when he sent me here that you'd come and play and now you won't. It's the worst humiliation anybody could have."

Ivanhoe played a little arpeggio on the rough table with his right four fingers, and then again and again.

"Musicians set their prices—you can't just fling them a bone, you know, and expect them to bark and jump around. I'll play for your father's party if I can sleep on the best bed in the house and have breakfast with all of you afterward."

"What! Are you crazy?—why the best bed? He'll never do it."

"It's not what you think. If he wants to come and guarantee it, I'll waste a little time on him. My boat goes in the early morning."

"You're stubborn!"

"I've got to that. An improvement, eh?"

"Thank you for the help on the piano. Good-by, Mr. Keeler."

It was almost an hour before Dunshee came into the lobby, straight, thin, erect and furious.

* * *

Dunshee had a big house. The principal bedroom, he explained, had been assigned to Governor Briggs with two other rooms for the immediate members of his party. He himself was sleeping in a small semiattic room—three steps up to see the roof. There was simply not room for Ivanhoe and no occasion for his demand. "Dammit, sir, I'll have any food and any drink you want sent down here punctually, but don't you see that you'd crowd me out of my own house? And put the governor in a small room?"

Ivanhoe was apparently weary to the point of sleep. "I see that very clearly, sir. But the demands on an artist—you understand. Why, there's no difficulty! You can have my room here!"

"I sleep in my own house, sir!"

"By God, that's more than you could do in your own tavern. You notice that my mattress is made up on the floor. You can't use that—it's a very expensive mattress. You will use your own reverent springs."

"By Jehovah, you'll hear about this!"

"Use plenty of postage. I'll be halfway to St. Louis this time tomorrow."

Dunshee smiled thinly. "You don't have any investment about here, I suppose. No house, no barns, no acres?"

"What makes you say that?"

"Somebody's pouring out money up along the valley."

Ivanhoe shrugged. "Eccentric millionaire."

"Momentary millionaire, perhaps," said Dunshee. "I know that you've had a good season. But successful business is done largely on credit in growing country, young sir, and if I guess correctly you'll have a section of land and your buildings to pay on for a while to come."

Ivanhoe yawned. "*You* wouldn't lend me money if I brought the Vatican Choir and Hector Berlioz over to accompany me." He straightened and his voice was hard and severe. "Listen, you! I'm a busy man. The proposition is straight out and open and I won't move from it an inch or any part of an inch. I'll play for you and your governor as much as you please, but when I get through I go to bed in your best chamber on your best mattress. Take it or leave it."

"You're crazy! You're threatening me! What is this lunacy about the best bed in the house?"

"Look. I don't want to seem unreasonable. Come on up-stairs with me."

He hurried ahead up the stairs and Dunshee had nothing to do but follow him, grumbling protests.

Ivanhoe stripped the covers from the mattress on the bed with one savage jerk. It revealed a sagging swing of denim, cobbled with uneven springs; in the valley at the center the mattress was merely depressed and dead.

"I'm going to make a speech," Ivanhoe announced. "Don't interrupt me or I won't talk to you at all any more." He cleared his throat and waved an eloquent hand at the mattress. "You call that a mattress! *There's* a mattress—on the floor—sit on it, lie on it, jump on it; that's the best mattress that can be bought in the city of St. Louis—on the floor.

"When I left home twenty years ago and more, I slept two nights on the ground in the woods. Then I slept on a board bunk in a steamboat cabin and after that for years I mostly slept on the floors of taverns that never had any beds left to rent. It was three or four years before I began to make enough money so I could go to Cincinnati to a concert once in a while and sleep on a real feather mattress.

"Years went by. I slept on pallets in the woods and on rope webbing in little frontier cabins and taverns. I was in this country before you ever heard of it, sleeping on dirt floors and playing for the first settlers. I've rolled in the berths of ocean steamers on stormy nights and scrunched myself together in railroad carriages. I've slept on battlefields with and without tents—I've even slept on horseback.

"So, I come back here to seek some creature comforts and maybe settle down in my declining years and, by the great Jehovah, I find this country that I practically helped to settle tyrannized over by a cheap, Yankee Caligula, Torque-mada and Bloody Jeffreys all rolled into one. Not content with stretching out your claws over the foul web of wealth you've woven over the country, by God, you ordain in your might that helpless travelers to your empire must stretch their weary bodies out on such diabolical and ingeniously and awfully inhuman wrecks of a torture rack as that contrivance there.

"This is a fitting cause for me, in itself, but you have seen fit, sir, to treat me lightly as a wandering fiddler and so I take it also as a symbol. I am not a fiddler—I am an artist. I have played before audiences whose least member would have considered you a virtually indigent villager; an uncouth Yankee backwoodsman. You have made a bad mistake, sir, as you now learn when you need a fiddler."

Dunshee, from being enraged, had now grown amused at Ivanhoe's diatribe. "Pshaw, man, put your mattress on the bed if it will make you feel any better. But you can't ignore the governor's own request."

"I can't? I'm going to accept two of my invitations and play for him in Keokuk and Farmington. You've heard my terms—whether I play for him in Pittsville is entirely up to you. Good day, sir."

Dunshee shrugged his shoulders. "We'll find some other musician for him around the county, or near by. Please don't forget that this room will be engaged after the end of the month."

"I'll have other quarters by that time. If you change your mind before I come back from Keokuk you can leave word with Jake at the desk."

Dunshee left in a queer humor—amused, angry and uneasy. The damned young puppy with his high-flown speeches! Yet, somehow, during the spring he must have made himself something of a figure in the state or Briggs would not have mentioned him. It was also a chance to show off Evelyn's playing for Briggs and his party—he doubted that Evelyn would consent to play alone; she always insisted that she wasn't good enough. Good enough! She was good enough to play every other evening with that young popinjay that she said was an "artist." Poor Ernie'd hardly had a chance with her at all—it was a good thing that that was practically settled.

The devil of it was that the fiddler would most certainly

stick to his guns unless something could be invented and pro-
posed—something—anything. But Dunshee had no ideas.

Ivanhoe sat thinking for a while after Dunshee had left,
then he grinned and went down to find Sammy. Davenport
was too far away but he might ride over to Burlington and
wait for the governor to arrive three days later. No use to
tell anyone where he was going—he'd said he was going to
St. Louis. Dunshee would have to change his mind fast when
Ivanhoe returned because he planned to return with the governor.

*   *   *

Burlington was a bully town, though too nearly vertical
in spots. Close to three thousand people at the very least,
Ivanhoe guessed, but down toward the docks it was, like St.
Louis, big enough for a town three times its size. Ivanhoe and
Sammy arrived in late afternoon, found a tidy livery stable
and accepted its proprietor's advice on a tavern. Ivanhoe sent
Sammy out to find the man whose name was on the telegram
and treated himself to a bath and a change of costume.

He then sat down and practiced on his violin till he
could get word from Mr. James Edwards, the proprietor of
the Burlington *Hawk-Eye*.

The word that came was Mr. Edwards himself, announced by Samaliel. The two men shook hands warmly.
The Burlington *Hawk-Eye* had been particularly warm in
reporting Ivanhoe's concert some months before and Edwards, together with other citizens, had been insistent that
Ivanhoe must come back and give some concerts in the park
during the summer.

"Good Lord, man, you gave us an awful scare. We were
almost sure you would reconsider, but some of the committee
said you never could tell what a musician might do and
we've been shaking in our boots all afternoon. We had a
notion you wouldn't want to go as far as Davenport and so
did the governor's party, so they asked us to make a special
point to see that you were here. You must have started about
ten minutes after you sent us your message."

"I did. I ran into business that will keep me in Iowa for

a while and affairs in St. Louis can wait. I figured I could bring word myself in about the time and a lot more accurately than the telegraph machines would bring it."

"Well, we're sure glad to see you. You know why Briggs has made a special request for you, don't you?"

Ivanhoe looked at him stupidly. "I suppose he likes fiddle music."

Edwards laughed. "Don't come the rustic on us here, Ivanhoe—we folks in Burlington know the difference between a fiddler and a violinist. He wants you for the same reason he wants this tour. Iowa has been pretty wild, free country—when I called our folks Hawkeyes I was thinking about the birds as well as their eyes. The first governors are always in a bad spot—it takes taxes and diplomacy to improve a country and new restraints to order it. Briggs has had two terms but he's got a duty to his party and he wants the state to understand just what the Democrats have done for it and plan for it."

"I'm a Whig," said Ivanhoe. "Like my old commander. Look how the Democrats treated him."

Edwards grinned. "That's all right—you can be a purple-pated gazoombus if you feel like it, but you'll find that Briggs is a fine man, and we're too busy with our own affairs back here in Iowa to let the shystering back in Washington bother us. Parties will relocate on slavery in a few years anyway, and then I think you'll be a Democrat if toting a nigger all over America and Europe and Mexico is any criterion."

"First thing I did when I bought Sammy was to turn him free."

"Free?" Edwards laughed. "Yes, that made him a worse slave than ever. Didn't you say he had a family in St. Louis? Why isn't he with it?"

"I'm fixing to get them all settled up here on free soil."

"Did this free slave suggest being settled with you up here in Iowa? Did he suggest coming here?"

"All right—I couldn't get along without Sammy but he couldn't get along without me, either."

"The little I saw of the two of you, I think there's no doubt of that. But this isn't a matter of slavery—I shouldn't have brought it up. It's a matter of helping out one of the first big men in the state of Iowa. If you're going to be one of us up here you ought to be one of us the whole way through. Now, I don't think the Whigs have seen your particular importance, your possible usefulness, to a little raw state whose international background is a tendency to damn England and the Frogs for irrelevant and obsolete reasons, and damn the rest of Europe as being connected with them over across the ocean; and a state whose cultural accomplishment thus far consists of a few horrible ballads and funerary verses for the newspapers and some artistry at doing hymns on old parlor organs."

"Crayon pictures of ancient Scottish castles and bowls of pansies," Ivanhoe murmured.

"And colored enlargement of daguerreotypes. That's it. You could be a useful citizen of this state, Ivanhoe. You're known and you're popular all through the east and southeast. Every time there's a dance, from Davenport to Keokuk back to Mt. Pleasant, there's bound to be a dozen people there say, 'Too bad they couldn't get Keeler to fiddle for the dance and play us some music.' You see, they don't underestimate you even when they talk about 'fiddling' for a dance—that's the best music for dancing but they know that's the least part of your art."

"You are about the oiliest, most flattering, cajoling son of a gun I ever ran into, if you'll pardon my saying so, Mr. Edwards. But I am flattered that you'd take so much trouble to think up these beautiful inventions. But in short, you want me to be the dancing bear for Governor Briggs's entertainments."

A look of the most exquisite anguish crossed Edwards's face but his eyes twinkled. "Mr. Keeler, you insult the great art of music when you say a thing like that.—And it honestly isn't quite true. Wait till you see Briggs. He's got another speech for you if mine doesn't work."

Ivanhoe laughed at this bit of candor. "I'll see the governor. If he seems to be as represented, I'm not enough of a partisan—except for what the Democrats did to General Scott—to let it stand in the way. If he doesn't seem to be quite my style—which is no criticism, mark you—I wouldn't get mixed up in the business if he were running with the Twelve Apostles on a platform of free manna for everybody."

Edwards nodded. "We expected that. You won't be able to pick a hole in Ansel Briggs. We'll count on you."

"Not yet," said Ivanhoe, smiling. "We'll hope for the best."

"There's one other thing I want to ask you about—purely as the proprietor of a newspaper."

"Fire ahead."

"Did you ever hear of a brewery in St. Louis whose president has the same name as yours?"

"Oh, yes. Funny, isn't it?" Ivanhoe said casually.

"Yes. It's funny, too, that they'd call the brews—they're getting very popular along the river—'Serenade Brews'—sounds like a name a musician would pick."

"All the Germans are great for Ständchen and sentimental music."

"It's even more curious, Ivanhoe, that your head is on the kegs."

"It would take a newspaper editor to find a resemblance in a brand picture."

Edwards laughed. "What's this masquerade? I haven't published the story yet because Briggs's tour was being planned two months ago and when I got the facts it was obvious that you wanted to remain incognito, but I know almost all about you from the Sue Ellison business to Europe, and then from Europe where your friend Charley Hoskin almost whipped Bendigo from St. Louis down to Mexico and on through the war. You've got the Purple Heart and three citations and you got that scar at Chapultepec. Your man is one of the very few colored men ever to have been mentioned in the orders of an American army. I got the whole history of the brewery from their salesman. You're one of the richest men in Iowa if you stay in Iowa. What's your idea?"

Ivanhoe looked at the editor thoughtfully. "I don't know quite whether I can make it clear—all the things you're talking about just happened to me. But I started out to be a violinist and that's what I got to be without luck. I had a lot of fun this winter; apparently I helped a lot of people have some and I made twice enough money to keep Sammy and me without trying. I'm not a brewer—why should I go around being a big brewer when I'm a violinist?"

"I see what you mean. It'll come out, of course, but you're pretty well-established up here in your proper person. I'm not putting any pressure on you, understand, but if you could add a solid place in our Iowa affairs to what they already know of you, they wouldn't say, 'My God, that's the rich brewer from St. Louis.' They'd say, 'Oh, yes, that's Ive Keeler—big man in the state. He's got a big brewery somewhere, too. He's a dandy violinist.'"

"No—no pressure. I'll think about it but I want to see your governor."

"Only one thing I want to ask of you—let me know first when you're willing the word should be let out. Make me a nice story for the paper."

"All right. Give me two weeks. I've got one item of business back in Pittsville and then I'm going down to St. Louis. My man and his family will stay here—I've got business for him. I may be gone for a while. I've got a notion I may need an ocean trip."

"Nonsense, man! You look as if you'd bust out of your clothes if you were any healthier."

"I'm healthy. But you never can tell when you might need an ocean trip."

Edwards chuckled. "You're a strange one—but I like puzzles. Well, if you'll pack your things we'll put you up at Silas Hudson's, where the governor is going to stay. Silas is a Whig but he's a friend of the governor's. He knows everybody in politics; he's an old-timer. Great friend of Honorable Abe Lincoln over in Illinois—the young fellow that made such a fuss about your war; so watch what you say about the war."

"Whigs making a fuss about the war!"

"All tarred with the same brush," Edwards said, smiling. "By the way, Briggs was in favor of it, Democrat or no Democrat. So was I."

"Perhaps if the objectors been down there and seen the condition of that country they might have had other ideas. Santa Anna's no better than a good brigand and outlaws run the country."

"You can't argue with me about the war. You haven't unpacked many of your things, have you? My carriage is downstairs."

"Your man Briggs sounds all right. I wish this Lincoln fellow could have known General Scott and Lee and Grant and Jackson and some of the people who were fighting down there and thought they were doing the right thing. They might have given the fellow some ideas."

*   *   *

Ivanhoe met Governor Briggs three evenings later in the fine new house of Silas Hudson. The two evenings of waiting had been two receptions, for it would not have been possible for Ivanhoe to stay in any great house with pianists available about the city and not play for his supper or, at least, out of good nature. He was a little bit puzzled at the deference that met him everywhere until it occurred to him that Edwards might not have been completely tight-mouthed about Serenade Brews.

The governor was a dignified man in the best of his mature years, but he was a politician, as a man had to be with frontier voters who were likely to shy, kick and bolt at the slightest excuse, for the fun of an argument or just general hellishness. He was as candid, however, as Edwards had been in an oblique way, and he and Ivanhoe liked each other. He was much interested in the war and the political side of the war as the soldiers had seen it. He shook his head and clucked sympathetically as Ivanhoe told of the nearly disastrous insubordination and enterprises of Scott's Washington generals.

"You can rest easy about that, Captain Keeler—the country suspected those generals and the suspicion is growing."

"It will grow a good deal faster when the last soldiers are back from Mexico, sir."

"No doubt. But the party quarrel will soon be Free Soil and the Constitution. No one can see yet what will come of it. Webster is an irritable old windbag, but he's powerful."

"I have nothing to say for that Yankee, sir, after his appraisal of the value of our new territories."

Briggs chuckled. "Not enough boulders and timber wastes in them for a New Englander. How could they build fences without any rocks? What would they do for stony mountains to keep their cattle exercised?"

They had a very good time for the next week. From Burlington they cut back to Mt. Pleasant to speak at the little new college there; then back to Burlington where they caught the boat to Ft. Madison and afterward on down the river to Keokuk. From Keokuk they went up to Farmington on a boat specially decorated for the governor, and there Samaliel, who had been sent ahead, came down on his own horse, leading Ivanhoe's, and Ivanhoe promised to greet the party at the Pittsville dock in the morning.

The news of Ivanhoe's attachment to the governor's party had preceded him. Old Jake was startled and he attempted to be obsequious when Ivanhoe came in at three o'clock in the morning.

"Is the governor with you?"

"No, they won't be in till morning. Coffee hot?"

"Oh, yes, sir! Everything's ready for any emergency. Mr. Dunshee thought you'd be up on the boat, but we've all stayed ready."

"They won't be here till the morning boat. Sammy, throw out the coffee and fix some for us out of the bag I got at Keokuk."

Sammy took less than ten minutes to grind the coffee

and boil it. Ivanhoe gave it the usual treatment with a bottle from one of his bags and he and Jake sat across the table and enjoyed themselves.

"What goes on?" Ivanhoe asked.

"What doesn't go on?" Jake said. "Don't look so blazzy. Governor here on the morning boat—we've heard about you, Colonel Keeler."

Ivanhoe looked at him quickly and laughed. "I'll stick to 'Captain' among friends, Jake. Or even 'Ivanhoe.' How'd you hear?"

Jake sipped at his coffee, made a horrible face and licked his lips. Then he turned his old head politely as if he were about to sneeze or cough or utter some other unpleasant emission, but it amounted to nothing but a soundless laugh.

"We got all new mattresses yesterday, Mr. Keeler—colonel—Ivanhoe."

"Too late," Ivanhoe said. "I'm going to run this tavern out of business. Don't you worry, Jake. One of the reasons I'm going to put it out of business is that I'm going to hire you. Best damn clerk—manager—I've ever seen, working under blankets. Huh! Blankets is right. You'll get a real chance to express your art. Sammy will be the steward but you'll be the manager. It'll be my hotel and you two won't disagree."

"Colonel Keeler!"

"Captain."

"Colonel Keeler—can you really do it? You do about what you please, but Mr. Dunshee—"

"A hollow shell. Don't you worry, Jake. If you stick with me I'll give you a thousand dollars, no matter what happens." Ivanhoe took some more coffee. "I'm tired as all hell. When did Dunshee get the mattresses?"

"The *Hawk-Eye* came down four days ago, colonel—saying you was a colonel on the governor's staff. There'll be more than forty people here from Keokuk and Farmington—so Mr. Dunshee changed the beds. We got what they had in Keokuk and there'll be more from St. Louis on the morning boat."

"Sammy!"

Samaliel, in the kitchen, making some hot sandwiches, heard that voice as he had heard it on battlefields and back-stages.

"Yes, sir?"

"Get our things ready to move on the evening boat to-morrow. The old snake has outguessed me on the beds." Ivanhoe put his finger at the corner of his nose and smiled. "We did a good work here. It's a victory of sorts. Now we'll get back to somewhere else."

"The house, sir—the hotel?"

"The deuce with them. Send the horses back down to Keokuk. I've got the bit in my teeth, Sammy. We're going to Cincinnati, Philadelphia, New York, Boston—back to England and Paris. The governor's folks can sleep in good beds—don't forget to bring our mattresses. I'm all through here."

Samaliel's smile was to himself. "You promised the governor—"

Ivanhoe hesitated. "Yes. We'll catch the morning boat next day."

Sammy said, "About Mr. Jake?"

"Good God! Can't a man open his mouth? He can go down to Dick—Dick will find something better than this for him."

"Then I'll pack, sir, for next-day morning."

"I'm going to bed."

*　　*　　*

On his bed, though, he reflected. He couldn't take Sammy away from the home and the projects he had assigned him and his family, and he had his promise to Briggs.

He grinned at the new beds and also at the fact that when Dunshee got ready to buy steamboat landings or rail ports he would be blocked by two miles of acres along the river. In a day or two men would be digging at the founda-tions of what would be the best hotel in Iowa.

After the long life contained by his few years he frowned at the idea of Evelyn, so exquisitely and essentially desirable. But there had been other girls without whom he could not live, and the rude and dusty answer was that he still lived. He sang himself to sleep on the lesser Guarnerius, his old love—he could make it husky and rich, or shrill and specific as he chose. The girl never argued or failed to respond. When he wanted a chord he always got it.

He was wakened by Jake. "Governor's boat sighted at Shultz's Bend, Colonel—Captain Keeler."

"All right, thanks. Sammy!"

"Yes, sir." The communicating door opened.

"What do you suppose I ought to wear, Sammy?"

Sammy was emptying a jug of hot water into a small basin. "If you'll sit over here, sir. I've got your uniform in order, sir. Since you got your commission, sir, I think you'd be proper in military dress."

"Sword shined up?"

"Sir?"

"I'm sorry. Go ahead, Sammy."

The dockside was gay with the costumes of a thousand people from all the county. The little river boat let out a continuous whistle from the time it became visible beyond the corner of the oxbow till it was dragged and virtually held by some hundreds of eager hands on the ropes at the Pittsville pier. The crowd stood back respectfully for Caesar, Dunshee, Agnew, Jesse Ellison, Beggs and all of the selected committee.

Caesar made a speech—short and sensible, Ivanhoe thought. There was a good, sound, realistic streak in Sue—these two must understand each other, for Caesar never used a hundred words when three would do.

Dunshee welcomed the governor in the hundred words that Caesar had omitted, and some other hundreds. The governor received this with a gentle, appreciative and dignified smile. Then he came down the plank and shook hands for fifteen minutes. After a while he extricated himself and he and Dunshee rode up the hill together in Dunshee's car-

riage, with the party following in the other carriages that
had been arranged. Ivanhoe had stood back from the affair,
awfully admired by all the children of Pittsville, who regarded swords highly.

It was not ten minutes after Ivanhoe had returned to
the hotel before Jake knocked at the door.

"Mr. Dunshee, sir, didn't know that you would be here.
The governor has asked about you. They wonder if you
would join them at lunch."

Ivanhoe grinned. "Listen, Jake. Dunshee knew I was
here the first thing this morning, didn't he?"

Jake looked at the corner of the room.

"All right. Tell him that I have eaten but that I want to
be of as much help as possible. Give him this. Tell him to go
ahead and use it." Ivanhoe put back his inlaid Tourte bow
and took one of his practice bows. With two twists he re-
moved the hair and gave Jake the empty frame. "See that he
gets that."

Ivanhoe lay down on the bed and got the rest of his
sleep.   *   *   *

Dunshee came about six o'clock while Ivanhoe was still
in bed. "You've got me. I've been putting the governor off
from minute to minute. He's surprised that you didn't join
his party at the boat, as you promised."

Ivanhoe gave a small gasp and took a short, deep breath
for an eye-opener. "I was there. There was such a crowd
and a lot of talk."

Dunshee did not wince. "Well, we want you up there
right now, to plan for this evening. There's a talk in the
park and a reception at my house."

"Good! Briggs is a nice old chap." He gave up the sock
which he was measuring, apparently, to see if it still fit his
foot. "I'll find out about it tomorrow. Your servant, Dunshee." He rolled back on the bed and closed his eyes.

"Keeler! I could overlook—you can't be impertinent to
the governor!"

Ivanhoe raised his eyelids slowly. "Not impertinent to

anyone. You are the one who's impertinent. I asked for a trifling accommodation. You didn't find it convenient."

"But the *governor* has to sleep in that room!"

"Too bad. A politician ought to learn to sleep in all kinds of beds."

"Do you think a fiddler ought to outrank the governor?"

"A fiddler? No."

"The hell with you, you conceited pup."

"The same to you, you overstuffed jackass, if compliments are in order."

Dunshee slammed the door and stalked down the hall. At the stair, he paused. Ivanhoe grinned and gave a credible "sizzz-hoooosh" of deep slumber when Dunshee came lightly to his door. The rap came immediately.

"Good God, sir! I need a little rest! I rode last night."

"Never mind. You can have the bed. I have to do it, but we'll have some more affairs a little later, Mr. Fiddler, if you don't run away."

"That's unfriendly. What time is supper?"

"At six. I don't suppose you mind hours but this is at six, promptly."

"I'll come in a little before. Miss Evelyn and I will want to plan the music.—Eh! I don't use a pillow—sleep with my back straight. If you want, Sammy can shave you after he gets through with me. He shaves better than any barber you ever heard of."

"I don't want."

Ivanhoe shook his head. "Too bad. You underestimate Sammy!" He shook it again. "A general failing of yours, Mr. Dunshee, if you don't mind."

Dunshee smiled, the elderly and patronizing smile of greater age, but he held his lips tight in a promise of things to come.

Ivanhoe called, "Sammy!"

"Yes, sir?"

"You'd better touch me up with the razors—I've got to

go to a party.—No, no—don't hurry off, Dunshee. I can talk while Sammy shaves."

"I'll see you a little before six."

*   *   *

There was another rap on the door just after Samaliel had finished and Jake entered. "A gentleman, sir."

But there came the high and hearty voice, "The hell with that! Ive, will you let me in or shall I come in and drag you out?"

"Charley! (It's all right, Jake.) What are you doing here?"

Charley was a mirror of fashion from his gray top hat to his varnished boots. The tailor had draped him, Ivanhoe observed, so that the great shoulders and enormous chest were quietly Doric and the timber trunk, which was as straight up and down as an elm, had a false suggestion of a narrow belly and narrow hips.

"Beau Brummell himself," Ivanhoe murmured. "No, I can't use any beer today."

"If you'll send Sammy and those razors away I'll tear you into the littlest pieces. What are you doing up here, you blasted fool?" Charley reached into his pocket for a notebook. "We've sold Dubuque, Davenport, Rock Island, Muscatine, Mediapolis, Oquawka, Burlington, Ft. Madison, Keokuk and now we're going in-country. But the main thing that is worrying me and Dick is what you're doing up here. I ain't let anything out but the first thing we hear is that there's some crazy, good fiddler going around with the same name as our president. I've put in a few ale pumps on the strength of 'if the brew was as good as the music.' "

"Well, then, what's the matter?"

Charley looked at his boot solemnly. "I don't know, Ive. It's your trouble. It's a girl, of course. A 'farm'! Hunh! I came up to see what was what. When you spend eight thousand dollars in a month in a little place like this, Dick and I don't object but maybe you'd tell your old partner—"

"Maybe, Charley. Tomorrow I'll show you the eight

thousand and some more of my own. River bottom, pasture, and the best house in Iowa. Then I'm having a hotel here—that will be Sammy's under my name. Color doesn't mean anything in this free state, except that the place had better not be Sammy's. Let Sammy brush you and we'll look around and go to a supper. The governor."

"Tell me about the girl, Ive. Who is it?"

"What do you mean? Why a girl?"

"It's always a girl, Ive, as soon as you can think up a good enough tune to make yourself believe it."

"I haven't written any tunes about her—oh, quit grinning! Sure there's a girl—very nice one. Just a friend. In fact, she's practically engaged to one of my good friends."

"Practically," said Charley. "Good thing I came up here. I suppose your good friend will be hunting you with a musket in a couple of weeks."

"Not a chance. Why, to show you—soon as the governor leaves tomorrow I'll help you sell the coffeehouse some Serenade and we'll both go back to St. Louis. I'm going to tour some. How're the old dusters, Charley? How about us going back and getting some more pounds, shillings and pence?"

"You mean—" Charley looked at him keenly. "Another ocean trip, uh? It's come to that already. I wondered how you got over Alwine so fast. Dick and I were all set to give you credit for the beginnings of a little gumption."

"Oh, I've got a lot of gumption. Wait'll you see my farm and my horses. I'm going to be a big man up here, when I get ready to settle down, Charley. Been traveling with the governor the last week. Wait till you meet him." He put out two fingers close together. "He made me a colonel last week, so I'm your superior officer—in case you're thinking of any more remarks about gumption."

"No!"

"Yes. There's my new sword over in the corner. I still wear the old one and the old dress uniform, though. If I go on fiddling and keeping out of fights I'll probably be the general of the American Army pretty soon."

Charley loosed a short burst of his deep, grunting laughter. "Not a bad idea. You could come riding up on a white horse and play the enemy songs about home and mother and their darlings far away. Then when they started bawling and was all busted down and their eyes full of tears so they couldn't aim we'd come shoot the roosters.—Well, come on, general. Put on your pants and shoes and let's take a look around Pittsville. Any fun here?"

Sammy appeared with the hip bath and hot water and Ivanhoe began his day's toilet.

"Any fun? I'm amazed at you asking a colonel and an intimate of the governor of the great state of Iowa a frivolous question like that. This afternoon I have to precede the address of our chief executive with a display of my art in the Courthouse Park before the free electorate of Van Buren and adjoining counties. This evening, the governor and I and—uh—you, I suppose, will have supper with that commercial Titan and leading financier—by golly, I never did hear his first name—Dunshee, after which there will be a reception for me—the governor will be there, too. After that you'll come down to your miserable room here in the tavern and I will be a house guest of Mr. Dunshee, along with the governor."

Charley grinned. "You make any more snooty speeches and you'll be house guest of the Burlington Coffin Factory. No, they make right comfortable coffins—too good for the like of you. I'll pitch you in the river."

Sammy was making a lather and Ivanhoe was putting on his underclothing and socks. Ivanhoe sighed. "Always violent—and always thinking up some impossible project. That reminds me, what about that tour?"

"It ought to remind you—impossible projects! Did it ever occur to you that I'm a married man with a wife, a sturdy and quarrelsome son and a house? Or that you are paying me no contemptible monthly salary to sell your beer? And that Dick wouldn't like it if you went chasing off again just when he's almost finished hiring a symphony orchestra. God, our plant ain't livable! You see a guy soaking hops and all of a sudden he begins to gargle the second violin part of the Limburger Symphony of Umlaut in Q-flat. You see a guy wheeling a sack of barley and he's fingering the piccolo Allegro from the Windy Quartet of Sauerbraten on the truck handle. It's a hell of a brewery. Dick is wild because it's taking you so long to get out of whatever mess you're in up here. He's got a concertmeister that can whale hell out of a piano—studied under von Beelow—or play a good violin or direct. So he's superintendent of casking—well, he's all right but kind of hard on the coopers. It's the blamedest brewery I ever saw."

Ivanhoe chuckled. "Well, I won't let Dick down. We'll have the first rehearsals next week."

"You mean it, Ive!"

"Yes. I'm going to split things up now—spend the proper seasons with my orchestra and the rest of the time up here with my horses. Come on, let's get some breakfast and then I want to show you my farm!"

They rode for two hours while Charley exclaimed over the rich bottoms and beautiful river hills that Ivanhoe had acquired. The house was nearly completed; two stories in the central part of the building with one-story L's branching from the center. It was all the hard gray limestone from the ledges of the creek that ran through a virgin pasture a half mile north of the house. Purplish slate for the terraces and the roof had also been split off the edges of a coal vein that had been revealed by the river down at the bluffs of the oxbow. The walnut floors and beams of the interior had been hand hewn from the cheap native timber, and the floors so carefully smoothed and jointed that each seemed like a single piece from some enormous tree that could have grown only in Brobdingnag.

"Wing for you when you visit, wing for the tenant and I'll take the middle to keep you apart. Fellow from Illinois moving in in a week or two—he's bringing an orchard with him on one of his wagons—good four- and five-year-old stock. All that bottom land will have corn on it the next time you see it."

Charley stood in the big central room and looked up at the high-eaved roof and the gallery which led to the occasional rooms.

"I'd better get out and get to work. Going to take a lot of beer to furnish this place."

"Not so much. We've got a top-notch cabinetmaker who's making most of the big pieces out of native timber. There'll be a cherry room and a walnut room and a hickory room for you and a chestnut room and I'm having pine shipped for the music room and the master bedroom. There's a spring for the two kitchens and the water closets and another spring and two cisterns for the stables. I'll have a well dug for the house later—there's ground water all over the hillside.—Good Lord!"

"What's the matter?" Charley asked, alarmed.

"You darn near made me betray my country—keeping me gassing here about my country estate. The electors will be waiting for me in another hour and we've got to get some provisions. Come on."

Charley laughed and they got on Ivanhoe's mares and cantered off to Pittsville and the coffeehouse, where they could have a mug of ale with their roast. Samaliel's missionary efforts for his master were evident when the loin cuts of venison came in roasted and then lightly pan-simmered in wine, with raisins and cayenne in the sauce.

"If you had this in England, now," Charley observed after a mouthful or two, "you could get the royalest duke in the land to thank you for an invitation."

"Op," said Ivanhoe, meaning "yes." He swallowed. "I can remember the time when I'd give the finest joint of venison in the land for a pound of good smoky bacon or a plate of oysters. Game—game—game—I dreamed about a leg of lamb once with caper sauce and mint jelly."

"I was an old frontiersman, too. The next time I ever settle I'm going to know enough to take along plenty of pigs and plenty of tobacco."

"And pepper and enough onions for a winter."

"And coffee. Lord, what we drank for coffee!"

"Those were great days—let's hope we never have any more. I've got to dig up the governor and see what he wants me to play. Come along. You're the big brewing man from St. Louis—but not a word about me!"

"More tomfoolery. I want to get a look at this girl."

*   *   *

"This girl" was not at the afternoon meeting, however, and Charley had to dismiss all the young women who greeted Ivanhoe after the program as not "this girl." Ive was too easy with them. The big man met the governor as an old army friend of Ivanhoe's and Charley was immediately invited to the festivities of the evening—supper, reception, dance and music.

Charley unknowingly tantalized Dunshee by his careful explanation that he was an investor engaged in realty operations in St. Louis; he was looking at lands up the Mississippi and had dropped in on his old tentmate.

Dunshee's mind immediately turned to the big farm and the big house outside town. This must be where the fiddler had got his backing, if it was really his house, as seemed almost certain.

"Pretty place your friend is building up above town."

Charley looked puzzled, then his face cleared. "Oh, that. Yes, a nice little country place for Ive. Cheap place to keep his horses."

So it was Keeler's, all right, but what did this big, obviously prosperous, simple and substantial man mean by "nice little country place"? A chill of doubt struck Dunshee. It was very possible that all that simplicity of Hoskin's might be assumed; that he might be nothing but a very good swindler, or even someone brought in by Keeler for effect. But that idea did not hang together. The house and the land were there without a cent against them—the whole investment might run well into five figures. No one ever spent money like Keeler and saved fifteen thousand dollars or so from fiddle playing. There was someone solid behind this and it might most probably be this Hoskin.

The only alternative was that the damned young scoundrel had fascinated some rich and gullible people in St. Louis as he had the governor and half of the feather-headed inhabitants of Van Buren and that he and Hoskin were partners in some newfangled swindle. This didn't seem too probable, either—the governor knew about Keeler's war record and it would be hard for a man as invariably conspicuous as the fiddler to take to his heels. Hoskin must be put down as a victim, too.

Dunshee reflected that he had land to sell and projects to finance. He had planned a power dam and a series of mills to refine the products of native agriculture—wool, grains and lumber—he had plenty of ideas for using money but the country was new and the people who understood its possibilities had chiefly come here for the uncomfortable reason that they had not enough money for their needs, let alone investment.

The dam and factory project would have taken Dunshee's whole fortune and, though it was only slightly speculative, he did not want to take such a risk by himself.

" 'Little house,' " he said agreeably. "I guess you're used to bigger houses than we have around here, sir."

"Oh, no—I mean it's little compared to the house Ive could build if he felt like it."

Dunshee had another shiver of doubt. He knew Keeler's history by pieces—Ellison and Caesar Crawford had known him when he was fiddling in taverns for pence and shillings; he had wandered over half the world, fiddling and wasting his money; he had certainly made no fortune in the Mexican War and he had come almost directly from that venture back here to Pittsville. Of course, he had done well here—but thousands of dollars!

There was no doubt that Hoskin was doing a little harmless boasting for his friend—or perhaps from the height of some great fortune he credited everyone close to him with his own resources.

"If you're interested in land up here, Mr. Hoskin, I'd like to talk to you in the morning. There are some real opportunities here. For instance, there's a fall of water up the river—eleven feet in two miles—that is simply gaping for a dam and a mill—"

"Oh, that's out of my line—you'd have to talk to Dick—Richard Byerley—about that. He's our financial expert. Tell Ive about it—he'll know all about the location and he can see if Dick is interested enough to come up and go into it with you."

"Richard Byerley—Richard Byerley—I don't just remember—but I know the name!"

"Visit St. Louis often?"

"I have it—the brewer. Serenade Brews, they call them."

"Not so much a brewer—though we've got the biggest and best brewery west of the Mississippi. But he makes our big money in real estate. We've got property that will sell for a million five years from now if the town doesn't grow any faster than it has been. Dick's a wizard. First time I saw him ten years ago he had a little gin mill and eight hundred dollars. Now he's worth half a million if he's worth a nickel and he'll be a millionaire inside five years. I'll be well off, myself. Anyway, I wouldn't sell my ten per cent for a hundred thousand. Pays me ten per cent and my salary and commissions double that."

"He let you buy in—would he sell more stock? I'd be glad to come down and investigate if he's interested in more capital."

Charley grinned and shook his head. "Closed corporation. We couldn't buy anything with the money better than what we've got. If we needed more we'd just cut off dividends and live on our salaries."

Dunshee nodded. "I'd like to meet your man Byerley, though. We have some things up here that might be closed corporations, too, but, frankly, they're too big for me without outside capital."

"Oh, sure. Run in the office the next time you're in St. Louis.—I've got to traipse down and change for supper, sir. Lucky I can dress properly. Can't tell what you may need on a selling trip so I've got my dress uniform. If Ive tries to give me any orders because he's a colonel, though, you'll be short one guest."

Dunshee went home in a sad state of bewilderment and unease. If this Keeler was really a pet of rich people he could have been serviceable; very serviceable. Dunshee was never slow to admit his errors—to himself. He felt that he had been unreasonably misled by Ellison and Caesar Crawford and their smiles about Ivanhoe but there was no use to reflect on that. The fellow had some wretched sort of magnetism that had taken in these St. Louis millionaires, the governor, the local farmers and townspeople, and even Evelyn to some extent.

They had had some sharp exchanges but that could be gradually turned off as bluff playfulness if he now took Ivanhoe into favor. And that house—he probably got the money from the St. Louis friends but it was paid for, along with more than a thousand acres of very desirable land. And if Ivanhoe could influence men like this Hoskin, Dunshee felt that he would be doing them a favor to get some of their money into a sound project rather than into the Spanish castles of an itinerant fiddler.

* * *

Ivanhoe and Charley in their dress uniforms very nearly shared honors with the governor at the governor's reception. Ivanhoe, naturally, had to be next to the piano with Evelyn but Charley had to beg to stay off the receiving line. This did not prevent him from having his own private reception with the county's only captain in the war, one attended by all the young ladies at the party and everyone else who could get within listening distance while the two compared the campaigns of Scott and Taylor and the parts of Mexico in which they had been conducted.

It was after eleven before the retirement of guests began to show a purposeful progressiveness that meant that the party was ending.

Evelyn was good-humored after her small quarrel with Ivanhoe, in fact, she seemed amused by his presence and its conditions but neither of them said anything about it; they were kept too busy for conversation by the demands of the party. Only in the pause between dances late in the evening was Ivanhoe able to put down his fiddle and bring her a plate of chicken wings, salad and cocoa. Dunshee was a tee-totaler but this was the governor's party, so Ivanhoe was able to supply himself with a mug of rum punch and a heaping plate of what the buffet afforded in the way of food.

"Getting tired?" he asked Evelyn.

"No, why should I? I enjoy playing. And I rested this afternoon instead of practicing."

"I could go on all night. Charley and I had a nice ride in the country this morning and a couple of quarts of bitter ale with lunch—some Charley brought up with him. The stuff at the coffeehouse is terrible."

"If you have all that rum on top of it you won't be able to hit the notes."

"If I ever get to a point where I can't hit them I'll be so far gone I won't care. We're about through now, anyway. I'll have another mug, I think, since I probably won't get a nightcap."

"No, you probably won't," she said, wrinkling her nose very slightly.

Ivanhoe wrinkled his nose up, too. "That's the way I feel about it. Any house that sends a guest to bed without a nightcap. Well, probably the omniscient Sammy has packed a flask of cold punch with my dressing case. I can put some hot water in it from the jug. Shall we give them a tune and stop for the evening?"

"Do you have to drink liquor every night before you go to bed?"

He looked at her with wide eyes. "Of course not—I don't have to play the violin, either—I like to. Do you do everything you do because you have to? How silly! If a man can't occasionally declare himself independent of necessity in his behavior he might as well black his face and go hire out in some cottonfield down the river—might better."

"Father hates liquor."

"I don't know the pertinence of that. I hate boiled turnips. No harm in a preference. I don't think any the worse of him for it—or very little."

Her eyes narrowed for an instant. "You do just as you please, don't you, always? Go where you please, say what you please, act as you please."

"Within legal limits, mostly. Is there any harm in that?"

"The world will take you as lightly as you take it."

Ivanhoe shook his head. "Mmmm. Calvinist influence, no doubt. What a foolish idea! 'The world will take me as lightly as I take it.' Did you ever hear of Voltaire—or, no—did you ever hear of St. John the Evangelist? Who took the world more lightly than those two? Now, I'm a profane man, fiddle, sing, drink, curse occasionally, brawl in a good cause, flutter around gaping at things, feeding my body with the best I can find and tossing my soul a bone if there happens to be one left over. Your father, if you'll pardon me, is a God-fearing man—no more honest than I am—but inclined to take the world seriously; certainly as much of it as is likely to appreciate in value—and he doesn't know as much about the Appassionata, or poor little Chopin's cries in the night as a pig knows about Sunday. He's never stood on a mountaintop and seen men dying all around him while the bright sun came up over glittering green valleys and almost heard the Revolutionary Étude thundering in his ears. It is essential for any man who can take any large part of the world to take it lightly. There hasn't been an Atlas for some time."

"I don't know about all that, but I do know that Father has lived an honest, Christian life."

"It's not hard to do that under favorable circumstances. If he'd been down at Chapultepec he might have found it necessary to shed a fellow Christian's blood. However, that's enough. Your father is an estimable person if only on his daughter's account. What about the Kleine Nachtmusik to speed the parting guest?"

The attempt was successful, for the last guests were leaving when they finished the fourth movement.

*   *   *

Ivanhoe slept late in the morning. Sammy had come up, according to orders, entered without arousing Ivanhoe and laid out his kit and his civilian clothes. As soon as Ivanhoe stirred he hurried down to the kitchen for hot water. Ivanhoe lay and stretched in the pleasant sunlight of the master bedroom. He was, after all, in Dunshee's bed, waiting for a better shave than Dunshee could get.

He thought seriously of his conversation with Evelyn the evening before—he supposed he would have to apologize for that. No, be damned if he would—it was true, every word he had said, and her patronizing remark which had started him off had been merely an empty platitude.

She would expect him to apologize, too. He grew more and more indignant as he went down the stairs to breakfast; he was still three steps from the bottom when the simple derivative of all of the sound arguments he had been giving himself for withholding his apology came to him in a flash.

He went into the dining room gaily. It would have been a reflection on Sammy's various skills if he had not been the best-dressed and groomed man in the room. The governor and the intimates who were traveling with him were still working through an enormous Iowa breakfast—buckwheat cakes, sausage and bacon with eggs, porkchops or steaks and potato cakes with hominy, lots of coffee and open-face apple pie made from tart dried apples. A duty of the good politician in the time and place was to be a hearty eater and Briggs, with a platter of breakfast steaks in plain view, was taking a second helping of sausages, eggs, potatoes and gravy.

Evelyn, the weak vessel, was toying with a reasonable slab of pie on which she had poured thick cream.

All the men gave a little lurch as a symbol of rising from the table, and went on eating.

"Morning," said Ivanhoe cheerfully, addressing the company and a stack of hot cakes which had appeared instantly. "Sorry to be late. Fine comfortable bed—room of your own with no clerks or visitors makes you sleep late. What's become of our host?"

"Up betimes," said the governor. "We'll have to give

him our thanks at the boat. Your friend Charley wanted to look at some land for a little country home and Mr. Dunshee is showing him some sites."

"Charley? For heaven's sake!"

"You're great friends, aren't you? He told me about your fiddling and fighting through Europe and Mexico."

"Yes, but Charley's got a house in St. Louis."

"Well," said the governor, smiling, "he seemed to think that you wouldn't have built the house you did unless you expected to marry and settle down in it pretty soon. He is thinking about a country place somewhere near."

"Charley—what makes him think—oh, Charley's always had a few loose cogs in his head. I just got my place for a headquarters. Everybody ought to have a headquarters. I've got three trunks of music, for one thing."

The gentlemen all smiled at each other and Ivanhoe stirred up some remarks for Charley's private ear. He did not know why it was so disagreeable to him to have them all think that he had a sweetheart somewhere.

"Charley just got married—well, not exactly that—he's got a baby—but he got married just before he went to war and he thinks if you do anything a little bit out of the way, like build a house, there could only be one reason."

"It usually turns out there is only one," the governor said. "Two families like yours and Charley's would be a great addition to the state."

"Don't count on me," Ivanhoe said. "I've been footloose too long. I'm going to lead an orchestra this winter—St. Louis, Cincinnati, Louisville—might even try farther east if everything goes well. My agent down in St. Louis has been collecting the company all spring."

"Bring them up here, my boy. We'll give you a great reception at Iowa City and Davenport, and I know they will down the river."

"I might do that."

"It's worth considering." The governor rose and his party with him. "I've got to circulate around town a little and then get our boat off. Ivanhoe Keeler—colonel, if I may remind you of a little mark of the state's esteem—we'll always count you one of us. I value you, sir, for a great many more things than your violin. If you do by any chance come back here—to settle down—we would have use for a man with your experience of the world and military record. If Washington—Congress—would interest you, we'd be glad to talk about it with you—I have no doubt it could be managed."

"Thank you, sir. I'd never thought of anything of the sort. But I'm afraid they wouldn't let me play my violin in debate."

"Most of the debates are settled outside the House. I have no doubt you'd be as useful as anyone we could send. Good-by, colonel—Ive."

"Good-by, governor. And I hope you won't wait for my wife to invite you to come and visit me the next time I come back here. The house'll be finished then."

"I'll come in any case, but I don't think your friend Charley is a fool and particularly not about you and your behavior."

Evelyn saw them to the door. After the prolonged good-bys which were saved over from settler tradition—when strange families might become lifelong friends in a few days of bad-weather tarrying at a convenient cabin—she returned to find Ivanhoe rising from the table.

"Nice old chap, the governor. Wouldn't I look like a guy in Congress? I believe he meant it, though. Thank you, Miss Evelyn, and you thank your father for your very delightful entertainment. I'll give you one more music lesson now before I go—I'll almost certainly go down the river with Charley for a while."

"This evening?"

"We'll ride to Keokuk and let Sammy come on with the luggage. It's a nuisance lightering all the stuff over the lower rapids, changing boats and so on. Charley and I have a lot to talk about and we've both got good horses. They'll need me in St. Louis—I wasn't talking through my hat about the orchestra. We'll have summer concerts—those Germans are crazy about music—at any rate, we'll be ready for the season. If you come down, let me know."

"I haven't been in St. Louis since we came through there on our way west. I don't know when I'll ever be again. St. Louis is a long trip for us who haven't traveled all over the world."

"Oh, no. The boat's fine and it's fast. Make Ernie bring you down on your honeymoon."

"Aren't you taking some things for granted that don't concern you?"

"Am I? Aren't you being rather nasty-ladyish this morning? Come on. I'll talk to my concertmeister about you—he studied under von Bülow—and have him send you some advice and music. I hate to tell you, before you've finished, but you could be a good accompanist and perhaps a concert player. My conscience makes me do what I can for art."

"Thank you, maestro."

"Not at all, child. Come on."

She went on and touched the string for Ivanhoe to tune his violin.

The E string snapped. Ivanhoe pawed impatiently through the pocket of the case.

Finally he stood up impatiently. "That was my last one. I guess it was just as well. I didn't want to play, anyway. I wanted to tell you something."

She looked up quickly at his change of tone. "Me?" she said lightly. "What do you want to tell me?"

"A long story." He told her a long story, the first of it much the same as that he had told Charley, of his flight from home and his first days as a fiddler.

"And so you see, it has always been deep in me that I am a fiddler. Those other things—Bull and Spohr and David; the stages of England and France; playing my way through the war—made me feel the honesty of my art, but none in myself; I loved my violin but my contempt for a man who merely played a violin through life increased from the days when I caught shillings and fips around the taverns.

"Some profound way I must have accepted the appraisal —and in myself, too. My heart's been broken a dozen times— I suppose they could all see that I wasn't as solid as my violin, which is reasonably hollow. All right, we are hollow, but you couldn't lift the weight that's tightened across that little bridge and bears on the fine wood below.

"Once it almost came to me from Spohr—old Beethoven had met the Empress and her court on a walk. 'They must give way to us; not we to them,' he told Goethe, and walked straight through them.

"I suppose that was a little in my mind last night while I was dreaming—in the governor's bed. Though I'm not Beethoven.

"And it came to me a little at Chapultepec. I had been a dancing monkey for the fighters all the way from New Orleans—oh, they liked me well enough, and I had given some of them lessons with the light saber so that they respected me, too, but for most of them I had the low-bred taint of being a fiddler, until Chapultepec, where I fiddled with a steel bow that had only one string and one tune. But after that I fiddled again.

"This morning I reflected that I would leave you today, and all these other things went through my mind and it occurred to me that all the accidents of my life have not been accidents—that every particular of my life has been strong except for my own deep-held mistake, my youthful idea that fiddling was a cheap expedient for gaining comforts without fighting for them.

"It has come to me that that is not so. It is a gift that must be perfected at the cost of continual struggle and polished momentarily. It is one of the great struggles, but that little violin has been a weapon, hardly mastered, but powerful. I am not sorry that I did not break the acres that Jesse Ellison has conquered or master the mildewed precedents and equally mildewed manners that fit Caesar's attorneyship. I am not a solid man, but I have bested solid men in everything but love, which is essentially conservative.

"In short, your scribbler, your rhymer, your dauber,

your fiddler, have their ways in this world with their own weapons an unreasonable number of times. Now I know that I am not less manly for being one of the company—so it is fit for me to love you, as I have not quite been able to keep from doing since I first saw you, Miss Dunshee."

Then he saw that her eyes were large and serious and it steeled him to his last gesture.

"This is my darling of many years, Miss Dunshee," he said as he picked up his violin. "This is no empty token." He brought the violin down against his knee. "Leb' wohl, Schatz," he said to the old sweetheart.

She cried out and rushed to stop him. "Oh, cruel—"

He caught her as she plunged toward him and the broken violin fell to the floor.

"I wondered when that would come to you," she said in a few minutes. "I was afraid you might never notice."

And some minutes still later she looked at the violin. "What a pity!"

"It's only the fingerboard broken off, dearest. It can be fixed."

THE END